Praise for *Addio, Love Monster*

"In rich, descriptive prose peppered with _____ :o gives us a penetrating look at several gene_____ 1- ily. Bookmarked on either end of this no_____ ng upon professional mourner and matriarch ___seppa Millefiore, who teaches her family that "everything dies"—but not before the entire clan loves, laughs, and dips deep into the gusto that characterizes Italian-American life."

—Rita Ciresi, author of *Pink Slip* and *Sometimes I Dream in Italian*

"Joyce had his Dublin, Ferrante, her Naples, and for Marrocco it's Mulberry Park, where not much seems to happen, and yet something's always going on if you look beneath the surface. Marrocco finds the extraordinary in the lives of the folk who inhabit this sleepy suburb of Chicago, creating stories of individuals that she forms into a lively word tapestry, capturing days of lives gone by, reminding us that everyone has a story to tell."

—Fred L. Gardaphé, author of *From Wise Guys to Wise Men*

"In *Addio, Love Monster*, Christina Marrocco has created a world that pulses with life. At the center of that life is the Millefiore family and their iron-fisted matriarch, Giuseppa. Set in fictional Mulberry Park, a suburb of Chicago, on the largely Sicilian-settled Singer Street, Marrocco's novel-in-stories creates a place that is both familiar and wonderfully strange, a slice of a past time where families and neighbors squabble and gossip and judge, but most of all, they share a love that outstrips those lesser emotions. A wonderful first book by an author with a keen eye and a skillful touch."

—Patrick Parks, author of *Tucumcari*

"With a unique and captivating voice and astounding attention to details, Christina Marrocco immerses us in the lives of a multi-generational immigrant family with her debut novel. I *know well,* these people of Mulberry Park, her fictional, working class, Sicilian-American neighborhood near Chicago. In this sharply focused snapshot of the midcentury Southern Italian immigrant experience, Marrocco populates *Addio, Love Monster* with people as real as it gets. I love this book."

—Karen Tintori, author of *Unto the Daughters: The Legacy of an Honor Killing in a Sicilian-American Family*

First published by Ovunque Siamo Press
OVUNQUESIAMOWEB.COM

ISBN 979-8-9862692-0-7

Cover photo by the author
Book design by Adam Robinson

Addio,
LOVE MONSTER

Christina Marrocco

OVUNQUE SIAMO PRESS

ovunquesiamoweb.com

For: Mom

ACKNOWLEDGEMENTS

Much appreciation to my family, particularly my husband Guy, who read every one of these stories aloud to me so that I could listen to them as I revised. To my mother—to whom the book is also dedicated—for reading the manuscript with care and an eye to history. To friend and colleague Rachael Stewart and the entire Monday Night Writers Group for encouragement and careful reading but also for putting a non-Italian eyeball up against the work so that I could see how it played in the larger world. To my friend Carol Szabo for listening in as a quiet reader with excellent cultural insight. To Michelle Reale and *Ovunque Siamo*, this wonderful press for valuing my work and the work of Italian American writers at large. To all my children, and particularly my daughter Tiff who died of cancer while I was finishing this book—she'd have been so proud it is finished. And dare I say to myself, for doing the work, sticking in there and doing it even when I wasn't sure where it was going, even when I'd rather have been gallivanting about.

NOTES

First important note: This novel takes place in a fictional suburb of Chicago. All characters are fictional, as are their stories. No character represents any person living or dead.

Second Important Note: The fictional town of Mulberry Park is a working-class suburb of Chicago. While during the time of this novel it is heavily populated with people who are the diaspora of the *mezzogiorno*—southern Italy and Sicily—it is also home to many others. It, like it's neighbors, Melrose Park and Maywood (which are real places) were once heavily populated by German immigrants and Irish immigrants. Mulberry Park is transient in that after these stories end, it will shift to new groups of immigrants—it will not be preserved as a "true" Little Italy. And that ties into what we need to understand about the languages of Mulberry Park. Because language is a living, breathing aspect of living, breathing people, the way the people in these stories speak is true. It is not always pure and it is not without the influence of the other languages that surround it or the specific family peculiarities of the speaker. The Sicilian/Italian/German and English language here is constructed to show flux and movement rather than adherence to ideals of language purity.

CONTENTS

(handwritten annotations): Jena & Nicky Lost Twins · Nickey Malagone · Agata/Benla · Nicky wife Leala · Mr & Mrs contralto · Dandelion Lady

Freda & Frank dies
Lena's Twin

Guiseppa Millifore

Josie Jobs

Womens Lib

Teddie millifore 7/4 mom Lena prejudice

Teddie Grandma dying

#2

Addio, Love Monster

ONE

A Professional Mourner's Birthday Party

Really bad 1st sentence

Giuseppa Millefiore's bottom lip pooched out like the spout of a chipped fountain in some Sicilian courtyard, chiseled into being long before people became so lazy in the head. Before they understood life only in dull absolutes of good and bad, young and old, sinner and saint. Giuseppa had been made when the sacred and the profane still rode the same horse. Hers was a lip made for kissing everything from broken fingers and the tender heads of newborns to the cheek of a corpse and the hem of a priest's frock. A thin brown stream trickled from this pooched lip into a rivulet that ran down her chin and finally seeped through her quilted housecoat. Then to her silk undershirt, and finally to her skin. It was the juice of snuff, a delightful product she'd used for decades, but which now sometimes caused her to dribble like a grasshopper. And yet, she sat regally before her half opened living room window, catching the breeze. Her features and the skin pulled over them were resilient enough to carry old age with apparent indifference.

From her chair in the parlor, Giuseppa could hear her two grown daughters gabbing away in the kitchen. About the soldiers coming home from the war, about how Hitler had killed himself before anyone else could do the job, about the price of sugar. They spoke in Sicilian now, and as she listened, she pressed her rounded shoulders against the padded back of her platform rocker to straighten out her neck and lift her ears. Giuseppa had rocked for some part of every day in this very chair, for most of her life. But it had never been the mindless rocking of leisure until today. Still, the chair's Victorian solidity, the squareness of the platform itself, reassured her that, somehow, she still belonged in this changing world.

Today would be her seventy-fifth birthday party, and because of that she had been told, as if she were an infant, to wait patiently for her party to begin. Even though she was strong as an ox and capable of helping. She had been told this by her eldest daughter, Lucia, who preferred to be called Lucy and who would determine when it was time for Giuseppa to get up. Lucy liked to be in charge, and that made Giuseppa bristle. In fact, there was a lot of bristling between the two. This mother and daughter, had they been *Americani*, would have been estranged but because they were still Sicilian such a thing was impossible. So, they made do by never looking one another in the face at the same time.

Her other daughter, Filomena, who was also in the kitchen, was easier. And then there were all the boys. But, of course, they were not in the kitchen helping prepare. Just her daughters, her youngest and oldest children. Giuseppa thought about that, how the girls were like clasps at either end of a long rope of beads which held her six sons.

"Oh my *god*, she's all dripped up again," Lucy griped to Fil, her hiss floating out of the kitchen with the dust motes.

"Would you just look at her—like a big brown shit from head to toe."

Giuseppa heard Fil murmur an agreement.

"And she won't wear a bra, not even today. You just watch, she's gonna ruin this party."

It was a lot of words to say about someone in the next room, Giuseppa thought. But then again, easy for a big mouth, *molto facile*. The old chair creaked as she rocked it fast, readying something to say. She took a deep breath.

"Just-a so you know, no bra, no never" she called out sweetly. "*Non mai.* You hear what I say at you face?" Giuseppa chose her English words carefully. And she never shouted. It wasn't necessary.

Shouting was *brutta figura*. In Sicilian, she added for good measure: "you may wear what you prefer, I will wear what I prefer. You want to wear a bra? You want to wear ten bras? Please do. You don't have ten? Here, here's my pocketbook."

When she was finished, Giuseppa leaned back and enjoyed the feel of her silk undershirt everywhere it wasn't damp. Silk, warm in the winter and cool in the summer, was all a woman needed against her breasts. Bras were harnesses meant for horses and prostitutes. She knew she was in the right. *Assolutamente.*

Pulling her chair closer to the kitchen so she could see a bit as well as hear, Giuseppa saw Lucy panting against the stove, hot from the heat of the oven but from the change too. Lucy rolling her eyes so violently that Giuseppa thought it must hurt to do it. Fanning herself with a flour-sack dish towel, flapping it like mad. She watched as Lucy pulled yet another tray of cookies from the hot oven, throwing the flour-sack towel over her shoulder. She marched over to the round-topped Frigidaire and yanked the chrome handle to release it, pulled open the little ice box inside and tried to stick her entire head right in, but there wasn't room. The box was all iced in.

"Okay, you look at her, Fil," Lucy said, "look and see what she's doing now."

"No, you look; I'm crackin' these eggs over here."

"I can't, Fil. Please."

Giuseppa saw Fil crack one more egg.

She closed her eyes most of the way to look like she was asleep, not listening in at all.

Fil's head poked around the corner.

"I think she's sleeping now," Fil whispered back to Lucy. "Or else she's faking it again."

Giuseppa waited a few minutes to be safe and then slowly opened one dark eye to peer into the kitchen. She found she could hear better with an eye open lately. But all she could see was Lucy's broad back and one meaty arm. The arm seemed to float in the air as its hand filled trays with *cuccidati*. They began to speak again. If it was in

3

English, then Giuseppa knew it was to keep her from understanding. When it was in Sicilian, Giuseppa knew it was to make a point right in her face. Today, it was that mix of both languages—and Giuseppa knew *this* was done to confuse her. She listened and, indeed, found herself bewildered by the rapidity with which her daughters jumped between languages. Now she saw Lucy turn and jerk herself up the aluminum step-stool like a big stringed puppet carrying a full cookie tray, wanting to store it atop the tall Hoosier cabinet until the party.

Giuseppa's kitchen had no built-in cabinets—instead there were free standing ones with enameled pull-out counters. It was an old-fashioned kitchen, and all the things were well-made and heavy. Lucy had said she should replace them with something more modern. Some Formica. Some black and white floor tile, but Giuseppa always refused.

While she was up the ladder, eye level with the top of the tall cabinet, Lucy must have spotted trouble because she shouted to Fil for a wet rag. Scowling over her shoulder, she teetered a bit and then handed the cookie tray back down to Fil. Giuseppa watched her scrubbing away at that grease coated dust up there, the worst kind of dust there is. Giuseppa could see it *skeeved* her. Lucy called for a spatula to scrape it. Then she called for the Kitchen Klenzer. And when all was clean, Lucy slid the cookie tray into its place on the top of the cabinet, but she hesitated at the top, as if she were afraid to back down the step ladder. After all, she was fifty-nine and should stay on the ground. Why they went overboard like this, Giuseppa never understood. If it was up to her, Giuseppa would have simply put out confetti almonds and coffee. Lucy had dozens more *cuccidati* to arrange and then, Giuseppa knew, she would begin the rosettes, which she was practically famous for. Yes, they were always light and airy as angels' wings and collapsed on the tooth. And yes, Giuseppa was proud of Lucy's rosettes, but she never told anyone that. It was not good to brag about your children.

What a big culo that one has, Giuseppa thought as she watched Lucy backing down the step stool, like a ripe tomato, and all because she won't stay away from the sweets. In her old age, Giuseppa now found she had no desire for sweets anyway and preferred a plate of dark cooked greens with oil and salt to almost anything else. She decided that she wouldn't eat any of the *cuccidati*, not even one. She called through the rooms to whoever was listening, "Don't give me any *cuccidati* at the party, maybe tomorrow for breakfast, but none today. Too hot! Too hot!" She paused for effect and added, "In Sicily, we never made *cuccidati* except for Christmas, you know."

"Well, well, she's awake," said Lucy as she made herself completely visible in the archway, taking one *cuccidati* and devouring it. "Fine," she said. "I'm eating yours, Mamma. *Va Bene*, and suit yourself."

Giuseppa often thought that had her eldest daughter not married such a very poor man with so few aspirations and a very bad back—and had she not had too many children herself—she'd have made a business woman, maybe even opened a bakery. Instead, she was too poor in her own kitchen to make much beyond what could be fashioned from the plainest of ingredients: flour and lard, a little sugar and a little salt, some oil, maybe an egg. But Giuseppa knew that everyone had chipped in for her birthday, and so today Lucy had all the ingredients she could want. Everything. And she watched as Lucy let figs and raisins and candied cherries stick to the tips of her fingers like jewels.

Giuseppa heard the ticking noises the pot made as the oil heated. She saw Fil sift the flour for the rosettes and carefully set out more eggs. Her daughters talked about nothing but the rosettes and the heat of the oil for a while—was it ready? Was it not? Were there any weevils in the flour? Double check. Sift it again. When Lucy dipped the rosette wand, long and dripping with batter, into the pot, the oil began to sing. Giuseppa lifted hands to the scant breeze that came through the open window. Bored, she exercised her lungs, pleasing herself with how deeply she could inhale and exhale despite old age. There she sat expanding her diaphragm, pulling in deeply the sugary oil smell. Breathing it back out again and again. Feeling invigorated, she helped herself to another pinch of snuff. As soon as the snuff found its way to her bloodstream, sounds came louder, vision clearer.

When Lucy began talking in the kitchen again, Giuseppa heard every syllable, but suddenly she didn't want to hear it anymore. How it grated on her. She wondered why, why was this daughter so much harder than all the other children? Giuseppa liked to answer her own questions, and in a split second—no longer—and in a way that reassured her that her mind was still sharp, she knew. It was because a first-born girl always wants to be on the top. That was why.

Giuseppa summoned memories to distract herself like a snake charmer summoning a cobra to rise from a basket. And soon she felt the exact sharpness of the grit she'd once trod along the road from Molano to Palermo under her slippers. The road she'd walked with her husband and tiny daughter, the next child already growing in her belly. She felt the exact angle of the hot Sicilian sun heating her brow, too. And she saw, like in a film, the moment when tiny Lucy—*una picola bambina* then—had spun around in the center of the road and announced loudly to a pack of perfect strangers who walked behind them that they were heading to America. And as if that weren't enough, little Lucy had added—in a particularly strident squeak—that they had bread in their canvas bag strapped right there to the donkey and a mess of coins sewn into their pockets. Said it to *straniere*. Giuseppa still couldn't believe it. Luckily, the strangers had turned out not to be *banditi* but just another family traveling to the port of Palermo, fleeing Sicily. So, instead of robbing the Millefiores, they'd only laughed.

"That one will do well in *L'America* with her mouth already wide open," the father of the other family had said, bending to spit on the ground for luck. "But you had better crack her in that mouth anyway, just to be safe. She needs to learn now."

"See?" Giuseppa had growled at tiny Lucy, "They only want me to beat you. See how *straniere* are? That's why we don't tell our business to anyone but family, Lucia." Lucy had stared at her mother, round-eyed as a field mouse but unapologetic.

"Do you understand?"

Little Lucy just shrugged her shoulders, which was a thing Giuseppa could not stand. And so Giuseppa had taken the stranger's advice and given her small daughter a crack in the mouth with the back of her hand. How the little mouth had trembled, but the child did not cry. Her reaction was only to walk more slowly now, dragging her feet through the dust of the road, leaving furrows deep enough to plant winter wheat.

Not hard, Giuseppa reminded herself in the living room chair that it had been just for show. How could she have guessed this daughter would be a grudge-holder? The sting of the remembered slap tingled across her left hand—the sinister one—and Giuseppa rubbed it against her housecoat, hiding it in the quilted folds.

Giuseppa startled when Lucy appeared in the living room, rushing past her chair without stopping on the way to the window to fling it the rest of the way open.

"As if I'm nothing more than a spindle or an arm-rest, a flattened cushion," Giuseppa muttered, "such disrespect."

Giuseppa could see how Lucy chose not to hear her, how she only wrestled with the window, yanking on the painted handle with all her might. It would not fling even an inch.

"*Madon*, it's hot in that kitchen, Ma. Where's the fan? Do you know where the fan is? Where's the fan, Ma?"

Giuseppa said nothing.

"Ma? Ma, where's the fan? Ma?"

Giuseppa shrugged her shoulders.

She watched Lucy straighten her spine and cast her eyes to the ceiling and then rest her eyes on the plaster-framed oval portraits that hung above Giuseppa's chair. First, she focused on the portrait of her papa, benevolent with his bristling broom mustache and his long, calm face. And then her eyes wandered, maybe without her wanting them to, to the portrait of Giuseppa next to it. Giuseppa knew how young she looked in that portrait, how haughty and strong in her striped dress. She'd been beautiful. And now she was not. She watched Lucy look away and back at the portrait of Giovanni.

Of all the people on this earth, it was Lucy who had known Giuseppa the longest time. Of all people who had *ever* lived. And the opposite was true as well. Lucy was the only child who had been born in Sicily. All the other children had been made in America.

Well, except the boy who'd been born on the ship, but even he had been *headed* to America when he came to be. Lucy had breathed plenty of Sicilian air, and though she'd been young when they'd left, Giuseppa was sure she still recalled the sound of the bells ringing out from the Basilica of San Pietro of Molano, the thinness of the air in the mountain village, the sun on clay brick. Lucy had been born nine months to the day after Giuseppa and Giovanni's wedding—a fact that proved both Giuseppa's fertility and chastity in one fell swoop. So yes, she'd been useful to Giuseppa from the very beginning.

The labor with Lucy had been so very long ago, and even though other women swore every mother forgot that pain, some vestigial memory of agony lingered in the darkest marrow of Giuseppa's bones. Birthing Lucy had been worse than all the others. Giuseppa was a midwife and knew she should have forgotten about that long ago. She pushed it from her mind.

She reminded herself as well that it's in the nature of eldest daughters, that they have no choice, but to become second-mother, scrubber, washer-woman, short-order cook. That there is less time to pet and kiss them than there will be with children who come later in life. For this, Giuseppa often felt something akin to regret, a heavy sadness, but then she soon found herself annoyed with it. It was just the natural order of things and no one could say otherwise. When she imagined Lucia at the age of ten or eleven what she saw most often was a pensive girl staring out from some corner where she folded a diaper or stirred a pot or wiped a dish.

Giuseppa watched Lucy take a breath, groan, and give the window one last enormous yank. Finally, it squealed, dropping its weights down its thick white ropes. Then Lucy clomped out of the parlor to find the fan. Giuseppa knew Lucy would be able to find it because Lucy never gave up. She looked forward to seeing it held in the jaws of the window, a wave of cooler air pushing against her body. These modern luxuries she enjoyed most of all: lights at night, the big round radio that played music and voices, water that ran inside the house instead of a well, seeds that came in neat packets for sale at the dime store, and electric fans. She wondered idly if those same things had come to Molano as well by now and how much different Molano might be than when they'd left it. Probably not much, she decided.

Of course, when Lucy returned to the parlor, Giuseppa didn't look Lucy in the face either. But it was a daughter's job to make amends. There's nothing, Giuseppa thought, nothing I wouldn't have done for my mother. But Giuseppa's mother had died before Giuseppa could even memorize her face. So, she had no idea what it was really like to have a mother at all.

Lucy heaved the fan into the window, clamped it in place, drew the black and white cloth cord across the floor, and plugged it in. Giuseppa smiled as Lucy snicked the dial to the highest speed. But then Lucy stood in front of that fan as it drew in cooler air from under the pear trees just outside the window. She blocked Giuseppa's air. Her plain black dress and untied apron blew against her body; her long-out-of-style iron-gray finger-waves rumpled out of place. In the window, the fan spun so fast that it transformed itself—Giuseppa imagined—from a dangerous looking blade to a round disc, to a plate, to a face. A clown's face? No. A dog face? No. A baby face? Yes. *Lucy's* baby face is what it reminded her of. Round and full. Nothing like that *faccia funga* she dragged around with her now.

Finally, Lucy went back to the kitchen, but then, suddenly, Giuseppa heard the Mix-a-master whirring something like crazy. Frosting? She didn't like frosting much. Too sweet. Too much.

And then a fuse blew. The house went dark; the fan in the window slowed, then stopped.

"Sonofabitch!" her daughters yelled in the kitchen.

"Sonofabitch!"

"Sonofabitch!" Giuseppa chanted to join them.

They were right; the electric was a sonofabitch. And her window fan had stopped. But then she thought she heard them laughing at her. She fell silent. Someone hurried to the basement to change the fuse. It sounded like Lucy, like her shoes, anyway. Little thuds. *Ciucciarella*, hooves and braying and all. The kitchen whirred to life again. And in the parlor, the breeze from the fan came back. It reached out for Giuseppa's hair and tousled it into knots that would be difficult for her daughters to comb out.

"I know we told her to replace that electric box a thousand times!" Lucy complained. "She won't listen. Always gotta have someone running over here day and night, night and day."

Giuseppa decided it was time to speak again from her chair: "it's fine," she said as loudly as she could without yelling, in *l'inglese.*

"It-sa good electric. Best-a electric. Only time is a sonofabitch-a—that's when *you* in the kitchen. Lucia. Always use-a that Mix-a-master. Just use a spoon, you! Is-a good enough!

There was silence, except for the Mix-a-master pummeling frosting. Giuseppa found the silence worse than the laughing, so she broke it, in Sicilian:

"I'm just saying it, Lucy-Lucia, you always got something to say, but you never say *the thing.* You've got something to say? Come on, say it."

The room went quiet, and no matter how Giuseppa looked, she could not see her daughters, not even with both eyes opened wide and her entire body leaning forward—almost tumbling—from her chair. They must be by the back door out of the kitchen, where the little pantry shelves lined the wall. Maybe Filomena was petting Lucia's arm and telling her, "You know she don't mean it, Luce," and "Not now, let it go, Lucy, let it go. It's supposed to be a special day." And maybe Lucy did let it go. Or maybe, thought Giuseppa, she added them to the big pile of angry she kept in her head.

And Giuseppa had a pretty good idea *what* the biggest angry against her was. It had all gone truly and completely to vinegar when Giuseppa had been pregnant with her last baby—Filomena there in the kitchen—and Lucy had been pregnant with her first. Mother and daughter both pregnant—the mark of a truly healthy family Giuseppa knew, *anyone knew.* But Lucy lost her mind. Avoided her own mother. This left Giuseppa, weighed down by heavy cotton maternity skirts and hobbled by swollen ankles as well as a varicose vein burning down her inner thigh, searching for her. When she caught up, Lucy, *furioso,* turned pink and raced away, shouting over her shoulder, "Like cats! Disgusting!"

When Giuseppa no longer saw Lucy on Croaker Street, she asked the shopkeepers and soon found her daughter had taken to doing her shopping in the evening, when she knew Giuseppa would be resting with her feet up. Giuseppa had also heard from the neighbors that Lucy's husband, for his small part in the drama, was not pleased to have a wife on the streets shopping in the evenings. So, he threw a fit here and smashed a plate there, yelling in Lucy's face. She knew that. She also knew that Lucy was always the last customer of the day in every shop. The very last. That Lucy had to make do with what was left—and that often it was discounted, a pound of tripe and two tomatoes or three thin *Barese* sausages, a withered onion, a loaf of stale bread. The butcher told Giuseppa he thought maybe Lucy was having money problems, and so did the vegetable cart man, but the baker and the rag man, they said that Lucy was *mortified.* And that annoyed Giuseppa.

But despite her annoyance, and because she had the second sight, Giuseppa had seen how night after night, Lucy, a new bride who wanted very much to impress her husband with her cooking, leaned over her little gas stove frying sausage and peppers or gently stirring her tripe in tomato sauce and cursed her mother. Back then Lucy had long brown hair worn in a loose chignon to keep it off her neck. Her long sleeves always brushed the fire as she bent over the stove. Lucy was careless about herself from a child, always standing too close to gas flames and fires. So, Giuseppa had put a protection from fire on Lucy that would last through every day of her life.

And still, even all that was before Lucy truly went over the edge. What sent her was that Lucy's baby was born before Giuseppa's. And this, Lucy believed she knew, was because Giuseppa had *held hers in.* In fact, Lucy was so certain of this that she'd gone to her brothers, to her husband's family, to neighbors and accused Giuseppa of making sure the nephew would be born before the uncle just to prove a point.

"She can do that," Lucy had moaned to whoever would listen. "She can do it because she's a *stregha.*" Neighbors would offer her a *caramello* in cellophane paper from their pocket or a pear from a backyard tree—to calm her. They'd take the new baby from her and soothe its crying, tell her she needed to keep it in the house until it was six months old. Smell its *culo* to see if it needed changing. Try to change the subject. Nothing worked. And since Giuseppa really was a stregha, they'd stayed even further out of it than they might have otherwise. The foolishness of it all. "Everyone knows," she told the fan, "that no woman carrying a change-of-life baby wants to stay pregnant one extra minute."

The back door opened with a whoosh and Lucia yelled out, "Ma, we're going over-across to Lena's for a cigarette. Be right back. Just take a nap so's you're fresh for the party." They were gone before Giuseppa could remind them only loose women smoked cigarettes and to make sure they waited until they were inside Lena's house. The inlaid wooden snuff box was handy in her pocket, and she opened it again. Alone in her flat, she felt larger than when they were there with her.

Giuseppa stood up slowly, pushing her cat to the floor. She padded to the kitchen. There were trays of sweets on every flat space: table, counters, and balanced carefully on top of the rounded fridge as well. All the bowls and baking sheets were washed and drying on spread-out towels. The floor was swept. And the Mix-a-master gleamed like a jet airplane in the corner. It looked like someone else's kitchen. Giuseppa decided she might as well have a *cuccidati* after all. So, she crept up the stepladder very carefully and removed one perfectly pillowed cookie from Lucy's neat tray, leaving an empty space. Then she crept back to her chair, nibbling the tiny candy balls from the top first, then licking the sugar glaze, and then, finally, biting into the soft figgy center with her bottom teeth. When she'd brushed the crumbs from her lap, she counted off three rosary beads with her stained thumb. She implored the mother of God to correct her daughter's thinking so that things could get better.

Giuseppa knew that at that very moment a great many grand-children were signing her birthday cards while having their cowlicks slicked down with mother-spit. One great grandchild, too. Everyone would flock to the house in a little while. And of course, her six sons and their families would come. Those boys who Giuseppa often noted had never been strong on her. Never. But they were weaker in their bodies than her daughters were, weak like her husband had been. They were her six worries. You couldn't tell how susceptible they were by looking, but she knew. She was their mother after all. And so, she could still hear the croupy chest-rattle of each baby boy, feel the cold winter as she had carried them out into the snow banks to open up their throats. Year after year. And then there were the worms; these she had cured by making the boys sit over buckets of garlic, for hours, until the creatures had crawled out their *culos*. It had to be done. And so, yes, despite their wiry quick actions and their veined muscles, those boys were fragile, as boys are. And now they were all bald. Every single one. She'd watched their hair come in and she'd watched it go out. Their skulls gave her pause.

Giuseppa was still considering her sons' bald heads when Lucy finally stepped back into the doorframe. She hadn't heard her daughters come back into the house, but here they were, silhouetted by the afternoon sunshine spreading into the living room. Giuseppa was picking her nose just a little. It itched.

"Ma, stop it."

"Ma, we're gonna get you ready in just a little bit. We're done in the kitchen and just getting everything ready downstairs, OK?"

"I'm already ready."

"Yeah, okay, Ma. But I'm gonna do your hair up and put you in a fresh dress and some nice shoes."

"No."

"Yes."

No matter what she said, both daughters would be coming for her, Giuseppa knew, to make her presentable. She could do it just fine herself, but they liked to dress her up, so she might as well let them. But not, she thought, too easily or they'd take over completely. Speaking toward the kitchen in her deepest, most precise Sicilian— which she kept for formal social occasions—Giuseppa pushed her toes into the orange and white hooked rug in front of her chair.

"No bra! No bra, I said. We agreed. We agreed, and now you are trying to trick me!" She paused for a moment and grew wilier even than before. "It's for strangers, isn't it? The *In-laws*. You want to impress the one from Bari or the *Napoletana*, and the Polack—oh,

the Polack. And worst of all, the tight-ass over there from Palermo."
She rubbed her neck. Lucy yelled what she always yelled: "Stop call-
ing Lena the Polack, Mamma. First of all, she's German. And second,
Polack is not good to say."

Giuseppa thought the Polack was nice enough but still unfamiliar
despite the fifteen years she'd been around. Her skin made Giuseppa
think ricotta spread over toasted bread with little bits of cinnamon
and sugar over it. Odd but not bad. What *was* bad was how this
Lena spoke no Sicilian, not a word—she wouldn't even *try*. That was
who her youngest son, Nicky, had married. Sometimes when she
thought of her daughters-in-law, Giuseppa felt unnerved. Her hands
shook a little. She digressed in her thoughts. But it was Giuseppina
from Sicily—yes—she pulled herself back on track—Pina who really
got her goats. Always asking how much money Giuseppa had in the
bank, bossing people around. What made it worse was that Giuseppa
herself had ordered Pina from the matchmaker in Sicily. And there's
no problem more annoying than the one you cause for yourself.

She waited patiently for her daughters to come with her clothes.

Just beyond the window was the wide front porch, painted glossy
gray with white railings. It was just there that Giuseppa's husband,
Giovanni, had dropped dead after gulping down a glass of cold water
she'd handed him. It had been too cold; she'd realized too late. The
glass broke as he hit the planks and it cut his hand. She'd seen that he
was dead even as he fell.

After work at the factory that morning, he'd taken his dented
wheelbarrow and a shovel and headed to the tracks like he always
had. She could imagine him there, even now, stooping to pick up
the chunks of black coal along the shining rails. Bent and already
old, he gathered things that fell off the trains from the weeds along
the tracks every weekend and after work on weekdays. And on that
steaming hot day he'd died, Giovanni had left his wheelbarrow at the
foot of the steps, his work-boots on the first step, and then—with
a thud—his body in the center of the porch. And just like that, the
husband was gone. Just. Like. That.

She could still feel that thud under her feet, whenever she stood on the porch, as if it were the singular beat of a drum. And she could feel the sun on the porch floor, too, as it had been that day. How the hot of the porch planks had radiated heat through her long cotton skirt when she'd crumpled beside his body. She'd shaken Giovanni, shouting out for help even though she knew nothing could be done. Fil, just a girl then, had run out and fallen down next to Giuseppa, confused.

And as they'd walked up the block, from their Saturday work, wrapping papers at the news agency or shucking corn at the green-grocer, the boy children joined Giuseppa and Fil on the porch. The family formed a loose circle around the body and looked to the heavens for help. The prairie sky had nothing to offer but a long clear view. Cloudless. What would become of them?

Two laboring men on their way home from Saturday work happened upon the scene and took their hats off in sorrow. One of them ran to the village hall to summon the new ambulance. But it never came. The ambulance system was new that year—you couldn't count on it. News travels fast, though, and Lucy, pregnant with her third by then, had run to Giuseppa's house before the man made it back. She'd thrown herself into the pile of people there. "Papa! Papa!" like a child, she wailed. Maybe, Giuseppa guessed, she'd feared for her siblings and her Mamma—who would keep them from the poorhouse? But probably she feared much more for herself. Trembling like she was at the thought she might be needed back in her mother's house to help care for her mother's children again.

Giuseppa had never before and never again seen her oldest daughter so wild with emotion, and she'd stretched out a hand to Lucy, to comfort her—her own cries stopping in her throat. But Lucy had swatted her mother's hand away as if it were a crow's claw. Wordless.

"Papa! Papa! Don't go!

But I never chose him. I never liked him. I never wanted him, Giuseppa reminded herself, running her hands more quickly back and forth along the smooth wooden arms of her chair. He'd been a funny-looking man, she thought. Not handsome, not ugly. And with an odd manner as well.

She'd always known that, as a boy, Giovanni had come to her baptism, looked at her in the cradle, and solemnly handed over the gift his family had provided to seal to their engagement, a thin gold bracelet for the baby Giuseppa had been then. Once he'd finished presenting the bracelet—exactly as his big-eared mother had instructed him to do—Giovanni had run outdoors to play ball with the other boys at the celebration. He'd left his tiny *fidanzata* in her cradle to squall. The priest had joined the ball game in the dusty courtyard, too, risking his vestments and sweating in the heat, pink faced. The way Giovanni told her about it, it had been a beautiful day. But also, the way Giovanni had told her about it, always irked Giuseppa. He tended to tell it after too much grappa, laughing, slapping his knee about the priest. And continuing to laugh even when Giuseppa had no smile on her face. The more he'd laughed, the more he'd annoyed her because it reminded her how she'd had no choice at all.

Scooching in her chair, Giuseppa turned her thoughts from Giovanni because she felt it important to think of her own mother on this, the commemoration of the day of her birth. And she'd saved her for last. But try as she might, she could not envision her mother. The longed-for mother-face seemed, as always, made of eels. Slipping into the background. And in its place, intruded the face of her old grandmother, dreary and looming large. This was the old woman who had taught her *la via vecchio*—and her ways had been not merely old but ancient. Ways hatched from eggs made of fossil, older than the volcanic dirt, older than Jesus or any of the saints. Far, far older. This is not to say the ways did not include Jesus and his family. No, certainly they'd been folded in as well, like glace fruit into cannoli filling.

On this, her birthday, Giuseppa prayed to the mother of mothers to send away the grandmother's hard face and show her the face of her mother, but still she received no more than the general shape—a roundness framed on both sides with ropey, dark, looped braids. True, again, she couldn't see her mother, but at least she could conjure her smell, for smell is the first sense. A smell of milk and sweat and lemon trees. Of eternity. Giuseppa twisted her hands in her lap and forbade herself to cry for her mother. Her crying would disturb her mother in the spirit world, and she would not do that.

The grandmother's face returned again, uninvited as it was. But her *nonna* was not a villain, Giuseppa knew. And her ancient ways were real and useful. But she'd been a hard one. All those years Giuseppa had stood at that old woman's dry elbow learning to grind dried leaves of yarrow, gray green and dusty. How she'd learned to remain silent unless asked to speak. Learned to be useful. The two of them rustling out into the street together, in dark of night, their heads covered with heavy scarves despite the heat, hurrying to help draw a baby from the body of its mother, most often in life and sometimes in death. Giuseppa had learned the best healing cures and protections. She'd also swept floors and invigorated bread dough, kneaded it till it lived, carried the loaves on a board to the village oven in the evening and went out again to bring the hot loaves back before the heat the next morning. She'd formed macaroni after macaroni after macaroni until she saw macaroni like moving creatures when she shut her eyes even to blink. This was how she'd been taught all the crafts of the kitchen, of the midwife, of the *stregha*. But of these, the kitchen always made her itch. She'd have preferred to do only the healing and the apothecary, but she swept obediently.

But there had been pleasant times as well, times when she and her *nonna* walked together into the small courtyard's garden, under the wide mulberry hung with silkworms and sparrows. There Giuseppa and the old woman had squatted close to the ground and dug into the soil with little awls, early in the mornings—pulling weeds and leaving wild herbs to thrive. It was only in those fleeting moments that she loved her old grandmother, that she could let go of missing her mother. And this was mainly because she saw the wetness in her grandmother's black eyes and knew they were missing the same person together but could not speak it and, in those times, they scraped the garden soil in unison. But then she'd had to leave her grandmother, steaming away on the *Archimedes* to *L'America*. The old woman never to be seen again. And so, even this grandmother, she'd lost.

17

There had been small boys who'd lifted their trunks from the donkey cart, carried them up the gangplank at the port that last day in her Sicily. Those boys had walked upon feet that looked like little hooves—built up into hard calluses that covered the bottoms of their perpetually shoeless feet. And they'd tapped up the wooden gangplank. She could still hear her own voice as it had sounded then, too, musical, a voice accustomed to singing along with her father's trumpet. She'd warned the hooved boys to take care, not to bang the trunks around so much. In the smaller of the trunks was a tiny inlaid wooden box into which the grandmother had tucked a sprinkling's worth of soil from the courtyard garden. And on that soil, the old woman had put a strong spell for germination and growth. They'd dug it up together with a silver spoon under a silver moon by the light of a full moon. Giuseppa had watched the old hands wrap the box three times over to keep the earth inside from spoiling the snowy white the box would lie atop. The grandmother had kissed little Lucy on the head and had taken Giuseppa's face in her two cool hands. She gave Giuseppa's face cheeks a hard squeeze. Then she'd looked at Giovanni who had green eyes, green slanted eyes, like a foreigner. Like a Saracen, but with silly over-sized ears. The old woman whispered in Giuseppa's ear that the baby Giuseppa was carrying would have those ears as well. What could she do about it? Nothing. It didn't matter. He would be healthy and ugly enough to go through the world without being envied.

At this point in her reminiscing, Giuseppa wished one of her daughters would come in to bother her, to give her a break from these old memories. But they were finishing up in the kitchen, not thinking of her at all. She considered getting up to help them, even though they'd said not to, now that the heavy work was done. But knowing they would likely refuse kept her in her chair. She petted Gatto-Fred, who'd crept up into her lap again. Her hand automatically felt rheumatism in his bones, and she made a spell for healing, just a prayer really, simple but effective if done daily.

Lucy had brought this cat to this house. Yes, it *would have* been Lucy's cat living at Lucy's flat, but Lucy's husband was a known cat-hater. So, the black kitten arrived at Giuseppa's inside a wicker basket that hung dejectedly from Lucy's elbow. He rested neatly among a few tins of cat-food Lucy had spent her egg money to buy. This daughter, and the younger one too, had walked like a team of mules, very slowly, up their mother's porch stairs with the basket. As if the basket were made of marble. Giuseppa had watched them approach through the same window she faced now, hoping maybe Lucy had been bringing bread or an almond cake in that basket. But the hope had vanished when Lucy had come up enough of the stairs that Giuseppa could see her face. *Faccia funga*—too sad for cake.

Giuseppa had opened the door and met her daughter on the porch. She hadn't been in the mood for having them in the house that day because it was a mess, and she didn't want Lucy cleaning it. The three women had stood there in a circle, and Lucy asked Fil to ask Giuseppa if the little black kitten could stay at the house. It was urgent. Some of Giuseppa's sons, who'd been working around the house with hedge clippers and dandelion diggers, wandered over and up the porch steps. They'd tried to say no, that the last thing their mother needed was a cat in the house. They were getting full of themselves, and that irked Giuseppa. So, she'd said yes to Lucy. Giuseppa picked up the kitten and scratched it under the chin. She also put a new black mark on her son-in-law's name in the book she kept in her head. Him, she had come to despise because he gambled and ran with loose women, kept Lucy poor, and now had refused her even the solace of a cat. He could suffer with whatever *malocchio* came his way. She'd never help him.

While still standing on the porch, Lucy had told Giuseppa the kitten's name was Fred. But Giuseppa re-named it Gatto.

"Why, Ma? Fred's a good name."

"Because it's my cat now, Lucy. And Fred is something I just do not like."

Almost done with preparations, Lucy peeked in at Giuseppa from the kitchen. She made a little noise with her teeth to call Gatto-Fred, but he stayed right where he was, kneading Giuseppa's lap with sharp claws and lifting his rump into the air. Giuseppa could never pet the cat without thinking about how husbands are too strong on their wives. It made her think about how, when her husband died, his silly ideas and small controls had vanished with him. How thoroughly refreshing that part of it had been. It wasn't that she was *glad* he'd died. She wasn't. But at the same time, she wouldn't bring him back if she could. And she didn't feel guilty about that.

Yes, sure, it was true she'd taken to her bed after the funeral, after all the guests had left, and stayed there for a week, and then another while her boys had run like wild animals through the neighborhood. It was as if someone had wrapped her in cotton so tightly that every bone ached. And when, after weeks, she'd finally staggered to sit in a chair in the kitchen and then to prepare a meal for her children, she'd found that she no longer served dinner on plates and instead plopped a pot of food onto the middle of the big kitchen table and handed everyone a spoon. Sometimes, she'd dreamed of the little hooved boys of Sicily. They'd come trotting through her dreams, waving but not smiling. If her children became hooved, they'd be taken away from her. In America, shoeless children were removed and sent to orphanages or poorhouses. Bad boys were locked up in Juvenile Hall. Or sent to the army to be shot at back in Europe. It had been so very hard.

She looked around to make sure she was alone before she whispered it to Gatto Fred. *Molto difficile.* But bad and good luck always come twisted together. Before Giovanni died, Giuseppa had never gone without a chaperone to the market—one of her sons, her husband, her terrible son-in-law. This was the tradition they had brought with them, just like saplings or the dirt of Molano. That tradition, however, she found she could stop once she was a widow. Her sons tried to tell her, "No, no Mamma, it's not right for a woman to be in the street without a chaperone; you'll disgrace us. All the other boys will talk."

"Get out of my face," she told them.

After that, Giuseppa had walked all over town—to the dentist to have her rotten tooth pulled, to the poultry man to buy a live chicken, to her people who needed healing. Sometimes she walked to Creme Crunch Donuts and ate a donut alone in the gangway alongside the building. She still didn't like eating alone inside with the men looking at her while they drank their American coffee from big mugs. The donuts reminded her a little of a *sfinci* and so a little of her grandmother and a little of Sicily—a place she resented a lot but also longed for at the same time.

Giuseppa had never held any intention of re-marrying, and turning seventy-five now, she knew that had been the right decision. Widowhood had suited her well enough and, besides, she would have been a fool to risk all the harm a stepfather could have brought down on the heads of her boys. She knew how men were, it was better for her sons to run wild than to be squashed by the hand of a strange man in the house. Midwifery had opened the doors of a thousand homes to Giuseppa. She'd seen a lot.

To survive her early widowhood, besides continuing her midwifery, she added tatting and crocheting. Until her fingers twisted. She made bedspreads and tablecloths to sell. And she'd mourned during the day—professionally. Yes, Giuseppa Millefiore had become a professional mourner, traveling the sidewalks in a black veil and cape. Joining the small group of such women who served the Sicilian parishioners of Holy Cross over on High Street in this way. She'd chanted and wailed the death wail at the wakes and funerals in earnest. The Irish, with their keening, had nothing on the *prefiche*. No, the Sicilian mourners were equal and maybe even better. Perhaps, she thought, she was so good at it because she'd never known her mother and had been sad for that all her life. Or maybe it was the loss of her husband and the need for money that had driven her closer to grief, that had opened her heart to mourning for others. All in all, she felt proud of her skill, plus it paid well.

Giuseppa smiled to herself as she recounted how well she mourned for the people. She thought, I am good at it. I called up the tears for my mother, and for my father who never came across the ocean to join us. And I called up the tears for that still-born baby boy back in New York.

Besides sewing and mourning and healing work, in those hard days, Giuseppa had also taken more ruthless measures to keep the family afloat. Ruthless was the word Lucy used against her. *Spietata.* One day Lucy had come over to Giuseppa's door to holler about it. And Lucy had gone home still hollering down the street, people looking out their windows and shaking their heads. No matter how Lucy shouted, Giuseppa did the ruthless thing anyway: she removed all of her school-aged sons from school. After all, even the youngest had finished the seventh grade already. The people she'd healed over the decades found her boys jobs in factories, in carpentry, and on the railroad. They even helped one start a small music shop. Much-needed money came into the house, and Giuseppa collected it, kept it safe.

Until her sons married, she'd made a new tradition of sitting on a big blue chair directly at the top of the porch stairs, on Fridays, to collect their pay as they streamed home from work. She combined it with any money of her own. And she paid things off or saved it to invest in houses. Of course, she'd always have Italian coffee for them on the big wicker porch table, and lots of questions about their day at work. And it wasn't like she waited for them only on paydays. She waited for them every day. To hear how the railroad was running, what was happening at the music shop, what songs the gandy-dancers sang that day—in Polish, Hungarian, American.

She'd put the money away, never in the bank, only in the walls or under the floor, until there was enough to buy two more houses from certain men who ran such things in Mulberry Park. The houses were in need of work, and she had her boys there evenings and Sundays dividing the houses into two and three flats. As they'd married, their families filled the flats, and she would never be far from them or from her coming waves of grandchildren. This arrangement still suited Giuseppa very well.

Sometimes Lucy had come over to sit with Giuseppa and the boys on the porch, but never on payday. And she always came with a twitch in her eye. The boys lounged on the porch talking excitedly about life, blue cigarette smoke drifting out to the street. Sometimes Giuseppa noticed their wives peering out the windows of the flats across the street. They can wait, she thought, they can wait a minute. She'd have Filomena bring out more coffee and cigarettes for her boys. And really, when Lucy came by, it was brief and always to bring something, a third-hand nylon scarf or a colored piece of stationary for Filomena. A pack of Pall Mall for the boys to split. Nothing at all for Giuseppa.

"You're her slave *now*," Giuseppa had heard Lucy say in Filomena's ear one rainy autumn day. Her *sah-lave*.

Giuseppa had a good ear for whispers, and she'd heard that one clearly. And she knew what it meant, somehow. She'd glared at her elder daughter who sat on the steps, and at her younger who sat narrowly beside leaning in with a sideways smile. It was partly true, though, so she couldn't say anything against it on *that* account, but it was a disrespectful thing to have said—as if it all could have been done any other way. Everyone had to carry their weight if the family would survive. And Lucy's whisper, she recalled now, petting the cat in a way that made him squirm, had sounded much like a hiss. Meant to be heard. This is why I have an easier time with boys, she thought. This.

Giuseppa had known for a long time that her daughters-in-law called her the Iron Fist, and she knew it because one day Lucy had told her what they said.

"Yeah, that's what they call you. You earn it! They hate you."

Lucy had spouted this after a little disagreement about how to best de-flea Gatto-Fred. Lucy had tried to take what she'd said back after, but it was done. So, they called her the Iron Fist; well, well, well. She liked the sound of that, mostly. Sure, she might be the Iron Fist, but they all ate, didn't they? And they were going to send some grandchildren to college. One boy and one girl. A girl at a university and still complaining?

She counted the rest of her black beads and thanked Mother Mary, the dark one, for all this. It was a lot. Her daughters-in-law should learn to be grateful too. The smell of lemon oil reached Giuseppa. Someone was oiling the kitchen table. Why? Why were they oiling the table when the party was going to be in the basement like all the parties? The basement had its own kitchen with a hard tile floor, and it had outside concrete steps that led down to an aluminum screen door, that banged as each child bounced in or out, so no one had to come into her house unless they wanted to. And nowadays it even had a toilet. Some nights, they removed the long tables, put them on their sides up against the wall and made room for dancing.

This year, Giuseppa knew her hip would keep her from dancing. She also knew seventy-five was a good age to live or to die. A big number with strong angles: She liked how it looked and she could recognize it when she saw it because she could sign her name in her own hand, and she knew numbers. She planned to go on a while longer, though, she thought. At least to eighty, God willing. She packed in another generous pinch of snuff and rubbed her bare feet together like a cricket.

When she heard her girls coming with the hairbrush and the fresh clothes, she pinched her cheeks pink as she'd done when she was a girl. She wanted to look well when they came in. There's no harm in your daughters finding you beautiful. As Lucy came through the arched doorway between the kitchen and the living room, followed by Fil, Giuseppa asked for a glass of anisette. But they had it for her already. Lucy reached down to remove Gatto-Fred who tried to cling to Giuseppa's housecoat and to scratch Lucy on her arm. And at the same time, somehow, Lucy managed to hand her mother the tiny glass. Fil lifted the rosary from one spotted hand and the snuff box from the other, setting both on the side table

"For now, Mamma, just for now."

They had brought a washcloth and a basin of water, too. They asked her to spit out the snuff into a tissue. She did. Then Giuseppa's daughters had her stand and lift her arms to remove her tobacco-stained layers of clothing. They washed her with her favorite lavender soap and rinsed her well so that she wouldn't itch, taking care because her skin was getting thinner and she bruised easily. Someone tickled her neck, and she laughed a little, like a child—despite herself—which made both of her girls jump. Then, her daughter dried her with soft white towels and made her raise her arms, like a child again. She closed her eyes, as you do when clothes come down over your head. Someone slipped a clean fresh undershirt over her. After the silk undershirt, and clean underpants, a dress swirled with flowers of blue and purple, like irises. No bra.

"Ma, you look fabulous!" Fil pronounced, "Don't she, Lucy?"

* * *

Giuseppa closed her eyes and enjoyed the hair brushing, sighing with exquisite pleasure. She complained only a little when Lucy shoved her tender feet into big black shoes just like Lucy's own, and she sneaked a look at Lucy's face. Just a small one. Just for a second.

"Just slippers today. These shoes hurt me," she said.

"No, Ma. Not today," Lucy said. "Please, not today of all days."

"But these shoes *you got me*; they hurt me. Yours look softer."

The basement screen door began to bang open and closed. It was a very aluminum sound. Loud, familiar voices rose up the inside stair-case. Discordant against the late afternoon. Giuseppa heard Lena the Polack's heels clicking across the basement floor and imagined she was carrying trays of hot food she'd brought from across to street—okay, but not really delicious—setting them on the long folding tables. Bossy Pina shouted to Lena—which table for what. A balloon popped. A baby cried. It was time.

Giuseppa looked down at her purple-blue dress and the nice shoes Lucia had taken from her own feet to put on Giuseppa's. She was comfortable now, and she *did* look gorgeous. And so did her daughters. *La bella figura!* She mouthed with real conviction. The girls helped her down the steep stairs and into the basement; Filomena held her hand to steady her. Lucy carried the snuffbox care-fully, like a priest might carry a relic into the catacombs. "*La bella fig-ura*, Mamma," she whispered into the air. Giuseppa descended into her basement like a queen.

By all accounts, the party was a success; people laughed and ate and had a wonderful time. All the grandchildren—babies, toddlers, kids, teen-agers, a couple of young adults—were in attendance, and Giuseppa beamed at them as they surrounded her. They played with her silver hair and called her Grandma as she liked, not *nonna*. She felt modern. She felt she was still part of their world. After dinner, the daughters-in-law danced the tarantella and the polka to the record on the player until it was finally time for dessert. Everyone raved about Lucy's cakes and cookies. Giuseppa watched Lucy eat a few *cuccidati*, and far, far too many Rosettes. She shouldn't with her high sugar.

Giuseppa watched her sons prowl around with the movie camera, taking turns blinding everyone with the lights. Trying to capture the family in movies. They talked loudly. They smoked their cigarettes and patted their full bellies, saying *panza-panz*. They relaxed. They even went to Lucia and rubbed her sore feet, got her to take them out of those uncomfortable shoes. We could have been sisters, Giuseppa thought, me and Lucia, the closeness in age, but of course we weren't, and maybe that made all the difference. Who can say? Giuseppa was right. Maybe they were simply too different, or souls simply too similar, to ever be at peace with one another. Giuseppa was just about to call Lucia over to her, to say thank you even though for some reason it was hard to do, but then her terrible daughter-in-law Pina came and tried to take her snuffbox away, and that distracted her. She looked away from Lucia putting her head down on the long folding table. Let her rest, she thought, turning to resist Pina.

Within an hour the sugar diabetes overtook Lucy there at the long eating table, right next to the one loaded with her beautiful sweets. This came to light when her brothers went to get her up for the four-generation family photo. They splashed water in her face, shook her, felt for a pulse. Someone ran across the street to call the ambulance. And it came. But Lucy had already gone. And all Giuseppa could do was sit in the folding chair and watch everyone try to help. All Giuseppa could think to hope was that it must be true that Lucia remembered the mother who at the end of the long walk from Molano to Palermo—after the strangers and after the slap—had wiped away Lucy's gritty tear streaks with her own spittle, her hot thumb and her best handkerchief. Had kissed the child's forehead. It must be true that Lucy knew even as she departed, her still head cradled by her own arm, her mother had loved her.

It must be true.

It must be true.

* * *

Giuseppa wore her own pinchy shoes to her daughter Lucy's wake, having given back the borrowed ones for the coffin. She gave out anise candies to her littlest grandchildren in the coffee room at Zimbardo's Funeral Parlor. And to Lucy's grown children, she gave hugs. But those grandchildren were always stiff with her, pulling away. The room was dark, and the priest unmemorable. The casket seemed too wide open, and Giuseppa looked away and back again. The straight eyebrows, the fair skin speckled with age, the old woman's hair—was this truly her first born child lying inside? The priest swore to it, as did the undertaker. In death, Lucy looked so vulnerable, so changed.

And here was her other daughter Filomena: black hair, black dress, black eyes, pacing in front of the casket. And here were her boys: hooked noses, bald heads, white starched shirts, shined shoes. And here were her daughters-in-law, stunned, their permanent waves clinging to their heads as if terrified. Their cat's eyes glasses reflected everything in the room. There was always one of them by Giuseppa's side, holding her hand. Though she couldn't ever say which.

Giuseppa did not sit with the professional mourners now, of course. No, now she sat in the front row, where family always sits. And when the casket was closed, she wailed more loudly than she had ever wailed before. Both eyes open. Her tears, they wouldn't stop.

TWO

The Three-Legged Stool

Big Enrico Salvatore la Mostra Secchione carried his stool like he carried his name: with great care, great pride, and great determination. He'd decided earlier that week he wouldn't need a ladder. No, no, a stool would be enough, even though he was not a tall man. And so, his three-legged stool pinned like an overgrown hen under his left arm, Big Enrico made his way over the neighbors' cold front lawns on a dark spring night. It was important that he take a look inside the widow woman's house. Important that he make sure she was as good as he believed she might be before he set about courting her. Big Enrico was an old man, this he realized, and so he knew he had little time left in this world, none of which he intended to spend with an inferior sort of woman.

The truth was, and he had said this to himself in the mirror back at his son's house even before he'd combed his sparse hair straight back and put on his quietest shoes—the brown leather ones from the city—the truth was, well, it was this: his Janetta had been the perfect wife for him, and so, of course, no one would compare. She'd been serious and quiet and obedient. She'd been pretty early in life and handsome later. She'd been nice. And clean. And not just clean— she'd kept his shoes shined and his undershirts ironed and folded. And it didn't end there. She'd gone to church every single day to pray for his soul because he never went. She'd given him time to listen to his opera as loud as he liked, and to sing along, which he did—while she was at church. And most importantly, she had been a good mother to his children.

As he made his way, Big Enrico wondered what the widow woman wore to bed, and he aimed to find out. Janetta had always worn a white cotton gown with lace at the cuffs and a tie at the neck, and never was there a spot of grease or a crumb of cookie on her white gown. Like an angel, she'd been. In his mind's eye he conjured the sight of Janetta's thick silvery braid that had lain over one shoulder, her right, tied with a black something or other—he'd never figured out exactly how that worked—and he sighed. She should have worn a halo all her days—and wings. If only Janetta could come back, he'd not have to bother with this Millefiore woman.

But since the kids had moved him out of the city and into this village, he'd become very aware that the woman three doors down was in need of a husband. And very aware that Janetta was gone forever. He thought maybe he would benefit from having a wife again. He was lonely even in his son's house. Little Enrico had talked him into selling the old place on Taylor Street in the city. They'd gotten a good price and put all the money in the bank. Little Enrico had shown him the passbook many times—it had both of their names on it. Little Enrico kept it locked in a desk on the sleeping porch with other important papers. Sometimes, Big Enrico had asked if he could get the money out of the bank and buy his old house back, but Little Enrico always said no.

"A place like that is too much upkeep, Dad, and besides, someone else lives there now; why would they give it up for you? Besides, it's 1946—it's a new year, a new age; you can't live in the past." Little Enrico always talked to him in that martyr's voice. A voice the kid had picked up back in puberty, just when his mustache had come in like baby mouse fur and he'd hidden himself away in his bedroom. Little Enrico was fifty now, but he still had that voice. A voice that made Big Enrico feel stupid and burdensome.

"And anyway, this is better. We can help you with everything, and you can be with the grandkids, and not have to cook for yourself, so..." was always how Little Enrico finished the discussion.

It *was* good, Big Enrico thought, to have such a son, in many ways. He was lucky to be included and looked after. But when Little Enrico had to go on vacation to the lake house or needed to do big, noisy work in the house with saws and drills, he sent Big Enrico to live with the other grown children for a few days. Big Enrico didn't like being uprooted like that. And he didn't understand why he wasn't invited to come on vacation to the lake house. Or why Little Enrico's wife wouldn't let him rearrange the furniture in the living room so it would fit better. It was enough he'd been shoe-horned out of his place in the city, but now he'd come to a place where he didn't quite fit.

Big Enrico had been very quiet when he sneaked out of the house. Tiptoeing past the big bedroom of Little Enrico and his bossy wife, and the little pink bedroom of his three granddaughters, every single one of them snoring away. He'd set down his stool quietly, opened the front door quietly, and made his way out, shutting it quietly behind him. Generally, he was more nervous in life and might be dropping or banging things as he went, but he'd thought of that in advance and given himself a glass of wine in the kitchen for fortification—the stuff they'd all made together from the big purple grapes two years ago in Chicago. He'd smacked his lips quietly thinking about how the grape man who came to the city was superior to the one who came to this village—city grapes were more robust. Full of vitality. And that's not all, he thought, if you asked him, everything in the city was better. The roar of the traffic—louder. The height of the buildings—towering. The houses—brick, not wood. Yes, the city was powerful—the city was a man. The village was a woman, nice enough but docile. He was quite struck by his metaphor and stood stock still a few moments to let it spread through his mind, the stool waiting on the stoop for him to take it up again.

Yes, this village hung onto Chicago like a snail on the leaf of a succulent plant. And, well, it did not inspire him in any way. He'd once been a teamster, a teamster in the City of Chicago. He felt his sense of self inflating on the cool lawn, and it was about time. Here he was, with his fortified brains and his solid city stool, in his brown city shoes, striding out of Little Enrico's house in the dead of night.

Smart to do so. He'd put on his flat wool cap before leaving because it kept his head dry from mist, and also because it looked smart.

Just the week before, the priest over at Holy Cross had told him, as if making a closed sale to a family friend, that the woman was a particularly good catch—if he were interested in such things—and that she was the kind of woman—while very skilled and good—who might well turn evil if left to her own devices. Like a tyrant queen. And so, it would be good for Big Enrico Salvatore la Mostra Secchione if he were to marry the woman, and it would be good for the woman as well. In fact, it would be good for all of Mulberry Park and the surrounding villages of Forest Park, Maywood, Bellwood, and Melrose Park—for the whole world. The priest made a good case, and in that silver tongued way of priests who'd spent real time in *Roma*, he made Big Enrico feel like he was getting a deal—*fare un fare per Dio*—he thought he heard the priest say. But he couldn't be sure. He needed hearing aids and just hadn't gotten them yet. Too expensive.

"It's just," repeated the priest into Big Enrico's ear, "that she needs a good husband to set things into their proper order and to get her back into the church." Father Crespello, his wire rimmed glasses electric with candlelight in the front pew where he chatted with Enrico, had looked more pious than even the statue of St. Joseph, which is almost impossible. He'd put his palms together as if to pray, but blurted out, "That woman needs to put away her old ways!"

Big Enrico had stared as Fr. Crespello completed his holy hand movement, making a church of his palms, rolling his eyes heavenward to implore God to make it so. These village priests were much more open than the city ones. But in the end, Fr. Crespello had made Big Enrico feel important, a tool in the hands of an almighty, if distant, God. This pleased him greatly, but it also made him uneasy. A little sick to his stomach. What, exactly, was wrong with this woman's soul? He wanted details. You wouldn't buy a mule, he told himself, without a good look at its teeth. Priest or no priest.

Big Enrico had seen her in the neighborhood, sure enough. She was handsome and sturdy with a broad face that seemed carved from marble. She was old like himself, but not at all frail, also like himself.

Her hair was white and thick, and her skin was a sort of golden olive color. That was all satisfactory, though he felt she had no fashion sense and often had mud smears at her thighs where she'd wiped her dirty hands, probably while in the garden. But, he supposed, that was to be expected outside of the city proper. He could help her with that, among other things, lots of other things. Big Enrico felt a sense of excitement, suddenly, like a young man—as if there were an unknown future again. He wondered again what she wore to bed.

The pear trees in all the front gardens, including hers, sighed in the night air as he passed them, their arms raised to the sky as is the habit of pear trees. The avenue was quiet—it was well after midnight. No lights were on in the houses, but the half-moon lit his way over the lawn. Dew dampened his toes, even through his good shoes, but that only made Big Enrico feel even more alive. He forgot the pain in his knees from the years of laboring and driving, forgot the curve in his spine, too.

A cat's yellow eye glinted his way as it slunk across the street, stopping to watch him at intervals. Accusingly, he thought. He waved his arms at it but stopped short of shouting so as not to blow his cover. It stared some more. Big Enrico shook the stool at it in rage, and finally, thank God, it left him. Big Enrico knew he was in the right, he was sensible, in how he felt about cats. They were known evil-doers—sneaky, like snakes. He started moving again, looking down the street to make certain the cat had completely gone.

The south side of her house was his best bet. He paused to admire the concrete foundation, solid. Two windows faced him, one to the parlor and one to what might be a bedroom. He set his stool on the lawn before the parlor window, rooting its three legs back and forth on the lawn to dig them in so he wouldn't tip. He stepped up, grabbing at the wooden trim of the window to raise himself. The asphalt shingle siding rasped at his trousers as he pulled himself up. He hoped it wouldn't mar the fabric—they were his favorites.

Big Enrico was not big—he was small. In fact, Little Enrico was much larger than him, as were all his children—and their wives. It wasn't his fault. Big Enrico hadn't always had food as a child, and this, he felt, was the reason for his slight stature. But what could he do? Nothing. His smallness is why, despite the stool, only the eyes of Big Enrico and the nose of Big Enrico rose above the bottom of the window, but it was enough. He looked. The moonlight shone into the parlor, and the teetering man could make out a few things clearly. There was furniture that looked large and dark and heavy. Old. Nothing weird except a strange sort of shroud thrown over what might be a wooden box in the corner. There was no one up in this room, not her who lived alone, and no visitors. It looked relatively *normale*, cozy even. He liked the balls of yarn and some embroidery hoops on the floor, though she really shouldn't leave things scattered like that. As his eyes adjusted to the dark, they became keener, and he spied not one but three cups and a spoon littering the side table closest to the window. A little messy, but that could be adjusted. After all, a lonely woman has little purpose and might well forget to tidy up her cups. He felt quite benevolent and progressive in his attitude, advanced in his understanding of how women's minds worked. A modern man.

He'd saved the bedroom window for last, and he was pretty sure he knew which one it was. He took his stool over to it, felt for level ground, and balanced it carefully. Using his technique from the previous window, he pulled himself up to her bedroom window.

This window was a bit higher, he thought, than the other—but why would that be? Maybe the ground was sloping away from the house here. Either way, only his eyes rose above the sill, and those just barely. Big Enrico clung to the asphalt shingles and wooden window frame like a bat to a cave. He moved his eyeballs as close to it all as he could. The window was open at the bottom, just an inch or two to bring in fresh air. It was strange, he thought: she should still have her storms on. Nor was there a screen. If he'd been taller, he could have stuck his head right into her room. What was wrong with her? Letting night air and any intruder right in? Did she have a fancy man who visited her? Was she a *putana*? No, no, maybe she was just forgetful. He let it go.

There she was, in her bed, propped up on big pillows like a sort of queenly doll. A wide stripe of moonlight fell diagonally across her and the bed, which was old-fashioned and iron framed. A rosary hung from the headboard. Tall wardrobes lurked in the corner, and a dark Madonna statue rested on a long chest of drawers, much darker than the Madonna at any church he'd been to.

He saw what looked like artwork from her grandchildren, and birthday cards from them as well, decades' worth, all round the thick door molding to her bedroom, and it made the door look like a frilly cave entry. He wondered what all that was for. Why not keep it in a scrapbook, like Janetta did? Though it was hard to balance on his stool, he remained, not sure of what he was waiting to see. He could see her eyes were closed. She was sleeping as she should be at this hour, not up doing questionable things. He was glad for that. She looked normal enough, he thought. It was strangely fascinating, though, to watch a stranger sleep. He'd never done such a thing before. He sniffed, and he could *smell* her room. It smelled of her, which was a smell he'd not smelled before as he'd only ever passed her outdoors and, even then, at a distance. It stuck in the back of his throat, and he wouldn't have been able to describe it to anyone except to say it was good in general, maybe a little like anise and old mahogany. He sniffed up more of the air from the room and breathed it back through the open window.

He supposed he'd seen what he'd come to see, and it was time to go back to his bed at Little Enrico's house. But he felt too awake. If he were still in the city, he'd have gone somewhere. Gone somewhere like he'd done in his youth before he'd even been married to Janetta. Back when he'd had a life during the hours after midnight, under street lamps and inside bars with friends. But he had no friends here to go with anymore. However, if he knew where a tavern might be—one that was open late—he'd like to enjoy a Campari and soda or two and congratulate himself on finding out what he needed to know. And to plan his wooing of the widow and, really, of her comfortable home, in which he would very much like to live—with her.

Yes, he should have gone to wander the village in search of a tavern to celebrate, but Big Enrico found he couldn't tear himself away from the window just yet, lost in the feeling as he was. He felt a bit like a dirty old man pressed up against the side of the house. High above the ground realizing how much he missed the warmth of another body while he slept. Even dogs slept in piles for warmth and companionship. *Look how lonely, this woman, solitary in her bed. A bed alone is like a coffin.* Yes, he would definitely marry this woman and sleep in that bed with her for the rest of their lives. It would make living in this place better. And besides, he could visit his grandchildren three doors down whenever he liked.

Once she'd agreed, he'd take some of his money from the passbook to help her fix this place up right, no matter what Little Enrico said about it. It needed new wood around the windows, better siding. Big Enrico felt good about his impending generosity—preferring to do for people rather than have them do for him. He sighed a little too loudly into the window gap. Barely too loudly, really, but how was he to know she was a light sleeper.

When her eyes flew open, he knew she saw him right away—or really just his eyeballs—there in the window, and she fairly levitated from the bed, her hair standing straight up like a cat's. To Big Enrico's delight, shock, and horror, the woman was entirely nude, and the covers fell away in one whoosh.

Despite years of marriage and advanced age, Big Enrico had never seen—in the flesh—a naked woman head to toe——not covering herself. His Janetta had always worn that big white gown and lifted it modestly and strategically as needed. But here, in the half moon light, came at him a brazen, naked woman, thumping her bare feet across the bedroom floor. She was still powerful in her limbs. And her breasts, though they seemed to be a bit longish in nature, were undeniably breasts. They swung with surprising velocity as she reached for the statue on her dresser.

Enrico didn't know what to say or do. He figured it would be best to just pronounce his love here and now rather than launch into a long explanation or wait to ask her sons, and so, he said plainly and in his deepest voice, "Signora Millefiore, will you marry me?"

He said it right into the gap between sash and sill at the precise moment the woman yanked wide open the mouth of the window to get a clear look at what kind of degenerate lurked outside her bedroom window. She looked down onto the top of Big Enrico's flat cap and screeched.

The screech was not what he'd expected, and it unsteadied poor Enrico so much that his cap flew off and his stool tilted, then fell away from under his brown shoes. Clinging to the sill now, dangling, he kicked like a mule at the stool trying to right it, but he could not though the toes of his brown shoes skimmed it over and over again. Terrified to let himself fall to the ground and maybe break a hip, he had little choice but to simply hang there as long as he could.

He figured she must not have heard his proposal because she hadn't even replied—and instead was shouting something so obscene he wasn't sure he understood its meaning—so he repeated his offer: "Will you marry me, please?" This second time, though, it came out in a panting voice as he was tiring out hanging there. His arms were about to give out.

She lifted the Black Madonna high above her head, obviously meaning to brain him with it, but then she hesitated. She bent at the waist and stood the statue beside herself, on the floorboards. She still didn't answer Big Enrico. Instead, she walked toward him and calmly pried—one at a time—each of his thick aching fingers from the white painted sill. He tumbled to the ground below. A cat caterwauled in the distance.

He lay there for a few minutes, wondering what was broken. Then she came, now wrapped in a bedsheet, to the window. She raised it wide open and leaned her entire top half out. She spat at Enrico who was rocked over on his back like a beetle on the lawn, seeing if he could get up at all. He felt a little humiliated but also lucky that he hadn't fallen on top of his stool, which lay beside him, looking equally ridiculous in the moonlight.

The woman threw a few furious Sicilian hand signs at him. Then she said something he understood completely. She spoke in Sicilian and she spoke everything she'd heard about him. How he lived with his children instead of them living with him. How he stunk up the bathroom so that his daughter-in-law could barely breathe. How he sang opera whenever he could, and not well at all. Oh, she knew it all. And what did she want with it? Nothing. Nothing. Nothing.

Big Enrico got up on his knees, used his stool to get to his feet, looked her in the eye, and said nothing. He gathered himself and put his stool under his arm like a hen again. He staggered away toward Little Enrico's house, his ankle threatening to crumple out from beneath him. As he left the scene, he heard her window shut behind him. He heard her turn the lock on it. He hoped she wouldn't tell her sons about it. It was the kind of thing he knew would not look the way he'd meant it.

But he also felt vindicated. Obviously, this woman didn't have a proper temperament. It was a good thing he'd checked her out. His Janetta would never have come to the window naked and swearing even if the house were on fire. He missed Janetta more than ever as he limped back through his son's front door. His twisted ankle, nearly bringing him down. Nearly bringing him to tears.

Inside, he came across Little Enrico—still with a sparse mustache but also now with the under-eye circles of middle-age. He was seated at the kitchen table playing solitaire. The ceiling fixture in the shape of a massive bowl of fruit—bananas, grapes, oranges—threw a brilliant light that hurt Big Enrico's eyes.

He tried to look nonchalant, mumbled something about how he couldn't sleep and all the pear trees needed pruning. Then he made the motion of cutting branches with his arms, to make himself more believable. He liked his family to imagine him outside all night working on a neighborhood charity case—which he reasoned was somewhat true, if you really thought about it. But on the inside, under that fruity kitchen light, he also felt himself filled with some level of shame for having looked in on Giuseppa Millefiore and having seen her naked. What would he say to the priest at Wednesday night service?

If he craned his neck just right, here near his card-shuffling son, and looked out the kitchen window, he could see the light on in that woman's bedroom. What's more, he couldn't get the vision of her nakedness off of him. He swiveled to look at his son in an attempt to replace one image with another. It helped a little. Big Enrico thought Little Enrico looked lonely too, so as the son slapped the queen of hearts on top of the king of clubs, the father poured them each a swallow or two of that city wine from its gallon jug. Big Enrico also suggested a game of pinochle instead of solitaire. The son declined, preferring to stew in his own misery. But being a thoughtful son, he handed his father a fresh pack of playing cards so that the old man could start his own game.

When morning came to Singer Street, Big Enrico heard the cardinal, brave and scarlet, atop the tallest pear tree and trilling itself into a mating frenzy. It sang out its entire repertoire for the chance to share a nest with a mate, who, dull-brown, unconcerned and unappreciative, wanted nothing more than for him to finish. He imagined the female bird sitting safely in the tangle of last year's trumpet vine. He heard the heartbreak in the male's tone. The cardinal's song meant morning, and so it ended the solitaire games at the Secchione kitchen table. Big Enrico finally limped to bed. A single bed. In his son's house.

And there he slept through breakfast and lunch, dreaming of Janetta, of her white cotton gown and her sweet, simple face. He held his pillow as if it were her. His false teeth sat, speechless, an open jaw on the three-legged stool now beside his bed. On the floor, his portable record player and his stack of 78s on top, all opera. Under the tight bed, his brown shoes, still damp with night dew of this alien village.

THREE

Because of the Thalassemia

Anthony Nardone peered out the picture window from his easy chair. He looked up and down Singer Street, a little uneasy. He felt he was much too young to sit in such an old man's contraption. But there he reclined because his mother had told him to. And his mother had told him to because of the thalassemia. The rotten old thalassemia sure had his mother brooding, and it had his doctor jotting down notes faster than the school secretary and rolling his eyes toward heaven.

"The condition, when it's full-blown like this, never ends well," Dr. Barron-Once-Barroni-Who-Changed-His-Name-To-Get-Into-Med-School had said just last week. Oh, Anthony knew all about the doctor's name change because sometimes he used to listen to his parents talking at night out in the parlor. He had very good ears and could hear through walls. At least he used to—when they talked more, before the thalassemia got so bad. He wondered about his own name: Anthony Nardone. What if he needed to change his name to get into medical school or politics or something? It seemed no amount of moving or chopping letters would make it sound American. The best he could do was Nar. It seemed impossible.

Last time he'd come over on a house call, Dr. Barron had looked just like a mope when he was talking to Anthony's mom about the disease. Like it was one of the worst diseases ever—so bad it had two names. But Anthony was a boy who relished words and sounds, and he liked both names of his disease. Liked them a lot, actually. Thalassemia and Mediterranean anemia sure had a nice ring to them. Not ugly like those other ones you might hear around town. Croup or gout or that sort of thing. If you've got to have a disease, Anthony reasoned, it would be worse to have an ugly-sounding one.

Outside his window, the neighborhood kids tramped home from school, cupping light snow into snowballs that couldn't fly and fell apart mid-air. Anyone could see it wasn't packing snow. If Anthony had been out there, he'd have known to blow on the snow in his hands to melt it a little, to make it stick together. But the kids out there seemed to have forgotten about that since last year. They screamed and yelled and laughed—Anthony could tell by their open mouths. He tried to make out what they were saying, but only the faintest strains of the highest pitches came through his window, sealed tight until May.

Pretty Margery Sullivan was out there, her rabbit's fur earmuffs vanishing into the mass of black curls that sluiced over the collar of her pea jacket. Anthony liked her more than a little, so he leaned forward to tap the window and wave. But his mother must have sensed his impending exertion and she called to him from the kitchen,

"Anthony, you just sit still. Don't tire yourself for them kids."

Her voice was soft and high, still with the accent, "If them kids had any heart, they'd come in over here to see you, sick as you are!"

Anthony's mother had meant to say more, but as a woman who was naturally prone to nerves, she'd promised the priest and the doctor and her husband to "cut out that crying in front of the boy." She merely set a bowl of pastini and a glass of warm milk—atop a braided wicker placemat—on the end table for Anthony, who was still peering out the window. She stood silently for a moment. Took in the curved back of his dark, little head, the pale ears, the splotchy birthmark on the back of his neck. And then, Anthony's mother fled the room.

Anthony hated pastini because *everyone* knows pastini is nothing but food for babies and old-timers without teeth. He tried to ignore it there on the polished end-table, hot in its deep bowl, the spoon already stuck-in for him. *As if he couldn't put his own spoon in.*

It smelled real good, though, of chicken broth and butter and salt, of grated cheese. Heavy steam billowed from the bowl to fog the window and his horn-rimmed glasses so thoroughly that Anthony could no longer see the boot prints Margery Sullivan had left behind her in a trail down the sidewalk. Even amongst all the others, he'd have been able to pick hers out. She was probably almost in her own house by now, getting ready for her afterschool snack—whatever Sullivan's ate—maybe potatoes or bacon or cabbage or something. He sneaked to the window and wiped the fog off with his fist, but it just came back again.

The mirror across from him was an old one, blackened with age, yet Anthony could still make out his own face in it. Papa said they'd get it re-silvered someday soon, but Anthony thought it was better this way: like the surface of a lake with black lily pads floating every-where. He thought it was certainly a lot like the pond Ol' Miss Tobin said Narcissus had gazed into. Anthony missed school—though he knew most boys his age wouldn't have. And he missed Miss Tobin, too. She was a square-shaped woman who wore blue dresses, white collars, and wire spectacles. She'd smelled of Wrigley's Spearmint and pink erasers, and he missed that as well. Most of all, though, Anthony missed Greek Mythology class, which Miss Tobin taught.

Miss Tobin said Anthony was the only boy who loved the mythology as much as she did. And even though she'd been teaching forever and a day, no other boy had ever compared. And the girls this year didn't even come close, either. She often told Anthony that if he kept up with the mythology, he would go far in the world. He might even become a professor of Mythology, despite his being Italian—surely, he would.

In fact, Miss Tobin believed in Anthony so much she'd sent a big book called *Mythology: Timeless Tales of Gods and Heroes* to the house the very week Anthony's mother had told the principal Anthony couldn't come to school any longer—because of the thalassemia. The book had arrived wrapped in white butcher's paper, accompanied by a suede bookmark, soft and cream colored with gold embossed letters—A.N.—which stood for Anthony's name. It was the only monogrammed thing he'd ever owned; the kind of a bookmark meant only for book lovers who keep their books and bookmarks up off the floor and don't dog-ear the pages.

The book itself was heavy and overfilled Anthony's lap. The pages were smooth, the ink wondrously dark. The illustrations inside thrilled him with their deep blues and mellow ochres, and he liked to slip his fingertips over the silky, glossy paper, tracing the trees and skies there. Yes, yes, he adored the illustrations, but it was the *words* that truly carried him away. So he read that book. And he read it. And he read it. He read it until mother thought he'd ruin his eyes and begged him to listen to the radio instead. But Anthony ignored her. What did she know about it all? If he ruined his eyes, he'd just get thicker glasses, wire-rimmed ones like Miss Tobin had.

Here, then, with his small face looking out from the black pond mirror, he thought about how he'd look in Mrs. Tobin glasses—handsome of course. He also thought about how he disagreed with his mother a lot of the time, not just about reading. He even thought about how he even disagreed with Miss Tobin sometimes—though he would never have told her so in case she lost faith in his potential to go far. It wasn't that he loved being disagreeable; it was just that he had thoughts of his own these days that he could never give up. For instance, there was one that flew in the face of how Miss Tobin understood the story of Narcissus. *She* said Narcissus was punished for his vanity. But Anthony didn't see it that way. He didn't think it was much of a punishment at all, what happened to that fellow. In fact, he thought old Narcissus had it pretty swell—how bad could it be to turn into a flower and live forever beside a pond or stream or whatever?

He'd come to this conclusion the day he first saw a real narcissus, all white and a little yellow. It was the one Miss Tobin had brought to class in a little red clay pot. She'd put it right on her desk, near her daily red apple—which the students took turns bringing her—and her paper guillotine, which no student was allowed to touch.

She'd cleared her throat, pointed at the flower, and sang out "Let this flower serve as a reminder, nay, a warning, to all youth: *This* is what became of young Narcissus!"

Anthony had smiled at her and thought to himself, "That's one swell-looking flower."

He sat back in his recliner, picked up his spoon and ate just one bite of the pastini. Swallowing it with a sigh, he looked back into the old mirror. He was very white, he thought, like the narcissus flower, and a little yellow, too. And his neck was thin as a stem. He swayed in his bed-coat to mimic the breeze the real Narcissus would have felt near his pool of water.

Carla Nardone, Anthony's mother, often passed by her own window on her way between the kitchen and the door out of the house. She wore thick, square-heeled pumps and real silk stockings every day, from morning until it was time for bed. Those shoes of hers tapped along the red linoleum kitchen floor with purpose. She favored multi-colored house dresses, hems below the knee, and moved with a quick pace that put a person in mind of a rock hen. She would have appeared determined and reassuring to anyone who might see her there, though it was rare anyone ever did. Until now.

It used to be that she spent all day alone in the modest bungalow flanked by elms and set back precisely as far as every other modest bungalow on this end of the street. But now that Anthony was too sick to go to school, he was here with her every day. It used to be that she gave herself over to the unhurried business of kitchen-ish and laundry-like things that could easily fill a day with quiet satisfaction if done properly. And it used to be that each time she'd passed the blue china bowl of lemons on the table, she'd smiled at its unexpected beauty—surprised though it had been she who'd placed the bowl there and carefully arranged the lemons inside

Similarly, she'd waved at the canary in his cage, whenever he sang. Always pausing to listen up at him behind thin wires, much nearer to the ceiling than she. In fact, she could pass beneath the birdcage without ever ducking because she was quite short. This is why Mr.

Nardone had fashioned a pulley, so that Mrs. Nardone could lower the cage whenever she needed to feed the little creature or change his newspaper liner. In fact, Mrs. Nardone and Mr. Nardone were both short people, short enough to put a person in mind of the little china figurines on top of wedding cakes down at Palermo's Bakery.

Dr. Barron had told her years ago that Americans were all tall because they drank milk, and that made some sense to Carla Nardone. She had grown up with no milk to drink, and here she was tiny as could be. Like an ant. The Americans ordered bottles of milk delivered to their stoops, and they were nearly all tall. The cause and effect was easy to see, so she ordered milk delivery and thought about milk quite a lot.

Since her Anthony had become very sick, sick enough to be permanently excused from school, Carla no longer noticed the lemons in the bowl, or the canary, or the lovely red linoleum with gold specks everywhere. She was busy tending to Anthony in the easy chair, but it was more than that. Sometimes she just stood stock-still in the kitchen doing absolutely nothing, thinking absolutely nothing, looking out her little window and seeing nothing at all, nothing but the inside of her own mind, which seemed gray and misty. Yes, he was home with her now, always. No truant officer would come to the door to drag him back to school because he was excused. It would have been better that he was a hoodlum, she mused, than a sick, sick, sick boy.

When she'd told Doctor Barron about her milk idea, he'd said milk wouldn't cure Anthony, that there was no cure for the anemia. That it was because both she and Mr. Nardone were both carriers. It's the chance you take, he'd said, when Italians marry Italians. But Carla thought maybe Barroni-Now-Barron didn't know as much as he thought he did, and to her mind, if milk could make a boy grow larger than his parents, it might just cure the anemia as well. Who could say? This was America where all manner of things were possible.

Sure, sure, she knew about the anemia back in Sicily—some people had it, and none of them ever got better, true enough. But maybe that was from lack of milk. The Nardones weren't rich, but her husband had a good job with the Zenith factory, and there was enough money for all the milk they could drink.

These days, Mr. Nardone worked late, so Carla left his supper plate under a neat turquoise cloth with red whip stitch along the edges. She'd made it especially for that purpose. After she covered the food, she put Anthony to bed and put on her nightgown and went to bed herself, before he came in. The neighbors stayed away now, too—the Italian ones thinking maybe the evil eye was afoot, and the others never having come around much to begin with. If the Nardones had had family in the neighborhood, that would have been different. But they didn't. Everyone was back in Sicily or else dead. Carla and her husband had just gotten here fifteen years ago, come on a plane. They were not like the old-timers who lined the street, who'd come on boats before 1900, who spoke very old-fashioned Sicilian, who were busy with their generations of American children and grandchildren. And they were not like the Americans either. They had only one another. Really.

Carla dropped oil into water and made incantations—and when those didn't seem to work, she called in a professional *stregha*. The old Millefiore woman who'd come over in 1895 marched around the house burning herbs and mumbling even stronger incantations over Carla's Anthony in his chair. After the witch left, Carla went a step further and tied a thick red string around her boy's wrists and more red strings around the posts of his bed. He already wore the gold horn, but she removed it, spit on it, polished it, and put it back around his neck, reinvigorated.

Carla also said a thousand Our Fathers and countless Hail Marys, her dark head bent in prayer in the kitchen, in the church, at her bedside. She made daily one-sided pacts with Jesus; Jesus, because God himself was too intimidating. She felt the younger one was more likely to help. After all, he was his mother's son. Also, she made sure not to forget St. Anthony, her son's name saint, who was not just good at helping find lost items but also known for health-related miracles. And according to the doctor, a miracle was what they needed.

But no matter who she prayed to, or how many promises she made, her child continued to weaken in the window. And Carla's husband, a man who had the sighing kind of breathing she'd recently discovered gave her the *agita*, that husband, he worked longer and longer hours. She found his whiskers like black pepper stuck to the bowl of the bathroom sink, his dirty socks on the floor, his piss sprinkles at the base of the toilet: all evidence he still existed. And she cleaned it up.

He wasn't a bad man, she thought, just weak as men and children may be in this world. Too weak to watch the boy, their only child, turning colors, shrinking away, all except for his round belly, which grew bigger by the day. Her husband just didn't want to see. Alright, alright, Carla understood that. So she decided to pity him as if he were another small boy, sometimes. But he was not. He was a grown man.

Oh, that doctor and him, and the priest, all three of them who'd told her to stop crying for the sake of the child. Told her as if she were a child herself, needing to be disciplined. How she wanted to pull the noses off their faces.

And yet she had. Yes, Carla Nardone, somehow, had stopped crying altogether.

"*Va bene!*" she'd said, "You want me to stop. I'll stop."

This stopping of crying is why she was able to deliver the pastini dry-eyed, and fluff the pillow without a sound, tune the radio to suit the patient, too—all of it without a single hitch in her breath. All this, Carla did, moving like a *mezzamorte*, her black pumps no longer lively, plodding hesitantly over the floor. And she never looked in the mirror anymore, either. And when she brushed her hair, she did it staring at the blank wall.

One night, before she fell asleep, Carla had a fleeting thought: what, she wondered, would it feel like if her child, her Anthony, died and suddenly the weight lifted. And then, on the tail of that unbidden and fleeting thought, though not immediately, guilt punched her right in the face. Struck dumb, she lay there in bed, still as her own tongue until morning. What kind of a mother, she interrogated herself, would ever think such a thing? It was such a very bad thing—evil really—that she couldn't confess it to the priest.

And besides, she'd begun to hate him a little anyway. He'd reprimanded her for having the *stregha* over—twice. How he'd even found out was anybody's guess, but he had eyes everywhere. And when he'd spoken to her about it, he went on and on and on. A priest never understands about having a witch over—it's true, but he didn't have to be so loud about it. No, Carla would never forget when Fr. Molloy had bellowed at her in the crowded narthex, how he went both white and flaming red, how he'd meant to crush her into obedience. Meant to shame her. But Carla had neither cowered nor shed a tear. She'd looked past the priest and found the door.

Later that night, she'd gone into the basement laundry room where earlier she'd hung and draped the wet laundry because it was too cold outside for hanging—what with all the wind and snow. It all waited patiently for her, her whites drying on poles, colors on the wooden racks, silk stockings on little wall pegs. The warm little room in the underbelly of the bungalow smelled of Roma powdered detergent and bleach and Fels Naphtha. Carla pushed her small face into a wall of very white sheets, drew a deep breath, and summoned tears, attempting to moan out a cry—more out of curiosity than need. To see if she could still do it. And she tried for a long time before she gave up and went to the kitchen to pour two tall glasses of milk. She added Ovaltine for good measure, clinking the long spoon against the amber-colored glasses, one at a time, as she urged the milk and the powder to join together. They resisted. Carla felt the brown powder was a very strange substance, like chalky soil, but the man on the radio promised it had all the vitamins and minerals a body needs.

The tin tray on which she carried the filled glasses had a red rose painted in the center, small white roses all around that, and a little rim to keep the glasses from slipping off. A good buy from the five and dime what seemed a lifetime ago. When she reached her Anthony, she saw he was fast asleep already wearing the blue flannel pajamas she'd gotten him last Christmas, with the white piping on the collar. She set the tray down on the floor with care so that she could lift the enormous book from his lap. It was open to a big picture of Persephone and Demeter.

Carla-Nardone-Once-Having-Been-A-Girl-Named-Carla-Pernice-Who'd-Loved-Stories-Herself recognized Demeter in her blue cloak. Immediately. Demeter looked very like the Madonna in light from the table lamp, but she was also different. Carla traced the illustration of golden sheaves of wheat with her small finger, and the outline of the chariot Demeter drove in her great search. She traced the nose of Demeter, the feet of Demeter, the hem of Demeter's robe that stirred in the wind of the page. This Demeter also came from *Sicilia*—and her plight to save her child was achingly familiar.

How long Carla stood rooted to the carpet beside Anthony's window, holding the massive book and staring at the glossy illustration, no one can say, but she stood there until her legs finally grew tired, her arm ached, and her mouth grew dry. And then she stood there a little bit longer still.

When Carla finally closed *Mythology: Timeless Tales of Gods and Heroes,* she placed it on the table with a little bump—though she didn't mean to—which woke Anthony. She sat him up with her hand on his back, smoothed down his hair, which was sticking up like a coal grate, and gave him one glass of Ovaltine. She drank the other herself, perched herself beside him on the wide seat of the easy chair, green and nubby and enormous as it was. In fact, the old chair was so much larger than Anthony and his Mamma that a third person could have fit. But no one else was there.

The old mirror with black spots hung in front of them, and they watched themselves drink down the Ovaltine. They each saw their own faces and they each thought their own quiet thoughts.

FOUR

To Be a Cat is a Fine Thing

Gatto-Fred knew what was what. He knew how to appreciate the way the weather had not been too hot nor too rainy nor too dry all summer long. He knew how to make sure he was fed every day and could avoid eating rats and mice in general, except for those stupid enough to come into His Woman's house. Those he ate, not because he relished the taste—they were just alright—but because catching and eating them was pleasing to His Woman. He knew not to eat the sick ones in the alley.

So, Gatto-Fred knew his needs, but he also knew his responsibilities—and always his needs and his responsibilities aligned because he was a natural cat. For instance, he walked beside His Woman to the shops and waited outside the door of each as she shuffled in over the thresholds to take things away from the men who stood behind the counters. She was old; he could smell the old on her, and he liked her that way.

Today, like many days, Gatto-Fred sat and watched His Woman's baby buggy to keep other cats away while she was inside the shop made of wood. He had seen other women, young women pushing theirs around with babies inside, but His Woman was cleverer than that—she pushed food in it. And when she came out of the shop, he sniffed the bag she carried for fish heads. He wasn't disappointed. There was *always* one for him. Sometimes they went to the next shop for some soft cheese as well, which he truly enjoyed. His best times with her were when they were alone in the kitchen on some rainy afternoon. She would feed a smear of cheese to him from the tip of her finger. He was always careful not to bite, only to lick.

When His Woman had finished taking things from all the favorite shops and the buggy was full, he watched her put her fist to her chest and pound three times, which meant it was time to walk home. A sign. And so, of course, he walked her all the way home, his paws padding the warm sidewalk, his tail straight up and hooked to the side with pride, his one eye watchful. People admired him as he strutted past, but he did not look at them, only at her, His Woman. He noticed other cats stuck behind glass windows, staring, as he made his way with the lovely scent of fish and cheese like a fog around them. These other cats, trapped and stupid, he knew must wish they were him.

Gatto-Fred was unafraid of the traffic in the street, as he understood it stayed on the street. He kept to the sidewalk, taking care not to get caught beneath the wheels of the buggy, full of brown paper sacks, or under the square heels of her shoes. He meowed for good measure, every once in a while, to keep things moving.

When they arrived at home, His Woman wrestled the buggy to make it go up the steps to the front porch. It reared up on big back wheels and she grunted. He waited for her at the top, like always, looking down and urging her as best he could. When she finally opened the screen door, as was custom, Gatto-Fred slipped in first. He was a cat, so that was what was expected of him. Also, it was what he wished.

Gatto-Fred trotted straight to the kitchen for water. He leapt onto the sink to drink directly from the faucet. She opened the tap for him so that it came out in a perfect thin stream. He put his paw into the stream over and over, licking the water from his fur. He preferred to drink that way rather than put his face up to the stream and get water up his nose. When he was done, he leapt down to let her know she could close the tap for now. He was satisfied.

Next, Gatto-Fred helped her by going inside one of the empty brown paper bags that lay on its side on the floor while she put away the things. He was glad that His Woman didn't touch him of her own accord but always waited for him to head-butt her arm or drop down from the high dresser onto her shoulder. Hugging and squeezing and picking up were things he just could not abide, which was why he disliked children. And he especially hated babies. Whenever there was one of those around, other women came with them, and these other women would chase him out of the room with a newspaper the second he got anywhere near the baby.

But no matter, there were no babies here now. No one but him and His Woman. So he sat in her lap while she fed him a cut up chicken kidney from the ice box. He let her stroke his thick fur— even letting her rub the little hollow place between the pads of his paws, where there was no fur, with her finger. Gatto-Fred closed his eyes and spread his toes so she could get in there better. But it wasn't all just convenience for him, no, Gatto-Fred really *loved* His Woman. And because he loved her, he made sure no other cat ever got close to her. This task kept him busy in the home and outdoors.

That night, like every night—after his dinner of fish head, Gatto-Fred meowed to His Woman so she would open the front door to let him outside.

Mow! Meow! Mow! He liked to change it up to let her know when he was in a hurry.

She used her front legs to push herself up from her chair, and he twined himself between her back ankles helping her move along the floor. When she finally opened the door, she held it open for him as he went in and out a few times before leaving for the night. This was to let her know it wasn't easy to leave her—it wasn't done lightly. He told her not to let any cats, dogs, or babies into the house and he'd see her in the morning. But once he did go, he never looked back at her—though he knew she stood with the door still open and watched him go. He could feel her gaze on his shoulders.

At liberty, in the dark of night, Gatto-Fred conducted his business.

First, he made sure no other cats were near the home, not in the bushes, up the trees, in the vegetable garden.

Second, he shit in the neighbor kids' sandboxes.

Third, he sprayed all over the neighborhood. From the place where the giant, long car-thing screamed along the tracks to the house where the three horrible long-haired dogs lived, on the other side of the busy road. It was why he'd drunk all that water at the faucet. It took a lot to do a good job.

Gatto-Fred liked to make love before he fought, but the other way around was fine as well. He walked the tops of a few wooden fences looking for queens in heat or male cats to batter and bite. Tonight, like most nights, he came across the two at once—and he was so delighted, he didn't know what to do first.

So he simply let his wildness take him.

The knot of fighting-mating cats, of which Gatto-Fred was central, spun like a child's top around the neighborhood without any thought to direction or location, feinting and leaping, sexing and scratching. The weather was fair and still—dogs barked, but only from behind fences and on clotheslines and chains up and down the alleys. So the cats did not care. They knew any dog that could get them would not come barking. Barkers were nothing.

In time, they found themselves in front of the house of the man who smelled of wet chickens. That man had a little gun and cracked the gun at cats whenever he liked. One night, when the snow had just melted, Gatto-Fred had seen a small cat get hit in the neck and a big cat in the belly. The first died while it was still running and the second many nights later in a terrible state.

It was long ago, when he was younger and not as careful that he'd been up on the old fence ready to leap down on a couple of new orange cats—find out what they were about. He'd never heard the window open or seen the little gun. When it hit him, it blew the eye right out of his head. He'd run and run through the neighborhood to get away from the pain, but it followed him. He'd hidden in an empty shed for a long time, for many nights, before he staggered back to His Woman. She put water and plants on his eye and raised her voice at him. And ever since then, he always tried to stay away from that wet-chicken-smelling house. But the other cats were headed there, and he fell in with them anyway. Like most nights, he had no choice.

In front of that house, they yowled and fought, mated and screeched some more. It was alive. They were alive. They called the man and his gun to do their worst. They dared the dogs to break their chains. Until they heard the window opening. Then they streaked away into the night—in a dozen different directions.

The man barked horrible noises into the air, from his window hole, as they ran. That chicken smell coming from his open mouth and the air behind him.

Gatto-Fred felt his missing eye ache as he flew past chain link fences—a hollow sort of feeling in his skull. His heart pounded and ached a little. He needed a rest, so he decided to call it a night, go back home to look in on His Woman. He always felt the best view of her at night was from the pear tree, so when he got there, he clawed his way straight up it. He could see into the open window of the room where she slept. Even in the dark—of course he could. There she was, in her bed, snoring like a darling. The human purr.

FIVE

Waiting for Butch Bobko

The blonde man lifted his trousers from where he'd draped them the night before—over the heavy walnut footboard—in the tiny spare room off the kitchen, in his sister's flat. The smells of lard and sugar from the donut shop stole in under the sash and made his stomach growl. Five-thirty in the morning, and traffic on the main roads was already vibrating, most of it headed east to Chicago. To the Water Market, to the building sites, to the demolition sites.

At this hour, there were very few fancy cars on the road. Five a.m. and the lawyers and accountants were still in bed snoring. This was the commute time for candy pourers, metal bangers, ditch diggers, gritty men of all sorts. They rode in trucks and panel vans, and Reinhold Ruhe knew his ilk well. Their collective breath smelled of black coffee, unfiltered cigarettes, and Listerine. They often nicked themselves shaving and wore bits of tissue on their chins until they fell off naturally. They told off-color stories on the way in to work and bounced in the seats of trucks with poor suspension. Normally, Reinhold would not be among them, bouncing in the seat of Butch Bobko's old red moving truck, wedged between Butch and another helper, aggravating his sensitive condition. But today Butch would be picking him up late; something had come up. Reinhold hadn't asked what—Butch was the boss, so you just didn't. You just made sure you were ready when he showed up.

The vinyl Roman shade in Reinhold's window, at half-mast, showed the garden, only a shade lighter than it had been in the night. There was the tired brick wall of Creme Crunch Donuts. The holly-hocks he'd helped his brother-in-law Nicky plant. The wooden picnic table, painted green to match the house, but still looking black at dawn. The holly-hocks stood along the fence to the alley like soldiers. He watched them.

A white mulberry tree, lush and wide as an oak, made Reinhold understand that he was a short-term guest here, and he looked away from its gravity to the cotton clothesline. He'd never actually seen his sister Lena carry the laundry as he was always at work on Mondays. But he noticed the wooden pegs clinging to the rope like straight-backed men with big heads. Clothespins hadn't changed a bit since he was a child—his sister's were just like his mother's had been. Just like his wife's were.

Reinhold Ruhe was the sort of person who didn't think in words—he didn't tell stories in his head. He didn't plan out what he would say or should have said. And it wasn't a choice, it's just how he was. Instead, he thought in images and flashes and sudden knowledge. He wasn't sure it had always been this way, but maybe it had. Or maybe it was more so lately.

As he maneuvered one lanky leg into yesterday's work pants, Reinhold envisioned the mouth and big smooth chin of his wife Ida, floating between ribbons of green corn leaves, in Wisconsin. The long hairy leaves flopped this way and that in a hot summer breeze, and her mouth looked like a prizewinning strawberry. But the corn. The corn looked real bad, dry at the edges and thirsty. He blinked fast, and the image left him.

A cat skirted the top edge of the brick wall of Creme Crunch Donuts. Reinhold yanked the shade down to release it up, and it furled, clearing the window entirely. He followed the sightline of the cat. Blue jays circled and shrieked over it, but it moved on unflustered. When the cat slipped out of sight, Reinhold groaned forward on the edge of the bed to pull on his socks, worn but clean. He'd washed them in the bathroom sink the night before, dried them in the window sill. The socks smelled of Fels Naphtha and of a private kind of cleanliness.

Summer had just begun, but when it ended, Reinhold planned to return to Wisconsin. Five years earlier, and with a spurt of courage that surprised himself, he'd upped and taken his Ida and their adopted son Freddy away from this city. They'd sold the little motel they'd owned in Oakhurst, and everything in it, to buy the farm in Hillsboro, a farm of their own. Wisconsin, where no one knew his troubles or pitied him for them.

But in Wisconsin he'd failed—failed so miserably that this was the third summer running he'd had no choice but to take the Amtrak back to Chicago for paying work. His brother-in-law's friend, Butch Bobko, had hired him to move furniture. It was back-breaking work for a young man, and Reinhold wasn't young. He wasn't old either. He was somewhere in the middle. The moving job had been just enough to keep him from losing the farm, but, of course, it required him to leave the farm behind all summer long. Chicago people always moved in the spring or summer, and you couldn't blame them for it.

The sun was up now, and back at the farm, without him, Ida would be feeding the dog, slopping the ten pigs, driving the tractor like a man. It was early July, so she'd be putting up jam. If he closed his eyes, and he did, he saw the jars red as rubies, but dimmed by a coat of sand dust. Sand dust which blew in through every chink in the clapboard farmhouse. The farm had sandy soil left behind from the glaciers that had once ground down sandstone cliffs into nearly nothingness as they slid southward. The old timer who'd sold them the place had coughed into his big red handkerchief saying, yes, yes, the land would produce—you just had to think through how you went about things because sand is sand.

Ida would be sun blistered from the hard work outdoors, patting vinegar onto her pink nose and then walking the rows. His son Freddy would be at the school on the other side of the town, glum that he'd been taken away from his cousins and moved to godforsaken Wisconsin. Reinhold hoped he'd appreciate it someday, when he inherited the farm, but nothing came easy on that land for Reinhold and Ida. Sand snakes slithered atop the furrows, and the poor excuse for soil blew into the barn to make small drifts. It gathered into the eyes of the pigs who ran squealing to hide under the pines. Reinhold drove all the visions from his mind—though the pigs were slow to leave and looked over their shoulders at him with no little resentment as they faded away.

Smoothing the chenille bedspread, Reinhold made the bed tight like they taught him in the army. He plumped up his pillow, which smelled of goose feathers and the sweat from his own scalp. He buttoned his trousers.

His sister Lena had married into Italians, and there were Italians everywhere on the block—in fact Mulberry Park was mostly Italians now. A quiet man, Reinhold often felt the Italians were far too much. They yelled out windows and from porch to porch, sometimes laughing, sometimes cursing in their language. But other times he felt freed by them because they appeared to be without subterfuge.

Reinhold could never ask his sister why she married an Italian. He could never ask her if she was content with it or if she were lonely, though he'd like to know. He was able to ask her some things—could he set the table for her? Repair the hinges on the shed door? Scrub the front steps? But nothing prying.

Reinhold heard Lena's house slippers over the kitchen linoleum, and then the sounds of her lighting the stove, filling the percolator, pulling a store-bought coffee cake from its brown bag atop the icebox. Nicolo was already gone to work at the railroad, and the children were still asleep, made lazy by their long summer vacation. Lena called to him, "*Reinhold, komm. Kuchen und caffe ist da*. She always spoke German to him—low-German with its drumming regularity and instinctive humility.

"*Tööf mol kort*," he opened the bedroom door a crack to whisper into the kitchen. On my way.

Before leaving his little room, Reinhold turned towards the small round mirror on the bedroom wall and combed his tufty light hair as down as he could get it. He put on his strongest face and pushed the bedroom door open, directly into her kitchen, his suspenders up over his shoulders and his back like an exclamation mark.

The Chicago Daily News rested, neatly folded, near his cake plate. Everyone said that the '48 Olympics were going to be the best ever, but Reinhold had little time for sport anymore. Lena had given him the biggest mug in the house and cut him a generous wedge of crumb cake. Turning away from the sink, he watched her tighten the belt of her red-checked housecoat, tuck her red hair behind her pale ears. She wore new cat's eye glasses, and Reinhold thought, more than anyone else he knew, she did truly look like a cat in those. An orange cat, the friendly kind.

When they sat down together at the green Formica kitchen table, the vinyl seats of the chrome-legged chairs sighed like bellows under them. Lena reached across the table and poured Reinhold's coffee and then her own. Reinhold wondered at this woman, his youngest sister, who was both familiar to him and not. As familiar as anyone, really, but then again, they'd grown up mainly apart.

The twins, Lena and Frida, had been just nine months old when Mutti had died of the Swine Flu. Reinhold didn't need to close his eyes to see his mother dead in her bed—dark circles ringing her eyes and her lips without any color at all. And yet her chest had looked to him like she might begin breathing again any moment. He saw the twins squalling in their shared cradle, laid head to foot in order to fit. He saw Vatti, too—strong farmer that he was—burning up with fever in the bed beside Mutti. And that was it. That was all. After that Mutti was gone forever. And Vatti was never completely well again.

Even here in the warm summer kitchen, Reinhold felt the chill of that long gone, cold winter in his feet. It had been too cold to dig graves. And because of that Mutti, and all those neighbors who died of the flu, had been stored in the church basement with the windows cracked open for some weeks. When they finally went into the ground, his father was still in the bed, too ill to stand at the grave. Reinhold had stood there, though, with his older sisters, and he could still hear the raspy sound his small handful of dirt had made when it scattered across the top of Mutti's casket. He had carefully stepped around the graves of the other people, so many mounded high since the epidemic began.

If he'd have been a man then, he'd have taken care of his twin baby sisters, but he'd been only a little boy. And in the family, no one had been willing or able to take on two babies at once. Too much they all said. He was five then, it was water long under the bridge, but even now, the memory of such utter helplessness made his Adam's apple jerk. The vision of little Lena, the colicky twin, she'd been sent to Tante Grunda, who already had four children of her own. The happier twin, Frida, was sent to Oma and Opa. After all, she was the namesake of their dead daughter.

Frida had lived as an only child for eight years until Opa and then Oma died. In those eight years, Frida had grown fat and sassy while Lena, in the house of Tante Grunda, stayed thinner and smaller, more hesitant. The once-shared cradle had gone with Frida to Oma's, and Lena had been put into bed with her girl cousins. He knew this, though he'd not seen it for himself as he'd never been to Auntie's as a child. But somehow, he had witnessed baby Lena wedged between Cousin Birte and the wall to keep her from falling from the bed. A flash without words. Her little brow was sweaty and her tiny fists clenched tight in determined sleep. Somehow, he saw it.

He saw Lena check the time on her watch. He feared he was holding her up. When he left, she'd get dressed for her job at American Can, then she'd wake the kids and send them across the street to their cousins. They'd switched her to days again. He watched her carefully consider words meant to reassure him that he was no bother at all. He saw how she feared he'd feel by her mentioning it. He saw she changed her mind. He accepted the second cup of coffee she poured him, and he was glad she poured one for herself as well. It wasn't as late as he'd thought.

Reinhold heard Lena asking him about the farm. Crop rotation. He heard himself talk about the sandy soil with her. He felt his eyes cast themselves down at the rag rug beneath the table—crazy colors pulled together in never-ending rings. Mustard, purple, red, sand, soil, water blue. But he felt apart from where he was.

When he picked up the paper and scanned the articles about Eisenhower, he swam in the black and white ink instead of reading.

And he saw glimpses of Mutti's kitchen in the white spaces—heavy kraut crocks lining the long wall. A butter churn in the corner. A plum cake resting under a tea towel. Neat, rectangle calling cards from the neighbor women set in the china bowl on the little shelf. Mutti's hair fell in two long plaits to her waist, and the plaits danced with the rhythm of her churning. In his vision, his oldest sister Minka soon came to help, then Anna, then Mina, and then himself. The paddle was warm to his palm, but he wasn't tall enough to make it churn. It didn't matter; the girls had done the work already. Mutti took a short knife and cut a fat sour pickle into four long slices. She handed a slice to each of the children and then licked the pickle juice from her fingers.

Lena brushed crumbs from the table with a tiny straw whisk broom into an equally tiny dustpan she kept on a nail on the wall. He saw that she hoped his injury wasn't paining him, but it was in such a place that she would never ask about it, No one would. Only his doctors and his wife knew exactly what damage lay hidden there. How he'd been injured was a story, and he didn't tell himself stories. But he saw his draft papers and he saw the Ardennes. He saw. And he felt.

Reinhold had never spoken to any of his sisters about the war, but he knew they'd heard enough. From a cousin who'd been fighting nearby. They'd heard how Reinhold had sliced wide the ass of a dead cow and crawled inside as the real Germans marched over his head, shooting everything in sight. How he'd been still inside the cow's body when the bullet found him. Still and quiet. He watched Lena rub the vinyl piping on the edge of her chair's seat with her thumbnail as he remembered the inside of a cow—dark, warm, suffocating.

Lena's second cup of coffee was drunk black, like the first, and she sipped it slowly as she spooned clabbered milk over her second slice of cake. She told him she could go in late today. He thought black coffee was a habit she must have picked up from the Italians. Click went the cuckoo clock on the wall behind them. Humm went the traffic on River Street seven doors down at the corner, smoother now with bankers and salesmen, teachers and managers. His sister stirred her coffee though there was nothing in it besides the black. Clink, clink went the spoon.

She had that guilty look, the one she got when she was about to say how the twins had been the lucky children. He was sure she was thinking it. Then she said it aloud, rubbing his shoulder, *we were the lucky ones.*

Yes, Minka, Anna, Mina, and Reinhold remained with Vatti— nine, seven, six, and five. Reinhold had been one of those white-blonde boys. Now he was dusted brown from sun, wind, war, and age. Forty-five years of scanning horizons. Lena patted his hand, and he allowed it. Three short pats.

Her hand was warm and freckled. Reinhold smudged out errors he made in the day's crossword puzzle. The puzzles, he found, kept him from conjuring too many images. But he didn't have the education to answer most of the questions. Vatti in those first months after the great flu, his mustaches overgrown like brooms, his whole tired body like a fish hook bent over Mutti's black Singer, his foot pumping the pedal. He mended their clothes. He bent over at the stove helping little Minka to make dinners—oats, potatoes, eggs, kraut, pickles.

Vatti had kept the farm going. His face was long with grief but pulled itself into fleeting smiles here and there. One day a distant cousin from two towns over had come out to help for a short time, but when it became clear she was after marrying him, Vatti had sent her away as fast as he could. The children had been glad. This cousin had made good cakes and hadn't slapped them but once, but she wasn't their mother at all.

"May I have another slice of cake?" Reinhold asked Lena.

She cut a square, lifted it onto his plate, and slid the dish of clabbered milk to him.

The little brown crumbs tasted of butter and cinnamon. Lena pressed her fingertip on those that had fallen into the bottom of the cake plate and ate them from her finger. The way her face looked now made Reinhold see that day he'd come with Vatti to collect Lena for a family photo. Her face had been sticky with tears, and she'd sobbed that she didn't want to go. But Reinhold had handed her a sticky piece of horehound candy from his corduroy pocket and so lured her out from under the dining table. They'd all rode to the photographer's studio in the wagon full of squashes and turnips and making a creaking noise, their father stiff and straight in his black suit.

Vatti had made do in the house well enough without a wife, but the farm was another thing. The summer Reinhold turned six, Vatti hired two farm hands. One of the men had been a bad one. Mohr was his name, and he'd crept up to the house from the fields in the early afternoons when Vatti and the other hand were toiling in the sun. A dark shadow that crept up the slope and in the door of the plain-faced farmhouse. Other fathers would have put the children to work in the fields, but Vatti had sought to spare his children hard labor at tender ages.

Minka, the oldest sister, had tried to hide the rest. She'd shoved Reinhold and the other children into the oaken chest, in the grandfather clock, in the larder amongst the canisters, when she'd seen the bad man coming up the hill. At first that had worked, but eventually the bad man found them anyway. Each one. Mohr, like bad men of his sort everywhere, threatened them all. He told them he'd kill Vatti should they tell. And they believed he would.

But then came the sores and fevers. Vatti brought them to the doctor. The doctor had seen this before, in the last war—venereal disease. The children were questioned by the doctor and Pastor Able; and they cried as they told what had happened, believing Mohr would come back to kill Vatti.

But Mohr never came back. Instead, the children were sent away. To the sanitarium. For months. And so, Lena was right. Only she and Frida had been safe, on the other side of town. So far away. Stir the coffee. Stir the coffee.

Lena rummaged in her housecoat pocket, pulling out a tinker toy and a cough lozenge before finding three dimes. She laid them on the table, glinting. He could see she was thinking about his debts.

The dimes made him see the collection plate at St. Matthew's. Pennies and dimes. When they came home from the sanatorium, cured, the people at church refused to sit in the same pew with them. So, they sat in a pew all alone with Vatti, who wasn't allowed to handle the collection baskets anymore, miles of space on either side. Other children weren't to play with them after school, either, nor were they invited to birthday parties anymore. They were dirty children.

A young and stupid fly crawled near Reinhold's hand, and he caught it in a cupping way, rising to let it out the back door. Lena heard the fly buzz under her brother's fingers and watched him take it away. Each blinked. Where was Butch Bobko anyway?

Pastor Able had taken the children away from Vatti. He'd given Reinhold to Uncle Heine, to a home where he was not allowed to sit at the table with the family. Where he worked in the field and lived in the barn. He was just seven years old, then. They beat him.

Reinhold returned to his chair and asked Lena about the weather forecast, had she heard how high the heat might go today? Reinhold saw his Ida and their big fluffy dog, Cap. They were walking in circles around the farmhouse waiting for him to get home. Ida looked impatient, flustered, maybe even annoyed. When she'd married him, twenty years ago and just before he'd left for the Army, how could she have known he'd be shot down there? He'd once thought she might leave him. He'd almost hoped she would, but his big wife laughed and said, "it's okay." She'd found a baby boy to adopt: Freddy. Now, sometimes Ida went out late with other men. Reinhold couldn't blame her. He pretended she was out with women friends, out to a show maybe, or a card game.

Butch Bobko finally pulled up in front. The rounded hood of his big truck looking like a big, red clam. Reinhold and Lena watched through the kitchen window as Butch pulled his cap tight over his big head and walked up the sidewalk. Reinhold rose from his chair with a tiny grunt.

Butch pounded on the door, "I'm here, let's go, Rein!"

"Comin' Butch!"

While horning his stocking feet into his farmer's work boots, Reinhold closed his eyes and envisioned a plan, a story, really.

It was simple. He would shoot himself in the head with his army pistol, which was back in Wisconsin. So, he'd have to wait. But that was good. It would give him time to make the full summer's earnings to give to Ida. He would do it out of doors and while Ida was out. The pain below knifed him as he put on his cap. It knifed him every time he moved, and nothing helped, not even whiskey—he'd tried it.

Reinhold carried his plate to the sink, scraped it, rinsed it, and dropped it into the soapy water that waited. He placed one hand flat on each side of his baby sister's head and drew her to him. He had never kissed his sister before, but there he kissed her among the thousands of freckles just above her eyebrows. She smelled of Ivory soap and cinnamon. Her cats-eye glasses bumped his nose.

"Take those dimes and get yourself a Coke and a sandwich." she said to him, smiling. He picked up the dimes from the tabletop, dropped them back into her housecoat pocket, and smiled back at her.

"It's okay," he said. "I'll wait until dinner."

Spring Races

Spring of 1952 opened itself late into April. It had been a hard winter, the kind Midwesterners moan over in long-suffering nasal tones, hands chopping the air as if freeing themselves from under the ice of a frozen lake. And yet, like all things good or bad, that winter had indeed finally come to an end. The day's soft breeze held distinct warm and cool threads blowing in a tremulous way. And it was the warm streams that tricked the children into peeling off their wool coats and dumping them right there on the sidewalk.

Teddie Millefiore, less than a month away from her sixth birthday, handed out fat plugs of railroad chalk from a tin pail. Her real name was Teodora, but no one ever called her that. Her daddy brought the chalk home from the railroad yard for her on Fridays, and she had loads of it. The pail scraped against the sidewalk as she dragged it here and there, to this child and to that. A group of fifteen or so crowded the sidewalk in front of the dark green house, all intoxicated by the simple change in the season. They chattered and twirled not unlike the birds in the trees above them, robins and red winged blackbirds just come north and juncos and chickadees gathering to head south.

Teddie's big sister Dolores, age ten, was so enchanted with the sudden warmth that she not only removed her heavy coat but escaped from her socks and shoes as well. Tiptoeing on pallid feet over spalled concrete and into the front lawn where she stood still, letting cold water squelch up from the earth to fill the spaces between her toes.

Dolores was looking down at the way the mud made shapes when she felt eyes on her back from across the street. In one ungraceful movement, she pushed her heavy horn-rimmed glasses up her nose, licked her lips, and turned to see Mrs. Contralto framed, like a painting of immense and dark proportions, in the direct center of the plate glass parlor window across the street. The woman's mouth was wide open in shock.

Mrs. Contralto rapped her strong knuckles and shook two fists at Dolores and the other children. Dolores took a breath of disappointment and began to mince her way, this time walking on her cold, numb heels only, back across the sidewalk to where she'd left her stockings stuffed into the necks of her heavy winter shoes. She knew even though she obeyed Mrs. Contralto's cross-street command, the old witch would still tell on her. It was an unspoken rule, and they all knew it: there was to be no removal of coats, socks, or shoes until after Mother's Day.

While Dolores felt the eyes of Mrs. Contralto early, the others looked up only when the rapping came cracking on the breeze a second time. Little Teddie dropped her hunk of railroad chalk, looking up from where she lay on her belly. She'd been stretched longwise on the sidewalk, carefully inscribing the number six, which looked a lot like a tadpole, into a hopscotch square. Her cousin Daniel, age seven, dropped his chalk as well—halfway through designing the Blue-Sky exit square. Bossy cousin Carmella, eleven, crouched like an old woman picking beans at the foot of the hopscotch path, her rosary in hand. She'd been praying over the entire affair in her bossy voice, making it drone. All the kids, and everyone in the neighborhood, knew Carmella was going to grow up to be a nun, which was why she got to be bossy—she was no less than God's fiancé on the sidewalk. Mrs. Contralto's intrusion brought Carmella's forty-ninth Hail Mary to a sudden but short pause. Carmella looked at the Contralto woman and rolled her own eyes heavenward. She made the sign of the cross before resuming her Hail Mary, chanting more loudly, walking as slowly as she could toward her coat.

Many of the kids on the sidewalk were cousins, but there was also a smattering of non-related neighbors; a couple of Sullivan sisters, a smaller Straglimiglia boy with cherub hair and dimples, two LaPrimas from the end of the block who sometimes picked their noses at the exact same time, an uncounted mess of LaRoccos, and one kid no one had ever seen before—he must have wandered over from another neighborhood. He was even weirder than Dolores with his hoppy steps on the hopscotch trail and his unknown face, but they'd given him his share of chalk and the job of finding hopscotch rocks alongside the road. He was busy making a mound of them, all flat and well-suited, when he too noticed the crazy woman banging the window and pointing. It was loud and commanding, but the stranger had no idea what it meant.

"She's a mean old dishrag," Teddie informed him, "and she'll tell our mothers whatever we do."

The stranger boy stared at Mrs. Contralto, and then at Teddie, and then at his pile of hopscotch stones. Perhaps he imagined Mrs. Contralto tracking down his mother, six full blocks away—his mother learning he'd wandered those six blocks when he was only allowed to go one.

"Goodbye," he said, and ran back from where he'd come.

The rest of the children shrugged themselves back into their winter coats in full sight of Mrs. Contralto, hating her. Hating her with a hatred so reverent and pure that it nearly made them glow. Her face remained in the window, long and dark, edged by its unbecoming sideburns. She watched them a while longer to make sure they didn't take those coats off again.

Dolores and Teddie noticed Anthony Nardone staring out from the window of the house next to Mrs. Contralto's. Anthony's face was very close to the window and his hands were waving, trying to catch the eye of Margery Sullivan. Everyone in the neighborhood knew he was in love with Margery, but they also knew he was going to be dead long before he could marry her or anyone else. That's why he was never allowed to play outdoors.

Lucky, Teddie thought, that Mrs. Contralto's window was even with Anthony's. It made it so the woman couldn't see Anthony's waving at all; if she had, she'd have knocked at his door to tell his mother he was tiring himself out again. Teddie gave him a quick wave and Dolores waved too with wild vigor, her lips spreading into a smile that showed off her extra-big new front teeth.

Mrs. Contralto mistakenly believed the girls were waving at her and was taken aback. When she was satisfied that all the *bambini* were properly clothed, she turned her attention to an equally pressing situation: the spaces under her husband's dresser drawers, where she was sure he was hiding dirty magazines.

She marched into their bedroom and yanked the drawers out. One, two, three, four, five, six, big ones, and then the little two on top. Nothing. She found nothing hidden there but a rat's tail comb that had fallen through the seam in the wood and an old love letter she'd written him years ago. She didn't bother to read it; she already knew what it said. And besides, she was in a hurry. If she had found the magazines, she'd have left the drawers out, overturned in scandalized piles on the bedroom floor, but as it was, she had to slot them back in before he got home. He wasn't going to make a fool out of her. And she had to hurry because she still had the summer house out back to search.

It was only because Mrs. Contralto was so very occupied in her hunt for contraband that she never saw Tommy and Terry Sullivan amble up the sidewalk toward the hopscotch crowd. Margery Sullivan's older brothers were what Mrs. Contralto called "rough Irish." The kind of Irish that didn't move out with the rest when the neighborhood changed to Italian—because they couldn't. Mrs. Contralto had heard the Sullivan boys had a German mother, and she knew it to be true, but she discounted it in favor of simplifying things. Rough Irish is all they were to her.

The Sullivan boys did have a rough exterior, indeed, like birds that have flown through a windstorm and lost some pinfeathers. This was because they had been knocked perpetually askance by the beatings their father administered, not just to them but to everyone in their home. But, still, the boys got the worst of it. As they entered their

earliest teens, they began to stomp brashly, they began to forget caution—because caution had never kept them safe enough. They began
to feel like bad boys, not hoodlums or criminals, no, but simply
wrong. Under their lawn-thick crew cuts, their hazel eyes squinted
hard as cowboys', but inside their Sears and Roebuck work boots,
their ankles were still soft as those of infants.

Tommy and Terry Sullivan weren't about to play hopscotch—a
game for girls and babies—but they weren't above playing games
in general. Though they were older than any of the other kids on
the sidewalk, Tommy and Terry Sullivan, at twelve and thirteen, felt
drawn to the other children, to the industry and happiness on the
sidewalk. To the sunshine there. They'd not have admitted such to
their school friends, but between one another, they had no secrets.
There were lots of things they didn't like other people to know—that
they still played like kids along the railroad tracks, that when they
were bad their father made them sleep without blankets or pillows
on the basement floor, that the cement-cold seeped into their bones
to bend them like old men which was the real reason they slouched.
Or that they worried their mother would run away one day never to
be seen again and they'd be left behind with *him*. Their sisters knew
some of it, of course, but never spoke it.

As they met the children on the sidewalk, Tommy approached
his little sister Margery first and gave her his handkerchief to wipe
her runny nose. He tightened her lopsided red scarf so that it stayed
nearer her neck, and he gave her a shove.

"Whadd'a'ya say we do somethin' more fun?" he asked the lot of
them. They swarmed him and Terry with shouts and cheers. These
little kids were always excited when big kids came by. But what
would they play?

Tommy thought hard: "I know, we'll get our wagon and you all
get your wagons, and we'll have a wagon speed race."

The group set to action, scattering and then coming back
together like a murmuration. The Sullivans fetched their wagon;
Tommy pulled it alongside himself as he ran it across the street, his
rolled dungarees tight at his ankles. It was a little squeakier than last
year, and a little rustier, too. But it was still solid.

Little John and Daniel brought another wagon, smaller and "gimpy" they said. And Dolores, squinting at the sun, wandered back to the sidewalk with hers as well. The race, Tommy announced, would happen in the train station parking lot, where they could race all day if they liked because it was Sunday and the lot was pretty empty. Tommy lifted up a cigarette butt left on the sidewalk by some adult and reached into his pocket for a match, which he struck emphatically, smoking as they pulled their wagons to the destination.

"This is the spot," Tommy cleared his throat, "of the first annual Mulberry Park Speedway Races!" He coughed out a little smoke and made a series of additional announcements culminating in the very basic rules: no cheating and no crying.

The first leg of the race soon commenced. Over the parking lot they went, shrieking, laughing, faster and faster, sunshine in their faces laughing back at them. Carmella brayed like a *ciucciariello*, her short, stocky body pulling with real might. Little John kicked and kicked at the asphalt, skinny Daniel urging him on, yelling "Mush!" "Mush!" Big Tommy Sullivan kicked off too, and his legs were longest. They had the pogo-stick quality of impending manhood. He plunged his wagon into the lead. Six-year-old Teddie, her banana curls stretched behind her like two slinkies, gripped the handle and tried to steer— as was the passenger's job—pulling it to the left and then to the right. Faster and faster they went. The youngest and the oldest together, toward the final curb that indicated the finish line. Tommy turned his head to look over his shoulder. Behind them he saw Carmella's determined mouth yelling something as her leg churned, driving forth the clattering wagon Dolores steered. Little John's wagon was so far back, he might as well have quit; and his passenger, Daniel, showed a long face collapsing in disappointment. Tommy's brother, Terry, cheered from the sidelines with the other kids who were waiting their turns in following races. Tommy Sullivan gave one final kick and he and Teddie surged toward the finish line. And as they did, the handle of the wagon wrenched mightily, escaped Teddie's small grasp, and came down on her forehead with a thwack to split it.

74

A mighty caterwauling ensued. All of the other children, including Tommy's brother Terry, wailed at once. The blood. The blood. The blood. Teddie Millefiore screamed loudest of all, and she certainly had a right to. Tommy could hardly think what to do, but he managed somehow. He pulled his sister's red scarf from her neck and wrapped it around Teddie's forehead, a terrible headband. And then the whole lot of them, wagons and pullers and passengers, solitary runners and audience members, they all raced up the Singer Street sidewalk for help. Teddie was still wailing, but feeling pretty special as well. Margery and Helen Sullivan blew her kisses as they ran. Dolores bawled for her baby sister's split head. Carmella yelled, "Make way! Make way!"

Tommy was sure Teddie's family would attack him on the street for everyone to see, and he was equally sure he deserved it. He knew Teddie's Pa would strangle him half to death for busting the little girl's head—and Teddie's Pa was a golden gloves boxer, you know. And then, later, he also knew his own old man would choke him in the basement. But still he ran toward the source of his own gory end, because all in all, he was a good boy, even if he was a bad one.

Alerted by the grumphing noises speeding wagons make on an uneven sidewalk, Mrs. Contralto raised her head from where it had been, down near the floorboards of her backyard gazebo, her knuckles rapping them to see if any might be loose and hiding a secret space. As her eyes reached the height of the screened windows of the summer house, she gasped at what flashed in her peripheral vision. An arrow shaped herd of children moving with far too much determination to mean anything good, and at the head of it, that rough Irish, Tomaso Sullivan. And there with him, his brother Teredo, twice as bad again—him with the lazy eye.

Mrs. Contralto sprang to her feet and rushed through her backyard, around her house, and towards the phalanx on the sidewalk. Some would later say she was frothing at the mouth, but just a little. Further enraging the woman, she was slowed when she twisted her ankle in a garter snake hole along the way. She shrieked in pain and frustration. Heads poked out from open windows up and down the block, responding to the cacophony of noise and the flash of red wagons.

Giuseppa Millefiore made her way out her front door and down the porch stairs at her house.

Sick little Anthony Nardone pulled himself to standing next to his easy chair and stared through the picture window, mouth agape, at the crowd across the street.

And in her flat, in her kitchen, Lena Millefiore heard Tommy Sullivan calling for her with a primal fear caught in his vocal cords, a strangulation of sorts, "Teddie's Ma! Teddie's Ma! Teddie's Ma!"

Had he called out "Mrs. Millefiore" he might have had six or seven women rushing at him ready to kill, so he'd narrowed it down to the appropriate one. Tommy had a good mind.

Lena made one last snip with the scissors she was using to cut bunches of green grapes into small clusters—manageable so that her family wouldn't pick the spine of the grapes bare like wild animals—as her brain registered the fact that the hysterical yelling was for her. That it was now both Mrs. Contralto and a Sullivan boy screaming. Lena, Teddie's mother, felt her heart drop onto the top of her uterus, and she felt her uterus push the heart back up to her throat. She knew her child was hurt, and she knew which one—the *baby*. She swallowed and flew out the front door, into the street, the grape-snipping scissors still in her hand, her freckles standing out in constellations against the dead white of her frightened face.

When Lena got to the crowd in front of the house, Mrs. Contralto already had Tommy Sullivan by the back of his shirt collar and was swinging him in circles, but he evaded her full grasp to a degree, twisting and floating, and so they did a strange dance in the very middle of the street. Cars going around them.

Tommy didn't cry, and Mrs. Contralto interpreted his dry eyes, not as a sign of strength or weakness, but as sheer defiance, and she swung him more rapidly until she lost her grasp on his twisting, ripping collar and he found himself suddenly free. He rushed to Lena and now he *was* crying. Choking out the story. He told the truth. All the children nodded their heads, even poor Teddie, who looked like a bloody Halloween monster from Hunky Huckster's Haunted House. Cousin Carmella added a quick Our Father, which she performed in front of Mrs. Contralto in the way she might one day perform an exorcism, holding her pilfered mass card like a shield. She said "protect us from evil" as the loudest words of all.

"You're never gonna be no nun," Irene Contralto spat at her. "I know you run around without pants under your skirt. I know you kissed your cousins, and not just the boy ones, either."

"Back, *beastia*," Carmella spat in return. "Saints protect us." And then she smiled her most beatific smile. Normally that smile would have gotten her a great many hugs from her aunts, but though they had all streamed out of their flats, they were preoccupied with Teddie's bleeding head.

Mrs. Contralto would have liked to grab Carmella Millefiore by her coarse little pigtails and give her some of what she'd just moments ago been giving to Tommy Sullivan. She had plenty to go around. But by that time there were Millefiore everywhere, and they were in no mood to have their children receive the discipline Mrs. Contralto believed they so desperately needed.

The Millefiore women gathered in a tight knot around little Teddie on the sidewalk. Teddie could see nothing but them, not the street, not the sky, not the sun. Their hips and legs, a stockade fence of real proportions. Their high-up faces were like multiple moons, all full, full, all familiar: Mamma, Aunt Agata, Aunt Pina, Gramma, and the rest, and now, gently pushing her way in after having run blocks from her home on Fifteenth, borne by the news, Aunt Fil.

Fourteen stitches went into her blank forehead, and Teddie fought the doctor the whole while, watching the needle from the corner of her eye, kicking the white cot, flailing until the nurse had to lay across her to hold her down. She left with a decoration in heavy black thread, a line the very shape of one edge of the handle of Tommy Sullivan's Radio Flyer wagon handle.

Tommy Sullivan, to his great surprise, was neither strangled by Teddie's father, nor attacked in any way that day. In fact, the neighborhood took no action at all. Instead, they chose inaction. They did nothing. Mr. Sullivan had been away that day, and there was no reason to include him. Know-it-alls say that there can never be a conspiracy of more than three people—that secrets cannot be kept in groups. But those know-it-alls must not know the Sicilians on Singer Street. Secrets there depended not on the number but the need. As much as Teddie Millefiore needed stitches and ice packs and chocolate ice cream after her ordeal, Tommy Sullivan needed to be acquitted. And the neighborhood, well, they gave him that without a grudge, even impressing Mrs. Contralto, their very own informant, to keep her mouth shut. Many of them nodded at Tommy Sullivan in cryptic ways, with their black eyebrows high on their heads, or in knowing ways with a shared slyness that wrinkles around the nose. They did everything they knew to indicate to him that he was safe with them, that it wasn't really his fault—though maybe he *was* too big to be playing with the small kids anymore. Though they never came out and *said* it.

But, of course, Tommy Sullivan was Irish—and German. He couldn't clearly translate all that secret face-language. And so, he told on himself the very next morning, as his father slurped his coffee, read the paper, and ran a rough hand through his high waved hair. He did it before someone might. And when, days later, he recovered from the beating he received, Tommy pinched a small stuffed bear with black glass eyes from the five and dime to bring to Teddie Millefiore as a get-well present.

When Teddie's mother answered the door, Tommy attempted to hand the cheap toy to the woman, and flee, but he found himself invited in, so in he went. Little Teddie received her gift graciously in the living room, perched high on the green sofa, her small feet swinging in circles above the floor. The sight of her stitches terrified Tommy, and he gulped in rapid succession. Little Teddie offered him two cookies from her half sleeve of Oreos. Her strange sister Dolores spun like a gangly ballerina across the wood floor, observing it all.

The neighborhood watched, too, from their windows, waiting for Tommy Sullivan to come back out, and they knew, most of them, that he was a good boy. They hoped he wouldn't turn bad.

SEVEN

Diamond in the Rough

Lena Millefiore perched at the edge of the examining table in an examining room, the second in a set of adjoining rooms, each meticulously sanitized and gleaming with stainless steel instruments. The air smelled of isopropyl alcohol and bleach. Lena waited for the doctor, trying not to swing her legs or check her watch. Her low-heeled blue pumps waited under the upholstered chair opposite her, where she'd carefully placed them after wrapping herself in the hospital gown. The shoes seemed disembodied, as if they might shuffle out the door of their own accord. Maybe heading out to Creme Crunch Donuts for a coffee and a sweet. Maybe skipping the procedure altogether.

Lena's husband Nicky had taken the day off work at the railroad to accompany her. He waited impatiently in the waiting room where he'd been pacing by the window when the nurse had come to bring her back. His long face drawn, running his fingers through his thinning hair. He'd stopped pacing to kiss her on the top of her head as the nurse led her out, the reek of cigarettes and coffee on Nicky's breath, reassuring in its familiarity.

Even though she'd really finished the *McCalls* magazine back in the waiting room, Lena held onto the magazine because of the recipe for Moroccan Pound Cake with peanuts on page 127. She wondered if she had lost her marbles—thinking about a cake recipe when she was about to have the procedure. Stealing down from the table to hunt for a pencil and pad in her satin clutch, she kept one eye on the door. She'd hate for the doctor to enter and find her rummaging instead of waiting motionless as she felt was expected. But there was no pencil in her clutch, just her pink rat's tail comb, a metal compact, and her rubber change purse that opened like a mouth. She climbed back up on the table's edge, flipped to the pound cake recipe again, and tried to commit it to memory: 2 sticks of butter, 2 cups of flour, 1 T. mace, one half cup peanuts. But no matter how she tried, it kept slipping free.

"Something is wrong with your female parts, which is why you have this strange bleeding," was what Dr. Manzo had told her two weeks earlier, "Some kind of blockage that needs clearing." He'd put one of his hands on her shoulder to reassure her, and with the other, he waved the speculum he'd just used on her like an obscene pair of salad tongs—for emphasis. She'd blushed.

"I'm sure it's what we call fibroid activity. We'll simply dilate and remove it. And then, we'll look at it under a microscope to see what's what." He'd pointed the speculum at Lena, "as soon as possible."

Of course, she'd set up the appointment immediately. She was not a woman who questioned doctors. No, she was a woman who'd not finished high school and instead had gone to work in the homes of doctors, nannying their children during the depression. And there, when she was still very young, she'd learned to respect them. Also, she was tired of the dark thick blood that layered itself in her underwear every few days—what her sisters called *mittlesmerch*. She was tired of the heavy feeling in her insides.

The fibroids were one particular problem, but they weren't alone. Problems generally travel together, and Lena had another substantial problem, a long-term one. That problem was Nicky Millefiore, her husband. Nicky, who she knew now paced in the waiting room— tipping his cigarette ashes into the brass urn each time he passed it. Slicking his eyebrows straight with his thumb to make sure he was presentable.

Nicky was a problem for just one reason: twice a year, like clock-work, he beat her up. There would be an argument—any mundane thing—then there would be a fight, and he would wallop her. It's not that the Millefiores didn't argue more than twice a year. And some-times they were vociferous arguments. But it was only twice a year, no more, no less, and not on any ordained or guessable day, Nicky pummeled his wife.

This problem was like a nest of bees living in Lena's lungs, hum-ming even when she slept. It made her nervous and clammed her up when she felt like talking. It made her say stupid things when she felt like being quiet. It made her hair shed and her nails become brittle. She couldn't accept it.

For some time now, she'd felt the solution was to change Nicky's behavior, not by herself of course—she'd tried that for years—but through the help of another, someone he respected or someone he feared. And since Nicky wasn't afraid of anyone, it would have to be someone he respected. With this theory in mind, she'd begun with family. She'd talked to her sister-in-law Agata about it first, but Agata had only been able to cry in commiseration and hug Lena, python-like, an embroidered handkerchief flopping in her little fist. Lena appreciated the sentiment, but she needed someone who would set Nicky straight.

She'd talked to her own sisters about it, and they'd made their high cheekbones even higher and sang to her nearly in unison around an old dining room table, "Well, you did marry an Italian when we told you not to." And then they'd taken swipes at her individually: Minka said that Nicky was a good provider, and those don't come a dime a dozen. Anna said, "it could be worse" and cautioned Lena to be sure not to upset Nicky and *make* it worse. Frida—who was in the similar sort of situation herself—shrugged her shoulders and looked away. When that was over, Mina—who hadn't weighed in—cut everyone a wedge of Sacher Torte from the German bakery down in the city. She did it with a flick of her wrist that made clear the conversation would now move on to more pleasant things.

Well, what do you expect? She'd told herself. What can my sis-ters do about it? Nothing. So she'd simply gone home and waited until the next time Nicky hit her. She knew it wouldn't be long, and she planned to call the police. It was her last resort. An act that would never be forgiven. But, surprisingly, she didn't have to call them because during the next beating an unknown someone had summoned them. It was the night Nicky fractured her jaw. The officers had asked her questions, but somehow, despite her clear words, Lena had been unable to make herself heard over the wails of her old Sicilian mother-in-law who stood lowing in the middle of the street. "My Nicky, he a good boy! He a good boy!"

When the old woman pulled at the policeman's sleeves and knelt on the pavement with her hands to her chest, everyone was afraid she might collapse. Even Lena.

The neighbors remained in their houses as was the custom for such things.

The young cops had spoken among themselves, nodding their black curly heads like sheep, not because they believed the old woman—what's to believe or not believe—but because they recognized her like they recognized their own grandmothers.

Within the hour, by the light of the streetlamps, mother-in-law and the law had worked something out. Nicky, the ex-golden gloves boxer with the mean left hook, would sleep elsewhere for two nights just to cool down. It was a compromise, the police had said. Nicky agreed, contrite and rubbing his bulging eyes.

"And, you better," the officers added," cuz we don't wanna hafta come out here again."

Lena sat on the curb in the dark, rubbing her swollen jaw and staring down at the dark reality of things. She watched her husband vanish into the night. She realized no one on the street would ever help. Her sister-in-law Agata sat beside her, holding her hand and picking the pils from her flowered housecoat. In the house, Lena and Nicky's children looked out—Lena could see them even though they hadn't turned the inside lights on, like shadows flitting in the windows.

The next morning, after she had her jaw looked at, Lena had wound her way from Mulberry Park to Elmhurst, where a Lutheran pastor could be found these days. She'd had to take the bus. Her damaged jaw—fractured not broken, everyone said—ached. She'd yanked open both front doors to St. Luke's, marched with verve through the narthex.

Pastor Schiff had peered at her and offered her a paper cup of cool water. He'd listened to her story and told her it was a shame she hadn't been to church regularly in years. Told her to pray for guidance. And whatever she did, not to get a divorce. That, he'd said, would be a sin.

On the edge of her stainless-steel examining table, Lena planned to ask Doctor Manzo—in his starched white coat which carried formality and respect—to speak with Nicky about his behavior. He was her last best hope. Surely, he could break through.

When the doctor and two nurses finally made their way into the little room attached to hers, she saw and heard through the window in the door that they were chatting to one another about the weather, the sound muffled. She saw the doctor wash his hands at the deep sink, smearing yellow soap up to his elbows and scrubbing away until every germ was gone down the drain. Lena realized she was terrified of the procedure the very moment Dr. Manzo shut off the faucet with his elbow. "Dilation and Curettage," he'd called it the last time she'd seen him. "D&C for short," which made it sound only a little less frightening.

He looked at her now, through the little glass window between the rooms. There were thin pieces of wire inside the glass, and she wondered why that was when he rapped on the door between them, she raised her head to say, "come in," but Dr. Manzo let himself in before she could speak, so she was left saying the words after the fact, and they rolled out of her mouth without any real volume, useless as they were. The doctor stood smiling and freshly shaved, flanked by his two nurses, Carol and Donna. Lena knew them from her previous visits, but not well, of course.

The nurses smiled and nodded while the doctor ran over the procedure for all present. He patted Lena's hand and made reassuring sounds to her. He said in his clear and precise English—educated English—that she'd feel "good as new" in two days or fewer. Maybe better than ever.

Despite her plan to ask Dr. Manzo to intervene in her marriage, things happened too quickly for Lena to ask much of anything, and, really, she thought, perhaps it was not the best time. Someone put a mask over her face. Someone else lay her head back on the table, which made Lena a bit dizzy. Someone else told her to count backwards from ten.

"Ten, nine, eight, eight, ummmm," and Lena, a rag doll. A nothing. Gone from the world.

When she rose back to consciousness, Lena had the feeling of being hollowed out, like one of those black plastic recorder flutes the kids brought home from school. Air might blow through her being unhindered. Dr. Manzo hovered nearby, leaning over her. He reached to pat her hand again but changed his mind. He opened his mouth to speak, but something in Lena's gullet finally pushed its way to the front, and she interrupted him before he could start.

With surprising precision, considering her condition, Lena Millefiore put forth a complete and detailed summary of the abuses she'd endured: jaw, the twisted arms, bruised thighs, pushes and shoves—the backhands on the front porch and those in the backyard, the full-force punches. Dr. Manzo listened. He nodded. He sighed. He murmured sympathy. The long black hairs on the back of his hand were like a pelt. Lena tried not to look at them. And still she continued to speak. She asked for help, bluntly, explaining her logic. She asked for it there in the surgical bed with the warmth of leaking blood beneath her.

What she'd expected, she couldn't have said, really, but whatever it was, it was not what she got. Dr. Manzo continued to gaze down at her with something he likely felt resembled or *was* compassion, and he said, "Mrs. Millefiore, my dear, please, please realize that your husband is a fine man—a very fine man."

"But that's not..."

"One of the very finest. Now, I know he's spirited."

"But it's bad."

"But really, Mrs. Millefiore, he's improving every day. Nicky Millefiore is a diamond in the rough."

Lena's hand went limp, and she ground her teeth despite her jaw. Dr. Manzo took a breath and finished, "And if you don't mind me saying so, it's for you to polish him, Lena. Because he's *your* diamond."

Stoic in his white coat, the doctor said no more on that subject but moved on to the next, and now he gripped Lena's hands more tightly, his eyelids lowering in sorrow.

"Lena, I must tell you, and there's no easy way for me to say this, but it must be said. Lena, there was a complication of sorts during the D&C."

His eyebrows knitted like tangled rugs, but he kept talking.

"All indications were that you were suffering from fibroids, small fibroids—you had classic symptoms. As we discussed some time ago. However, I'm sorry to tell you that when we began to scrape…"

Lena convulsed a little under her sheet. What sort of horrible growth or rot had they found? Was it cancer? Something worse? Was there something worse? But why should she expect more from this life than her own mother got? Where were her shoes? She wanted to leave.

Lena wriggled her hand loose from the doctor's and gripped the sheet as if it were the handrail of the Parachute Rides at Riverview Park.

"I'm sorry to have to tell you," Dr. Manzo took a breath and continued, "there were two fetuses there. We had no idea. But there was a small fibroid as well. So, there *was* a fibroid."

She stared at him dumbly.

"Two fetuses?" She felt ill.

"Babies."

"I know what a fetus is."

Her mind crashed and careened from the imagined terror to the real horror. Her tongue became thick and she moved it slowly in her mouth, finding some words.

"But. You. Said."

"There was no way to know. The tests showed only fibroids, and you showed no signs of pregnancy."

The room spun, and Lena's fingers fell slack from the hem of the sheet. How could she have not known? She'd had three children already. She knew what it felt like to be pregnant. How had she missed it?

"Are they alright?" She asked, backtracking desperately to something vanished—grasping.

"No, I'm sorry."

Lena Millefiore turned her freckled, moon-shaped face to the wall and wept. The doctor sat beside her for some time fidgeting with his stethoscope and saying things she could no longer hear. His powder-faced nurse, Carol, stood right behind him, a hand on his shoulder. Finally, with a groan, Dr. Manzo rose to get Nicolo Millefiore from the waiting room—to be told.

Through her tears, which ran soundlessly down the sides of her nose and dropped onto the pillow Carol was busily wedging under her head, Lena, managed to see—through the dividing window— her husband led into the little room that joined hers. It was the room not just for scrubbing up but for giving bad news to husbands, she realized. Nicky's striped summer shirt was rumpled, and sweat marks showed under his arms. His eyes were round and wide. *Popeyes*, she thought, ridiculously. Through underwater-ears and the muffling of the door she heard a few calm words spoken by the doctor followed by an outraged squawk.

And then she saw the Diamond in the Rough launch, punching at Dr. Manzo, whose glasses flew into the air. Lena strained to sit up, yelling, "No, Nicky, no, not the doctor!" But Nurse Carol pushed her back down into the cot. She struggled to sit up and look. Now Nicolo had Dr. Manzo by the neck like a small terrier with a giant rat. Now by the head. Now he was giving him an undercut or two.

The other nurse, who had moved on to changing the pad under Lena, trying to pretend nothing was happening, stopped mid-clean-up, a bloody rag in her hand and a look of pure amazement over her face.

Dr. Manzo could be seen trying to hold the short, wiry Nicolo back with his longer arms, and heard trying to reason with shouted logic. But the pin had been pulled from the grenade that was Nicky

Millefiore, and there was no putting it back in. So, Dr. Manzo was forced to truly fight rather than simply attempt to deflect.

Lena and the nurse watched as the little window in the dividing door broke under someone's fist, the wires in the glass holding up some fragments and letting others shimmer to the floor. They heard the instrument cart tip over like an avalanche of stainless steel.

Then silence.

Then quieter talking sounds.

Dr. Manzo, now looking more like a regular man of the neighborhood than the GP, opened the door to the waiting room and poked his bloodied nose into the crowd who'd gathered around that door trying to see what was going on. He announced to them everything was fine and there was no need to call for help. All the people there looked slightly ashamed that they'd never even thought to call for help, but they nodded and went back to their waiting seats. And then he pivoted, and into Lena's room, came the doctor's whole head. Nicky would be in shortly, he informed them, after he composed himself. Everything was fine. Any man would be so upset about the loss of babies.

Nurse Carol took Lena's face in her pudgy white hands and said, in a voice like sharp cider, "Mrs. Millefiore, you will need a divorce. As soon as the children are grown."

Lena counted off the years as she had many times before. Eight years until the children were grown. That would be about sixteen more beatings, she figured. She nodded at Carol who had gathered up Lena's clothes to help her dress. Lena reached out for her bra as she counted the years she'd already spent with Nicky. She was more than halfway there. Yes, eight more years. Eight more years to raise the children and eight more years to mourn these lost twins. And she'd better make sure there were no more babies or she'd have to start all over again.

"Valium?" Nurse Carol asked, filling a white paper cup with tap water from the little sink.

"Yes, please. Two."

EIGHT

Violeta Scrubs

Whenever <u>Violeta Eloise Contralto,</u> **on hands and knees,** backed her way out of the Contralto front door and onto the Contralto front porch, neighborhood children—mostly boys— waited under the mulberry trees across the street and on the front porch next door. She seldom disappointed, and on the 14th of July 1952 shortly after three in the afternoon, as expected, her ample *culo* emerged, wrapped like a plush ottoman in the broadcloth of her yellow summer dress, patterned in roses. As big and yellow as the sun.

No one else in town scrubbed their sidewalk by hand, the steps maybe, but not <u>the sidewalk</u>. That belonged to the village, so generally, a quick sweep would d<u>o. Violeta alone</u>, with her bucket of hot soapy water and her wooden-backed <u>scrub brush</u>, grunted and swiped at the rough concrete, erasing every bit of leaf-soil, every grain of dirt. Therefore, Violeta Contralto's mother-in-law—the formidable Mrs. Irene Contralto—enjoyed the cleanest steps and sidewalk in the neighborhood, thanks to Violeta. Though she told people it was unnecessary.

Violeta wore thickish stockings that ended at her thighs and were held in place by sand-colored garters. She wore holes into those stockings as she scrubbed, but she never went out without. Every few moments, a flash of high thigh appeared as she worked the steps and then the sidewalk down to the street, that flesh bordered between the stocking tops and the hem of her dress like no man's land. Her shoulders moved this way and that, and her rump swayed to the off-beat. Almost always, her dress shifted as required to keep her mainly covered.

Rarely, though, if the boys waited long enough, and if they didn't look away at the wrong moment, these children could see everything. It was because Violeta Contralto did not wear underpants when she scrubbed. She may not have ever worn underpants at all, but that was not known one way or the other.

Of the five boys and one girl who waited on this particular day to catch sight of the fantastic, none knew who in the world had been the first to discover it; that's how long it had been known. The fact of Violeta's nakedness was common knowledge in the same way that thousands of things were: in the same way every kid knew Mrs. Kraum kept a still in her wall, in the same way that every kid knew Mrs. Covino's son was connected to the outfit, and in the same way that every kid knew young Daniel Wohlwebber's dad, Daniel Sr., laid himself out like a dishrag in front of the flophouse three blocks down—a bottle stuffed into the waistband of his dirty trousers.

Young Daniel waited breathlessly for Violeta Contralto that day, and while he waited, he tried not to think of his father at all. But the flophouse was a reality in the neighborhood. One that often made young Daniel feel ashamed, and that shame pressed into his mind. Sometimes he had to pass the flophouse corner no matter how hard he tried to find another route. When he did, he always moved fast, squinted his eyes, and hoped that his father would be absent. But more often than not, he *was* there, and so Daniel would run past on the other side of the street with his head turned over his thin shoulder, away from his father, watching the buildings pass. This technique kept his father from seeing him, he thought. From recognizing him, anyway. Sometimes Daniel moved so fast he wasn't really sure if his father was out there anyway—not *really*. Because, really, the men who sprawled across the concrete steps leading up to the boarding house resembled one another so completely in their crumpled, collapsed way as to become nearly identical. They had a habit of only raising their heads when absolutely necessary, so usually their whiskery faces were all turned down to the sidewalk. Because they were indeterminate men in some ways.

The thing was, about once a year, Daniel's dad would sober up and move back home. He'd get a job with someone local—a mason or a butcher, the greengrocer. Nothing fancy. But he'd cut his hair and get a tooth or two pulled. Spruce himself up. At those times, Daniel's mother, Filomena, would smile hopeful little smiles and hum as she swept the floors and polished her nails. But then, far too soon, a bottle of Old Fitzgerald would be discovered hidden in the attic rafters, and then another peeking out from behind the cotoneaster bush on the shady side of the house, and finally, like clockwork, the mouthwash and the little jar of vanilla would go missing. Over the spiraling course of the following two or three weeks, Daniel Wohlwebber Senior always wound his way back to the concrete steps on the corner at Dick Dacey's boarding house. Daniel's mother would scream and collapse as if she'd been put in an electric chair. Daniel's uncles would threaten his father, maybe even beat him up pretty good, but nothing could stop the wheel that was rolling over them.

Daniel decided he preferred not to think about Daniel Sr. if at all possible, and so he concentrated directly on Violeta. And that did the trick. In just a few minutes, Daniel Wohlwebber had completely forgotten his father in favor of sunnier things. Young Daniel was accompanied by two of his cousins, and each boy sat cross-legged under the grand mulberry trees in cousin Big John Millefiore's front yard. Here, in the shade, Daniel kept a lookout for the private areas of Violeta Contralto, like a sailor watches for land. He knew they might pop into the sunlight across the street at any moment. His gaze never wavered.

Some small amount of dappled sunlight fell across his own face and turned his brown eyes nearly amber. It drew out freckles across the bridge of his nose, and just beyond, but most importantly it illuminated the scene before him—the Contralto sidewalk, steps, porch, and Violeta backing her way closer and closer. Every now and then, Daniel heard the rain-like plunk of a mulberry dropping to the lawn before him or behind him. His fingers plucked thin blades of grass—the soft kind that grows only under big trees—one by one.

Big John was smoothing his strange spiky cowlick and reading Gulliver's Travels silently; Daniel's oldest cousin had a knack for reading and writing and always carried a library book with him. He was Daniel's favorite older cousin, and Daniel would let Big John know if anything happened with Violeta so he could look up. Big John was thirteen to Daniel's eleven. He had glasses from reading so much and had been to Bug House Square to hear the communists with his mother. Big John knew a lot of neat stuff, and he never ever went hyper.

Little John sat on the other side of Daniel. He had the look of a boy whose older sister is going to become a nun, because that was the case. This is to say, he looked full of himself and still more than slightly frightened—as if someone set off firecrackers too close to his head every day. Daniel tried to ignore Little John whispering to him about the "dilemma of sin," about how he prayed the private part and the hindquarters of Violeta would remain under her dress so that he wouldn't have to confess to Father Sephio about having seen them—yet again. He argued with Daniel, even though Daniel wasn't arguing back, that watching for, but not seeing, something shouldn't really require a confession at all, not technically.

"Why are you *even* here, then?" Daniel hissed.

"Because you're here."

"What kinda reason is that?"

"I dunno."

The conversation was going nowhere as usual, so Daniel rolled his eyes and told Little John to just shut up. Little John was accustomed to doing what he was told, so he did shut up, but not before taking out his rosary beads and mumbling a quick Hail Mary at Daniel. Daniel wanted to biff him, but he couldn't because the Holy Mother wouldn't like that. And if she was real, he didn't need problems with her on top of everything else.

Daniel could see the Sullivan boys across the street, on their own front porch, craning their short necks to the side to see Violeta while sharing a comic book between them. Their younger sister Margery was there, too. Well, it's not every day a kid might see a grown woman's naked bottom, so Daniel felt Margery had every right to watch. The Sullivans were closer to Violeta, but their view was not nearly as good, obscured by the angle of being directly next door. Daniel felt as if he were sitting in the front row at the movies. All he had to do was stare straight ahead.

It wasn't that Violeta Contralto was a particularly beautiful woman. She was quite old, maybe thirty-five. She was solid and a little ruddy. Her ankles were a bit thick. Her hair was dark blonde and pinned up all over her head. She wasn't even as pretty as Daniel's own mother, but that wasn't the point at all. The point was seeing the part of a woman he was most curious about, curious with a curiosity that nearly ate him alive. And even though he'd seen the shocking sight before—on several occasions—he felt it wasn't the kind of thing you just see once. It had kind of knocked the wind out of him last time and the time before that. It never got boring.

Also, Violeta wasn't *bad*. Not like the bad women in Chicago he'd heard about, women who wore big hoop earrings and went out with men every night of the week. No, Violeta was simple; that was what all the big people said. They also said she wasn't right in the head, but they didn't say it mean. They said it nice.

Every few minutes, Violeta sat up like a prairie dog and looked over the work she'd done. And when she did this, Daniel felt disappointed because the dress lowered safely to the backs of her knees. What if she just got up and went into the house? All that time he'd spent waiting would be for nothing. Daniel, like his mother, was a worrier by nature.

However, Violeta wasn't about to quit. You could count on Violeta. Back down she went. The scrub brush rasped—shhhhp shhhhp shhhhp—across the concrete. The scent of Murphy's Oil Soap drifted across the street and right up Daniel Wohlwebber's left nostril and into his sinuses. He thought he might ask for binoculars for his birthday in March. Besides this, he thought he could use them to watch birds, and if he was ever invited to a White Sox game, he'd bring them along to that, too. Maybe his grandma would get them for him, but probably not. They were too expensive. *Non sono una spendachona,* she'd say right into his face until he dropped it. His grandma was a miser; that was what his mother said. Like the King Midas. That was where the word came from after all. And his mother should know because Grandma was her mother. No, he wouldn't ask for the binoculars, he decided. It was better to wish forever than to ask for something and be told no.

The clouds were high in a blue sky. The house in front of Violeta was bright white, nearly gleaming. She was still scrubbing and swaying away, when a persistent wind arose, new on the scene, and finally lifted the hem of Violeta's dress up over her back.

Daniel couldn't speak, so he hit Big John instead, who carefully marked his page with a dog-ear and set his book down in the grass. Little John, transfixed, let his string of beads drop like a snake, at the same time his mouth dropped open. The entire pack of Sullivans froze stock still like deer hunters on their porch. Daniel took all this in at once as he also gazed upon the round cheeks of his strange muse across the street—and the mesmerizing pelt-like part that now showed below. The dark fantastic there put him in the mind of a sort of magical stole. It was all like watching a shooting star. Or a jack-in-the-box. Or a murder. He felt changed. He felt strange. He wanted to move closer. But that would break the spell, so he simply leaned forward.

Violeta's yellow dress stayed up for quite a while, a surprisingly long while, really, and young Daniel found himself wondering whether he should finally look away. How long was too long? But no one else did, so neither did he. Birds flew over. A truck horn blared over on Seventeenth Avenue. A cloud moved itself and covered part of the sun. And still, as if it would never go away, the most interesting part of Violeta Contralto presented itself to him. He coughed quietly and felt more than a little dizzy and weak. Violeta just scrubbed and scrubbed. Surely, she could feel the breeze on herself, Daniel thought.

Daniel and his fellows, those under the tree and the Sullivans on the porch, were still so mesmerized that they nearly failed to notice Violeta's father-in-law, Mr. Contralto, come home very early from work. The usually sleepy little man walked up from the corner bus stop and then trotted. The children saw him only as he sprinted the last few feet. Mr. Contralto dropped his packages to the ground and stooped to lift Violeta from the sidewalk by her hands, gently. She rose and they faced one another. Violeta still held her scrub brush. Daniel could see by Mr. Contralto's face that he was not even angry with Violeta. Also, he was not embarrassed of Violeta. Also, he did not try to see Violeta's private parts for himself. No, Mr. Contralto, Daniel saw, took a lollipop from the square pocket of his sleeveless dress shirt, and handed it to Violeta. He smiled at her. The smile was broad and quiet, and it lifted Mr. Contralto's jowls all the way up to his bald head.

Daniel was sure Mrs. Contralto would come raging out the door any second, as she almost always did when Mr. Contralto came home. But she did not. And he was glad. He didn't like to see how Mrs. Contralto beat up on Mr. Contralto. No one did. But his grandma and his mother said it's no one's business what goes on behind closed doors, nodding their heads together. Daniel thought this was inaccurate because what Daniel saw went on right in the front yard, but no one listened to him.

He watched Mr. Contralto pat Violeta on the head like she was a little kid. And he heard Mr. Contralto say, in a voice that carried, "Violeta, dear, this is the cleanest sidewalk in Mulberry Park, maybe in all of Illinois. And that, Violeta, is because you have done such a very good job, *hedda*"

He paused and picked up the tin pail of soapy water.

"Violeta, now," he added, "it's time to come inside and wash up for dinner. Yes, yes, the sidewalk is finished."

Daniel and the others pretended to be reading or pulling weeds or praying the rosary while they watched as Mr. Contralto led Violeta up the stairs. When he reached the top, the little man looked at the children gathered where they were. Daniel felt he looked right at *him*, right into his eyes, like a teacher or something. Maybe Mr. Contralto was going to let him have it.

He didn't, though, not really. There was no yelling, no screaming, no threatening. The only thing was Mr. Contralto looked so very disappointed. His eyes were sad, and his jowls dropped down even further than where they'd been before. He telegraphed straight into Daniel Wohlwebber all that was wrong with a bunch of perverts sitting around trying to get a peek at the naked rear end of poor Violeta, who was not right in the head. The disappointment of Christ shone in his eyes, the disappointment of the Sacred Heart, beating like a snare drum. It rolled across the street like a boulder, flattening Daniel, and maybe on Big John, too, though Daniel wasn't sure because Big John was back in his book, turning pages loudly, as if he'd not even seen Violeta's privates at all.

Daniel suddenly knew right from wrong on this account—like he really hadn't before. Well, he kind of had, maybe, but not like this. It was clear. He made an oath to never lie in wait for Violeta's dress to rise again. He'd keep his mind on baseball and his chores at home, and how to take good care of his dear mother since his father was a ne'er-do-well. That alone was a big enough job to keep him away from the three pm weekly gathering.

Just then, Daniel heard the tinkling of forks and knives from within the kitchen of the Contralto's. Mrs. Contralto's soprano voice trilled in a sort of gripe, but there were also the sounds of Violeta's laughs and the quietness of Mr. Contralto saying nothing. In not too long, the grown Contralto children would come home, including Violeta's husband, a narrow quiet man named Silvio, who had married the simple-minded woman. Daniel wondered if that had been on purpose. Daniel wondered if Silvio Contralto cared that his wife scrubbed the sidewalk like she did. With a naked behind jumping out all over the place. He wondered what it was like to be Silvio, but he didn't wonder for too long. He was hungry himself, and it was time to go home and wash up for dinner. His mother would be waiting.

Daniel watched as Big John closed his book and Little John closed his gaping mouth, and Daniel hoped they wouldn't talk at all about how Mr. Contralto looked at them. The Sullivans lowered their heads and crept back into their house. It was suppertime everywhere. Daniel couldn't forget the eyes of Mr. Contralto. He pulled his baseball cap down tightly, past his eyebrows, and he left toward home, a zealot fully resolved never again to lie in wait.

But by the time he'd sprinted past the flophouse with his head turned over his shoulder, he was only pretty much sure he'd never return. And by the time he stood over the sink in his mother's kitchen, washing his hands for dinner, young Daniel Wohlwebber had completely given up on his reformation. As he rinsed the soap from his hands, he wondered what color dress Violeta would be wearing next time she scrubbed the sidewalk. Blue, he hoped. It was his favorite color.

NINE

Little Big John and the Atheism Problem

Big John Millefiore was thirteen and a half and seven days old, and he rode his bicycle with considerable skill and care toward the library, on the sidewalk. He rode carefully because he wanted to survive long enough to go on to do better things than were generally done in his neighborhood. Better things like his friends on the other side of town did—friends who talked about going to Northwestern and DePaul when they finished high school, friends whose fathers arrived home with briefcases and papers, their faces and necks clean. Men who announced themselves with the snip, snip, snip of their polished shoes coming up the walkways to their very solid front doors. Big John's own father, Nicky Millefiore, by comparison, came home sooty and with lumps of railroad chalk in his pocket. He came home with a sweaty face and a dirty neck. He came home in boots that clomped and dragged up over the porch but no further. Boots so dirty they had to be taken off outside. His father then crabbed into the house in stocking feet, trying as hard as possible not to bring the dirt in with him.

What Big John really hated, though, was when his father lay down flat on his stomach on the living room rag rug and made whichever of his children was closest take off *their* shoes and walk slowly over his back and shoulders to work out the lumps in his muscles. It was hard to not fall off his back, and they were afraid of hurting him. And what's more, they could smell his exhaustion and it made them feel like they were the cause of it. When he'd been properly walked upon, Big John's pa would raise his shoulder to indicate to the walker to dismount. Then he'd groan and hoist himself off the rug to go soak in a hot bath, water gone white with Epsom salts Big John's mother had sprinkled in. Big John thought it was pure gross that his father didn't bathe *before* the foot massage, but it would have been very foolish to suggest a change in the ritual.

Whenever possible, Big John made sure he was out of the house when his father arrived home from work on the railroad, which was only his first job. On weekends his pa worked a second job with Butch Bobko's moving company, so Big John tried to be gone when his pa got home on weekends, too.

He imagined his sisters having to do the back-walking, and he felt not even a little bad about it. After all, they didn't mind it as much as he did because they were young and not as smart as him. But his father liked it best when Big John walked on his back because Big John was the oldest and the heaviest. He flattened out the lumps best.

Big John's school friends never had to do such things; he knew it. It wasn't *fair*, and when he had children, he vowed he'd never make them walk on *his* back. His mother said life wasn't fair; get used to it. But he wasn't swallowing that either.

He stood up on the hard pedals and hovered over the seat of his green Schwinn, sailing up the sidewalk toward the library to return his small stack of books. The cement raced below his gym shoes, but despite the pedals and the sidewalk, the bike and the books, he could still feel the knobby muscles and sinews of his father's back under the balls of his feet.

Big John knew a lot. He'd read every *National Geographic Magazine* the library had, devoured them in the cool Naugahyde library chairs—you weren't allowed to take them home—and every volume of *Encyclopedia Britannica* as well. Sometimes he sniffed the leather-bound spines as if they were perfumed. Whenever Big John's mother took him to Bug House Square, he stood in front and listened intently to the speech makers—pushing his glasses this way and that until his focus on them was perfect. He felt like a German intellectual trapped in the body of an Italian peasant. This, he often thought, was part of the unfairness of being behind half and half. If his mother had just married someone else, another German or even a regular old American, well, he'd have had an easier time. But no, she'd chosen his pa. And thus, he had to live with the Italians and their ways, which he felt were limiting his options.

Sure, he looked like *them*. He even loved them. But on the inside, where it counted, Big John Millefiore felt he was nothing like these people at all. He was—but he felt uneasy to mutter this even to himself because no one likes braggart—something somehow better. Better but also in constant danger of falling completely in with them. He stood on the precipice, in danger of being completely wasted in a filthy, dirty factory or at the Mulberry Park Roundhouse, toiling mindlessly with the neighborhood men. Moaning about his aching back. Sometimes, he felt panic over this. Sometimes he felt guilt. But most times, he felt only vague desperation that he must be different.

Big John lifted his front tire into the bike rack in front of the library among the few other bicycles and a tricycle. He unbuckled his leather bike satchel—a Christmas present from his parents—it was roomy enough for several books as well as his notebooks and pencils, and he was proud of it. Besides books and papers and pencils, he usually kept his rock in it. It was a geode he'd bought from an Indian boy in New Mexico last summer, on the once-a-year train trip all the railroad families received. The other boy had called it a Thunder Egg and cracked it with a chisel right there in front of him. It split open on the table from which the other boy sold his wares, near the railway station. There had been tables of wooden carvings and of beaded change purses and of dolls with feather headbands, but only the rocks interested Big John, who spent all his vacation money—which was not much—right then and there—on a rock. On the outside, it looked very plain, but on the cut edge, it was an explosion of sparkles and clear bits, and rings of color. Big John knew and fully comprehended exactly how his geode, a sedimentary geode (he'd looked them up at the library using photos and lots of time), had been formed. Formed in a pre-historic time of dinosaurs and zero people. None. He loved the idea of holding something from a landscape before human foolishness.

After he purchased it, he'd stood shyly with the boy who'd laid out before him so many marvelous stones. He'd have liked to buy them all, but he was sensible and measured, and now he was broke. He'd taken half of the geode and put it into his pocket and hurried back to the train to join his family. The other half was returned to the table, to be bought by someone else. When he arrived back at the train, his aunts and mother were smoking cigarettes, and his sisters and cousins simply stared at the wide vistas open-mouthed. Like the simpletons they were. No fathers had come on the trip—they stayed home to work. It was great.

Big John never mentioned the geode to any one of them. He knew they'd rib him about paying for it when you could pick up a rock from the ground any time back home. He'd say it wasn't the same and show it to them, but they'd refuse to understand anyway, and this kind of thinking made him want to peel himself into a different way of life even more. It was the kind of thinking that made him keep the rock out of sight from the first moment he had it.

Big John never left his geode unattended. In front of the library, he removed it from the satchel and wedged it into the pocket of his stove-pipe dungarees. His shirt was white and crisp from his mother's ironing, and he knew he cut a fine figure as he carried his books up the library stairs. He hated to return *Gulliver's Travels*, even though he'd check it out again the next day to re-read it. There were several books he checked out repeatedly. Books he felt were his. And no one could stop him from having *Gulliver's Travels* over and over again, but there was always the chance that some other boy—or worse, some nerd girl—would check it out and never return it, leaving it to molder unread beneath their bed. There were kids like that in his town, and he knew it. They were always doing things like that.

Of the many things he loved about Jonathan Swift, the most important of all was that the man—separated from Big John by so much time and even more ocean—had defined Yahoos for him. And that gave Big John a reference point he much needed to understand what went on inside the houses up and down his block, in his own house as well. Had Swift been still living, Big John would have written him a very long letter requiring multiple stamps due to weight. And in it, he would have asked Swift about God, or rather, the obvious lack of God. Big John felt relatively sure that, like himself, Jonathan Swift would have been an Atheist.

Big John knew all about atheism, or a lot about it anyway. He'd looked it up when he was seven—when he'd determined in a spurt of huge thought that not only was there no proof of God, that the very idea was highly, highly unlikely. More unlikely, he decided, than regular fairy tales, which were not true at all either but at least were direct and to the point. He figured that people just wanted to live forever and told themselves stories that fooled themselves into believing they would. They were just afraid. And simpleminded. And he was surrounded by them. Even most of the librarians who looked up from their filing as he dropped his books into the slot, holding on to *Gulliver's Travels* the longest before it disappeared into the hole.

Big John had been an atheist almost half of his life now, and really, he thought, you couldn't count the ages zero to four because, well, you're pretty much a baby then. So in reality, yes, most of his life he'd been an atheist. And it was a lonely road, indeed. He couldn't tell anyone in the neighborhood. Only his friend James Allen who lived blocks and blocks away knew. James Allen and Big John would talk for hours about the subject of atheism, and also about agnosticism, and socialism, communism, and pacifism, and journalism—which they felt was directly related in many ways to all the rest. They would talk into the late afternoon, until James Allen's father's polished shoes snipped over the threshold into James Allen's neat brick ranch-style-house. That father would smile, set down his briefcase, and push his horn-rimmed glasses up his nose as he greeted the boys in precise, well-modulated proper English.

James Allen's mother would pour a drink for the father, a gimlet, and she'd push up her glasses too, and then they'd all watch the evening news on a television together before dinner. No one talked back to the newscaster or took their shoes off. Often, they'd invite Big John to stay for the news, and the whole lot would perch on the sofa, peering from behind glasses at the news of the day, and commenting

from a like-minded space. Big John felt right at home at the Allens'
though he was seldom invited to stay for dinner. In his house, if
someone was over when dinner was being cooked, the person was
definitely invited to stay. This was the one thing he didn't like about
the Allens, and he chose to overlook it.

After checking in his books, Big John thought about riding over
to James Allen's house after the library, but then he remembered he
had homework to do. Lots of it. Latin, Math and Geography. He
thought he'd better just go home and do his homework in his little blue-walled bedroom where no one dare disturb him. Especially
not his little sisters, Dolores and Teddie. Just the week before they'd
broken all the tips off all his pencils, and he'd had to re-sharpen
them—twenty-two pencils in all. So he'd given them a good talking
to and hung a Do Not Disturb sign made of cardboard and stenciled
in careful printing on his door. They couldn't even read cursive yet.

But before he left the library, and despite the amount of home-
work that waited for him, Big John hunted the stacks for new books.
He selected a few: *The Complete Grimm's Fairy Tales*, Unabridged,
Killer Fish of the Amazon, and *Das Kapital.*

The librarian stamped the first two books with a gap-toothed
smile, but her hand halted mid-air above the stamping place of *Das
Kapital,* and she hissed.

"I don't think this is appropriate."

Big John's heart sank because the book looked fascinating. He
wanted to scream, but that would do no good, and he absolutely
could not risk losing his library privileges. So, instead, he gathered
his resolve before she could sense his fear. And he said, as if without
a care in the world, "Oh, okay. My mother asked me to pick it up,
but I can tell her you said no, and maybe after work and making
dinner—if her neck's not hurting too much—she'll walk out in the
coming rain to get it." He smiled at the gap in the teeth with dis-
interestedness rivaling that of any Victorian Essayist he'd read, and
the stamp came down on the book. He'd have two whole weeks with
it, but he knew he'd finish it in days and then re-read it. And he
desperately hoped it would give him some answers about the mam-
mal he was. He also clocked—at that moment the stamp hand came

down—his superiority over this particular librarian, who knew nothing about the book at all and he was sure had only reacted based on her fears. This alone made her a dolt.

As he rode home, his new books, homework, and stone safely in his control, he passed the Catholic churches: Holy Cross and then Our Lady of the Flowers, and he rolled his eyes a little, but not so very much because he knew all the people who were inside those churches on a Wednesday afternoon. *All* of them. He pitied them with the benevolent insolence of a thirteen-almost fourteen-year-old boy. The opiate of the masses, he whispered to himself; The. Opiate. Of-the. Masses.

Because his mother was a Lutheran and his father a Catholic, Big John could waltz into either church or neither church at the age he was, and that was a rare position for a child of his neighborhood. And he hadn't been put through catechism. When he did go to the Lutheran one on the arm of his red-headed mother or the Catholic one on the arm of his bent grandmother, he worked out algebraic equations in his head for most of the service and wondered how much money was in the collection basket. A lot he figured.

Riding by the church put his grandmother in his mind—her hawkish eyes, her strong grasp, her pious marching in the procession with a black scarf tied over her hair—barefoot on the burning pavement—counting her beads. She was probably, he thought, the one most likely to attempt to beat atheism right out of him in the middle of the street if she ever caught wind of it. On the other hand, simply hearing of his atheism might well kill her outright before she could take any action at all. She was old, after all. He imagined her tumbling out of her front porch chair and onto the lawn below—quite dead. It was a strange mix of satisfaction and horror that he felt.

In the case of some boys, these thoughts might have caused a distance to be kept. Or at the very least, a quiet sneaking up the alley rather than a brazen riding openly up the street right in front of such a grandmother's house. But Big John felt he had to be strong or he'd disappear altogether, and so he rode right up to his grandmother's porch, waving at her, and she beckoned him.

"I can't, Gramma," he shouted, "I got homework."

"Only five minute," she said, "and I'm-a you gramma. Pick Gramma."

Big John parked his bike and came up her stairs onto her porch where she patted the seat of the chair next to hers. She had a little blue plate of *confetti* waiting there for him, as if she knew he'd be passing by. Or maybe she just knew *someone* would, and he was the fly that got caught in her web. He took one of her candied almonds and wondered about her traps. After all, she had six sons and twelve grandchildren on the block. It was just a matter of time.

Big John didn't want to talk about religion or atheism, not at all, but it seemed he couldn't stop himself, "You not going to church tonight, Gramma?" he asked, hating how he parroted her broken English, but he couldn't stop himself from that either. He felt the round ball side of the geode in his pocket, like protection from her.

"No, no tonight. Too nice out." She pointed to the purple blue sky of the autumn day nearing evening, and the orange of the maples, the golden mulberry trees, the sun setting behind them. The colors of impending sunset were mirrored in the sky to the east, which they faced like movie-goers.

"Sometime, I go Wednesday night. Sometime I no go. You go?"

"No, Gramma, I no go."

She nodded and urged him to take another almond, sweeping her hand across the sky and across the plate in one large arc, like an orchestra conductor, he thought. Her hands were strong and wrinkled, and her teeth were out, probably in the bathroom. Big John felt the candy shell crumble against his teeth.

"You my favorite," his grandma grunted. "tell me what it is bother you. I no stupid. I see you ride you bike. Ride here, ride there, ride here, ride there, like a dog with bones, looking for *un posto* to bury it. Tell me the bone."

"No bone."

"Yes bone. I'm old woman, I know bone when I see."

"No bone, Gramma,"

Big John was starting to feel uncomfortable.

"Why you lie to you Gramma? No trust Gramma? No trust Gramma even though you favorite?"

His grandma rubbed her forehead hard with all of her fingers at once and then dropped her head nearly into her lap. "You break-a my heart, Big Giovanni."

She looked truly miserable. Big John thought hard. Oh no, it was likely that she would tell everyone how, how she knew he was afraid to say it, but she was observant. She'd have made a good journalist in another life or in Sicily. She would tell everyone, and then they would pester him up and down the streets, from the youngest to the oldest—everyone trying to figure out what his secret was. And not just that, the things they'd suspect might stick, even if wrong. Those could be worse than the truth. He felt trapped. Her head was still down, and she looked like a small boulder.

"OK, Gramma," he said. I'll tell you but only if you swear it's only between me and you. You can't tell nobody. I mean anybody."

When she grinned, Big John knew he'd rightly sensed things. His grandma loved being the only one to know something. Anything. He knew she went to great lengths to discover information, and that— everyone knew—was how she'd broken her hip long ago. Climbing up on skids to look in a window to catch Aunt Lucy's husband gambling away the money for food. It was a legend that Grandma had said it was worth the broken hip to get the truth. Big John had heard this story by eavesdropping on adults when he was just nine, and he hadn't yet been forward enough to ask for additional details. It was part of why he liked his grandma despite all her silly old ways.

When his grandma agreed to the deal, he was not surprised, but he was terrified. Still, fear did not hold him back, and Big John laid out his Atheist manifesto like a feast table before his elderly grandmother, breaking only to stuff more *confetti* in his anxious mouth. It helped. She didn't interrupt him but listened quietly, though he wasn't sure how much she really understood. She sure nodded a lot. She nodded through his definition. She nodded through his explanations. She nodded at all of his examples of injustice on earth and his recounting of all the dead people in the family and up and down the street. He sweated a little in the cool breeze, and he looked her in the eye.

To make sure he was understood, Big John recapped his stance at the end, saying as loudly as he could without anyone else on the block hearing. "I think about everything, all of it, and there can't be a God. There is no God. People just made the whole thing up to make themselves feel better!" He said it with feeling, with emphasis, with surety, and with the kind of tears that come from strange relief. He'd done it. And now, let come what may. They could excommunicate him from the family, send him away to a monastery to try to straighten him out, but it would never work. He waited for a slap, or to be dragged down the stairs and off to church at the very least. He waited, needing a drink from all the sugar seizing in his throat, for a keening, a shrieking, a fainting. A crumpled old grandma on the lawn below.

Instead of any of these things—which he was prepared for—his grandma met him with a certain narrow-eyed conspiratorial look. She smiled broadly, showing all her gums and pulled a dime from her house dress pocket. She put it in the palm of his hand, closed his fingers around it so that it was safe in his fist, and kissed his knuckles in a slobbery smooch. Then she leaned back in her chair, looking at Big John, a little disappointed that the secret wasn't more monumental. She exhaled.

"*Everybody* know that."

Big John stared at her. What? He thought. What? He also was simultaneously relieved and disappointed, and maybe a little furious at the thought that it was all just a tale told to children. That the adults were all in on it. But why, he wondered, why then do all the adults go to church? Surely they must believe it. His logical mind spun and spun like the Tilt O Whirl at the Feast. He stared at his grandma's undecipherable face as she brushed crumbs from their laps denoting the finality of her comment. She pulled his face to hers and kissed him on each cheek. He could smell the snuff in her mouth and olive oil seeping from the pores of her skin. She indicated it was time for him to go home and do his homework.

All was well. All was well. All was well. It was no big deal.

As he left her to walk his bike across the street to his own home, she called after him a bit too loudly.

"*Si*, Johnny, you right *everybody* know that, but remember, God, he no like."

TEN

Pipe Dreams

Pina Millefiore stood next to her plastic covered sofa watching *Ding Dong School!* She rocked back and forth a little on the low heels of her black pumps. The convex eye of the screen held her favorite American, Miss Frances. A sort of beacon who smiled out at the world, beefy and patient but firm. Pina loved her. And though she could not follow all of the English, she gravitated to the brash musicality of Miss Frances' voice and figured out most of the words she didn't recognize by guessing. She especially loved the way Miss Frances showed everyone how to do things. Today, for instance, Miss Frances blew soap bubbles with a pipe. Yesterday, she taught proper hand washing with a song to do it by. Of course, Pina already knew how to wash her hands properly—she was a grown woman, after all. But still it was good to know the way Miss Francis thought best.

Pina looked around the flat to see if she had a pipe somewhere for blowing bubbles. There had to be one—and—when no one was around—which was a lot of the time—she just might try blowing bubbles with the dish soap in her kitchen sink. Then she'd be able to show a child how to blow bubbles one day. But there wasn't one, so she returned to the television. Her deep black hair curled in thick waves that stopped just under her chin, and her skin was the type of olive skin so thick it seemed to smooth out her emotions. Unlined, a face that appeared much the same now as it had years earlier, when she'd first come to America. But a keener observer would note that what had once been a quiet serenity had now turned to something else at the tips of her winged eyebrows.

Pina had learned, in her near decade here in America, that she had not been what her new family had once thought she would be. Of course, what they had thought she'd be had been a figment of their wild American imaginations. They'd wanted her, she thought as she touched her tapered index finger to the plastic sofa covering and watched a halo of condensation fog appear, to have flaws that were really *attributes*. But she had none of that sort. And neither did they.

Perhaps, she felt, the problem had been with the Matchmaker. Matchmaking was an art, really, practiced in closed off kitchens with symbols and omens—and then carried out into the world on foot—in spoken words. But these days the web of people of Sicily now stretched around the globe, and the matchmakers had to deal, sometimes, with people far, far away. Pina put three more fingers down onto the plastic to make halos that burgeoned into one another on the vinyl. It looked like when baby Jesus and John the Baptist and Mother Mary were painted together and their halos all came together. She looked around her neat living room and felt like a vase from another century, cracked as old majolica and surrounded by new things.

Pina understood she was the only wife in the Millefiore family who kept plastic on her furniture. But she did so because furniture was expensive and should last a lifetime. When she'd first found out about clear sofa covers, she'd been delighted. When she found out about vinyl carpet runners, she was delighted again. As soon as John brought them home from Polk Brothers, she'd laid them out in paths so that a person could travel among all of the rooms of the flat without ever touching the carpet. They'd had smelled so strongly of fresh vinyl that she could taste it, and she'd gotten to work right away, rolling them out with their spike sides up, certain the ridges of the tiny rubbery daggers that lined the long edges of each runner were intended to dig in and correct careless people from veering off the runner and onto her pale green wall to wall carpets. She'd been hurt when everyone laughed and told her no, no, no; those were for gripping onto the carpet beneath. "*Mamma Mia*! Just *offada* boat," she heard her mother-in-law moan, as she turned them over with reluctance.

Upstairs from Pina and John lived brother-in-law Lorenzo, sister-in-law Agata, and their two strange children, Little John and Holy Carmella—who everyone said was going to be a nun. Pina thought that unlikely as she'd recently seen the girl rifling through the common mailbox at the front door, opening envelopes and then digging into the pockets of coats that hung in the common hall. Carmella had stood there shaking the dimes she held in her palm like an old man getting ready to roll dice. And Pina had watched through her peephole, opening the door only when Carmella got close to her own heavy wool coat. The girl had run, banging out the front door and taking the dimes with her. She'd left mail scattered on the floor—a mess. Yes, this was the family Pina had come into, and she wasn't sure they were so good. But she'd adored her husband, and so, she'd tried to smile.

For years now, Pina had picked up the odor of Agata's place rolling down the stairs towards hers, like a *scirocco*. It was the smell of high-strung people who give in to their impulses and perspire uncontrollably—something of hot air and old garlic and older cabbages plus a thieving daughter who wants to be a nun only to get away with things. Of course, Pina knew the upstairs flat was hotter by nature, and she couldn't blame her sister-in-law for *that*, but surely Agata could open the balcony doors in front and the sleeping room windows in back to let some of that stink out into the air instead of pushing it down the staircase at her.

Just the day before, Pina had spent an hour pressing the sharp end of cloves into lemons so she could hang pomanders at her front door. So, she could push back the smell from upstairs. And it seemed to have worked. Lemons were her secret to daily cleanliness: lemon and vinegar, lemon and soda, lemon and salt—and though the lemons in America were small and dry they still reminded her a little of the lemons of Sicily. And of Sicily itself, where laundry hung out windows, high above dusty streets, blindingly white. Sicily where everyone around her knew her from birth. Sicily, where shoes could be both sensible *and* beautiful.

There, Pina had cared for her old parents—steeping their teas: chamomile before their siestas, lemon and bay leaf after dinner for their agita, fennel before lunch. She'd tucked their long thin feet under the clean sheets when they went to bed at night, and, in the mornings, she'd helped them into the courtyard when they wanted to take sunshine. She'd played countless card games with them, as if with children, always letting her father win.

When her brothers had come visiting, Pina served espresso and pastries to them and their wives, to their solemn children who said *per favore*, and *grazie*, and *prego*. It had been a solitary life among her own family in a way, and then when her parents died, Pina suddenly had no purpose. She moved from family caretaker to family liability: a mouth for someone to feed for perhaps another forty years. And though beautiful and sturdy, in Molano, she was too old for marriage. But in America there lived a well-respected *comare* named Giuseppa Millefiore, an old woman who needed—and right away—a wife for her bachelor son, called John. The matchmaker told the sister-in-law, who told the brother, who told Pina herself about this old Giuseppa's urgency and need.

At first, the story went, Giuseppa Millefiore had thought her son John was funny—one of those men who has no interest in women at all. *Finocchio.* The old mother had learned to live with this—after all she had other sons. It didn't matter. But then this American son, John, had fallen in love with a divorcee with children. That's when the old mother put her foot down. It was said that she'd boxed her son's ears in her backyard and accused him of tricking her. They said then she'd composed herself and written a letter to her second cousin, the matchmaker in Molano. That she'd learned to write in America. It had been a desperate letter in black ink on pale blue paper. But now Pina knew it had been Filomena Giaccina—the old woman's friend and niece—who'd written the letter. Giuseppa could neither read nor write.

Pina had been the first in the Millefiore family to immigrate by airplane, the last to immigrate at all, and that set her apart. When she'd come, her brother Bruno, the youngest of her six brothers, had accompanied her on the trip. This was necessary, to keep Pina and her well-seasoned virginity intact until she married her *fidanzato*, John. The families knew one another—or at least they had known one another fifty years previous when they were Molano third-cousins and neighbors. And likely they'd known each other for a thousand years before that. Bruno was also there to make sure this new husband was as good as it had been claimed he was—sound of body and mind with a good job.

On that fat plane that had carried Pina to her new life, her brother Bruno had looked to her like he enjoyed the flight far too much. She'd watched him stretch his legs and flirt at the stewardesses, parting his mustaches. And yet, he managed to flirt and be watchful all at the same time. He'd sat in the outside seat of their row so Pina wouldn't be brushed past by strange men. Bruno wore a lightweight suit and a red tie, and Pina a navy-blue linen traveling dress, real silk stockings, square heeled navy-blue shoes. These were their best clothes. On the plane, Pina's posture had been ramrod-straight, her eyes unblinking as two black ink spots.

She'd done her best to give no sign that she was terrified—what good is showing your fear? Besides, she'd also been excited. And she'd tried to keep that from showing, too. Excitement would have been unseemly. But from the first mention of the matchmaking, Pina's mind had begun to consider possibilities. She experienced the return of girlhood dreams—dreams of her own bathroom with a hot and cold vanity, her own pots and pans, dreams of a husband's affection. Dreams of children. Serving her parents had been neither a choice nor a burden; more of a sacred duty that had once seemed perpetual, but on that plane, she'd finally realized with full force, things were— certainly and suddenly—changing.

As the plane stuttered along over the Atlantic, from her bag, Pina had taken a blood orange. It had been carefully wrapped in blue tissue paper by the fruit vendor's daughter the day before, back in Molano. The wrapping had fallen mostly away from the orange inside the bag since then and fell the rest of the way off as she held it. She peeled it slowly, rewrapping the peelings in the paper. She hadn't known it would be the last blood orange she'd have, sweet and sour and volcanic. No one had told her that in America there were none. And because she hadn't known, she'd eaten the segments quickly without savoring them.

Pina had worried a little about the safety of her things in the cargo hold. One case had held her wedding dress, new and heavy—ivory silk. A row of silk covered buttons ran up the spine to define her straight back and graceful neck. The silk had been cut to flow, and when she'd tried it on in the dark dressmaker's shop in Palermo, it had, like water.

Her other large suitcase had been filled with embroidered bed sheets and pillowcases, cut-work tablecloths, lace bedspreads. Pina had been filling her hope chest for decades—just in case. She was ready with linens to last a lifetime. The smallest case, red and round, the size of a big man's face, held her trinkets and mementos. In it, her parents' best spoons, their playing cards, her own childhood Easter *capella*—in case she gave birth to a daughter in America—you never know. It was of fine woven straw with a yellow velvet ribbon. There was also a framed photograph of her six brothers and their families—everyone seated around tables made of doors and balanced atop saw-horses—arranged in the courtyard of the old home, covered with white cloths. Bruno, next to her on the plane, had been busy picking his nails with a pocketknife. He bore little resemblance to the Bruno photo packed into the case. It's funny, Pina had thought, funny how little people might look like their photos. It had been an unsettling thing to think about as she hurled through the air towards her new family, her new home, her new husband—whom she'd seen only in a small, grainy photo.

At her wedding, all the women in her new family had murmured within earshot that Pina didn't look a day over thirty, and a good thirty at that, though she was nearly thirty-nine. But then again, they'd added, she'd not been dealing with a husband or children all those years. No wonder she still stood straight and had a tight belly. They hadn't been wrong. As soon as she had a baby, they said, she'd be wrecked just like them.

The photo of Pina and John set on top of the television console, showed a woman, ageless. Maybe a little tired around the eyes from that long transatlantic flight, but still with the figure of a girl. The wedding dress had gleamed under the camera lights, and her face, free of any sort of make-up, looked out, serene. John, however, had looked every one of his forty-eight years, but Pina really didn't care about that; he'd turned out to be a kind man, eager to make the best of his new situation. He'd met her at the airport with a bouquet of yellow roses. It had seemed he'd forgotten the red-haired *divorcee* altogether, and if he was ever sad about having to bid her goodbye, he never let on.

The marriage had gotten off to a strong start: Pina's mother-in-law spoke to her in Sicilian—and enthusiastically and always. And that was good because having come over as an adult, Pina's American was very limited. It had seemed the old woman was glad to have someone from back home here with her. A *comare*. They laughed about having practically the same name, for you see, Pina's long name was Giuseppina—little Giuseppa. It tethered them a little. Her new mother-in-law had gotten to work right away, making Pina tonics of purslane and sage to drink. She'd come over on Sundays to tie amulets to Pina's bedposts and to her wrists. All to help her to get pregnant as quickly as possible. The mother-in-law had even brought Pina bloody beefsteaks from the butcher to strengthen her blood. She'd knelt before statues of the Madonna, the blue serene one at church and the special black one she kept in her bedroom, for hours. Pina knew this because they'd sometimes knelt there together. But despite the well-known powers of her mother-in-law, no pregnancy came. Each month, Pina's period had burst through, regular, dependable, and clot-heavy with approaching middle age. And she'd cried into her dish towels while she cleaned her kitchen.

By the end of the first year, the desire to have a baby had become pure anguish. Pina caught John staring at their nieces and nephews with frank want, and sometimes they even sobbed together—there in their full-sized bed, the Sacred Heart of Jesus nailed to the wall above them, looking benevolent but refusing to lend a hand. They'd tried so often to make that baby that the novelty of sex wore off before they were even done being newlyweds.

Mumbling after Miss Frances in English phrases could not save Pina from the specter of her mother-in-law's face floating before her. That vision didn't frighten her, it simply made her grit her teeth, and she swatted it away as she might a horsefly. That woman really got her goats. Things had become especially bad the summer Pina turned forty-one. That had been the summer they gave up on a pregnancy— the summer her mother-in-law suggested they turn to the *matchmaker* again.

Baby adoption—like wife procurement—could be arranged through the matchmaker in Sicily. This was because the necessary skill was, once again, knowing everybody's private business. Old matchmakers knew which daughters of which families, having somehow escaped a mortal beating by their male relatives, had managed to give live birth to a child out of wedlock. The matchmakers *knew*, even if that child were being passed off as the menopause-baby of its own grandmother. In Sicily, illegitimate children were hard to place because no matter how fine and healthy they looked, they were understood to be *unpredictable*.

In truth, any child from outside the family was unpredictable, but more so in the case of *bastardi*. So, far in greater demand by childless couples were the babies left behind when married mothers died in childbirth. But, in those cases, there might be grief-stricken fathers to contend with, men who preferred to take the babies to their own mothers or sisters to raise—or else men who would quickly marry again to provide a mother for their brood and get on with life. However, if the child were a first child, and a girl, and if the mother and the grandparents were all dead, something might be done. If the church hadn't already stepped in. A young father might agree to adopt out a first child because then he could remarry with a clean slate. It would have to be a girl baby because no one gave up a healthy boy.

There were also some legitimate babies and small children who had been let go for any variety of reasons. Everyone pretended not to know who their parents might be. Children who had the misfortune of conditions ranging from harelips to weak hearts to club feet. These were rare because Sicilians loved their children in ways Americans never would understand, Americans who built big buildings to house the mad, the old, the deformed. Of course, adopting an American baby was out of the question. The family would never know how to raise such a creature, and, besides, the Irish nuns in charge of American babies weren't likely to give them a baby at all.

From the start, Pina and her mother-in-law had disagreed about whether or not the Sicilian child must be legitimate. Their Sicilian was so fast and so cut-short that anyone overhearing them would have struggled to keep up. They switched sides over and over in a dizzying flurry of debate, but always stayed firmly apart from one another. At Pina's yellow Formica table with the matching chairs, the mother-in-law had said she'd get Filomena Giaccina to come over and write a nice letter like she'd done last time—to send for Pina herself. But Pina insisted it was *she* who should write the letter. After all, it was she who would be the mother.

"You're no mother yet," the old woman had let her know, "and I'm the mother of this family. And Filomena Giaccina was good enough to write the letter to get *you*."

The wave of heat that had run up Pina's spine nearly knocked her over, and she'd watched her own hand snatch the paper from in front of her mother-in-law. She'd grabbed her pen from where it rolled along the table top. The older woman had sat with her bony ankles tucked behind the cold chrome legs of her chair, bent forward over to look at Pina's paper. Pina put her hand in the way. When John came into the room and suggested they consider a child with a health condition as it would be a kind thing to do and improve their chances, they'd ignored him until he walked back out.

Pina had taken great care with her penmanship that day. She'd gone to school through the age of twelve and had always excelled with her hand. She felt the matchmaker would be impressed by a nice-looking letter. A letter like that would get them respect, and respect would get them a good baby. The mother-in-law tapped her foot.

Pina had been just about to sign her letter when she'd realized she didn't know the matchmaker's address—Dear Matchmaker would never get it where it needed to go. In town, they just pointed you to the old matchmaker, to her yellow stone house in the *piazzetta*. No one needed an address.

"How do I address this?" she'd asked.

"You're smart; figure it out," said the other.

Pina had stared at the old woman's face, balled up like a good-sized fist. The veins in her old forearms standing up like hissing cats.

"It's fine, I've already got one. I had Filomena Giaccina write it yesterday," the mother-in-law said.

Indeed, Pina looked and saw the letter peeping out from the old woman's dress pocket. She'd craned her neck to try and read the address. Then she snatched it from the pocket. And in return, her mother-in-law snatched *her* letter from her very hand. There, on the shiny linoleum—the only room without vinyl pathways—they'd each held the adoption letter of the other in her hands and then, simultaneously, each had torn the letter of the other into tiny scraps, letting those scraps flutter to the floor like confetti. The late afternoon sun shone under the back arbor and into the kitchen. There'd been nothing left for them to say, so they'd pointed at one another's faces.

The next day, John, in an attempt to draw peace out of acrimony, like honey from a nest of hornets, had proclaimed that *he* would write the letter—one letter—on behalf of the three of them. Pina had hissed that it wasn't about the *three* but about the *two*. *Was he married to his mother now?* But she knew well that her mother-in-law had the real connections, the old witch. So she didn't protest too much.

John, who had completed American eighth grade, wrote his letter very carefully, with Pina and his mother standing over his hunched shoulders, as close as they could get to him without being close to each other. Pina had been sure that if the old woman so much as brushed her, she'd lose her mind, run out the door, never return. She'd live on the streets if she had to. Like an *animale*.

It had taken hours of starts and many restarts before they produced something that could be grudgingly agreed upon. The letter did all of the necessary things, winding along formally and politely for a full page before it got to its point. First, it asked after the health of the matchmaker and her extended family, each by name. Then it told the curious tale of recent weather in Illinois and made pleasant small talk. Next, it offered up a detailed narrative, explaining the great need and great love of John and Pina and painting a picture of the wonderful life a child would enjoy with them as well as a kind and generous grandmother like Giuseppa close by—and aunts and uncles and cousins galore. And finally, after all that throat clearing, that letter had arrived at the business of the baby itself: "While all children are a blessing, we are hoping for a child from a good family with no one insane or idiotic, and, if at all possible, may it be a male child as it will likely be our only child." The women both nodded for John to write the final salutation and seal the envelope, and so he did.

"Settled," he said, licking the glue, and pounded the letter shut.

Pina had made espresso for all, and they'd sipped silently, standing around the table, feeling the psychic pressure of the envelope around their heads. Despite hatreds and frustrations, there almost always remained manners. No one would ever call Pina *brutta figura*. She'd felt sick to her stomach.

The next morning, she'd helped John put on his short-sleeved work shirt, straightening his collar, and giving him a kiss on the cheek. She'd watched him leave early for work so he'd have time to stop at the post office. She'd stared at the clock on the wall for ten full minutes, gauging his progress along the street in her mind. And while she did all that, she also used her mind's eye to re-read the letter they had written together in agreement. Suddenly she found it terribly unsatisfactory. It had no heart in it at all.

So Pina had sat down alone in her kitchen and penned her own better letter. The day before, she'd seen the proper address when John had addressed his envelope, and she'd memorized it: Sebastiana Solaro, Via Vecchia, Molano, Italy. She wrote it on the envelope with satisfaction. In her letter, she acknowledged the previous letter as if it were a prologue. Then she'd added her own thoughts about babies and what sorts of family traits, like murderousness, sloth, and weak lungs would probably be best to avoid—if at all possible—though, she was not one to judge. She described the welcoming interior of the flat with its orange goldfish in a clean bowl, sunny yellow kitchen, and fig tree in the back garden. She'd described the bedroom the child would have all to itself. But right across the hall from hers, of course, so that she could check on it regularly. She'd even mentioned the carpet protectors to show how frugal she was. When she'd tried to write of the love she already had for that baby, she felt foolish, so she'd signed off with great respect and deference.

In the middle of the day, after she'd fed the goldfish and scrubbed her kitchen floor, Pina Millefiore had walked her letter to the post office, paid for the airmail stamp, and handed the envelope filled with her big baby dream to the indifferent clerk, Mr. Falcone. She muttered to him in Sicilian, "just a birthday letter for my brother." She didn't need any witnesses.

On the way back to the flat, she'd had to duck quickly into a doorway near the Savings and Loan. There was the mother-in-law, jaw set in a straight line, pushing that old black baby buggy towards the post office from whence Pina had just come. That cat of hers with its one eye was trailing along like a bad omen.

Pina had known in an instant that the old crotch had a letter in her hand, probably dictated to Filomena Giaccina at the crack of dawn. But what could Pina say? Nothing. She'd just mailed her own secret letter. Despite that fact, she'd been tempted to accost her mother-in-law and rip the envelope away from her in the middle of the street. So tempted that she'd somehow decided to do it without even knowing she'd decided. Running past her rival, like an Olympic sprinter, Pina had reached out and plucked the letter from the arthritic hand. "What's this?" she'd asked, stopping to pant. "What are you up to, you old meddler?"

The mother-in-law had said nothing, just rolled her buggy right up to Pina. Dark eye to dark eye.

"You stay out of this baby business!" Pina snapped, moving her shoe away from the dab of spittle on the street. How did she ever get such a mother-in-law? *Mamma mia.*

"It's my grandchild, and you can't make me."

Pina had looked at the envelope now in her hand and slowly slit it open with her forefinger. She'd cleared her throat and read it aloud right there in the street—in a voice to mimic her mother-in-law's.

"Dear Matchmaker," she'd cried like a crow, "it would be a favor and an honor if you would include my personal wishes regarding the new Millefiore child as follows: it's best if the family of the child includes no one who has died of, or casts, the evil eye, no one who is a glutton, and please no Sciaffos. I'm sorry to have to say this but that family is known for producing criminals, and while America is good, it's a place that's very hard on criminals. I don't believe such a child would find happiness here." The letter went on, but Pina stopped reading there.

"How dare you?" she spat. "How dare you say that about the Sciaffos, you know very well they are my mother's second cousins." Pina found herself panting again.

"Well, that explains a lot, no? But, yes, I already knew that. It was something I chose to overlook when I got you, but I won't be so foolish this time. Now, you give that letter back to me."

Pina did not give back the letter. Instead, she'd prepared herself to rip it to shreds in a reenactment of the letter ripping of the day before. She'd held it up high, but the old woman, with surprising agility and steadied by one hand on the handle of the buggy, hopped up like a grackle. Got it back.

"I'm warning you," the mother-in-law told her, shoving the letter deep into her pocket, "I can have Filomena Giaccina write letters day and all night. We are old. We have little else to do. You want me to take out the part about those Sciaffos? Fine. Fine. That, I can do."

Pina had watched her mother-in-law wheel away toward home, which wasn't too far. The cat swayed behind her, and people on the sidewalks deferred to her like cowards. Because Pina's flat was in the house right next to the one the old woman lived in, she remained, standing in the street, not wanting to follow. While she waited, she'd asked herself about the kind of woman she was becoming in America. The kind of woman who fought in the street like a Sciaffo?

It was the fault of this terrible mother-in-law. Why wasn't she the kind of old person Pina could bring chamomile teas and read to? The kind that stared at the ceiling and smiled harmlessly? All her life, Pina had never known an old one this difficult. She knew it was wrong, but she longed to squash her mother-in-law like a hard-shelled beetle.

When she'd looked up, she noticed a set of clouds had finally blown in from over the lake, and the afternoon traffic had picked up. Finally, Pina had left the street for the sidewalk and stomped down to Creme Crunch Donuts where she reached into her skirt pocket for change and bought three of these things called crullers, one for her and one for John to eat later. And one for herself to eat now, alone, as she stalked home. The cruller wasn't bad. Kind of like zeppole but less so.

When Pina and John ate the other two donuts at home, she'd informed him about what his mother had been up to.

"You need to tell her to stay out of it. This is *our* baby, not hers, my love."

"You're both making me crazy, crazy, crazy," he said, swallowing the last of his cruller and heading out the back door to prune trees.

Pina had known her mother-in-law would never remove the hateful reference to the Sciaffos from her letter. The old liar. In fact, she'd probably make it even more insulting. So, Pina had had no choice but to write yet another letter of her own and as soon as possible. She'd state specifically that though she was not assuming the Sciaffos *had* not produced any children they could not at this time raise, should a Sciaffo child for some reason, any reason, need adopting, she would be happy—no, *overjoyed*—to have one, particularly as everyone knew Sciaffos were renowned for their honesty and good fortune. This was patently untrue, but Pina was loyal to family, and she knew the matchmaker would see that as a sign of good character on her part. She signed it and took it to the post office.

Then, a few weeks later, Pina had written yet another letter for good measure in case the earlier two had become lost on the way. She was worried as there was no reply at all from the matchmaker, though it had been over six weeks since the first letter had gone out. This new letter had repeated a few things to refresh the reader, but then it also made it clear that Pina would happily take a daughter even though the first letter might have made it sound like they had their hearts set on a male child. Really, it didn't matter. And, in fact, she'd thought it over quite a bit, and she didn't mind at all what family or where the baby came from or any conditions it might have. Any baby, she said, any baby that needs a mother is the baby for me. She'd wanted not to sound desperate or stand-offish, so she'd added swirls in ink at the bottom to show a friendly and artistic spirit. Last, she'd sprayed just a tiny bit of lily of the valley perfume on the envelope, a nice touch, she was almost certain.

Pina had wished she could just phone the matchmaker. But matchmakers, everyone knew, didn't have phones. If only she could have phoned the matchmaker from Lena's.

Another five weeks had passed with no reply. Pina had seen her mother-in-law headed in the general direction of the post office several times, and though she might have been going to the bakery or the Little Flowers of Italy social club, both of which were also that way, Pina was certain she was mailing letter after letter—ordering up the sort of baby *she* wanted, smearing Sciaffos left and right. And making them *all* look bad. Ruining everything.

With no way out, Pina had written still more letters to combat the ones she was sure her adversary was sending. Pina wrote letters heavy with perfume and swirls. Letters with little sense of pride or dignity anymore. Then, letters with none at all.

A year went by. A second began. And every hour of each day of those years, Pina had pined for a baby. She'd fingered the yellowing ribbon on her old easter bonnet. She'd fed candy kisses to her new nieces and nephews, some of them surpassing her in height as she waited and they grew. She'd wondered: who would be left for this baby to play with once it finally came? While she ironed her husband's clothes and packed his lunch boxes, she'd imagined packing her child a school lunch. And when she was at the five and dime, she'd touched the layette sets there, softly. But she never bought one so that she wouldn't jinx herself. Pina had sometimes cried along with the neighborhood babies when they sent their cries toward her. And yet, she kept her spine straight in public. Despite all the "pleases" in her letters.

In the fourth year of the letters, when Pina turned forty-four, a response letter finally arrived from Molano. It had come to her mother-in-law's address next door and was stamped all over with airmail stamps. Surprisingly, Giuseppa did not carry it to Filomena Giaccina to be opened and read to her there. Instead, she'd taken it carefully to John and Pina's flat, where John opened it with his pocketknife and Pina trembled.

> Dear Signore and Signora John Millefiore and Cugina Donna Giuseppa Millefiore,
>
> Your letters are many and strange. Every week there is a new letter that says this or that. Some are sprayed with perfume, some with what smells like tobacco. The ones from Donna Giuseppa have money in them. I've donated that to the church and also fixed the roof of my cottage, which had a bad leak. I did not ask for the money and I'm not sure what you intended it for, but I felt this was the best use.
>
> I'm not one to judge, but let me say again, so many letters. Regardless, there's some confusion here. I cannot get you a child nowadays—maybe in 1895—maybe even two decades ago with great luck—but not in 1953. That's all up to the church and the government these days. But you should know it would be a waste of your time to write to them. You should know, it's no use. I know the rules, and the mother must not be over 40. The father must not be over 50. All three of you are far too old to get a baby sent over.

The letter had gone on, but they had all stopped reading there. Pina did not keep the letter. She'd burned it over the stove. And that took some time and effort because it was an electric stove. Yes, she'd destroyed it, but she'd inadvertently memorized it as well. It now marked, in what she thought of as her soul, the very definite end of her connected feeling with Sicily.

Finito.

That letter, however, it must be said, also had done some good. The day it arrived, it had thrown the three of them together, clinging to one another in the kitchen. Wailing over the child they would never have—its cherubic smile, its starfish hands, its sweet dimpled knees—everything. And while this common loss had not made Pina like her mother-in-law one iota more, it had made her love the old woman a tiny bit. They'd squeezed each other's elbows for a moment, supporting John who threatened to fall to the linoleum in his grief.

But now, here in front of her television, five years later, Pina no longer felt that squeeze. She no longer dwelled on the letter itself. She simply watched television and kept herself company all the long days. Whether Pina was anything, anyone, in those long hours with no one watching, she wasn't sure. Sometimes she imagined herself emptying the savings account and flying back to Sicily to break into an orphanage and kidnap a mystery child, no matter what anyone said. She daydreamed of her crimes on the sofa, sticking to the plastic a little.

She also knew exactly how she would serve her husband pastini tonight. How she would tie a *mopina* around his neck like a baby's bib, to keep his clothes clean. She found that she babied him as much as she could, evenings and weekends. *Ding Dong School!* remained her favorite part of most days, even though she was a serious woman who kept a spotless home. She sat with an imagined child, a kind of chubby ghost who ate candy kisses, removing the silver foil wrappings carefully, bunching them neatly on the coffee table. In the daytime Pina knew she had to be her own child. Not easy in this flat with its plastic slipcovers and spiky runners, in this home where she could not find the pipes for blowing bubbles no matter how hard she looked.

ELEVEN

Constant Comment

Agata Millefiore opened the French door to the dove gray balcony with the white wood rail, stepped out onto it from her hot, little flat, and hollered to the children below.

"Don't sit on the curb in your swimsuit! Or you're gonna get piles!"

She wiped the sweat from her upper lip, a fresh permanent wave so high and tight over her smooth forehead that it hardly moved at all. It was always hot in the upper flat, no matter how many windows she opened. So, she remained a while on the balcony raising her arms, not above her head which would have looked foolish, but at least even with her shoulders, letting the breeze come in under the armholes of her sleeveless house dress.

The children she hollered to sat, her own two among them, tucked low over their legs, on the curb. They looked up at her and waved, sucking their Popsicles, shivering in their sprinkler damp swimsuits. Agata felt that the sound of her warning floated on by them in the hum of flies and buzz of traffic a few streets over—a symphony of nothing muchness. She watched them finish their Popsicles and read the riddles on the sticks very loudly to one another. Giggle. Then they chewed the sticks to get at any tiny bit of sweet left in the pale wood. And finally, they sharpened the sticks against the sidewalk, into spears. Hers, Carmella and Little John, looked up at her.

Maybe, she thought, she should go down and check them for mosquito bites, and bring the calamine lotion. They were big kids now, not babies, but she wasn't ready for them to grow up.

Carmella and Little John had nearly black hair, and it shone in the sunshine the way a black pony shines. Her nieces and nephews were shiny too, but lighter. She considered their colors and the way they spread out. It was as if someone had dropped a handful of old and new and in-between pennies onto the street below. She was unabashedly thankful in an almost dizzying way, to be able to look down on them, to protect them from whatever might come their way.

When the young people finally rose, having dried and begun to bake in the hot sun, they left wet marks on the curb—the odd shapes of their *culos* blotted there, like ladybug wings. Some were big, some were small, some were lopsided. "Look at all the *culos*! Aunt Agata," Teddie shouted up. "Carmella's is the hugest!" In response, Carmella pushed Dolores to the ground and sat on her back.

Agata watched the children spilling across the lawn, running along the side of the house across the street. They ran so fast. Agata was glad to see they didn't stop at the sprinkler—which she felt was directly responsible for all summer ear infections. Maybe they really were growing up. It oscillated, showering red climbing roses that blazed against the dark green house across the street. Better that they should nail worms to the picnic table like they did last week, than get wet in the ears. Making pemmican, they'd said, like their history teacher taught them about. Agata had no idea what pemmican was, but it seemed harmless enough and sounded a lot like "pelican" which was a delightful bird indeed.

Her brother-in-law Nicolo would come out soon and move the sprinkler around, but he wouldn't turn it off till night. She could hear the pressure in the hose even from here. Sounds seemed to come to her, unbidden. She looked down at her short-clipped fingernails and her wide hands, hands like little mittens. She hoped her sister-in-law Lena would come over soon, but she didn't want to be seen hanging around hoping, so she turned and went back inside her flat where it was as hot as hell.

Agata's parlor was quiet and dark and close as she sank into her ruffled chair, smelling anise biscotti, chocolate chip cookies, and her own sweat. Agata's husband Lorenzo liked his biscotti, and she'd made chocolate chips for the kids, from the recipe on the back of the package, *authentic American*. Agata knew how to keep everyone happy: she kept Italian bread and she kept Butternut; she kept mortadella and she kept hot dogs. She felt it was the best way to do things. She even kept American cheese, which she sliced into perfect slabs with her stainless-steel slicer. It wasn't that bad with tomato and giardiniera, though it was, she thought, shockingly bright yellow.

Agata believed that children should—in the main—be given what they liked, and she couldn't bear the sight of a child in tears, and so her children seldom were. Unless they were tormenting one another. And this accounted for no small portion of their personalities. She also tried to help make it so her nieces or nephews led tear-free lives as well. But of course, this was difficult because they were not her children, and she could only intermediate so much.

Everyone, Agata reminded herself in the dim room, liked *some* kind of cookie best. It was just a matter of finding the right one. The tin of Hershey's syrup on the counter was for chocolate crinkle cookies, and the almonds were too. She'd make those next, later, after the kitchen cooled off again. The cookie belief was only one food belief Agata used to feel her way through life. There were many, but the one she cherished most was this: Agata Millefiore believed in a God who made sure that each person, the night before they died, ate their favorite food. She had no *proof*. But she didn't care about that. This was just something she'd noticed. It was like God waited for that opportunity to sweeten the pot. When she pointed it out, people said nothing. Maybe they didn't believe her. Any thinking person with an urge to argue could have proven her belief patently untrue, but no one who knew Agata would be unkind enough to do so. People generally realized she was not a thinking person but a feeling person. And they realized that without this particular belief— and some others—there could be no Agata Millefiore at all. Even her mother-in-law let it pass, except for once to say her husband had dropped dead on the lower porch after a glass of ice water, and that certainly wasn't his favorite meal.

Agata relaxed into her chair and wondered what her own mother had eaten for her last meal—no one had ever told her. Maybe *pasta fagioli*, she felt. With fresh bread and good olive oil.

Agata looked down at her small ankles and wrists, winnowing away from plump arms and calves. She reminded herself of the drawings of a stegosaurus her son showed her in his schoolbooks, ruffs of bone and hollows of flesh. Agata was a grown woman of twenty-eight, with two children, and still, she was only as tall as an eleven-year-old child—though quite a bit wider. So, she hemmed her dresses drastically, at the bottom and at her sleeves, and she bought her shoes in the children's section of Kerger's shoe store, size four. The salesman there looked perpetually astounded—and impressed—by her dainty foot, insisting on measuring and x-raying her every visit, as if she might grow. She did not. She walked wherever she went in the most sophisticated children's shoes she could find at Kerger's, which was to say, she had to be very discerning. But Agata was used to being discerning; she ported secrets of unbearable weight.

She wanted to go out and sit on the balcony for air—and, really, to watch out for Lena coming now, even if it might be pathetic of her—but the summer had already turned her darker than anyone else. Her mother-in-law had commented.

She dragged her chair over to the window and looked out at Lena's front door, willing her sister-in-law-friend to come out. She knew Lena ironed everything in the house down to sheets, even though she worked midnights at American Can. This meant Agata often had to wait for so long that she feared maybe Lena wasn't coming at all for their afternoon coffee. Feared that maybe she'd never come again. Agata felt that fear today, and it made her rub her arms as if she were cold until she saw Lena emerge, pale, pale against the dark green of that house across the street. She smiled; Lena always came eventually.

It's a hard thing in families when some are fast friends and others aren't, when some feel left out and others feel guilty for leaving some out. But there's no way to make it fair. Agata knew this was why Lena slipped like a cat burglar from her own front door, a dull gray silk scarf tied over her red hair. Why she stepped off the curb, crossed the street, climbed the bottom porch stairs on tiptoe, and opened the door of Agata's building without knocking. Why once in the entry hall, Lena held her breath and tiptoed past Pina's door. It was also why Pina would be right behind that door, crocheting pointy-toed house slippers or watching television, alone, listening.

Agata heard Lena climbing up, stepping along the sides of the wooden steps—where the creaks were fewest. If Pina popped out, Agata knew, Lena would have no choice but to invite her up to Agata's, and then their talk couldn't happen properly. There'd be a different talk, sure, but not what she needed. If Pina came out then they'd be stuck all afternoon murmuring about weather and niceties, talking about Sicily which was a place neither Agata nor Lena had ever been. And Agata would be translating to Sicilian for Pina and to English for Lena. The three of them suspended at the table, and at the center, Pina, her flat queenly face showing no emotion at all, as was her way. She had the face of a strangely beautiful frog waiting patiently on a lily pad, Agata thought.

Lena made it up without Pina seeing or hearing her and let herself into Agata's flat without knocking. She wore sneakers and dungarees, a white shirt with rolled cuffs, and the scarf, very modern. Like a combination of a berry picker and a French spy and Lucille Ball. Agata rose from her chair and motioned to Lena from across the room—at the teapot on the stove. She kept Constant Comment and *pfeffernusse* in the house just for Lena.

When she tipped the teapot to pour a big blue mug for her sister-in-law she said, "I'm so glad you came." Agata poured coffee from the Moka into another mug for herself and set down a green Fiesta ware platter of the white *pfeffernuese* between them. The women put their chins in their hands and leaned their elbows on the enamel topped table, cool. Then their forearms against the table. Finally, Lena pushed her hot freckled face onto the cold enamel and they both laughed.

"Where did we leave off?" Lena asked.

Agata looked down at her Buster Brown penny loafers. The sharp smell of spiced tea and spiced cookies was blunted by the weight of coffee and tea in the room, and the hot coffee somehow cooled her. In this dark, warm room, stories were told for better or for worse with no interruptions. The afternoon sun slipped in through the venetian blinds like fingers, trying to reach the women. But they stayed out of grasp, in the corner of the kitchen, soles flat on the linoleum.

"Like I said, I practically lived my life on that stoop for two years."

Lena nodded.

"Sat there until late at night—the wee hours, you know."

Agata paused for a sip of coffee. Not a slurp.

"Because my father had bad women in his room."

She raised the cup again for confidence—to obscure a trembling upper lip—and she put it back down again. "Really bad women. The worst ones. You know what they are; I won't say it."

Lena never looked shocked. Lena never looked doubting. And Lena never—ever—broke a confidence. In fact, Agata and Lena called each other by a French word they'd heard somewhere: *confidante*.

"I've never been so cold since. And I shivered all the time, even when I was at school. The teacher put me nearest to the radiator. But when I was out on the stoop, no one would offer me a hot drink or a bite to eat because of my father. You know, he was such a disgrace, and I was his child. They thought I was a disgrace, too."

Lena nodded—her cat's eye glasses reassuring and eyes behind them even more so. Agata wore a matching pair of specs.

"My father was a careless man," she continued. "And my mother was dead years already."

Fiddling with the thick hem of her cotton dress—it was pale yellow and green—Agata wondered why she noticed it was frog colors when she'd bought it?

"But, you see, he wasn't all bad. I had a little red purse he bought me, you know, a sort of velvet purse. He gave it to me with three tootsie rolls inside. Three of them still in the waxed papers as they come."

As Agata told the story, she could feel the pressure of the old concrete stoop beneath her, not the cushion of her kitchen chair. That was gone altogether. Under her fingers, she could feel the thread-bare corners of her red velvet purse, worn from her loving it. She smelled the tootsie rolls and felt them sticking to her molars, the sweetness at the back of her throat. And then her father's whiskey breath came on the hot breeze through the window, his big white teeth in the glare between the blinds.

"It was only because he was lonely that there were all those women in and out."

That's what she said to Lena. And it was true. Sometimes, in the early morning hours, he'd cry out for Agata's mother: "Why did you leave me, you? Why did you do this to me, Malena?" He'd looked so pathetic that it still made Agata's heart hurt. She was never angry at him, not now, and not when she sat out on the stoop all those nights when she was seven and eight and nine years old. Ten, eleven, twelve and more. Agata didn't really know how to be angry.

"He wasn't a bad man, really," she told Lena, "But he wasn't a good man, neither."

Agata knew how Lena had a lock of her own mother's hair folded in a violet handkerchief in the maple secretary across the street. Agata had seen it. Even been allowed to touch it. Agata didn't have anything of her mother's. She pushed down the envy that always washed over her when she thought of the long chestnut lock tied with a black ribbon. Her father hadn't thought to clip a lock for Agata. Or to save a scrap of anything. She unstuck her molars and reminded herself that her father was only a careless man. She pushed down the anger—but envy was slipperier. Still, she managed it. Pushed it down, down, down to her loafers.

Agata was not glad in any way that Lena's mother had died, but she *was* glad Lena had a dead mother, too. A dead mother she'd never really known. It made them a little the same. Dead mothers are hard to live with, Agata believed, and no one with a live mother was worth talking to about your dead mother. She pushed the plate of *pfeffernusse* closer to Lena.

She took a big breath and continued.

"Those women," she recounted. "You could see them coming up the sidewalks, and they knocked real loud and he'd let them in and push me out. They stepped on me as he was pushing me out, like I was a doormat. He'd close the door behind them and say to me, through that closed door, 'You stay out till I tell you to come in.' And then he locked it. The door had no window, just planks. I couldn't even see in."

"But everyone in that old neighborhood could see me out on the stoop, and I was not to leave it."

Lena inched her hand across the table to hold Agata's. Agata liked that. She could feel the fine dust of flour still on her hands and hoped Lena didn't mind.

"You deserved better."

"Oh, I don't know."

Agata shrugged as an eight-year-old shrugs, head low in the clavicle, eyes closed. She really didn't know. Who deserves what? she thought. No one deserved my father, but my father didn't deserve my mother dead, and my mother didn't deserve to be dead. She looked at Lena and opened her mouth to say more but did not.

"Trust me," Lena whispered. "You deserve the best."

"I still want my mother, Lena."

"Of course, you do."

"I still want my father, Lena."

"Of course. Of course, you do."

"But if he was still alive, Lena, I'd never ever bring him here."

They held hands for a long time and could hear the singsong sounds of the children coming in the window, the scream of the jays, some pounding noises. Nothing enough to jolt them apart. They would release like coming up for air, and that took some time.

Before Lena left, both women put their faces to the cool enamel table top again, one cheek and then the other. When Lena got up to rinse her mug, Agata thought she looked so smart in her blue denim, really even more like Lucille Ball but softer and much more dependable. The two stepped onto the balcony, now shaded by the buildings to the east and watched the little world below them. They could see the old mother-in-law standing on her porch next door, whistling for the children to come and help on the garden plot. The little mob rushed over, whooping as Little John popped something into his sixth-grade mouth, a mouth that should know better. The kids loved Giuseppa, they had to admit it. There they were swarming over the curb to get to her, putting their shoes on as they ran. Agata and Lena watched Giuseppa and the children head off to the empty lot on the next street, a pail of hand-tools bouncing along in her black baby buggy, which the children helped her to push.

Agata and Lena on the balcony did not smile at the vibrant scene below. Nor did they frown. Leaving behind the worlds of their own childhoods was like wisping themselves out from a genie's bottle—it required dematerialization.

In time, though, they did feel the magnetic pull of the shade from the houses across the street move over the porch. And more from the craning mulberry in front, its arms heavy with quilted purple fruit. The east was becoming dark, cool, and relieved. It was time for a great many women to make dinner for hungry husbands, husbands who knew so few of their secrets but provided other things of value. Agata and Lena watched through their matching glasses, until they became fully conscious of their own children whom they could no longer see, children who seemed to own the street, the sidewalks, the summer. Children with mothers. And though *they*—Agata and Lena—*were* those very mothers—well, it was somehow odd to see such creatures in action.

When Agata hugged Lena goodbye, she pinched the pale cheek, squishing the freckled skin there. Next time it would be Lena's turn to tell a story. Agata knew she'd pick up where she'd left off last time, a five-year-old Lena in the home of her aunt who raised her, wanting the love of a woman of migraines, high expectations, and far too many children underfoot. It was likely she would begin with the broken crock incident and the subsequent switch. Agata knew the story well.

Agata saw Lena glance at the nibbled cookies on the little plate, the powdered sugar of the *pfeffernuese* like gleaming snow in the dim light. She urged her to take a last one for fortitude, to make it down and past Pina's door once more.

"What kind of cookies do *you* like best, Agata?" Lena asked, her speckled arm extended into the space between them as she opened the door to the hall to leave.

"Oh, I don't know. I never thought about it, really."

"I think you should," Lena said. "I really think you should."

Agata surprised them both with a single tear, one she managed to catch in her the crook of her elbow and then flick at the floor in a strange matador-like gesture.

But when the door closed behind Lena the rest of the tears came like hard rain, and Agata Millefiore sobbed as she ran herself a cool bath, sobbed as she removed her apron, her dress, her sweaty underthings. She sobbed into herself as she sat in the clean, clear water, crying out feelings without thought. Time passed, but she barely noticed her fingertips wrinkling or the water getting warm as the air. When she'd cried herself out, she plunged her face under the water, bending forward over her round tummy. She breathed bubbles out her nose into the bathwater, blowing away the salt of tears, snot, and sweat.

By the time she washed herself with the yellow soap and then pulled up the rubber plug, which only let go after a struggle, she was reborn in a way. Or at least reset. There was much to do: dinner to make, laundry to bring in, the stairs down to Pina's to sweep clean. And she needed to find her lost rosary, too. On top of all that, she knew she should pick out her favorite cookie tonight. She had no idea what it might be, but she was determined to find out.

TWELVE

Midnight Mass

Nicky Millefiore knew exactly what was going on across the street, at his mother's place. He knew it in the same way a piano player senses the keys in his mind rather than with his eyes. His wife and sisters laughing, their wide, lipsticked mouths like crescent moons. Their shoes slapping the basement floor as they bustled. All the children wriggling, shouting, and whining in excitement. In the center of it all, his old Mamma in her best dress, a wad of snuff under her lip, her silver hair held back in bone combs.

The children who understood enough Sicilian would be translating for those who didn't. Mamma wasn't usually a joker, but she had a Christmas Eve routine like a stand-up comedian, and everyone knew laughter only encouraged her: "Seven fishes?" she'd be saying. "Better you save your money. The airs of the ones born in America, they made this up to show off!" She would turn her head and pretend to spit behind her for emphasis, "Seven fishes, bah!" On second thought, he felt, maybe she wasn't really trying to be funny at all.

Nicky could just see how the overhead lights would be bounding off of the many pairs of eyeglasses—his wife's, his sister Fil's, his sisters-in-law's, the teenage girls', as well as two of the more bookish boys. A family that could afford glasses all around was a fortunate family. On the long folding tables in his mother's basement, there'd be the bowls of smooth white Jordan almonds and tiny demitasse cups of espresso—white with a gold rim. For the children, there was milk, as it had been since the depression ended all those years ago. And all the voices would be in soprano because the grown men were in their own flats busy with their Christmas Eve duties.

Nicky had work to do, but still he tuned into the high vibrations of sound and light flowing from that full house across the street, over the snow, and through the front door of his own flat—a large one in which he, Lena, and their children lived. It was owned by his mother. She owned three houses now, plus the empty lot for the garden. And she'd filled each house with her grown sons and their families. Some sons in some neighborhood somewhere might have felt an impotence in living in a house owned by their mamma. Or even resentment, but Nicky and his brothers did not. He paid his rent on time and felt an admiration, no, a fealty and sense of safety under his mother's dominion. Tonight, he also felt a wetness in one eye and then in the other. Setting down the hemp twine and scissors he'd been working with, he took a moment or two to weep, not in sadness but in something else, a welling of feeling he had no real word for. This was not unusual. Nicky also cried when listening to Caruso and when the Chicago White Sox won a game. He cried when old neighbors passed away and when babies were born. He cried at weddings. As did his brothers and his neighbors. As had his ancestors when singing at home back in Sicily. But he cried for just a moment or two because timing was everything on Christmas Eve, and there were quite a few presents jammed into the back of the closet still to wrap.

Nicky walked to the phonograph and stacked his favorite records on, setting "Ave Maria" to play first. He wiped his eyes with his shirtsleeve, his nose too. And then he wrapped the children's presents—carefully, but not as well as his Lena could do. He used brown butcher paper and the twine, and he marked each present with a name, using a squared off construction pencil to print, and taking care not to drag the heel of his hand through and smear his letters. He followed the directions—what for whom—on the list Lena had slipped into his pocket as she'd ushered the kids out the door and across the street earlier.

His brothers and brother-in-law had similar notes from their wives and wrapped in similar empty living rooms, crouched on similar braided rugs. Such was the tradition in this family. And because the men did the wrapping for Christmas—something the children could have never expected or guessed—the adopted mythology of the Santa Claus was an especially fervent belief of all the Millefiore children, a belief that sometimes had to be shaken out of them even after puberty.

Where were their fathers on Christmas Eve? What were they up to? Why did they never attend Midnight Mass? The children had no idea; they'd just never been there. If you'd asked the kids where their fathers got to, they'd have said it wasn't any of their business what their fathers did—ever. And if you had suggested those men—concrete finishers and movers and bookies and railroad workers—those men—were on their knees in their own living room floors fighting cellophane tape and shearing paper, the children would never have believed it.

Santa Claus, for this story, Nicky was thankful. He reveled in this thing called childhood, a thing that seemed like a real good idea to him, if it could be kept intact. Times *had* certainly changed, he thought, stretching his arms behind his back and over his head, an old boxing move to stretch tight ligaments. It felt good. It made his blood circulate. Imagine, he thought, just imagine such a childhood. It wasn't that Nicky had never been small or that he had not been loved; he'd been both, but the family was new to the country then, and not just them, hard-faced little Italian kids had populated the neighborhood when he was a kid. Children who picked up pipes from the street and smoked them. Children who chewed the tar that patched those same streets, just like chewing gum. Children with cinders embedded in their skinny little knees all the time. It had been a childhood, but then again it hadn't. Besides, most of it had been forgotten. He'd read in Reader's Digest or somewhere like that, this fact: many times, people forget the most traumatic experiences of their lives. But he seemed to be the opposite. *He* had forgotten what happened *before* his traumatic moment, as if his memory suddenly switched on when his father died, like an electric light in a dark, dark room, the glow exposing everything. And so his memory began at the age of eleven.

When Nicky's father had fallen dead on that hot front porch across the street, still wearing his battered work boots, well, in that very split second any belief in benevolent beings who kept people safe or who brought presents had dropped dead right beside him. *Mort.* For Nicky it hadn't been Santa, but the Befana, who'd vaporized. She never appeared again. It was also the moment that meant the end of schooling for him and his brothers. It was, of course, the absolute end for Nicky's father, *finito,* so he knew he had nothing to pity himself about, comparatively. He guessed it was one of those things people called a chain reaction. One thing ended another and another and another. Disappearances. Vanishings. The end of music in the house and of whiskery kisses. The end of milk in the icebox. At least that's what his sister Filomena had said. It was hard for Nicky to recall there ever being milk in the icebox or whiskery kisses, but he trusted his sister on such things. She helped him to miss what he could not recall.

Nicky, as all good parents do, worried about his own death, wondered what would become of his children if *he* dropped dead on his front porch, or here on the rug wrapping presents, or down at the freight yard any day of the week. He wasn't a young man anymore, not that *that* mattered. Young men died, too. Nicky's fear of his own death was why he believed so zealously in life insurance. Since he'd been in touch with Gerber, he knew that no matter what came, Big John, and Dolores and Teddie would not leave school to work, would not go milk-less, would not dress in rags. In fact, the insurance man had said, they'd probably be even better off than ever.

Nicky had a habit of thinking in paths that were constructed to avoid, but somehow always led to, the worst thing about his father's death. The very worst. Tonight, he wandered his mind-paths with care, wrapping a caramel brown and mint green wool sweater for Big John. He struggled, slapping at the sweater several times to get the long arms to stop flailing in the wrapping, which would give away what it was to anyone who might squeeze its finished package. But try as he might, both the arms and his own mind outwitted him.

That awful memory shuffled across decades to meet him like an old ghost, and it came out of that same basement where his children and wife now sipped espresso and sucked the hard shells off their confetti almonds.

There, a few feet past the folding tables and cold metal folding chairs, in the deeper corner of Mamma's basement, stood the cement sink. It was cavernous and double-sided with its bottom drains open wide like mouths. There was one just like it in his house now, and one just like it in every house up and down the streets. And yet, the one in his mother's basement was the most troubling one.

It had been two days after Papa's death that he'd seen—no, more than that—that he'd *watched* those drain mouths sucking down Papa's blood. He shouldn't have seen it; he should have stayed outside under the Bartlett pear tree where he'd been shooting marbles with his older brothers—a game to keep them out of the way—but he'd come down through the side door looking for his Mamma— there was a man banging at the front door selling pots and pans. The man said, please find your mother. And even though they'd been told to stay outside all afternoon, Nicky thought he'd better go find her. His mother was not in the basement, nor was her frizzy-haired cousin Rocca—who'd come on the train from New York to help with the death. *Zia* Rocca was a healer like Mamma, and maybe even more powerful because she was bigger and faster.

No, Mamma wasn't there, nor *Zia* Rocca, nor was the funeral director from Zimbardo's Funeral Company who'd come with his black bag to talk to Mamma about the arrangements and to sip coffee while Mamma stared at the wall. There was no one, it seemed. No one at all in the basement.

But when Nicky stepped further into the cool space, he saw his papa strapped to a board that hung low from the ceiling, angled and grooved like a carving board. And from that board his blood seeped and drained into the great awful sink with little intermittent gurgles. The same sink his Mamma used to drain chickens and ducks or to wash sheets. Papa was naked and horribly dead, and still, it was Papa, much worse than how he'd been on the porch.

Nicky screamed, but he didn't run or even back away. Yes, he was sure he must have screamed because very soon *Zia* Rocca came banging down the stairs and tried to drag him away, slapping him all the while. But Nicky was like a bag of cement, and she only moved him inches at a time.

"You!" she yelled in Sicilian, "you are not to be here!"

When he still wouldn't stop screaming, one of Rocca's big meaty hands came around his head and covered his mouth, and the other pinched his nose shut. He'd felt sucked inside himself, like he'd swallowed all his father's blood and then everything else in the basement—all four of the cement basement walls, the Formica countertop, the stove for canning, the cement sink, and Papa's naked body, especially his terrible dead penis, his blue toes, his still-strangely-human belly button. All of these things seemed rolled up in him like a lump of coal, gritty and cutting and globular—and shiny. "It has to be done," Rocca hissed. "That's life, and that's death, and that's why you don't open doors you are told to stay away from. Goddamn you, that's why you stay under the pear tree! Now get out before the mortician comes back!"

Nicky had found his feet then and ran from the basement. But he hadn't returned to the game of marbles, and he lost his cat's eye and his Conker that day because of it. Instead, he went to the alley and kicked at the pea gravel there. He kicked at it until well after dark.

A great many guests had come to the wake—which enveloped the next three days of Nicky's young life. Most of the parlor and dining room furniture had been shunted into the bedrooms and replaced by chairs and mattresses the funeral home dropped off. They also brought extra pots and pans and dishes. Nicky and his brother had been made to carry them inside from the cart. In the house were masses of flowers, strong smelling ones like gladiolus and gardenia. There were also some flies buzzing around, which *Zia* Rocca swatted to death with rolled up newspaper when no one was looking.

People had trailed into and out of the hot front parlor and looked at poor papa, now dressed in his old brown suit and placed inside his coffin like a sleeping sailor, on a sea of ice to keep the body cool. They brought with them food in bowls and jars and baskets, some of the women went to the stove and cooked, washed dishes, organized things. Everyone cried loudly to express their grief and their solidarity with the family—Nicky cried too, but it had come out strangled, like an old hen's cry. Rocca had looked at him with an eyebrow pointed up in a vicious sort of way. His oldest sister, Lucy, had noticed too. And she'd looked down his throat but saw nothing there but throat. She made him a poultice and fed him honey until she was satisfied with her effort. All three days of the wake, Lucy had yelled at everyone including poor Papa, the corpse. She had been both the most insane and the sanest person present. Mamma was mostly in bed.

Anyway, despite Lucy's ministrations, the lump of coal thing had remained, just under Nicky's esophagus, and it kept trying to come up in front of people. The lump made it hard for Nicky to eat bread with his brothers or to sleep lying flat. He nibbled the edges of strange cookies and little salty fish on platters that people had left on the sideboard. He slept with his day clothes piled under his neck to help keep the thing down where it couldn't choke him.

The people came and went until the last day; this was so that his mother rose and dressed in black. People made sure she never had to be alone with the body. At night his two sisters and cousins from the city slept on the floor in front of the coffin, whispering into the night, softly, though sometimes hissing.

Finally, a black cart had come to take the coffin away. Inside it were men who came into the house and closed Papa inside the box. Everyone shrieked, not the men, but everyone else, especially *Zia* Rocca, who had big black circles under her eyes as if she'd been punched, but she hadn't. No one would punch Rocca. She was just prone to circles. There were many old women there, looking a lot the same, and *Zia* Rocca said they were the *prefiche*. Said they were as old as time and that they chanted you out of the world. Their voices made the hair on Nicky's arms stand straight up.

Then the men from the funeral company used chisels and pry bars, and they removed the large square front window of the house, the parlor window, and they floated the coffin, which days before they had assembled in that room, out through the gaping hole. As if it were a feather. And into the waiting wagon it went. While they put the window back in and sealed it with putty, the family combed their hair and splashed cold water on their faces so they would be presentable for the burial. A crowd had gathered inside and outside the house. All of the women and girls wore black and covered their faces with veils, despite the heat. They carried more than one hand-kerchief to dab their upper lips and brows. Nicky could hardly tell any of them apart, but since they were all the same that day, it really didn't matter much. Everything was sad.

The crowd had followed the wagon all the way to Queen of Heaven cemetery, an entire town over. *Zia* Rocca said it was noth-ing—that in Sicily they walked up and down mountains and across deserts to get to the graveyard. She said Illinois didn't compare. She told him to carry her black bag for her.

Once there, Nicky, like everyone else, looked into the deep hole. They all cried some more, watching the gravediggers lower Papa in and then start to fill the hole up with good black earth. But they didn't finish—only a few shovelfuls went in, and that had alarmed Nicky. He wondered what the gravediggers were waiting for.

And then, in unison, all the grownups all dried their dark eyes and walked away, leaning on one another, so obviously and gladly alive. They left Papa behind. Lucy said they would visit on nice days, with cheese and bread, like they always did for the little dead babies who had been two small to live. They would picnic and water the geraniums. They would polish the marble headstone with lemon oil and visit all their dead. Nicky, however, kept crying, but he found that if he tilted his head down, no one could tell.

All that year, the year of his father's death, whenever he'd dreamed, Nicky Millefiore dreamed that his aunt and his mother and the mortician were draining *his* blood over the sink, even though he was still alive, and even though he was just eleven. Sometimes his father's corpse stood in the background, furious that Nicky had seen him naked, furious that Nicky hadn't helped him. He was mad in the dreams like he'd never been in life. Other times, his father-corpse just cried in loud wails with an open mouth and closed eyes begging his blood to come back into his body and up out of the drains.

After a few hours of morning time, though, the dreams would wear off and things were a little less scary. He'd go outside to play stickball. *Zia* Rocca was still around then, and she warned Nicky, several times, that he'd better not tell his mother what he'd done, looking in the basement, nosing around, seeing what he had no business seeing. What no boy has business seeing. So he didn't. No boy would. *Zia* Rocca was tough, so tough she'd once shot at her husband and hid the gun on a rooftop and then jumped off the roof to escape the police. So tough she would get him, he knew it. If she had to, she'd jump on the Penn Station train in New York and be off in Chicago and back in Mulberry Park in a day. She was magnificent and terrible, and for a boy who had never read a fairy tale, she moved quickly into his personal mythologies, twirling her frizzy hair and narrowing her big brown eyes. But finally, *Zia* Rocca left for home.

And soon, Mamma had gone back into her bed, silent. The healing woman from Melrose Park had come—as a courtesy—and the one from Cicero, too. But because Mamma was a *stregha* herself, it was harder to cure her, they said. A doctor had to come, and even he couldn't get her out. So, he left pills, and Lucy came by every day and made Mamma eat food and take pills and wash her face. Well into autumn, for the better of three months, Mamma had languished in that bed, the same one where all her American Children—except the baby who died in New York—had been born. For a while, her lying there made Nicky afraid that maybe she'd guessed what he'd seen by his long face, and his throat bulging from the lump.

But in time he figured it was only her grief and her fear of raising him and all the rest by herself. Maybe, he realized, as he wrapped the presents, she'd been having a nervous breakdown, and maybe she'd been resting up and preparing for what was coming. Laying plans. Either way, when finally, *Zia* Rocca took the Amtrak all the way back to Chicago and pulled Mamma out of bed, she threw the pills in the alley and stomped them into dust. Then Mamma got better, until she was wirier and stronger than ever. Nicky, on the other hand, was much the same for years with his sadness.

So, tonight, more than thirty years later, Mamma was over there across the street serving Jordan almonds and anisette, handing out envelopes with a dollar in each to her grandchildren, resting her feet and letting her grandchildren run and jump and skip about. If they spilled a drink or dropped their almonds rolling to the hard tile floor, she just laughed and waited for a daughter-in-law to clean it up. For a moment, Nicky wished he were over there laughing and sucking almonds. It might be nice for a change. Nah, taking a deep breath, Nicky knelt taller, upright on the braided carpet, wrapping away. He was fine, too. He was fine, he was fine, and his brothers and sisters were fine. *Zia* Rocca was dead, eh. But Mamma was well.

It was nearly eleven o'clock, so he knew Mamma would be overseeing the rinsing of cups in the cement sink, from her chair, and announcing it was time to bundle up the babies for Midnight Mass. He knew what she was doing, and she knew what he was doing. Most of the time, everyone knew what everyone was doing, it seemed. But, of course, there were exceptions. As far as the lump went, it was still there, but Nicky had grown big around it, so it hurt less than when he was a kid.

He spun around to grab the next present to wrap. Another sweater, for crying out loud! This one, sky blue for Dolores. Then there was a flat-faced doll, some jacks with a rubber ball in a blue cardboard box, a stack of encyclopedias from World Book, but not much more. He was nearly done. Through the dining room window, he saw them streaming up to the street level, from underground, like steam rising from a cup. Their caps and scarves wove them together at the head and neck as they shuffled along the walkway to the sidewalk. He stood up and went to the window to watch more fully. There was Mamma in her black coat, her strong nose like an elbow under her hat. Short and solid, she held her place at the front of the group, a grandchild at each elbow for support, old hip injury aching in the cold. He saw Lena and Agata tying extra scarves over their heads in tandem and leaning in to talk to one another. Banks of snow heaved up along the sidewalks and swirling snow adding more by the minute. It was the kind of snowfall that swallowed sound as it fell. Nicky liked when it did that. There's nothing quite as silent as a snow-thick Christmas Eve. The house lights glittered on the snow, and the smaller children kicked into it, sending the top layer flying. No one moved faster than the old woman, and she moved slowly, so they processed down the street in the direction of Our Lady of the Flowers under the high moon with calm, even though they were filled with enough caffeine and sugar to keep them up for the hour and a half Latin service and the walk home. When it wore off, it would drop them perfectly to sleep in their warm beds.

Once they turned the corner, out of sight, it was time to go. Nicky's work didn't end with the wrapping and the memory, no. The tree was also his to do. Every Christmas Eve, the trees on the corner lot went down to half-price. It's why Nicky always bought on Christmas Eve and left the tree up through The Epiphany when it began dropping needles like crazy. He knew already that he wouldn't pay more than three dollars for the tree. He went to the trunk for an old moving blanket, but then decided he didn't need one, there was plenty of snow on the sidewalks to simply drag it home. His records had finished playing, and the needle was scratching away at the label. He lifted the needle from the record and set the arm back in position with a click, silencing the phonograph. Shrugging on his thick car coat and pulling his hat over his balding head, he turned down the ear flaps. On went his galoshes and his gloves, and finally he stepped into the dark snowy night to walk the four blocks to the tree lot, singing "Ave Maria" to himself loudly and not caring who heard. Most nights he preferred to sing "St. Louis Women," but tonight was a special night.

The tree lot was looking picked over when Nicky arrived, but Christmas carols played from the loudspeakers on the telephone poles, and lights hung in swinging strings, flung this way and that by the snowy wind, so he was pleased. Nicky was ready to make a deal. He jogged in place a little, not making a scene, but warming himself up a bit, to prepare for the requisite haggling.

The popcorn man played hymns on his wooden recorder and slowly pedaled his popcorn wagon past Nicky. He looked like a red and white clown on the big tricycle, and the light of the glass popcorn machine and view of the popping kernels like a hot, square snow globe.

"Five cents a bag!" he hollered into the wind, "just five cents a bag!"

Of the twenty or so people in the tree lot, most were men alone, choosing trees with quick efficiency and with little or no regard for appearance. The best trees were long gone and had been for days. What remained tended to sparseness in spots and crooked trunks, but the cold December had kept them fresh and green. As it went each year, most of the people in the lot on Christmas Eve were known to Nicky, and nearly half were his relatives. He nodded at a few cousins, at his brothers in their long scarves, and to his brother-in-law, too. They all nodded back and pulled their caps down, not stopping to talk, only on *this* night.

When Nicky found the tree he liked, at the price he knew was meant to be haggled-down, he approached Manny, his money warm in his pocket. But Manny wouldn't come down fast enough, and it was cold, and Nicky needed to get the tree put up before everyone came back. He felt his hands tightening into fists, fists like mallets, and he wanted, with a rage that was very unbecoming on Christmas Eve, to box Manny-the-tree-seller right there. To fatten his stupid looking cupid's bow of a lip. Knock him into the line of Douglas Firs and tangle him in the strung lights. But at the last moment, Manny had laughed and stuck out his meaty hand.

"Okay, Nicky, three bucks is fine—this time—but know you got yourself a deal here and don't spread it around. I got a family to feed—and they're big fat ones!" Manny, large himself, rounded his arms before his belly in pantomime.

Momentarily disarmed, Nicky's fists relaxed, and he smiled as he handed Manny the pocket-warm money. He threw in an extra fifty cents, "Get the kids some candy canes from Santy Clause," he said.

Nicky left for home dragging a five-foot blue spruce by its crooked trunk and trying to decide if he'd be happier had the fight happened after all. Sometimes, he just needed a fight. He even thought about going back and starting it up again. But all in all, he figured, nah, not on Christmas Eve. He'd promised to turn over a new leaf for the New Year, and '56 was practically upon him, so he figured, he'd get started early.

Nicky left a broad path through the newly fallen snow, as if a giant's wife had swept the sidewalk with her giant broom. But with more snow falling the evidence would be hidden in less than a quarter hour. The kids would never see it.

His nose dripped from the cold, and his fingers ached. The wind blew his hat off twice, and into a snow bank on the west side of the street. He had to set down the tree to dive in for it. He had to knock the snow off the wool before he put it back on his head; it was still better on his head than off. He stopped and switched dragging hands several times. Nicky was inordinately proud of being a lefty, but tonight, he also valued his right hand. It helped with the cold. Things were much like last year, he thought, but windier, and he was older. But he was nowhere near *old*, he reminded himself. Still in his prime. With gusto, he swished that tree up the last remaining street to his house, its deep green cedar-shake siding, blackened by the night. A light he'd left on, glowed in the dining room.

The snow on the front steps creaked at him like Styrofoam as he climbed them and pulled the tree up. As he shoved it through the front door, tip first, snow fell from its boughs onto the waxed pine floor. He'd mop it up later. Nicky set the tree into the old metal stand and strung it with lights, big red, green, yellow, and blue ones—the size of a fat walnut each. He wrapped the garland around tightly and hung candy canes and German glass balls—Lena's. On the top, he stuck a pointy silver star. Then, Nicky swirled the red patchwork quilt from the sofa under the tree and then arranged the presents on it. When he stood back to survey his work, his heart swelled in the best of ways. This, he knew: a boy (or even a girl) would never forget. They might live to be one hundred years old, and still, when they closed their eyes, they'd see his tree. You could stand in front of this and stare all day, he thought. He double checked each of the brown packages to make sure he'd signed them right: S. Claus, and he had.

When the kids and Lena came home, they carried the smell of incense and popcorn and communion wafers in their hair. There were thoughts of mangers and wise men all over their faces, but at the first glimpse of the tree, well, poof, that all retreated.

Yes," he told them, "Santa had indeed come, in fact he'd run into him just on the front porch as Santa was leaving and Nicky was coming home from Barney's Bargain Barn. Santa said he'd decided not to use the chimney because of the coal furnace—too sooty, and anyway, he'd said they could open one present each tonight but the rest not until morning." And so, they did.

When the children were tucked into their beds, Nicky and Lena made chit-chat as couples do on a good night, forgetting past and ongoing misbehaviors, resentments, and brutalities—maybe even things they shouldn't—letting the cold cotton sheets warm under them.

That little coal thing in Nicky's throat seemed to have shrunken to the size of a baby's fingernail now, or maybe even smaller. And as he began to fall asleep with Lena, he put his cool feet on her warm leg. Maybe, he thought, that little lump was small enough to cough it up altogether, by telling the story. Spit it out like an oyster spitting out a black pearl, and then it would finally be gone.

When Lena asked him, as she sometimes did before they fell asleep, "is everything good with you?" He gathered up his guts to present her with his secret. His wide mouth cracked open, and his eyes looked up at the dark ceiling, and he took the deepest breath he'd ever taken filling his lungs with piney air.

"Huh? Yeah, I'm fine," he said. "I'm great, whaddya think?"

He twirled his hair—the part that wasn't bald—with his fingers. Just as he had as a child, until he fell asleep, the glow of the tree spilling in under the bedroom door.

THIRTEEN

The Summer House

The house-finches fledged in a hurry, it seemed. There had been three, but Mr. Contralto never saw the first two go. The third and last had somehow fallen to the floor of the Summer House and was now surveying the world from its new low angle. The nest above it was held tight against the arbor by twisting grape vines, a thing of some great beauty. Both were well constructed. And Mr. Contralto would know as he'd constructed the summer house himself years ago, when he'd been younger and less tired. Fancy people called it a gazebo, but people on this block always said Summer House.

So tiny was the birdling on the floor before him, that when Mr. Contralto rose, from the bench he had slept on that night, to get a better look, he had to bend at the waist just to see it. He thought he'd put it back in the nest to finish growing. He put out his hand like a scoop, but then, it showed him! The miniscule bird threw itself—not quite flying—straight into one of Mrs. Contralto's dense rose bushes, all done up in thorns and covered in twisted buds. Despite all the good reasons he knew for not touching baby rabbits and baby birds, Mr. Contralto reached into the thorny bush to pet the fledgling with just the tip of his pinkie finger. He was ever so careful and gentle.

"Don't you worry," he said. "I won't pick you up if you don't want." The bird moved further into the bush.

Early morning sunlight warmed the round, bald top of Mr. Contralto's head. He knew he looked just like the Saint from Assisi, everyone said so, but there was no one around to see him looking so Franciscan in his white sleeveless undershirt, his belt unbuckled from sleep. Only the creatures kept him company out here: honey bees, caterpillars, this reluctant bird.

The fledgling looked out at Mr. Contralto, wispy remnants of branching infant feathers still floating above its eyes, giving it that crazy-evil look of all baby birds. Maybe it was accustomed to his smell. Maybe that was why it didn't flee. After all, he'd been sleeping directly under its nest most nights and talking to it whenever he passed below since it was just a miniscule bluish egg. He felt proximity earned him some understanding from the little bird. He reached in further and it tolerated him, let him stroke its tiny head for a few seconds before throwing itself still deeper into the rose bush.

Baby grackles and the robins, it always seemed to Mr. Contralto, were tied by apron strings to their parents well into adulthood, the massive babies screaming and stalking the exhausted mothers (and sometimes fathers) across the lawn. You had to admire that kind of parenting. But the finch parents were nowhere to be seen despite all the scolding and chirping they'd loaded on Mr. Contralto while the young had been in the nest. Apparently when they were done, they were done. Mr. Contralto couldn't quite work out whether this finch parenting was practical or negligent. He looked up at the nest, more closely now, and saw it was already beginning to disintegrate. There were a few shit splats on the less white floor under it, and some more crusted on the wild grape vine that wrapped the nest.

Rubbing his gray whiskers and then his temples, Mr. Contralto considered the situation of late: he'd slept well here in the summer house the last few weeks, which was actually spring. And he was likely to be out here most of the summer and into autumn as well. His wife, he had to admit, was a class-A harpy, though Mr. Contralto would never have said so if he were in her presence or in the presence of any of her associates. He knew she'd soon be bringing him coffee and hard cookies and yanking him into the house to wash himself— all the while nagging him to, for once and for all, straighten up and

fly right. Oh, yes, with a good yank, she'd evict him from the summer house and drag him up the stone path to the back door. His
razor, soap, and towels would be laid out on the little painted bench
near the white pedestal sink in the bathroom, fresh underpants, trousers, shirt, socks folded neatly on the top of the wicker hamper. She'd
matter-of-factly help him out of his rumpled things and push him
into the bathtub. She'd draw the bath curtain closed with a strong
arm, making the hooks sing along the metal rod.

Oh, yes, she would be coming very soon. He knew it in his
bones and because this strange drama had played out, quite publicly,
in the warm months of the year for as long as he could remember
anymore. He'd like to put an end to it, or so he told the tiny bird in
the bush, but there was no way. And as the guys at the bar always
said, it takes two to tango, whatever that meant.

There were days he dreamed of running away, like a young boy
to a foreign land, maybe Indiana or even further down south. And
if he did, he'd never make a mess of things again in his new life. But
what would he do in such places where he knew no one? He supposed he could work in a factory like he did here, watching quality
control with his pad and pencil, but he didn't have the energy to
pack his bags, much less run. Besides, he told the little bird, he was
no quitter. It was one thing to be relegated to the summer house—to
be put outdoors by a wife—it was another altogether to be known
far and wide as a coward.

Mr. Contralto understood his wife's wrath to a degree. He was a
drinker and a gambler, and a drinker some more, and he knew that
these habits were a disgrace on Singer Street—to most of the neighbors. He knew that his disgrace spilled over onto his wife and kids,
and he knew the humiliation of it infuriated his wife. He also knew
his own humiliation—that equally disgraceful scene in which he, the
man of the house, was slapped and kicked by his wife in earshot of
his children and his closest neighbors as well as anyone who might be
driving by with their windows open and the radio down low.

The way Mr. Contralto told it all to his drinking and gambling companions just the night before was this: it was like a sort of
chicken and egg situation. He was the chicken and Mrs. Contralto,

undoubtedly, the egg. He was the only one who thought the explanation made any sense, so he'd had another drink so that he could explain it better. What else was there to do but lose yourself in drink and games of chance when your wife was so terrible? If it wasn't for her, he told them, he'd certainly be a different type of husband, a better type altogether. They'd looked at him for a moment with bleary eyes, until he corrected himself, insisting he wasn't saying there was anything *wrong* with gambling and drinking, wasn't anything wrong with them at all.

Sometimes, when he was at the bar, Mr. Contralto stared down into his glass for long moments, and his buddies patted him on his back. Because it wasn't just for the drinking or the gambling that his wife was after him. Sometimes she came roaring his way with the rolling pin held aloft only for leaving his socks on the floor, or for saying the wrong thing in front of company, or for nothing really at all other than she'd had a bad day.

"But," he always summed up with some shame in his face, "who would have known? She was a lovely girl with no temper at all before we married. A real angel, like in the movies. But I suppose I should have known by those beetle brows that she'd turn so mean."

"You know what?" he'd say, smiling a little, "My mother, God rest her soul, she warned me. Vittorio, she said, Vittorio, *filio mio*, that's the kind of lamb that keeps long fangs in her wool. My own mother told me that, and I married my wife anyway, though. Can you imagine?"

"Long fangs in her wool," his comrades repeated like a little prayer, and the lot of them made a toast to the wisdom of mothers. One even began to sing a short round of "Oh, My Mamma" with fat tears sitting in the corners of his eyes. The others had soon joined in. This they did, despite the fact that the monstrous Contralto woman—also known to them as "Irene-that-bitch"—was, in fact, herself, a mother several times over. This disconnect was not because they didn't realize she was a mother; it was simply because only *their* mothers were mothers to them. So, they didn't care much about that pesky detail. And so, last night, they had gathered the regular Friday night crew. Every single one of them gambling away the money for shoes and electric bills, for Sunday dinner that included meat, for new paint, and for drawing salve. The outfit guy at the table next collected their losses without a smile or a frown, his brown suit neatly pressed, his cufflinks gleaming in their hazy peripheral vision, like little gold suns.

The friends of Mr. Contralto always leaned on their elbows at the table and twisted their mustaches into points. They advised him. Generally, they advised him the same thing every time they saw him: to beat his wife soundly. This was honest advice because it was exactly what they would—and did—do. Often with little or no provocation from their own wives. Preferably with a belt, they added.

Mr. Contralto nodded yes, but his brain always swaggered in a horizontal and hidden "no." He imagined attempting to beat Mrs. Contralto. The image was like the slapstick he saw on the Three Stooges shorts at the movie house when he was in there sobering up. But the Stooges were funny. What he saw in his imagination was not. She was his Moe. And he was just an unfortunate lesser Stooge soon to be left blind or burned or toothless. She'd grab that belt right out of his fist and do him in with it, probably in the front yard where everyone could see. She'd drive him like a mule, lashing as she went, out the front door of the real house and around the yard to the back and the summer house until he collapsed. And if the neighbors couldn't see, she'd make sure at least they heard.

"Gambler! Wastrel! Degenerate! I'll show you to come home drunk again! I'll show you to gamble!"

The only place his own fists would be was over his own head in a futile attempt to shelter his skull from the buckle of his own confiscated belt. He'd read somewhere that the human skull was no stronger than a watermelon.

No, no, he'd never strike Mrs. Contralto with a belt, or with anything else, and he never had. Of course, Mr. Contralto couldn't describe what he'd just envisioned to his friends, so he nodded vigorously, changing the subject as best he could. Then he proceeded to gamble away the bulk of Friday's paycheck in the backroom of the bookie joint. That, he could do.

* * *

On the morning of the baby finch, Mr. Contralto waited like an errant schoolboy might in a quiet hallway. For the principle. Irene-that-bitch banged out the back screen door, a mug of black coffee in her right hand and a few biscotti in her left. Her hair was pulled tight into a knot, steel gray and thick. Her brows, still black as ever, made a straight line of satisfaction when she saw him. She couldn't see the bird in the bush, and he was glad for that. She marched with purpose.

Mrs. Contralto handed Mr. Contralto his coffee and biscotti. She inspected him, and he could tell she saw exactly what she expected to see, a rumpled mess of a man. He recalled how she'd pushed him right out the front door last night when he'd come home, before he'd even made it to their bedroom. He smelled, she'd shouted, in her blue nightgown with her hair curling like silver snakes in the electric light of the front porch. Smelled like the Primate House at Brookfield Zoo but only if the Primate House was also doubling as a distillery. It had been well after midnight and so she'd been the only sound up and down the block outside of gently ticking clocks and some wispy high pitched night-time insects. Everyone must have heard her.

She'd held her rolling pin high and demanded Mr. Contralto hand over what was left of his wages that very minute, and he did. Then she'd pushed him out the back door anyway. To sleep with the insects and animals. In winter, she had no choice but to keep him in the house so he wouldn't freeze to death, but in summer, out he went.

And he went as cooperatively as possible in order to keep the grown son and his wife upstairs, as well as the neighbors, from hearing more than they absolutely had to. It was his greatest fear that one of those neighbors would someday phone the police—as occasionally happened when Nicky hit Lena across the street. But never, in the history of the village, had the police been called for a husband beaten by his wife. Not yet. And if that happened, Mr. Contralto thought, he might just dig a hole in the backyard and put himself down into it forever.

That was last night, though. She must be in a better mood now. And he was right. She was. Mrs. Contralto sat beside Mr. Contralto on the bench on which he'd slept. His jacket balled up there for a pillow made her shake her head sadly. He didn't look her in the eye, but he could still see her staring at him from the sides of his eyes. He felt her assessing how to fix him and finding, for the ten thousandth time, that there was no way to do it. This fact gave him only a little satisfaction, but a little is better than none. And he didn't particularly want to be fixed, not by her and not by anyone else either. Had he wanted that, it would have been done long, long ago.

Mr. Contralto nibbled the almond cookie with his unbrushed teeth and sucked the strong black coffee from the thick ceramic mug. It was good. When Irene moved to get up, Vittorio flinched. He could see that irked her—her brows knitted. She took his hands and brought him to stand. She smiled a grim smile, the lips-turned-inside-out kind of smile meant to keep a person guessing at the future of things. She handed him the ball of his jacket. He saw her look at the bird splat on the floor and up at the nest, and he could guess she was planning to destroy it, but too late, he smiled to himself, too late. Sure, she'd be out there scrubbing the shit up and knocking the sticks down, but the little birds had fledged without her interference.

"Come on and get cleaned up before the kids have to look at you," she said to him. He let her hold his hand and walk him to the door—he was after all, a little shaky from the night before, and his head ached. Her hand was always surprisingly soft, and she smelled of fresh mint and fennel from her morning stomach tea, and of Ivory soap. He wanted to cry out that he loved her, really, and that if she just stopped biting at him like she did, he'd never go to Casa Madrid again. He'd stay away from Melrose and from Chicago, altogether. He'd quit gambling. He'd even give up the drink, because who would need it with a kind wife? He considered stopping her to say those words and make all those covenants right there on the path between the hollyhocks and the juvenile peach trees, in earshot of the little finch. But he was afraid it might all be a lie. Or, worse, a promise he meant to but could not keep. Or even worse yet, a promise he didn't even want to keep. But the worst possibility of all was this: maybe he would stop playing the games and having the nights with friends, but she'd keep on hating him anyway, hating him forever for all he'd already gambled and drank. If that happened, he knew, he'd have no pleasure in his life at all.

So, Mr. Contralto squeezed Irene-that-bitch's little hand with real love, but he said nothing. The coming bath would cleanse him, and the nap would refresh him. But tonight, or tomorrow night at the latest, he'd be out in the summer house. The fledgling would be gone by then, but he'd still be there, watching the house from a short distance. The light in the bedroom where his wife slept would be lit—she didn't like sleeping alone in the dark. It would remind him of the North Star—it always did. He would listen to the crickets and occasional police sirens until the birds began to sing dawn to him. He loved the birds. He knew there'd be a new nest coming soon— he'd learned that finches have two or three clutches each year. And he'd be there for all of them.

FOURTEEN

Porches and Stills

Her battered machete glinted—fingers tight around its taped handle—and her arm hung loosely by her side, swinging with the weight of the long, curved blade. In the pocket of her brick-a-brack smock she had a second knife, a short one. A harness of thick garden twine was strung over her back, and from that, she'd laced ten string bags jammed full of the dandelions. Bags-full she'd picked from along the train tracks, stooping, hunting, cutting, stooping, hunting, cutting, since first light. Now her shoulders and neck pinched. But she'd gathered the best and was done with that solitary part of the work. It was time to market her greens.

The Dandelion Lady stopped at the corner to take a long drink from the public water fountain in front of the town hall. What a country, she thought, with this kind of well for anyone to share. *But look at the chewing gum all around on the pavement.* She stooped close to the asphalt and used her short knife to pry up the wads that had re-appeared in the two days since she'd last visited the fountain. They stuck to her fingers as she flung them into the lawn that led to the park. *Madone*, she breathed, *madone a mia.*

When the Dandelion Lady closed her eyelids, toothed green leaves hung suspended there in a green mosaic. It's what comes from staring into greenery for a long time. The dandelion greens inside her head made her dizzy, so she opened her eyes and focused on the uneven sidewalk, taking care not to trip over its heaves and buck-les. Sunshine warmed her shoulders, and she waved to the rag and bone man as they passed one another along High Street. Their long wails intertwined in the still summer air; *raaags—chicoria—chico-ria—raaags aline, raaaaaaags aline*—like the bells of two churches ringing at once. And then they separated, him heading east, her west. His cart slowed him down, and as he walked away, she could tell his knees ached, that he needed a poultice.

The Dandelion Lady moved efficiently and rounded the corner on her way up and down the various numbered avenues of the vil-lage, to call the signoras from their kitchens for her bitter greens. They were tender and young in the early summer, and the season would soon run out. Then it would be her time to harvest *cardoons* from along the same tracks—they weren't really cardoons, of course, but they were what grew in America, and they were close enough to satisfy the people's hunger for the real thing from the old coun-try. Worse than the dandelions by far, these plants were fiercer and heavier, and they hurt her hands. They were also harder to sell— so much work to prepare them with the peeling and boiling and cooking again. Dandelion season was when she shone, when she had some jingle in her pocket. The weather was not yet stifling, the leaves were light, and she was still glad to feel the sun after a long winter.

Two young policemen approached the Dandelion Lady, their billy-clubs swaying like her own machete, their oiled hair glinting like obsidian. That high-nosed one was Domenica Giancarlo's boy, and the other she wasn't sure. He looked familiar, though. *"Assa binidica,"* they sang out in unison, *"comu sta, Signora?"* They were good boys, she thought, inquiring after her with respect and with true grins across their faces. She smiled back with her mouth held closed so as not to show her missing front tooth and reached into her pocket under the short knife to pull out two atomic fireballs wrapped in cellophane. *"Aspette, aspette,"* she said *"pacienza."* They waited before her until her hand unfolded, holding out the candies in her palm as one holds sugar cubes to horses. Officer Giancarlo and Officer Beddu snatched the candies without hesitation and waved happily as they left her, their heavy policemen's shoes hard on the pavement. She would have liked to talk with them for longer, but they had work to do and so did she. "Woo! Woo!" She heard them gasping as they rounded the next corner. Fireballs were boys' favorites, she knew it.

Sales were good that morning. Signora Palermo and Signora Greco each bought a bagful. Signora Giancarlo took two, turning back the flour dusted cuffs of her polka dotted housedress and sharing with the Dandelion Lady her troubling certainty that her grown children were turning into constipated Americans before her eyes. She was on a mission to make them regular. Her plan, she confided, feet planted on the third step of her front porch, was to stuff them with bitter greens until the end of June and then with chard through July and then with *cuccuzzi* for the rest of summer. Then they would be set up to get through the winter and she'd begin again the next spring. The Dandelion Lady agreed with Signora Giancarlo; the poor children must not develop sluggish American bowels.

The Dandelion Lady watched her satisfied customer climb back up the stairs with the two bags clasped firmly against her large breasts and held in place under her elbows. "*Grazzi, Signora Chicaude*," she shouted, "*e salute!*" When the door slammed shut, The Dandelion Lady turned and made her way back to the long sidewalk. She resumed her calling out and strode easily along the flat prairie streets of her new village. In the forty years since she'd come, she'd never gotten completely used to the flat land. Easy enough to walk on but nothing much to see. Nothing like her little city of Alcamo, in Trapani, where she'd once climbed up and down, up and down the vertical streets to the city market to take her place behind her father's stand. There she'd sung out the names of all the vegetables that lay in crates before her, mesmerizing in their purples and oranges and greens. Next to her, the snail monger had called just as loud, and beside him, the old woman who sold wild herbs, and then the eel merchant—a small woman with kinky hair who tried to drown everyone else out with her soprano screech. To be a foraging merchant in Alcamo had been to be part of the choir. Here it was solitary, *a capello*.

Today, the people were hungry for greens and she was down to just one bag left when she turned from Seventeenth onto Croaker, and there, at the second house from the corner, sat Signora Millefiore on her front porch. Signora Millefiore raised both arms to beckon the Dandelion Lady over. This woman did not like to yell from her porch like some did. The Dandelion Lady nodded and hurried up the walk, a small smile on her narrow lips, her surprisingly green eyes looking her customer right in the face. We are both old women, the Dandelion Lady thought to herself, she appreciates not just the medicine of bitter greens but the *taste* of them. I know she does by the look of her and also because she buys from me for years. She will prepare them the right way, cooked gently in water and served with oil and salt, a piece of hard bread thrown into the bowl, a few gratings of hard cheese, and a sprinkle of pepperoncini flakes.

Signora Millefiore rose to stand in front of her porch chair. The money was already on the little table next to her; two dimes. She took the Dandelion Lady's bag, and the Dandelion Lady took Signora Millefiore's money. When they smiled at one another, each noted how many teeth the other was missing, but not unkindly.

Signora Millefiore said her eyes were not up to needlework on this day. Nor did she have gardening to do—her garden was already planted with the help of her strong and obedient sons who lived in the houses all around her, and her house had been cleaned by her daughter who lived several blocks over. The Dandelion Lady could see how proud this Signora was of everything around her. Even the television, which Signora explained she hated. The television, with its tiny eye glaring in the corner, so she'd hung a *mopina* over it. She explained that the radio annoyed her as well—all in Sicilian and spoken quickly. She said she'd unplugged it earlier that morning, and it would remain so until her daughter came to clean her house again. She said that everyone she liked to chat with, her sons, her grandchildren, they were at work or at school.

The Dandelion Lady had always felt that Signora Millefiore was above her. After all, the woman owned her own house. She always made sure she didn't pay her more than the dandelions were worth by engaging in a few seconds of whole-hearted haggling, but no more. She always dropped her dimes down from her fingers to the Dandelion Lady's palm from her porch, never touching her. And the Dandelion Lady had always volleyed her string bag up, waiting only for Signora Millefiore to empty it into the kitchen sink and bring it back to her. But today, Signora Millefiore surprised the Dandelion Lady by patting the chair next to hers, asking her to sit a while. No one ever invited her to sit. She wasn't sure. But Signora Millefiore patted the chair again and the Dandelion Lady sat. She looked down at her stick-like legs, scratched by the briars that grew along the tracks. She pulled them straight in front of her and bent to yank her black socks up to where they belonged from the puddles they'd become at her ankles. The men's boots she wore were flaked with dried mud and rail dust. It was, she supposed, to be expected after all. She looked at Signora Millefiore's orange crocheted house slippers and wished she had a pair of those on at the moment.

Signora Millefiore said her old niece Filomena Giaccina couldn't come over today, and did the Dandelion Lady know her? No, but she'd heard of her. Signora nodded and got up to shuffle to the front door, calling out that she was getting the espresso. After some ten minutes, the woman returned with a tray, two cups, two tiny spoons, a plate of sugar cubes, two stale biscotti, and a box of snuff, all on an enamel tray. She and her tray clattered through the screen door with satisfaction, spilling nothing despite her bad hip and even though she'd left her cane behind on the porch. Baby squirrels giggled from the trees.

The Dandelion Lady waited for Signora Millefiore to take the first sip, and then she too sipped and dunked, feeling the nearly instant surge of the caffeine and sugar. The two stared straight ahead, side by side. Like a pair of donkeys. It was a fine morning, they agreed. Across the street and along the side of the big, green house, they watched two of Signora Millefiore's daughters-in-law, hanging out their laundry on separate lines. The laundry lifted gently in the breeze, and the daughters-in-law moved quickly. They had more work to do in these late morning hours—ironing, dusting, sweeping, polishing, and maybe mending. But before that, the next bushel of laundry to wash and then put through the ringer. The old women stared at the young with neither envy nor pity. Just interested in the patterns the flapping laundry made. Signora Millefiore wondered aloud why they carried the baskets in front of them with both arms when they could simply put them atop their heads and not ruin their backs. The Dandelion Lady agreed; she'd been wondering the very same thing and shook her head in confusion.

Next door, an old German woman named Mrs. Kraum crept out to her own porch, her son-in-law and grandchildren all gone for the day as usual. Signora Millefiore watched and told the Dandelion Lady that Mrs. Kraum's daughter was in bed with a black eye, hiding from the world. That Mrs. Kraum lived like a barnacle up at the very top of the three flat house next door—at her own house! Signora Millefiore said that Mrs. Kraum owned the building since her husband died, but her son-in-law ran everything. That Mrs. Kraum tried not to hear what went on below her, probably. But Signora Millefiore heard plenty and none of it was good.

Today, Signora Millefiore said, probably Mrs. Kraum had come to warm her old bones in the sun and look up and down the street. The Italian ladies could see the German lady looking into the yard across the street at Signora Millefiore's daughters-in-law who were lovely with their permanent waves fluffing in the sun. Mrs. Kraum frowned a little bit. Perhaps she was wondering, the Dandelion Lady thought, why they hung their underthings where they could be seen. Surely, they could string a line further down behind the house for that. Their husbands would be angry if they saw those things hung in plain sight. But times were changing whether old women liked it or not, and Mrs. Kraum better realize it.

The Dandelion Lady thought Mrs. Kraum looked surprised to see her on the Millefiore porch, shocked, in fact. She stared for a while before she seemed to realize it was the Dandelion Lady; maybe because she'd never looked closely at her before—and maybe because she never bought dandelions. The two Sicilians stared straight ahead again, like passengers on a train and sipping from itsy bitsy cups. They tried not to look at Mrs. Kraum so as not to disturb her, but they did anyway, from the corners of their eyes, and it was as if they could read the German woman's mind: Was it liquor? It was a bit early for that.

* * *

Signora Millefiore and the Dandelion Lady spoke among themselves. What should they do? The German woman looked miserable. The Dandelion Lady was surprised when Signora waved Mrs. Kraum over to their porch. First, Mrs. Kraum looked to her left, down the street to make sure she wasn't mistaken. And then to her right. But no one else was around. So, she pulled her purple crocheted cape around her round shoulders, took up an aluminum cigarette case and came over. She looked like a new girl entering the lunchroom with a fast heartbeat.

Now the three of them watched the clotheslines, the daughters-in-law, and the neighborhood squirrels. The language imbalance kept them quiet. No one was great at English. Signora Millefiore and the Dandelion Lady could speak Sicilian together, but it would leave Mrs. Kraum out. Mrs. Kraum spoke precise, clear German, but she was the only one. She signed that her English was no worse than that of her porch mates, but it was done differently. No matter, they soon realized. It was nice to sit with other ladies anyway.

The Straglimiglia boy drove by in his big car, looking strangely alone on the avenue. Anyone could see he should be at school with the other fourteen-year-olds. The women shook their heads together in disapproval. Signora Millefiore said he'd come to no good, that one. His mother's only boy and skipping school. The Dandelion Lady didn't know him personally as she wasn't from this street, but she could see what Signora had said was true. He combed his hair like a hoodlum, too. The car raced by again, gleaming mint green in the sun, and they snorted at him. They knew they were no more important to him than the trees or the grass or the birds that dropped their white shit all over his car. On his second pass he seemed to realize maybe they would snitch to his mother about him sneaking the car, and he swung his ship around and headed over to High Street— where he continued to roar up and down. They could still hear him.

Signora Millefiore offered Mrs. Kraum a cup of espresso which she took. In turn, Mrs. Kraum offered her Italian companions each a cigarette. Signora Millefiore waved her hand, no. She didn't smoke. The Dandelion Lady took one on a whim and let Mrs. Kraum light it for her with a wooden match. The match-head flamed up with vigor. She knew it wasn't right for a woman to smoke in public, she knew, but she felt safe doing what Mrs. Kraum did. Signora Millefiore opened her snuffbox and offered a pinch to the other two ladies; they each took one. The Dandelion Lady tucked hers into her cheek as soon as she finished her cigarette. Soon the trio were flying, red faced, and shaky handed. Somehow, they began to communicate in a frantic sort of impromptu community language supplemented heavily by hand movements and exaggerated facial expressions: they could approximate rage, sorrow, sly cunning, sheer joy. They could pantomime running, slapping, jumping, leaping, washing, cooking, digging, and killing. With all this going on, the Dandelion Lady lost track of time, and she didn't even care.

Signora Millefiore did a story about her cousin Rocca who'd followed her husband from New York with a gun. A woman with a gun! A disgrace. But still. You could understand. By the look on Signora's face, the Dandelion Lady knew her compatriot was stunned that she was telling such a story, but she went on and on anyway like a runaway train. Next, the Dandelion Lady, with flowing arms and upturned palms, found herself telling about how she was never chosen to be someone's wife even though she was neither ugly nor stupid, and how now she lived with her nephew in this village. How she sold dandelions to pay her way. She saw lots of things happen along the tracks, she let them know, things she wouldn't repeat.

Mrs. Kraum seemed to say, with lots of pointing and turning to the windows of her house next door, that she missed her husband and that her son-in-law was a brute, but there was nothing she could do about it even though it broke her heart. She pounded herself on the chest to show the other two how her heart broke. They nodded in understanding. She pointed to the window where her daughter slept and explained in the mixed-up language how she'd tried to help but what could she do? Really, what could she do?

Signora Millefiore said one more, one more. She told a story to cheer things up. How the old man from down the street fell and broke his ankle looking in her windows. They shouted together in English. It was a phrase they'd all heard on the news. A phrase that had stuck. Peeeeeping Tom!

The Dandelion Lady wondered if she should get moving. Perhaps she was staying too long, but then Mrs. Kraum slapped her hand on the arm of the porch chair she sat in. "*Komm* my place," she said. Eat. She opened her mouth and made a shoveling motion. Then she grabbed the Dandelion Lady's hand. And then Signora Millefiore's. She pulled the ladies up. It was a slow pull as they were all old and a little rusty. But the three slowly wound their way between the houses and up to the back steps to Mrs. Kraum's tiny flat. The Dandelion Lady and her new companions held tight to the handrail and skipped no steps as they climbed. It wouldn't do to fall.

It was cooler up in the canopy of elm and ash and sycamore—these inedible trees that shaded Mrs. Kraum's backyard. Where were the fruit trees? The Dandelion Lady wondered. When they got inside, they all sat on the twin bed in the sleeping porch and looked out through the leaves. No one could see them here. It was like a squirrel's nest. Mrs. Kraum backed into the tiny kitchen. The Dandelion Lady could see her cutting black bread and yellow cheese with a long knife. She fished pickles out of a jar and peeled hard boiled eggs. She said how she hadn't had friends over to her place since her daughter was a girl—since she lived downstairs and a renter lived up here. No visitors. Family, *Ja*—and the grandchildren ran up here sometimes to get out of the way of their father. But that was all.

The Dandelion Lady found Mrs. Kraum's food a bit dry and hard to swallow. The cheese was yellow as a school bus, but she ate it daintily despite her dirty fingernails, because she had been taught manners. She saw that Signora Millefiore did her best, too.

Mrs. Kraum chomped her pickle thoughtfully for a while and then rose and walked to a strange curtain in the side of the wall of the sleeping porch. She yanked it open like a shy magician. Behind it, built into the wall like a fountain, was a still. The Sicilian women were impressed with the ingenuity. Mrs. Kraum put her index finger into the air and motioned for them to wait as she turned her back and took two steps into her kitchen. When she turned around again, she held up a bottle of her best pear whiskey—made from the Millefiore pears that fell over her side fence, she said. It was medicine for after lunch. To help them digest. She poured the clear whiskey into water glasses. It was pure and it was strong. The dappled sunlight danced through the screened windows, and the ladies sipped and choked. They all began to feel very relaxed, tiny sip by tiny sip. The squirrels began to sing in the trees.

Each woman said one word looking into the faces of the others.

"Giuseppa," said Signora Millefiore.

"Elsie," said Mrs. Kraum.

"Claudia," said the Dandelion Lady.

They nodded all around. Giuseppa ran her fingers through her hair over and over until it stood up like the rays of a sun drawn by a five-year-old. Claudia took off her work boots and flexed her long toes inside her black stockings. Elsie giggled out the window at the trees. No one spoke, or tried to, and no one cared about that at all anymore.

They heard the knife sharpener grinding his way down the street. Claudia needed her machete sharpened, Giuseppa needed her chopping knife sharpened, Elsie wanted her shears done, but they were in no shape to make their way back down the stairs just now, so they just listened to him drone away toward Cherry Grove. They looked at one another and shrugged their shoulders and then flopped onto the bed, backwards, like young-old girls. Claudia, the last to fall into a drunken nap, thought she'd like to stay up here forever, on the edge of her new friend Elsie's bed. She heard the soft snores of her companions as she drifted away, pulling her knees to her chest as she'd done all her life.

She knew she'd never find herself here again, that her transactions with Giuseppa would return to their previous state. That tomorrow the woman's old niece, Filomena Giaccina, would be back on the porch. That they would become strangers again. Yes, this day was a ruby in a pile of straw, but she smiled anyway.

FIFTEEN

The Trouble with That Sort of Man

F rida Fenster awoke to find her husband still gone. First, she
inhaled the bedroom air and smelled that he wasn't there, but
then—groaning-tired and still half asleep—she reached over her out-
stretched hand, eyes still closed—to feel his side of the bed, just in
case. The sheets were cool and empty. *Ach du lieber*, she breathed to
herself, *ach du lieber, scheiskopf.*

She had to lie still and let the anger subside before she got up
to begin her day, lie there listening to the gurgle of hot water in the
radiators and the nondescript stirrings of her children waking in the
two bedrooms down the hall. It was a medium sized flat with the
bedrooms all to one end, and sound carried as if the long hallway was
an ear trumpet. She was still furious.

When she did rise, Frida bent to touch her bare toes ten times
in half-hearted calisthenics and then, immediately, made the bed.
She smoothed the corners neatly and soon the mattress looked like
a professionally wrapped present. It was a habit of order—one of
many impressed upon her in childhood by her Oma who'd raised
her. Frida was glad for that habit because she knew, had she not had
it, had she been able to walk away from that bed leaving it a mess,
she'd have been ruined. She slipped her pale feet into the pink scimitar style house slippers she kept beside the bed and walked them to
the bathroom.

When she opened the tap over the pink bathroom sink, the water went straight down—without the slightest hesitation at the drain—no clogs here. That was one good thing. She watched it gush away and prepared to brush her teeth—first dipping the bristles of her wooden toothbrush into the deluge and then tapping the wet bristles into a dish of baking soda. She polished her teeth and scrubbed her tongue. She spit quietly so as not to bother the children with intimate sounds.

Her reflection in the medicine chest mirror, the million freckles against the pale, pale skin standing out more than usual, showed that the tension of these last years had blanched her pale as an almond. She combed her baby fine, stick straight strawberry blonde hair into its pageboy shape and wished she'd inherited the thick chestnut hair of her namesake mother. Her mother who'd died when Frida and her identical twin, Lena, were only nine months old. Frida kept a photo of her mother hanging in the hallway, and a lock of that chestnut hair wrapped carefully in her dresser drawer—as did each of her six siblings. Sometimes—like now as she combed her own hair—she was sure she recalled sitting in her mother's lap with her twin, each nursing from her own breast and each pulling her own braid. She put her toothbrush back where it belonged inside the medicine cabinet and closed the mirrored door. She wiped the sink dry. It was hard to have been missing someone your entire life.

When she returned to her bedroom Frida whacked the hangers down the short rail in her bedroom wardrobe and selected a pair of high-waisted corduroy trousers and a simple boat-neck blouse for the day. If Frank should return home, she wanted to be put together well enough that she could hold her own.

In the kitchen, she mashed down the lever on the chrome toaster—it seemed to resist her. "*Fick Dich,*" she muttered. Frida spread the toast with soft butter from the covered butter dish she kept on the sideboard, and then she spooned on near-black grape jam from last summer's canning. She opened the back porch door and brought in the milk bottle, popped the cream off into a bowl, and poured three cups of milk for her children: two boys and a girl. She could hear them flushing the toilet and getting themselves into the school clothes she'd laid out for them after dinner the night before.

Calling them to the table with as much happiness as she could push into her voice, Frida also knew that by the time they reached the Formica table and pulled their chairs up to the chrome edge of its brimstone red top they'd have passed her open bedroom door and seen their daddy was not in the bed. They were perceptive children, and so they'd also know she'd left the door open so that they wouldn't have to ask at breakfast if he'd come home.

They ate quickly, all the while bickering about whose classroom pet was best—turtle, goldfish, lab rat. Frida stood behind the girl, untying the rags from her silky hair and twirling the curls into long bananas. She slicked down the boys' cowlicks, fixed their collars—and when the bickering reached a hysterical tenor—she slammed her palm down in the middle of the kitchen table to make it stop.

Once she'd herded the three out the door for school, Frida slotted one slice of bread into the toaster for herself and turned on the flame under her kettle. She ate her toast dry—chewing with her mouth closed tight and resting her head against the painted metal cabinets. The dry toast stuck in her throat and she sipped hot ginger tea to push it down while she watched her children through the square kitchen window—pushing aside its blue-checked curtains further for a better view. They joined the stream of other people's children, all in cold weather coats and rubber boots, all with satchels of school-books, all headed to the public school, like salmon upstream in the gray of February. Frida had no desire to be with them—no wistful urge to return to her own school days—her only wish as she sipped her cooling tea was to navigate her life well in what had become a roiling—and yet, somehow dull—river of uncertainty.

Once Frida lost sight of her three, she turned away from the window and pulled the curtains closed by their ruffles. She washed the breakfast plates and cups with a soapy sponge on a stick—which she'd just yesterday picked up at the five and dime on her way home from work. She rinsed her dishes in a separate dishpan of clear water—as she'd been taught—and dried each with a flour-sack towel. When Frida had wrapped the bread, covered the butter, put away the dishes, and hung the damp dish towel on the stainless-steel arms that jutted from the wall over the sink, she left her family flat, slamming but then stopping to lock the heavy door behind her.

Within ten minutes, Frida was leaning forward in a narrow side chair in her twin sister's flat. She rubbed her hands together to shake off the damp chill of February and confided to Lena—yet again—that she had absolutely no idea what to do about Frank anymore. Her own voice sounded tired and thin, metallic.

She paused while Lena set a small dish of pastel licorice snaps on the oriental-style coffee table next to the glass tray of hand-rolled cigarettes. She watched Lena drop into a matching chair opposite, and when her twin was settled, Frida took a breath

"No, not a word."

"Just like last time, Frida and the time before."

"No, the last time was five days—this time it's just four so far, but either way..." She chopped her hand at her throat like a little hatchet, "I'm fed up. *Ist genug.*"

Lena blinked. "*Naturlich*, who wouldn't be?"

Frida felt bad piling it on Lena, who had husband troubles of her own. But at least Nicky Millefiore never took money from his family—and he didn't disappear overnight. And because of this, Frida felt her situation ranked considerably worse.

Frida reached for a cigarette and then the lighter. The heavy table-top lighter almost slipped from her hand. But she recovered it, half dropping and half setting it down. She checked to make sure she hadn't scratched Lena's table.

"Don't worry," her twin said, bending low over the table to light her own and dragging smoke in deep.

Frida watched Lena, cigarette between pursed lips. That first drag gave her sister the look of a satisfied orange marmalade cat. She wondered if she appeared the same and took another drag of her own. Probably even more, she thought, more of an orange cat. When Frida looked at Lena, she couldn't help but notice the way fortune had played its game on them. Frida was larger—though slim. Taller, though not tall. Sturdier, though not sturdy. When their mother died, they'd been separated. Raised apart. Frida had been claimed by Oma, and Lena went to Aunt Grunda. Frida had been petted for the first seven years of her life—and Lena had been tolerated. In such ways they were made less identical.

It was their ritual to listen to the radio and play cards for an hour and a half before they left for work at American Can. Though Lena's flat had a TV right in the corner, the twins always left it off. They still preferred the radio for visiting so they could play Gin Rummy 500 and converse. This was often the best part of their day.

They weren't particular fans, but they'd been listening to *Dragnet* for years as the background to their mornings because it was on at the right time. Today's airing would be the last episode of the final season of radio *Dragnet*—ever. Frida looked up from under her pale eyelashes as Lena snicked the radio knob to on. The tubes warmed up and crackled, and then the familiar voice of the announcer announced the episode title—*The Big Moustache.*

"Well, at least they're consistent to the bitter end," Lena said, winking Frida's way, "it's always the big something or other." She tugged at her too-tight permanent wave in an attempt to loosen it a little.

"Yeah, what's it been so far this season? Let's see—*The Big Rod* and *The Big Cup,*" Frida said, blowing smoke like a dragon.

"Don't forget *The Big Pipe* and *The Big Sucker.*"

"And *The Big Broad?*"

"And *The Big Filth!*"

"That one sounds about right for today," Frida said. She'd been warned by her family that she had a sharp tongue all her life, and she could feel that tongue carving out space in the room for Frank's terrible behavior despite her best intentions not to let him spoil day—*schmutz.*

"Yeah, *The Big Filth,*" Lena echoed, blowing smoke at the ceiling.

Frida cut the deck and Lena dealt, snapping the faces of the cards against the table until each had 13. At the same time, the radio story unfolded into the living room—filling it with large male voices that were sure of what was what, who was who, and what was up. Joe

Friday's unwavering crusty righteousness lay like a woven rug over the card game. Frida tried to keep her mind on the cards.

But she failed and thought of Frank, Frank as she'd first seen him, dark-haired, golden faced, and fresh up from Kentucky crowing about his Cherokee blood and his high school diploma, which was no small thing. He'd winked at her before diving from the highest rock ledge at the quarry, knifing into the water. In that same quarry a year later, she'd felt the pressure of his hands on the top of her bathing cap, on her shoulder, and she'd smiled so wide she felt she might swallow all the water if she went under. Little fishes nibbled at her toes. She saw Frank laughing and tossing a baby in the air—catching it with ease—the baby laughing, too. A flash of Tom's white teeth. The bell shape of his laugh. The warm way their shins and ankles and feet wrapped around one another's on the sun-dried bedsheets. The sound of his nose in his voice when he said he was going out for the night, just the night. The timber-cutting rasp later when he cried out his sorries and promised to change, as had been the case the last few years. His hand, his hand, his hand on her shoulder as she ducked into the water for the coolness, quenching her sunburn.

But the trouble with that sort of man—Frida told herself in the voice she used to mother herself, scanning her hand for pairs—is that *everybody* is ready to love him. Her family loved him—especially Lena's Nicky. The neighbors loved him. The kids loved him. Strangers at the bar loved him. The trouble was that other women loved him as well and not infrequently.

What did *Frank* love? Why, Frida knew very well, he loved *her*— to be sure—and he loved his children. He also loved a good party, he loved scotch on the rocks, he loved floozies. Loved them a lot. And on top of that he loved to bet on the ponies. He was two men walking in one: the respectable foreman at Ferrara Pan Candy Factory who walked in the light, and the night-walking one who did things Frida did not have a clear view of, but which she could feel in her bones. The thoughts of which made Frida clench her teeth and forget to discard—meanwhile Joe Friday was gloating in the background. She ignored him.

Frida saw the cigarette dish was getting low, so she reached for rolling papers, fresh tobacco, and the snippers. She rolled ten in two minutes flat—her slim fingers flying—and she stacked them into a little pyramid in the dish as Lena rearranged her hand. When Lena melded, Frida lit a cigarette. When they were out of cards and the hand came to a close, Frida scratched their scores in railroad pencil on the same white paper pad they always used. It was nearly full but there was another waiting in the kitchen drawer. She knew it because she knew everything that was in her twin's kitchen drawers. Frida flipped through the tallies while Lena shuffled, cut, shuffled—two columns per page, page after page: Frida on the right, Lena on the left. The handwriting, no matter who had kept score, identical. It was almost time to go.

After work, Frida flopped-out in bed while a round-steak thawed on the counter. The children had changed out of their school clothes and were in the kitchen doing their homework, and Frida was flat on top of the chenille cover in an open robe—also chenille—her stockings and work blouse still on under it because she'd been too tired struggle out of much beyond her trousers. She had a pillow over her face as she blotted out light and sound in an attempt to rid herself of the headache that had come home from work with her. She'd also taken three aspirin and left the half empty water glass on the bedside table—*when would the aspirin kick in?* Her stockinged feet pointed toward the door, her arms were tight down by her sides, and she tried not to move a muscle, tried to relax her neck, her skin, her molecules. But Frida heard every single pencil tap and sigh the kids made. One was kicking the table leg. One was chewing an eraser; she was sure she could hear the gritty squeak against teeth.

And so, when the phone rang, it jolted Frida from under her pillow and made her groan.

"Mother, for you!"

She threw the pillow to the end of the bed and rolled to the edge, her hand to her forehead. *Him.* She felt that familiar sweep of relief and quick on its heels, the liberty to be truly angry. But she squelched her emotion and told herself how to react for the best outcome—firm but not *mean*. She'd let him know there would be

Swiss steak for dinner tonight—the kind she made in the pressure cooker—and buttered egg noodles—and the kids needed help with their math—and, hey, come on home and we can make things better. She'd even tell him she loved him—as nicely as she possibly could. She figured it was best to hold the rest for later, like a thousand hat pins stuck into her own scalp.

Frida was a little disappointed he hadn't spoken to the kids for longer when they'd answered—he was usually so happy to talk to them—but maybe he was nearly out of change. Maybe he'd bet away every penny he had.

"Yeah Frank," she said into the mouthpiece.

"Mrs. Fenster?"

"This is she." Her head throbbed.

"Mrs. Fenster, this is the Fox Lake police..."

"Fox Lake? *Wisconsin?*"

"No, ma'am, actually Illinois, but close. Mrs. Fenster..."

Ah, gott in himmel. "Just let him sleep it off." She wiped up the puddle the thawing round steak had made on the sideboard, tucked the phone under her ear with her shoulder, began to pull the heavy pressure cooker from under the sink.

"He has a car—I don't. I can't come to pick him up this time."

The kids stared at her while also pretending to continue their homework—she gave them the eye.

"I'm sorry, Mrs. Fenster—if you were closer, we'd have sent an officer, but I have to inform you that your husband, Frank Odell Fenster, forty-seven—of 162 Singer Street, Mulberry Park, Illinois is deceased as of 11:45 this morning, February 22, 1957. I'm sorry."

Frida stood with the phone at her ear, the lid of the pressure cooker pulling her phone-free arm to the floor. She didn't even say "what?"

"You need to sit down, please, if you aren't already. Because there's more."

She was sitting on the floor still—silent—when Lena and Nicky arrived and let themselves in. The kids were standing over with glasses of water, arguing whether they should pour them over her, to snap her out like they'd seen on TV, or not. She wished they would, but they just bickered. The girl still had the phone in one hand—having hung it up on the Fox Lake police and phoned her Aunt Lena to call for help. But she'd not put it back on the receiver.

Frida felt Lena and Nicky pulling her up from the floor, setting her in a kitchen chair. Lena knelt by her side while Nicky looked for whiskey and a glass. After two short whiskies, Frida could speak. Lena splashed Frida's face with cold water and dressed her in a fresh house dress. When Frida looked down to the end of her own legs, she saw she was now in a living room chair and Lena was pushing her feet—still sore from standing on the factory floor all day—into the scimitar slippers.

Frida was relatively composed when her oldest sister Minka let herself in, followed in quick succession by Anna and Mina. Their faces were soft but grim. They put the round steak in the icebox, put the pressure cooker back under the sink, hung the phone up, and put the children in coats.

"Where are you taking them?' Frida asked.

"It's alright, Frida, they're going down to our house with the kids," Nicky said. Frida looked at Nicky's eyes—she found them bulgy, like fishbowls. She wondered why Nicky hadn't made Frank stop and come home. Instead, like a traitor, he'd left Frank to his own devices.

"Fox Lake," she said. "He was with a woman in Fox Lake. Someone came to beat him up. He had a heart attack. He's dead."

She reached for her glass again, but Lena grabbed her hand, "No, no more."

"Lemme go, Leen. There's something else, oh, and you're never gonna believe this," Frida slurred. She got the glass and took a little gulp, spluttering on it because—really—she was a beer with an egg in it sort of woman.

"He was with a woman."

"Yes, you already sai—"

"It was *Hilde Dunner*."

There was stunned silence until there wasn't.

"Our *cousin* Hilde?" Minka whispered.

* * *

Two days later Frida received another call. It was to inform her that the Lake County Coroner had transferred Frank's body to the Cook County Coroner and Frida would be expected to ID it. She knew that was coming—anyone who listened to *Dragnet* did.

Nicky and Lena came over to accompany her. Nicky was wearing his suit. He greeted Frida with, "How's about you girls staying here, and I'll just go down to the morgue on my own?" Snow fell from his gloves as he talked. It had been a long winter.

"I don't know, Nicky."

"C'mon, it's the least I can do. Frank wouldn't want you to have to ID him at the morgue." He looked at her hopefully. "You'll get to see him at the wake. It's too much, Frida."

Frida felt like everyone was talking like characters from Dragnet. Even herself. It was ridiculous. She grasped the glass handle on the coat closet door and wrenched it open—it always stuck—and she took her mohair winter hat from its flowered box and her coat from a hanger. She turned to the mirror on the wall to pull the hat onto her head, noticing, as she always did when she wore that hat, that it brought out the blue in her eyes—bright and flinty. But then again, so did crying.

"Let's just all go together," she said, "and I suppose we can get some sandwiches after. It'll be on me." The idea of eating out after the task ahead made her feel guilty and queasy, but people have to eat.

The three made their way down the snowy outside staircase, carefully, clinging to the two-by-four rail, and then trudged to the bus stop bent forward into the snowy wind. It would be straight into the city and then two transfers to get to the mortuary—Frida was sure none of them had ever been there before—they'd only heard about it. They smoked the entire way, as did their bus driver and every adult on the bus. Frank looked terrible, but was, indeed, himself.

Frida never wanted to speak to that *schlampe*, Hilde Dunner, again. But she had questions that went beyond outrage and fury. She wanted to know who, precisely who, had killed her husband. The police didn't seem to know. So, she went to her little red address book and looked up the phone number of her cousin, and she dialed it, breathing hard. Her twin was with her, eating a dish of cottage cheese with salt and pepper at Frida's table.

Hilde answered the phone.

"It's Frida."

She heard Hilde inhale.

"I need you to tell me what happened." Frida promised herself that she would remain calm enough to get the information she needed out of this *schumtz* at the other end of the line.

"Oh, Frida, it was horrible!" Hilde sniffled into the phone.

"Just tell me the *facts*, Hilde. If this was about feelings you wouldn't be hearing from me at all."

"Okay. I'm sorry, Frida, but we were in the motel room, Frida, and three men came in and they beat him up—I mean they Beat. Him. Up, Frida. Brass knuckles and everything."

"Why was he hiding from them in Fox Lake?" Frida asked, motioning Lena to squeeze in.

"No, Frida, Fox Lake is where all those mobsters *live*. You would never hide from them there. We went there to bum around, you know, on the chain-o-lakes, have fun."

Frida did not know. Why *would* she? It sounded ridiculous.

Lena nodded her head. "They *do* all live there, Frida." she whispered.

"Who's *that*?"

"It's just Lena, Hilde, please get on with it."

"Well, it might have been about money or something like that. You know how he loved the ponies. Maybe he borrowed from them or something, but they didn't really say."

"Did he *pay* them anything, Hilde?"

"No, but maybe he was about to, I don't know, because when they were beating him up, he just had a heart attack while they were at it, you know. He just grabbed his chest and he died. And then they just left."

"That's it?"

"Well, they also said I better keep my mouth shut, Frida. So you can't tell anybody what I told you, please. I only told you because you're my cousin—and Lena can't tell either, okay Lena? And don't ask me what they looked like because they had stockings over their heads."

"And what then?"

"I ran to the front desk and said 'Call a doctor!' And the doctor came."

"How about the police?"

"No, I didn't see them, but you know, Frida. I was pretty shook up—*considering*—maybe they came after I went to sleep."

"You went to *sleep*?" Frida turned to Lena, "She went to *sleep*."

"Yeah, well the doctor gave me *some medicine, Frida*."

Frida could hear that Hilde was hurt. She covered the mouth-piece and whispered loudly into Lena's ear, "Poor her."

"What did you say, Frida?"

"I was talking to *Lena*, here—one second please." Frida held the phone against her chest and waited to calm down. It took a minute or two.

"Well, Hilde, it's really a shit thing you did to me, but I thank you for your help."

"I'm really sorry, Frida. I'm really sorry for you, I mean."

"What?"

Frida watched Lena lift her index finger and depress the receiver. With a little click, their cousin Hilde was gone. But the wrench in Frida's gut was laid open.

Frank's wake and funeral came and went—in a flurry of black wool and relatives lugging covered bowls of German potato salad, boxes of Linzer Torte from Hoffman's Bakery, plates of wursts. Hilde did not come, nor had she been invited. And no one spoke her name. There'd been the usual greeting of guests, the less usual suppressing of shocking information, and lots of crying. Despite Frida's efforts, most of the people knew Frank Fenster had died in a motel room with a mystery woman and they were not shocked. They'd known he was *that* kind of man as long as they'd known him and so it was a natural ending, as satisfying as it was upsetting.

Frida understood it was part of what they *liked* about him—that he did as he pleased when they felt *they* could not do as *they* pleased. And now, the manner and location and "situation" of his dying, had proved to them all that *they'd* made the right choices, that they were living different sorts of stories. Frida felt bitter toward them because the thing they liked about him, then, was the root of his mistreatment of *her*. She hated their tears and glared from behind her hand.

She could glare, but Frida had already cried out all her tears by the wake and funeral. She'd stood graveside looking at her fine-boned ankles in her navy pumps while they shuddered around her. She held her daughter's childish hand, the seamed white glove like a clamshell in her own gloved hand, and she'd felt the child tremble with grief. She squeezed the little hand. Her own grief was like a thousand helium balloons on very long strings, all tied around her wrist—not gone—but nowhere at all nearby. When she walked, her legs felt like the molasses that won't let go of the bottom of the jar. She'd smoked a cigarette as the crowd dispersed but stopped short of flicking the butt at the grave. She gazed at the casket before turning away, not without sorrow, to telegraph to whatever remained of Frank everything she had no words for. He'd left her with a *big mess*. And worse than that, far worse, he'd made her the object of pity and scandal, and she was a woman for whom both were insulting.

When burying time was past and she'd collected herself a little, a few weeks out, Frida sat with the newspaper articles she'd clipped. One in the *Chicago Daily News*, and one in the *Fox Lake Reader*— "Man Dies of Heart Attack, May Have Been Beaten" and "Third Motel Death This Year: Mulberry Park Man Found Dead at Sunset Motel."

"Call the reporters, Frida," she said to herself.

"What do you think I'm doing now?" she answered.

Frida called the reporters, indeed—those reporters and more. And she told them all she thought there was a big police cover-up regarding her husband's death because the police weren't even trying to find out who did it. They said thanks, Ma'am, and they'd check it out. Then she called the police and demanded some answers from her list of questions, which she'd written like the tallies for a game of Rummy on a thick white pad. She read them off in a terse voice to the police in Fox Lake and the police in Mulberry Park. Lots of questions and some ideas. She wasn't sure where she was getting all the energy. Frida had only fifteen minutes before she had to leave for her eight-hour shift at American Can, she picked up the phone and dialed the Lake County Coroner yet again.

After work on Tuesday, Frida took the kids to Prince Castle for burgers and square orange sherbet cones. Their bereft faces seemed to make her feet feel heavier and more swollen, but she would feel better about it all when she found and sent the murderer to jail, or was it prison? Probably prison, she thought, for something like *this*. *Murder*. She had a cone herself, and a burger with cheese—and it all tasted good.

It was late at night, when the phone rang—late enough that she rushed to it fearing there'd been another tragedy, stumbling and slipping across the kitchen linoleum without her glasses on, but she caught herself on the table.

"Hello?"

"Hello, Mrs. Fenster. Sorry to wake you so late in the evening."

"Oh, God, what's happened *now*?"

"Mrs. Fenster, listen to me. I'm a friend of Frank's. And I just want to tell you some other friends of Frank's are concerned about you calling the newspapers and the police all the time. These other friends know where your kids go to school. And they know where you live. What's done is done, Mrs. Fenster, and so I highly suggest you look to the future. It's what Frank would want."

The voice paused.

"Goodbye, Mrs. Fenster."

"You just wait a minute, you…" but the voice was gone.

It felt like a prank or like the most overdone episode of anything she'd ever heard. Frida walked back and forth across her kitchen imitating, no mocking, the voice from the phone. They weren't even scary. Who the hell did these people think they were?

Soon there was a knock at the door. Frida froze for a full minute in her robe and then pulled its belt tighter as she peered through the peephole. Should she get a knife out of the kitchen drawer?

It was just Lena and Nick. "Let us in," they said.

Nicky looked her dead in the eye and spoke as if he were speaking to a child. "Frida," he said, "you have to let this go."

"No."

"Frida, let it go," said Lena on the couch.

"Frida, they came to my house to tell me to tell you."

Frida heard little beads of cold rain plinking on the living room window and a siren yawning out from the station over on Thirteenth. She saw her bedroom light still glowing from the hallway she'd run through to get to the phone. She saw the closed door to her children's rooms—and in her mind's eye she saw them clearly. Frankie—his leg flung off the side of the bed as if he could not be restrained. Eric— his cap gun holster belted over his PJs. Susie—the rags Frida had tied in the child's hair after her bath peeping up against the softness of the pillow. She was momentarily overcome by their vulnerability.

"*Well*," she said—standing up to clear the ashtray. "I guess that's what he gets for running with *Italians*."

She watched Nicky wince but didn't feel sorry for him.

Wiping the smudges off her eyeglasses—polishing them with the hem of her robe—she decided to make coffee for everyone—they might as well stay up till morning now.

SIXTEEN

Garden Plotting

G iuseppa Millefiore's hip ached in the damp, and she groaned as she limped between the muddy rows in her garden. It was *primavera*. The tomatoes and peppers were still sprouting in her south windows, not yet ready to put down in the garden. But she knew exactly where they'd go come mid-May. Like those tomato and pepper plants, Giuseppa preferred hot weather. Today the cold and damp froze her tender marrow. Still, warmth was on its way and, already, she had peas and beans flowering on their trellises. She had greens of all sorts, small still, but their leaves crisp and succulent.

She bent to inspect the spot where, when the soil had reached the right temperature, she'd put in her big, flat cucuzza seeds—at the foot of the dead elm. And in no time at all, the vines would sling themselves up the dead tree in the middle of the empty lot. By July, fruits would dip down like pale green snakes. She loved her cucuzza—a plant you eat all of: the fruit cooked with tomato and onion and garlic, the tender leaves and stems softened into tenerumi soup. Her belly rumbled in anticipation of summertime.

Giuseppa already had a row of early onions up, and garlic. She could no longer crouch, so she slowly bent and thinned her greens, plucking beet, escarole, chard, and mustard leaves—laying them neatly in her wire basket to bring home to eat for lunch with garlic, oil, and salt.

When she'd first bought the empty lot, it had been neglected, mazed with chickweed and bindweed and creeping charlie. But also dotted with dandelions and something close enough to cardoons to eat, so they harvested the delicious and weeded away the pernicious until the ground was prepared.

Today she stood munching a few raw tender beet greens in this lot that had provided all the family's summer food since they'd moved to Mulberry Park, a lifetime ago. She wasn't sad, but it was like ghosts ran back and forth shouting in the garden today. Not really ghosts because most of them were still alive, but the spirits of their youth. How she'd made them work, pulling and planting, drowning slugs and squashing tomato bugs. Now they were grown up and couldn't remember the ghosts of themselves. But she did. A mother never forgets.

And Lucy, Lucy was gone altogether now—which was something Giuseppa tried not to dwell on. Especially in the springtime. These days, sometimes her grandchildren came to help, and she laughed and played with them, but they weren't workers. They were slow and always trying to play instead of work. But maybe they were American enough not to have to work so hard and they'd be alright anyway.

Her sons still did the shoveling and rototilling, the spreading of manure and compost. And, in late summer, her remaining daughter Filomena made *estratto* and *caponatina* and wine, while Giuseppa oversaw the production. Men always said women should never touch the wine—that they'd make it turn to vinegar while it was fermenting, but, meh, it was a lie. Giuseppa inspected her grape vines along the trellis—healthy but still dormant. She limped over to them to kiss their brown skin, to encourage them to grow well this year.

A demented little fly, the first of the season, landed on her nose again and again. She caught it in her hand and threw it down onto the ground. Her boys were all at work, and her daughters-in-law were cleaning their houses with that polish that came in aerosol cans. They said it smelled like lemon, but Giuseppa didn't think so. All her grandchildren were at school, some in high school some in grammar school—two over in the church school. There were so many children and grandchildren that she felt it a very strange thing that she would be alone much at all. But here she was alone in the garden. The rhubarb reared up the corner by the compost heap like a red mule. Scarlet veins standing out over its big green leaves. She smiled at it like an old friend.

In one pocket of her orange housecoat Giuseppa had packed in a tiny envelope of speckled bean seeds—*Romano*. In the other pocket, a mayonnaise jar full of the four o'clock seeds she'd gathered and kept from last year's flowers, hundreds and hundreds of them, black and round with little dimpled umbilicals. This year she'd plant the four o'clocks in a long line against the wall of the adjacent building. There they'd burgeon into a flower hedge: yellow and fuchsia, purple and red—all mixed together like a *festa*. Some people in the neighborhood these days preferred plain red geraniums in clay pots to all the colors. They also preferred white stone in place of black earth—white as bleached bones. Giuseppa found these types of people a little *fascista*, so she avoided them.

Reaching into her pocket for the smooth glass jar of four o'clock seeds, she thought about how she had no idea which seed would give her what color. You just had to wait and see. Like life all the time. The garden soil still held the cold rain of the night before and mud packed itself to the soles of her old black shoes. She found a stick in the garden and scraped the mud off, leaning against the brick wall and sending clots thumping against it. Then she took that same stick and bent at the waist to drag a straight line in the thick mud along the foundation of that brick building next door. Her line was at least thirty feet long and straight as an arrow, east to west. It would get the southern sun. When she reached the end, she dropped the stick to the ground, and poured the black seeds from the jar into her fist. Making her way back along her line, in the opposite direction, she dropped them, not one at a time, but with her fist as a funnel, the seeds as a stream. Some would say it was too many seeds, that she should place them gently, but Giuseppa knew this way only the strongest among them would sprout. There would be no ugly gaps. And if too many sprouted, she'd thin them. They were the only inedible things in her garden, an extravagance, but not useless. They would bloom in the late afternoon, letting her know it was time to stop working in the garden and head home to make dinner.

She looked at her decrepit cat, Gatto-Fred, who watched her from the dry sidewalk. He wanted something to eat. She could tell by his swishing tail, but she was well past the point in life where she hurried or rushed. He'd have to wait for her to finish. Before she could leave, there were just a few more things to do. Things that mustn't be skipped. She reached into her pocket for a pinch of snuff. She raised her hand to the sky and stared up into the gray day with no little gratitude. She cleared her throat as if she was about to break out into an aria, raised her arms, and spoke, thanking the sun, the clouds, the rain that lived in the clouds. She thanked the day and the night that came with skies. Then she bent to the earth, wincing, and took up a handful of it—of her soil, and she put that pinch in her mouth. She ate it.

It was gritty and alive on her tongue. As she let it slip down her throat, Giuseppa asked the soil to continue to feed the Millefiores into the future. She kept talking because she had a lot to say. She told the earth her plans for it this year—what she hoped they would grow together—good things to be eaten fresh, dried, stewed, canned, fermented. Next week, she promised, she'd have the boys unwrap the fig trees that stood huddled, swaddled in winter's burlap, against the alcove in the brick building's shape. She squelched down onto her knees in gratitude for what the garden would give her and hers but also for the victory they shared, both having emerged from the dark and horrible American winter together, yet again. She raised her arms, triumphant and calm.

But she soon found that it was difficult to rise again. If only she'd brought a cane along. If only she wasn't alone. Giuseppa knew she could have shouted for her neighbors or for her daughters-in-law. People would hear her and come out of their houses. But instead, she crawled the distance to the brick wall, cold and aching. The cat was no help, and it took her a long time. Every year, though, she crawled on her hands and knees along the hot asphalt of Seventeenth Avenue, in honor of Our Lady of the Flowers who floated above the crowd on the shoulders of white robed supplicants. She was used to crawling for good reasons, and so she did it with intent. Not hurrying. Placing her full opened palms into the mud and pulling her hip carefully. When she finally reached the brick wall, she pulled herself up, gripping its corner, rasping her left knee bloody through her black stockings. No matter. She shuffled back to where she'd fallen to retrieve her basket of greens, then shuffled over to her buggy on the sidewalk, then limped home to make herself a hot espresso and a fried egg.

SEVENTEEN

The Day Nothing Bad Happened

The day nothing bad happened was not famous because no one really knew what it was. But still it was real, and it was simple, and went like this: On a sunny Saturday in July of 1959, up and down all of the Singer Street neighborhood not a single bad thing happened. You heard right: nothing. Now, that's not to say a particularly great number of good things happened; just that bad ones didn't.

The not-happening started shortly after midnight, which is when a day truly begins, technically. The first instance—or non-instance—was that when Mr. Contralto, sneaking into the house late and stinking of *Campari*, cheap bourbon, *Negroni*, and Hamm's, was not met by Mrs. Contralto brandishing a weapon made perfectly for clouting his head. Because he was not met by his wife, who had not heard him come in, Mr. Contralto was able to slip out of his wrinkled trousers and creased shirt silently and then to carefully fold himself into the big double bed beside her. He sighed and fell into a relieved sleep as she snored softly away. He put his arms around her.

More deeply into the wee hours, who knows what time, the old cat called Gatto-Fred nearly fell from the edge of Creme Crunch Donut's flat roof—to his certain death—but he didn't. He should have flailed, yowled, and splatted, but Gatto-Fred remained on the ledge, somehow bopping on just one black paw while the others had only air beneath them.

At the very same moment, Mr. Prosperino, despite not having taken his requisite dose of Brioschi because there was none in the medicine chest for some ungodly reason, *and* despite forgetting to prop himself on a pile of pillows, and despite having eaten far too much *pasta al forno* at dinnertime, slept through his usual hours of anguish without so much as a belch, a groan, or a twinge. He did wake a few times just to notice how good it felt to sleep without acid gurgling around his esophagus, and he wondered what he'd done differently. But of course, it was nothing he'd done at all.

In the early morning, when the people of Singer Street began to rise from their beds, not a single grown-up had bad breath. No one had a charley horse and limped cursing along the floor, and not one old soul felt a creak in the back of the neck. The children, who were generally spared from those ailments anyway, looked out their windows and saw not a cloud in the sky and not a school day in sight. No one was compelled to hide wet sheets behind the dresser because no one had peed their bed during the night. Not one single person stubbed a toe on the way to the toilet, and no one choked on their hot breakfast cereal, not even those who had tried to eat without letting it cool.

Big Enrico Salvatore la Mostra Secchione, sick to death of life, braced for the usual sense of doom over coffee, the same one he felt every day when the caffeine jolted him awake just enough to re-realize there was little point to his carrying on since his wife was gone. Especially since he'd discovered with absolute certainty no other woman would ever compare. He waited, hovering over his cup like an old raptor, sniffing the aroma, but the doom did not come. He tried to *make* himself feel it. Still nothing. He felt a bit strange without his doom, but not terrible at all. In its absence, he noticed the profusion of red zinnias in Mrs. Kraum's side garden, and he wondered what sort of woman Mrs. Kraum might be—besides German, that is. He smiled at her when she looked out her window at him.

Even Mr. Sullivan, a very mean man—and the son-in-law of Mrs. Kraum—found not a single reason to slap or hit, or even pinch any of his children before he left for work—neither did he manhandle his wife. When he went whistling out the door to start work at nine, all five little Sullivans and their mother stared at one another for a full minute before they ran to the front windows of their house, to watch their tyrant amble into the shop where he worked. There was a long moment during which they worried he was tricking them—about to spring back across the street and in the door to grab someone by the nose. But he didn't. He had simply gone to work.

In the late morning, about eleven, Vinnie Straglimiglia took his father's car out for an illegal spin, which was his daily habit and tradition. As usual, he balanced himself precariously on the stack of Yellow Pages it took to give him enough height to see out the window. On other days, he'd have to pull over in a hurry once in a while to re-stack phonebooks. But on this day, the books never cascaded out from under him, and Johnny nearly forgot altogether how very short he was—and in forgetting that for a moment, he noticed how the pink steering wheel felt solid in his hands. Like he could drive to California without stopping for anything. And he would have if he'd had enough money, but he didn't. So, he just purred up and down the avenue contentedly.

At precisely noon, Carla Nardone knelt before her son Anthony's grave at Our Lady of Heaven. She'd prepared herself to find the clump of forget-me-nots she'd planted there to be once again yanked out by the overzealous groundskeepers, but the blue flowers remained. In fact, they were blooming so prolifically—out of season—that she gasped, kneeling back onto her heels and almost smiled. She wore her black dress and black stockings, as always. Usually, when she knelt in the grass, a sharp stone or two found her knee and ran her stockings, but today, there were no stones in the lawn. She cried her heart out in the sunshine, and best of all no one disturbed her trying to help what cannot be helped. No one stared at her from their kneeling at a different grave. In fact, no one even saw her.

At one in the afternoon, just after lunch, in the house at 159, Dolores Millefiore, so lanky and bony that people called her "String Bean" and "Skinny Malink" sulked across the linoleum toward her mother for her daily dose of cod liver oil—to build her up. Even though she was almost an adult, she still sulked. But when her mother swung the heavy refrigerator door open, the brown bottle was not there. Dolores felt the back of her throat relax, felt her salivary glands retreat and her taste buds come out from hiding, and she smiled up at her mother, who stated rather agreeably that one day without the stuff would do no harm. Dolores nearly cheered, and she would have if she'd been a cheering-type of girl. As it was, she smiled wanly and went away to get her favorite book.

In her warm backyard, Giuseppa Millefiore looked at a red rosebush that climbed the house. She felt so good without a backache or a hip pain that she went to the coop and killed not one but two chickens for dinner—so she could invite her grown children over, and when she swung the hens by their necks like pinwheels—both at the same time—each neck snapped instantly and painlessly. This was a gift to the chickens as well as to Giuseppa, who thanked St. Francis, the patron saint of animals.

When the streetlights came on at the end of that day, their light was met by ten times the usual number of fireflies, fireflies who found the evening simply perfect. They floated, all pulsing together so brightly that all the people inside their homes looked out their windows to see what was going on, and all the people outside their homes ran their hands through the air the way you might run your hands through the water if you were leaning out of a rowboat. Touching the fireflies.

By nine pm, all the people and living creatures on Singer Street felt a little stronger and a little better, and maybe just a little prettier than they had the day before. Even the babies—because they hadn't been stuck by diaper pins, swaddled too tightly, or made furious by colic. The spell or whatever it was wouldn't break until midnight and the people stayed up late, feeling so good as they did.

What was it, you ask? *Nun lu sacciu.* Who can say? It might have been magic or it might have been that the evil eye had simply taken a day off. It might have been because there was a strong *stregha* in Signora Millefiore. It might even have been that Our Lady of the Flowers, who lived in the church just down the street, had intervened for a day and a night because so many had marched in the procession the year before. Just the right number. Or maybe it was just a glitch in fate.

But the thing was, no one really knew that it had even happened. Each bad thing that *didn't happen* was taken in stride in the life of an individual or of a family—likely most of them went unnoticed altogether (the un-stubbed toes, for instance). The people never got together to realize. It seems sad to have such a thing go un-comprehended. Maybe it's for the best, though. For had the people of Singer Street comprehended the completeness of the non-happenings of that day, they'd have wanted all days to be like that. No other sort of day would have sufficed, and that, simply, cannot be.

EIGHTEEN

Josie Jobs

J osie Fabrizzi was a nice girl sophomore year of high school, right up through April. A pretty girl with neat hair, clean fingernails and a face that held no crookedness. Real symmetry, her art teacher said, without any bump on her nose, chipped tooth, or strange dimple. This in a school in which those distinguishing features appeared regularly, and not infrequently, all on the same face.

Josie was named after her paternal grandmother Josie—*Gelsomina* in Italian. But the family had shifted hard, in the main, to American sensibilities, and they found themselves comparatively sedate and somewhat isolated from their neighbors. Josie's namesake grandmother was the only remaining tie to the old country; she lived with the family but made no attempt to rule it. The old woman was shy for a person of her advanced age, though no one was sure what that age was because records had been lost and Grandma herself couldn't remember. Grandma lived quietly and made macaroni with the knife at the big square table; she wore thick yellow perfume made of the juices of violets which she bought at Woolworths. She hummed unknown tunes in a low voice. Josie knew her intimately, but then again, not at all.

What Josie could say about her grandma was that the old woman had never raised her voice at her, had never cracked her with a wooden spoon, never thrown a shoe at her. Such behaviors, she'd heard from friends, were practiced by some Italian grandmas when they lived in your house, but not hers. In fact, her grandma seldom said much at all, probably because she'd left her words in Calabria. So instead of speaking, she stared at Josie a lot, as if Josie were the second incarnation of herself, this despite many things which Josie thought should disprove such an idea. For instance, Josie was slender while Nonna was rather squat, Josie had a smooth moon of a face while Nonna was lumpy as a potato. The old woman moved by shuffling in children's house-slippers across the wooden floors while Josie stepped out smartly in saddle shoes. Josie loved her Nonna to pieces; she just didn't want to be the same as her.

As was, and often still is, the case with fifteen-year-old girls, the world of slightly older boys came crashing in. Few are spared their attention, and fewer still want to be—even girls who prefer girls—something which was never spoken about at Josie's school. In that neighborhood, all the girls might hunger for male attention, as it was a sign of *something*. And yet the attention almost always came as a shock to the system.

Josie twinkled like a star, highly visible to the upperclassmen when they returned from Christmas Break to begin the new year, 1962. For more than a week, the older boys had been gazing at her in the cafeteria, even as she turned her head to chew her Salisbury steak. At first, she'd wondered if there were drips down her front and grabbed her napkin to wipe, but there were none. Eventually, she'd stopped looking for drips and turned her whole back to them so she could eat her lunch without making a fool of herself. Because Josie had the late lunch hour, and her friends had the early one—all because she'd taken Honors English—there was no one she knew at the table to talk to or hide behind. Just some nerdy kids her own age—members of chess club—and some Freshman girls struggling with cosigns. She didn't know how to play chess and she was not particularly good at math, so she ate alone, really.

The new male attention wasn't limited to the lunch table gazing, either. Salvatore Nicastro and Michael O'Malley, who had not been seen near her locker ever before, began leaning against it every morning so that she had to ask them to move in order to get in there and

hang her thick winter coat, grab her books for class. Sally Nicastro
was the type of young man exceptional for his confidence. The
beauty and prowess of youth that animated him came effortlessly,
as is common, but the difference with Sally was anyone could see he
inhabited it. Or at least he sensed it. His waxing essential energy and
his intense looks, those attributes might well be fleeting in the larger
scheme of things, but neither he nor anyone around him knew there
was a larger scheme of things. No, it seemed to them that Sally would
be lithe and muscled with glossy black hair and eagle's wing eyebrows
forever, that his split fingered fastball would never slow down. That
his popularity—firmly in place since first grade—would never flag.

He was two years older than Josie, and so when he'd approached
her in the steamy cafeteria to ask her on a date, she'd stammered a
little, but she'd managed to say yes over her toasted ham and cheese
sandwich, "Yes, that would be nice." He didn't linger, returning
quickly to his friends across the cafeteria to let them know his foray
had been a success. They made a show of congratulating him.

"Be ready at eight!" Sally hollered over his shoulder, winking and
bowing. What did Josie think of Salvatore Nicastro? She really didn't
know, and she didn't really care. In fact, it hadn't occurred to her to
weigh him up at all. It was like she'd stepped on stage and there were
calls and responses to be made—and everyone knew their lines even
if they'd never even seen such a show before. This is not to say Josie
was unaware of herself as a human creature or that she was without
an inkling of things to do with sexual attraction and romance. No,
not in the least. After all, she'd kissed her classmate Malcolm Ross
behind the roller rink in eighth grade—several times. And she often
invented romantic stories before she went to sleep that involved
Steven, the college boy who lived next door, stories that made her
blush at the sticky cafeteria table recalling her tangled sheets and the
way Steven behaved in her imagination—the solid real-human-ness
of her goose-down pillow. Steven of her fantasies, you see, was not
always a gentleman.

As Josie straightened her ruby-red cardigan and put her notebooks and textbooks back into her canvas satchel, she realized it
would be impossible to keep her mind on her studies with her first

real date looming over such a short horizon. It was tonight. The last three periods flew by, and she raised her hand not once in any of those classes, lost in date fantasies of sorts.

Josie was allowed to date—with some rules, of course. The rules had been laid out for her at the beginning of the year by both her mother and father in anticipation of the first date. After all, she was almost sixteen. Her curfew was ten, and the boy had to come into the house to greet the family—every time. Furthermore, she was not allowed to date hoodlums or college boys. Also, she could wear lipstick and pantyhose but never mascara or eyeliner. Her best friend Teddie had other rules: no lipstick and no nail polish. No pantyhose, and no shaving of the legs like a prostitute. When a boy came into Teddie's house, if her father didn't like the look of him, he would call the date off on the spot without even getting out of his chair. In fact, of the eight dates Teddie had been asked on, she'd told Josie, seven had been called off by her dad. Mr. Millefiore, pointing some sad boy's way out the door, and Teddie running to her bedroom to slam the door. It all seemed so arbitrary to the girls who vowed that when they had daughters, they'd let them do whatever they wanted.

Behind the roller rink as early as seventh grade, other girls had hinted at things that what went on on dates—mainly things they'd heard from their older sisters or witnessed their older brothers attempting in parked cars in front of their own houses, but Josie had had no context to apply those bits of information. She had no older siblings. Or close cousins. What she had retained from the girls behind the roller rink, however, was pretty important: Don't trust boys. And don't let them get you pregnant.

As a bookish girl, fond of *Jane Eyre* and all those Jane Austen books her English teacher, Mrs. Brooke, shoved her way, Josie agreed that most boys could not be trusted, yes, at least most of them, well, really, not at the beginning. None of them at the beginning. But she had noted, if they loved you enough, they could—and *would*—become good. Like Rochester.

Josie could read while vacuuming the living room floor—one hand splaying her book open and holding it upright, the other dragging the heavy machine over the carpets, sucking up the edges on occasion. She could also read while walking to school—without tripping over broken concrete or being hit by the number seven bus. But best of all, she thought, was when she read in the bathtub, adding more hot water each time she began to shiver, and committing to yet another page. She draped her nightgown on the bathroom radiator to warm and sprinkled bath salts into the water. Josie was always careful not to get water droplets on the books, which would indicate to the world she'd been reading in the bath, which anyone could figure out meant she'd been reading naked. And while she wasn't *ashamed* of it, she felt that was just nobody's business at all.

When Josie got out of her baths, she powdered her shoulders with *Jean Nate* and gathered herself into her radiator-warmed flannel nightgown—which no matter how well she'd dried off, stuck to the damp places remaining on her skin. She tiptoed past Grandma Josie who dozed on the yellow sofa and into her room where she threw herself into bed to read some more. None of this is to say Josie was a wallflower—she was not. She had a nice group of girlfriends—those same who'd been separated from her at lunch—and she could make pleasant conversation with whoever was around, and if no one was, she kept conversation with herself—inside her mind—a mind she found quite interesting a place to be.

Josie liked to give comfort, and she liked to get along. She made French toast on Saturdays for her little brothers, and she dusted the entire flat twice a week as her main chore, other than vacuuming. She moved every knick-knack, cleaning behind and under them. But unlike many of her friends, Josie was not enslaved to housework. It might have been because she was only half Italian—also unlike most of her friends. It might have been because, she also believed, her parents were a bit forward thinking. Her friend Teddie referred to them as "permissive" with a look that combined envy, confusion, and suspicion.

That Friday night, when Salvatore showed up at Josie's family's flat to pick her up, she breathed on the panes of glass in the big living room window to clear her view of frost while he parallel parked in front of the flat, edging the car forward and back, forward and back, until he got it just right. He didn't hit her father's jalopy in front or the landlord's Buick behind. The silhouette of Sally's dark face was crisp under the street—cartoonish in its sculptured angles. It was a cold, crunchy late January day, not far into the new year, and Sally's '58 Rambler shone all muted salmon and chrome in the cold air. He slammed the door—as one must with a Rambler—and left it running—she could tell by the whale of exhaust clouding from the tailpipe. Josie translated this act as one of chivalry, and that was good.

Grandma Josie, sat at the square kitchen table pulling her little knife through snakes of semolina dough—the cavatelli piling up one by one. She'd been watching through the front window, too—as well as her old eyes could. She smiled a closed lip smile to cover a few missing teeth. Josie waited for the knock on the door before opening it—she didn't want to look like an idiot standing there with the door wide open as he climbed the outside stairs.

He smelled of Old Spice and leather—standing on the inside welcome mat in his pea coat with the collar up around his neck. Josie's little brothers—Andrew and Sam—still in grade school, circled this stranger, curious—then they ran to the window to admire the Rambler under the light. It sure was pretty.

Josie liked the way it felt as her date helped her into her coat. She pulled on her blue suede gloves happily, waiting for her father to come into the room from the back parlor where he dozed in his recliner every evening before dinner. Grandma kept grinning idiotically at Sally, and her brothers were now pulling his arms and trying to get him to sit in the stiff gold and white sofa so they could barrage him with questions about the car. With just a couple of hand gestures that swept over the bounty of rolled semolina in front of her, Grandma indicated that there were plenty of cavatelli and why didn't the young people just stay in and eat dinner with the family, save the money for a rainy day! All of the young people in the room ignored her as they saw her gesticulations, especially the little boys who firmly believed old people had the most boring ideas on a regular basis.

Finally, Josie's Papa shuffled sleepily into the room. He looked the boy Sally up and down. He looked out the window at the car, which was far more expensive and far less dented than his own. He looked at Josie who was dressed demurely and seemed very happy to be going out with this young man. Josie's mother was still at work at the Zenith factory, so it was up to Papa to give the final go-ahead—even though that had not been stated expressly as part of the rules. There it was.

Salvatore met him in the middle of the floor, under the amber light fixture, and shook the old man's hand heartily. "Don't worry," he said, "I'll have her home by ten, and a pleasure to meet you." Josie liked the way Sally took charge and got things moving.

With that, they were out the door. What a strange feeling of absolute liberty, Josie thought, and strangeness. The faces of her family floated in the window, her brothers pushing one another and rubbing out the fog made by the steam radiators so they could see. Josie felt their eyes on the back of her blue coat as she made her way carefully across the icy sidewalk, braced on Salvatore's arm. If she fell, it would be a dinner table story to last her life, and she knew it. But she didn't fall.

Sally opened the passenger door for her; inside, she sank into the warmth of that still-running car. Relieved. She waved at her brothers as the car pulled away from the curb, rubbing a circle much like theirs up above, to clear the condensation from the side window.

Josie wasn't hoping to marry Sally or anything, but she wasn't hoping not to either—a happily ever after was, after all, always potential—this was a known fact.

The young couple dined at Blue's Steak House, surrounded by middle-aged businessmen making deals, middle-aged couples order-ing their usuals, and some really old people at the tail end of the early bird special. They all looked wealthy to Josie. The women wore pearls and the men smoked cigars. Josie and Sally munched wedge salads of iceberg lettuce topped with bleu cheese dressing—which Josie thought tasted pretty awful—but she hoped she'd develop a taste for it as it was—apparently—what people ate in steak houses. They also had thick steaks—hers, the petite filet and his, the full size—plus fat baked potatoes topped with sour cream and chives. They drank Shirley Temples while the rest of the place drank Manhattans. For dessert there were wedges of baked Alaska followed by cups of coffee, to which they added great quantities of cream and sugar.

Sally talked about his school baseball team and all kinds of statistics that made little sense to Josie. She felt stupid for not knowing how these things worked and resolved to find out, so that she could be better company on later dates. Sally also talked about his job at his father's grocery the next town over. He was going to inherit it one day, he said, smiling very broadly and crinkling his dark eyes. He had some very major ideas for how to expand the business once his old man gave him some control. But he wouldn't bore her with that. Josie asked him to please tell her—she was interested. So, he did. He talked about Water Market Street on the docks, where all the goods came in, and how to advertise sales, and the differences between varieties of tomatoes until it was time to go, which was when the busboys ran the carpet sweeper right up to their table.

Josie was worried she might have to kiss Sally goodnight at the door to her house. She had only kissed that old Malcolm before, and that was just a peck in the relative privacy of the scrub trees behind the roller rink—not on her front porch under a light. To kiss him on the front porch would disappoint her father and her mother and Grandma. To not kiss him might disappoint Salvatore. Josie worried about what to do all the way back to her flat without ever really knowing what she'd do. She was relieved, then, when he simply walked her to the door and left her there, calling out goodnight behind him as he navigated the treacherous sidewalk back to the car. She let herself in the door with a new worry. Maybe he didn't like her, and he'd never ask her out again. Why didn't he try to kiss her?

Josie needn't have worried because the next Monday at school, Sally asked her out again, this time to a dance at the Catholic school. She wore her green crepe dress and high heels and, because she didn't have her own clutch, she carried Grandma's, which was black and beaded—and frankly, surprisingly beautiful. In it, Josie had stored a pack of Juicy Fruit, a small comb, a Lanolin Plus Lipstick, in Poppy Red, two dimes in case of an emergency, a small pencil from the mini golf course, and a safety pin because you just never know. Oh, and her lucky rabbit's foot. Hours before, Grandma had emptied her own stuff from the bag on the kitchen table, dumping it unceremoniously and grinning—a roll of butterscotch hard candies, a few old coat-check receipts, a fake ivory set of rosary beads, and a roll of antacids.

Sally was a good dancer, Josie thought, though he mostly danced from the waist down, which reminded her of a centaur—a centaur who could dance. The couple alternated between dancing and talking with Sally's friends around the cut glass punchbowl. Sally looked particularly handsome in his blue suit with a black tie, but in the Italian style. He played with the knife in his pocket—the one he used to cut open boxes at the market—while he talked with his friends, flipping it out of his pocket here and there, as if he were reminding everyone of who he was—a merchant, son of merchants. Or maybe, Josie thought again, it was unconscious or subconscious. What was the difference again? Maybe it was something vulnerable about Sally that *only she* had noticed. The knife twirled expertly between his fingers, until Sally put it away to pour a cup of punch for himself and for Josie.

There's no way to spike a punchbowl at a Catholic dance and not be caught by the monitors who are also drinking the punch, and thus there were great efforts and contortions made to ensure some amount of sneaked-in whiskey made it into each clear glass cup. Not a lot. No one wanted a scene. Just enough to loosen things up, as Michael O'Malley, Sally's best pal, warned the circle in his baritone whisper. Like Josie, who'd borrowed her clutch from Grandma, third baseman Michael had borrowed his silver flasks from his grandpa, but unlike Josie, he'd not asked permission. Nor had he asked permission for the whiskey he'd poured into its narrow neck in his dark basement before leaving his house. He confessed all this with glee to the group. He had three full flasks on him and two more in Sally's car.

Michael O'Malley, everyone knew, was always prepared to have a good time. Moreover, Michael was a gentleman, so he tipped into the girls' cups first and regularly. The whiskey was a good variety, though none of the youngsters yet had an appreciation for good Irish whiskey. In fact, Josie wished she could taste less of *it* and more of the orange sherbet and 7-Up—the whiskey seemed to bludgeon the sweet tastes. However, she wasn't about to complain or even wrinkle her nose as she noiselessly choked the concoction down.

There, along the back wall with its crepe streamers, stood, lined up, a great many girls with no date, all unseen, invisible, shuffling in their pinchy shoes and turning their heads to one another in whispers. By the end of the night, Josie knew they'd resort to dancing with one another rather than not dance at all. But not yet. They were still hoping. She knew all this because she'd been in that line before the new year, and that was what happened—or didn't happen—there. Always. She hadn't minded it much at the time, but now that she'd been a part of the popular crowd around the punchbowl for one evening, the line along the wall looked like purgatory to her, or maybe limbo. She wasn't quite sure. What was the difference again?

Josie danced the slow dances, the fast dances—all the dances. She did the pony and the mashed potato, the twist—even though it was getting hot in there. And she did the Watusi. In fact, she felt she'd never danced better. Sally leaned over and shouted at Michael, who Watutsi-ed next to him, "Whiskey makes her dance!" Josie laughed and danced harder, the crepe of her skirt swirling like a waterfall and her pinched feet feeling no pain. When her clutch spilled onto the dance floor, she crawled over the parquet tiles, unembarrassed and waving off helpers, to retrieve every article down to the tiny dimes that had rolled to far edges under the feet of the girls in the line. They watched her quietly as she sat up on her heels and snapped the clutch closed, black beads that made up its pelt, shimmering and rattling.

When the last slow dance played, Josie felt a little drowsy but happy and warm. She'd kicked off her shoes, and her feet, slippery in their panty hose, slid across the floor without picking up a single splinter as Sally swished her along. She burped up the taste of sherbet but muffled the sound in his lapel. Sally's hands, like a vice around her waist, felt fine. Very fine, indeed.

The cold air of February slapped Josie in the face as the couple moved down the stairs to the Rambler. Inside it was very cold, and the leather seats made noises of complaint. Michael O'Malley and his date, a girl from the Catholic School, sat in the back. The heater blew cold air on them all for too long, and they burrowed inside their own coats. Michael, his blonde hair standing up like cockscomb, fished out one of the extra flasks from behind the back seat and took a swig. "It'll warm you to the bone!" he promised before passing it to his girl, who passed it to Sally, who passed it to Josie. Josie took a swig and spluttered—it was quite a different thing straight, but it did, in fact, spread a creeping warmth through her body, and that felt good. Just then, the engine reached the point of generating enough heat to blow warm, and Josie felt altogether pretty wonderful.

It was definitely past ten pm, but though Josie wore her square-faced Timex watch—as she always did—she didn't look at it at all, or care what the time was. And when, rather than driving the group to their houses, Sally pulled the Rambler into the deserted lot at Thatcher Woods, Josie didn't think at all about getting home before curfew but instead admired the gothic nature of the big oaks and maybe the hickories, though she wasn't sure she'd ever heard of hickories from Austen or her ilk. Maybe hickories were only in the Midwest, and then they couldn't be gothic at all. But the way the branches loomed! Fantastic. There was something so nice about being in a warm car, where it was safe, while the forest primeval surrounded her—an insulation.

Josie knew that Mike and the Catholic School girl—was it Anne?—were kissing in the back seat; she could hear the sounds kissing made. Little pops of wet lips and rustling, shifting. Sally turned on the radio, and the nighttime DJ, Dick Biondi, screamed out from the dash all his excitement about music before giving the car a jovial dose of Elvis's "Teddy Bear."

"Man, Biondi's forever playing this one song," Sally snorted, "I mean, nothing against Elvis, but there's got to be something else he can play—just once in a while." Josie agreed and snuggled in close to her date. The radio gave privacy of a sort, and she wasn't surprised when she felt Sally's arms tighten around her, or when she felt him kissing her neck. In fact, she turned her neck to the side to give him more surface space to kiss. They'd never parked anywhere before, though Josie was no idiot, and she knew what parking was. Teddie's words of warning, while not her foremost thought, occurred to her. Her job was to not get pregnant. She'd heard of the pregnant girls—the ones who got sent to stay with "aunts" to help them out and came back to school silent and drawn or didn't come back to school at all, ever. She'd never seen one, but she had no doubt of their existence. Boys, Teddie said, didn't care whether or not they got you pregnant, not much anyway, because they could always say it wasn't them that did it. No one could really prove it was. And then you'd be ruined, and your parents would beat you up.

Josie, with the smell of Sally's Old Spice in her mouth and the new familiarity of his shoulders and chest, knew he wasn't the sort of boy who would get a girl pregnant and then deny it—maybe Michael in the back, but not Sally. Still, Teddie's words stayed close, like a net over Josie's face, and she pulled down the hem of her skirt when she felt it lifting. She moved Sally's hands from here to there and there to here. Things that felt too good, she halted—and somehow, she did this despite her whisky induced relaxation. She had no idea what was happening in the back seat, though, because she never looked. To each their own.

Josie felt power in response to the erection jabbing under her thigh, and a feeling of responsibility as well. Sally's movements seemed mindless, and so Josie felt as if she needed to relieve his feeling, one she sensed was akin to pain. That he whispered in her burning ear that she was beautiful and sweet, and an angel, made her feel unique. "Teen Angel" now floating from the speakers furthered the cause, especially because her mind was a little too dulled by endorphins and whiskey to remember the melodrama of the lyrics. She wasn't going to let Sally do what he wanted to, but there was a compromise to be had. And when he mashed her hand down on his crotch, they reached that compromise. Sally, with his dark eyes closed and his mouth gaping like a semi-attractive trout lifted Josie's hand, unbuttoned and unzipped his suit pants and shoved her hand inside. He let her hand lie there for a few moments but, impatient, closed her fingers over the thing that now pulsed in the open air of the car's inside, and moved her hand up and down. There wasn't much of a learning curve to master, and Josie was a deft girl. A practical girl despite her love of literature. Up and down her hand went, tighter then more relaxed, then tighter again. It didn't take long. Not long at all.

The rapidity with which Sally, minutes later, swiped at himself with a scarf, sat up in his seat, fixed his suit pants, and then engaged the Rambler in gear was a bit of a shock to Josie's system. Mike and what's-her-name were quiet in the back as the car left the forest preserve. Quiet until they said their goodbyes as each was dropped off at their home. Josie checked her face in the mirror that flipped down from the cloth ceiling of the Rambler. She wiped the lipstick off her smeared mouth and reapplied it carefully but lightly. She combed her hair. She popped a stick of gum in her mouth and reached out to hold Sally's hand. He gave her fingers a squeeze but then returned his hand to the steering wheel, for safety. When Sally dropped Josie off in front of her family's flat, though he didn't walk her in, he watched from the car to make sure she got in safely. She knew it because she heard the engine growl away only as she closed the storm door behind her. It was 12:30 in the morning.

At the kitchen table sat Josie's mother—her back at an incline forward, leaning her elbows on the wooden surface, her stocking feet curled back around the legs of the chair. She still wore her uniform sweater, from the Zenith factory, and she had auburn hair rolled tightly in pink sponge rollers. She smelled of Dippity-Do. The iron teapot slept in the middle of the table, on a crocheted trivet, four or five teabags squeezed and wrinkled cold on the saucer beside it. The cup in her mother's hand.

"Phew, glad to see everything's alright," her mother said, wiping her eyes. "I was worried you were in a ditch somewhere! Why so late?"

"Dance went long and then we went for coffee in the city." The lie rolled out smoother than if Elvis himself would have told it.

"Next time, call. If you don't, you'll be put on restriction."

"I will, Ma. Sorry."

And that was the end of it. Josie went to her room and snicked on her elephant light, a leftover from her infancy that she hadn't parted with. The gray trunk looked a bit penis-like, she noted. Maybe more than a bit. Maybe a lot. Her head hurt a little, but not too much, and she slipped off her dress and hung it carefully in her small closet. She went to the bathroom and washed her face with Noxzema. Brushed her teeth with Crest. She wondered what Sally was doing and if he loved her now. She fell into an untroubled sleep; her lies had been small, and she'd not risked herself in any way.

Things continued along the same path for some time, the only difference being all dates were now without other couples and all dates culminated in the Rambler being parked somewhere out of the way with Josie's hand moving (now skillfully) up and down in the front seat. It was a bit boring at times, but it was also very evident that Sally needed this. He did press her to do more on occasion, halfheartedly coaxing her head down to her hand, but she always declined. Josie figured all the other girls were doing the same—it was a good compromise.

But she was wrong. There was a game many girls knew how to play that she didn't—the game of purity and perceived value. This was a girls' game with rules written by boys generations ago. The boys' game was a drive towards full-on sex. The girls' game was pres- ervation of reputation. When Teddie heard Josie was doing this thing to Sally, she said to stop. Teddie for all her voiced carnal knowledge had none whatsoever that was firsthand—and she was, truth be told, a little repulsed by Josie's hand, not by Josie herself. Josie felt sad when Teddie grimaced, and she wished she'd never told her friend.

"Don't worry," Teddie reassured her, "you can just stop doing it. I mean, you don't want to get a reputation, so you gotta stop."

Josie tried to stop, or intended to stop, but she found that really, once you go so far, you haven't got a leg to stand on when you try to retract your warm hand. In fact, Sally seemed distracted lately and she wanted to keep him close. She felt his leaving. One night in April, after the customary vanilla malts and tamales from The Busy Bee and hand job in Thatcher Woods, Sally broke up with Josie.

Just like that.

He just wasn't in love with her, he explained. She was a fun girl and all, but, well, he wasn't ready to settle down with anyone—after all they were only teenagers. No, no, there was nothing wrong with Josie. Josie was swell. He just needed some time on his own. Josie tried not to cry in the Rambler on the way home or as Sally reached over to open the passenger door for her. She marched up the flat limestone steps to her front door. She told herself it wouldn't be the last time because Sally would realize he *needed* her. He'd come back.

But he never did. In fact, the very next night Salvatore Nicastro was seen by Teddie cutting the rug at the Catholic school dance with black-haired Anne Marie Moriarty. Josie was not there. She was in her bedroom attempting to drown herself in eighteenth century romantic novels. When those failed her, she stuffed herself with her famous French toast with jam and went to sleep. Teddie told her the next day.

Josie, bereft as only a fifteen-almost-sixteen-year-old-girl can be, anticipated she'd be alone for a long time, maybe forever. No one had been much interested in her before Sally, so why would anyone be after? For a few nights she didn't know what to do with herself. She ate fries and ketchup with tons of black pepper at The Busy Bee with Teddie, and she helped her grandmother roll cavatelli at the table—something she'd never done before. Grandma rubbed Josie's shoulders and smiled at her, but no one at home ever asked what happened to Salvatore. Josie supposed *they* supposed the romance just petered out. And she supposed they were right in what she supposed they supposed. What was there to say about such things? Sally had a right, she figured, to break up. She didn't hate him for it, but she was cut low. Destined for a life of solitude until she was at least twenty. This is why Josie was surprised when no more than three days after the breakup, Michael O'Malley asked her to see *The Manchurian Candidate* with him.

Some bit of information had moved or shifted in the world that April. And though Josie hadn't changed, her status had. For a few days, she said no, because she didn't feel it was right to go on a date with Sally's friend. But eventually she said yes. He was persistent and she was lonely. And, besides, Josie had heard the film was good. Mike took her out for fondue in the city first, and he'd tried so hard, with loads of brill-cream, to get his rooster hair to lie flat and spent so much on fancy food and the film that when, on the ride home when he'd pulled into an empty playground parking lot and put her hand on his crotch, she acquiesced. It felt different than Sally's and yet the same. Josie watched the swings blow in the March wind, unmanned.

As things go, Josie found herself asked on lots of dates, sometimes from boys who went to other schools. They waited for her after school. And each time, she'd hope they maybe hadn't heard what she could and would do, and so wouldn't expect it. But it was always the same.

The truth was Josie had developed a name. Not just a reputation, but a *name*. It was a joke or a pun. She was a joke or a pun. She was Josie Jobs. There was no shedding it here in town. She would be Josie Jobs forever. The name, with its double consonants, like Marilyn Monroe, rolled off the tongue and lodged in the minds of many. The first time she heard it, while standing in line for fries at the school cafeteria, she thought it was someone else's name, and was interested in there being a new Josie at school. But then she heard it again and again, with people covering their mouths with one hand, and she knew, with a chill, it was her. It didn't take Josie long at all to work out the pun.

Many girls did many other things, but without a defining name, they were not trapped like she was. As she saw it, our Josie felt she had two choices. To stay home alone forever being called Josie Jobs anyway or to go on dates and likely be expected to rub a penis at the end of the night. Young and energetic, she generally chose the latter. Though she hoped for better.

Some girls who had been her friends felt they really just couldn't be seen with Josie Jobs in public, and their drifting away was excruciating. Teddie and a few others stayed close and defended her whenever they heard the smear. It did nothing to change the moniker, but it made Josie know she had a friend or two, which quite likely saved her life.

Upon graduation, three years and some after her first date with Sally, boys and girls alike tittered "Josie Jobs" as she snatched her diploma from Principle Muehl's hand. Sally and Mike were long-gone graduates. Later still, when she worked at Goldblatt's, the stockboys would mouth "Josie Jobs" when she passed by, and they thought she couldn't see them. They'd also ask her on dates. By this time, she declined—she was tired of it all. Sometimes, Josie felt like dying. But she didn't. She just kept living and taking baths, rolling cavatelli in her grandma's spot at the table when Grandma died. Her brothers grew up, and she hoped beyond hope, they didn't know she was called Josie Jobs, or why, but she suspected they did. Only her parents and grandmother likely remained totally ignorant.

What Josie could not have imagined, despite her truly active imagination and her increasingly cynical nature was that at her fortieth high school reunion, middle-aged men burdened with bald heads and big bellies, when they saw Josie Farbrizzi's name on the guest list would whisper "Josie Jobs" to one another while their wives slapped at them, some playfully and some not.

It's a good thing Josie could not foresee the immortal quality of that name, she always thought it would end soon. It's best for Josie, and for us, if we remember that she was always the apple of her grandmother's eye, a good French toast maker, a lover of books, and one willing and ready to give some sort of pleasure when called upon to do so while also trying her best to keep herself safe. Anyway, that's how Josie, much later, will learn to frame it all on her therapist's couch, offering a stick of Juicy Fruit to him. She will pull it from Grandma's beaded clutch, which she keeps inside her modern purse. In that interior clutch, beside the pack of gum, are a safety pin, a roll of antacids, red age-erasing lipstick, and fake ivory rosary beads wrapped around a rabbit's food. My name, she will say, as she hands over the piece of gum, is *Gelsomina* Fabrizzi. I was named for my grandmother.

NINETEEN

To the Moon, Santina

S even hot dogs, dressed in mustard and relish and studded with sport peppers crowded side by side at one end of the sturdy cardboard box Santina Prosperino carried home from The Busy Bee over on Seventeenth. Paper packets of fries pointed up from the other end of the box, like a wave. As she hurried from up Seventeenth and around the corner to Singer, the smell of her food rose from the box and fell away behind Santina, layering with all of the other smells of Mulberry Park: donut grease from Crème Crunch, fully leaded gasoline from the corner station, diesel from the buses roaring away to Melrose Park, Oak Park, and Chicago. Vinnie Straglimiglia drove by and waved at her—The Beatles' "Eight Days a Week" drifting from his wide-open windows. Everyone knew Vinnie Straglimiglia sat on phone books so he could see out the windshield of his '57 Ford, and everyone understood those phonebooks made it harder for him to reach the brakes with his short legs. Santina waved back and stepped further into the sidewalk. She wasn't about to be run down, especially not today when she carried not just a box of hot dogs and a book bag but three very official envelopes in her coat pocket. Her lips practiced words designed around those envelopes, designed around convincing her parents to allow her to make her own way. The words left her lips in time with her footsteps—a march, a waltz, a march again. She rubbed her throat to push her heart back down from where it had flung itself, high and nearly bursting.

Late May 1965 opened in rumbles and chirps and roars all around her. Santina was a child of her neighborhood and had never lived anywhere else, and so she moved deftly, with a certainty that was altogether ignorant of any other state, though she often fantasized about leaving and then immediately recoiled in fear at the very same thought. She frowned as her book bag knocked the back of her knee over and over again. It was heavy with Mead notepads and big gummy erasers, triangle-folded letters from her girlfriends, a chain of bobby pins—all the things she cleared out of her locker as the school year ended. It also held the big flat yearbook filled with signatures and warm wishes.

The last few weeks of high school had been hard for Santina. Not because of her term paper or because all the reading that had to be finished in order to write that paper. Certainly not hard because of the math—she loved math. What had been hard for Santina Prosperino was that she felt just like she was crouching at the ledge of the John Hancock building, high above the city and surrounding towns, and that fastened to her narrow shoulders were wings she'd made carefully using math and physics, steel and fiberglass. She longed to soar from the ledge, and yet she longed to remain there as well—in a row with all the pigeons—calmly surveying the landscape. But most of all, she didn't want to be either prevented or pushed. She often dreamed that very thing early in the mornings, in that last dream before waking, and she savored it, lying very still under the heavy crocheted blankets her mother piled in layers until it was time to rise.

Santina was one of those rare students who adore school, and so her mourning and hesitance about leaving were practical as well as sentimental. From the first grade to the last, she'd completed every task and made every grade. She'd befriended each teacher and all the classmates she could. Despite racial tensions at school, she'd held tight to both her Black girlfriends and her White, which was no small feat. Had it been possible, Santina would have remained a senior at Mulberry Park High for the rest of her life. But, of course, only if her friends could have remained there with her, her teachers, too, everyone moving up and down the waxed tile floors, like limbo. Not for forever, just for long enough to fully prepare to do the import-ant things. Very important things. But on this particular afternoon, before the Straglimiglia goon had sped by, before she'd handed in the term paper on DaVinci's Moon Lakes, in those few seconds as she had carefully paper-clipped her lined note cards—in order—to her meticulously typed work, she'd decided. It was time to leap.

Santina bent her thin elbow at an impossible angle and lifted a fry from a packet, popped it into her mouth without slowing her steps. It was salty and greasy and wonderful—its brown skin left intact to prove its freshness. She chewed as she walked. In the pocket of her lilac cotton spring coat nestled her three envelopes—three acceptance letters from three colleges—full scholarship.

Hands full, she banged the metal storm door of home with her knee, taking care to hit it just hard enough to be heard without aggravating her parents. This she did without spilling a single fry, and nearly losing her balance only twice. When her tidy mother pulled open the door, Santina stepped over the threshold, out of America and into another place altogether.

It was some kind of minor kingdom or principality of Naples, and it was ruled by her father—King Massimo Prosperino. He sat at the kitchen table, a long-stalked bunch of *finocchio* his scepter, a shining white cup of black coffee his chalice. He needed no crown. Anyone would know Santina was the king's daughter—she wore his hawk's nose high in the middle of her face, just like he wore his. And he greeted her with paternal joy. But they were different as well— Santina tall and fluid, with a neck everyone thought swanlike and a head like a delicate egg—Massimo square as the sponge that rested on the countertop, his big head simply more of his overall square. He was the squarest king in the land. Yet, a king need not be graceful, and what Massimo Prosperino lacked in grace he made up for in dogged affection and protection, which he heaped generously upon his family, saving them from countless missteps over the years. Of this, he was quite certain. His children were only half-convinced, but of course they didn't mention that.

Massimo smiled to see Santina home from school, and he rubbed tiredness from his eyes. He still worked nights at American Can, keeping the books—maybe in a few years, when Herbie Rosenpflatz retired, he'd get the first shift spot. Or maybe not. There was no way to know. Neatly wrenching an arm of *finocchio* from the rest, he took a shining little knife from his pocket, and removed the fibrous threads. Then he sliced off shrimp-shaped pieces against his thumb, not all at once—this would have been eating like an animal. No, he sliced one, chewed it with his thick lips shut, swallowed it, made some conversation with his wife who was working at something in the corner, and then sliced the next. He piled the fibrous threads on a paper napkin with care. He wasn't the kind of man to leave a mess for his wife to clean up. The *finocchio* soothed his stomach, and so he had some every afternoon when he awoke—with a cup of thick black coffee, two lumps of sugar, no milk. His routine made him content if not peaceful.

Now, here was Santina with pink American sausages. He might have a bite or two, but he was better to avoid these types of food. His daughter put the box down on the table, like an offering. Massimo pronounced they would wait for the others, Santina's two older sisters—both at work—and her younger brother, still at the school, probably being kept late for being a dunce. Her Mamma nodded in agreement with the edict and laid two clean dish towels over the box to keep everything warm.

Santina wondered if this might be the perfect time, while it was quiet in the house. She hesitated and glanced down at her coat pocket, the white of the envelopes peeping at her. The muffled roars of buses seeped through the thick walls into the kitchen making Santina painfully aware of the world's pace. Mrs. Robinson, her guidance counselor, had said to be matter-of-fact about it. All the work had been done, and those offers were too good to refuse.

Santina Prosperino wanted, in her heart of hearts—and more than anything—to go to University of Illinois and to become an astronaut. Yes, she wanted to become an astronaut, not as a fantasy or a dream. As a reality. And for a thousand reasons—the martyred JFK, the Russians, angles and trajectories and mathematics, exploration and invigoration. But mostly for that reasonless reason. It was, she believed, *her destiny.* Under her bed, in a Buster Brown shoebox, was the model of the solar system she'd constructed in the eighth grade, and beside it, the special glasses for watching a solar eclipse as well as her sketches on graph paper of various rockets she'd read about. In the ninth grade, she'd listened on radio, as if enraptured, when her handsome president spoke of the moon, and of the means to get there. She'd felt, and still did feel, the giddy impatience alongside the solemn knowing. It would happen. Mankind would travel to the moon and beyond. Now, Santina Prosperino was no fool; she knew it was a longshot that they'd ever let a woman go, but like Mrs. Robinson said, why not? And even if they wouldn't let her at first, maybe later. She was a whiz with numbers and with physics—if she had to bide her time designing rockets and spaceships, so be it. She'd still be part of the race.

Mrs. Robinson had helped her write the submissions to colleges. Explained the various necessary degrees in hallways and from behind her solid desk. It was real. Yes, it was very real.

So, she went for it there in the roomy kitchen that smelled of coffee, mustard, and fennel. Santina smiled at her father and accepted a curve of *finocchio* from his short fingers with her long ones. The fennel smell was her father—all her life—and now he was in her hands, maybe. She prepared to shift the direction of the conversation in the room, away from weather and when to plant tomatoes—before or after Memorial Day—to herself and the moon and colleges. She knew full well that to this man, his black stockinged feet flat on the linoleum, the moon and colleges were approximately equidistant from the kitchen in which they now sat, each leaning forward toward the other on the plump vinyl seat of a chrome kitchen chair.

"Papa," she began, "I've done really well in school all these years. I'm at the very top of my class, you know…"

He nodded, beaming.

"I'm even valedictorian."

He nodded again. "This is so nice, to have such a daughter."

"And so, well, Mrs. Robinson thought, well I thought, well *we* thought, and even the principal said…I should go to college." She traced a seam in the kitchen table with her fingertip.

Her father sat back and closed his eyes.

She continued: "I wouldn't even have to leave home. Here, look, there are three colleges right in Chicago I could go to—only a short trip on the bus! And look, even better, it's free—they want to give me a scholarship! Isn't it *wonderful?*"

Santina could tell by the way his eyes were pinched shut that it *wasn't* wonderful. It was the same way he had pinched his eyes when she'd asked to have a beagle from the Basso litter, and the same way he'd pinched his eyes every time she'd asked to sleep over at a friends'. But she kept saying the word—wonderful, wonderful, wonderful— as if she could convince him that it was.

Her mother, now on the other side of the kitchen near the per- colator, wiping spilled sugar off the edge of the counter and into her cupped hand, said nothing. She looked in Santina's direction, though, flatness in her eyes, wire- rimmed glasses perched high on her face.

Santina carefully fanned the three envelopes on the table, each addressed to Mrs. Robinson's office. It felt for a second as if her teacher were standing there with her. Oh, if only she had been.

Massimo opened his eyes, "Mamma," he said, "*Brioschi, per favore.*"

The tall clear glass arrived with the spoon still in it. He stirred the antacid, swallowed, and sighed. Rising from his chair, he drew his suspenders over his shoulders. "*Mia, figghiaa,*" he said as he took Santina's slender face into his hands, looking up at her for she was quite a bit taller.

"*Figghia mia*, college is not for girls. Not for the girls. Now, lis- ten. I'm not unreasonable. I'm not saying you need to marry right away—or ever. I'm not saying you need to stay in the kitchen with your beautiful mother."

Mamma dropped her dishrag into the sink and sat down to pour herself a coffee. She wasn't a quiet woman, but there was no need for her to speak right now. Massimo would handle it, and they would talk about it later before they went to bed. Santina didn't even look her mother's way. She sensed the firm fingers on the coffee cup and the wall of refusal within.

"I'm not saying any of this," her father went on, "in fact, you can go to school, but just not to *college.*" Massimo held out both hands, as if he had a bird in each.

"I give you choices. You, *figghia mia,* can go to Beauty School or Secretary School. And then you will have a trade that is useful and proper for you."

Santina had never told either of her parents about her need to go to the moon because she knew they wouldn't understand, but now she gripped the underside of the Formica table and shouted about the moon.

"Moon? Moon?" Massimo shouted back. "What do you want to do? Kill your mother? Moon? You want to see the moon, go out in the garden. It's there almost every night."

"What, you don't even…"

"Listen, Santina, no moon. That's the end of it. You are not allowed to go to the moon. And no crazy college either. I gave you your choices."

"Secretarial School and Beauty School! Those will never get me to the moon!! *Non mai,* Papa, *mai!*" Santina's forehead hit the table as she flattened herself.

"Put your head up when I talk to you." He looked at her with real sincerity, "Hey, I see you wearing the lipstick all the time. You will like Beauty School. You will see."

"But I don't wanna *be that!*"

"Wanna? Don't wanna? No, wanna don't matter. You aren't going to college. You think I don't know what goes on at those colleges? I know! I know! What kind of a father would I be to send you into one of those places?"

"Nothing goes on."

"EVERYTHING goes on! If you try to go to these colleges, you hear me. Listen to me. If you do this, you cannot be my daughter anymore."

"But…"

"I mean it. YOU CANNOT BE!"

Massimo reached for his daughter's head again and kissed her on her sore forehead, bending it to him like one pulls the branches of a willow to cut a switch. She seethed and bent all at the same time.

"Heart of my heart" he whispered, "I will pay it. Beauty or Secretary. Your sisters, they will be jealous."

"But," Santina croaked. "It's not fair. I worked so hard."

"Not fair, not fair? Your sisters, I only sent them to work, but they were not as clever as you. Never with the As, only Bs. You work hard, and so I reward you. Remember this and be kind to your sisters."

Santina said nothing more, not aloud anyway. She was afraid of what she might say if she let even one more word out, and besides, there was no convincing her father—there had never been. His mind was made up about everything before his children had even been born. He had the map for life in his head and he would never deviate. To do so would have meant chaos to him. Santina knew this in her bones though she had no words for it—so familiar it was. There was nothing for it. She'd have to either run away and go to college or she'd have to listen to her Papa. And she knew she could do neither without dying. Fat tears dragged the mascara from her eyes to her chin and then along her neck. The letters still held their own, fanned on the tabletop, as if they didn't know they'd been slain. And Santina stood up from her chair, her mouth opened and silent. Massimo pulled a white kerchief from his pocket and dabbed Santina's face. She flinched.

"Yum," he said, "what's here in this box? Hotdogs, from my best daughter? I must have one! I cannot wait for the other children, those slowpokes." He lifted a hotdog, cradled it for a moment, and then munched it loudly, making a great show of it. Smacking his fleshy lips. He even ate a fry, cold as it was. It stuck in his throat a little and he coughed it up. This was still foreign food to him, but he did his best to make her believe he liked it. Santina didn't care whether he liked it or not anymore. She wished an enormous pit would open, a specific-purpose sinkhole, in the middle of the kitchen and suck her down into the bowels of the earth where there was magma. Her and the letters and the hotdogs. And then the hole would close back up as if nothing had happened. She knew this was impossible, so she went to her room and sat at the edge of her bed.

Outside Santina's window, old Giuseppa Millefiore shuffled almost imperceptibly along the sidewalk pushing her black baby buggy as she made her way home from the grocery. She used one hand to push and the other to paddle back a white chicken with a small red comb that wouldn't ride peaceably with the other shopping goods—cans and sacks of cornmeal and flour. Despite her great sad fury, Santina watched the scene pass before her, glacially. The chicken's beady eye looked at Santina and made her cry harder, such was the chicken's predicament. The old woman tried to stuff it back into the buggy with both hands, now pushing the buggy with her middle and bending precariously. The chicken disappeared from sight for a moment and all seemed well. But then the tiny head emerged with new vigor. The nervous bird struggled, and the woman shuffled inch by inch along the sidewalk until finally Giuseppa threw up her one hand that wasn't battling the chicken and halted in the warm May sun. She grasped the chicken's bony head with her bony fingers and swung the uncooperative bird in a great figure eight, snapping its neck. Santina screamed softly into her hand as Donna Giuseppa put the chicken back into the buggy, where it lay quietly.

She watched the dead chicken and the old woman process out of sight, removed her hand from her mouth, and wondered how she might proceed. Only Anglo girls ran away. Maybe secretarial school wouldn't be that bad. No, no, it would. It would be horrible! She had to figure something out. But she had no idea how to do that. Santina plucked at her chenille bedspread, making a small hill of plucked out threads. She sobbed and rocked and hatched impossible plans. But none of those plans could live.

In the end it was beauty school, though for no other reason than Santina's best friend from first grade on, Teodora Millefiore—granddaughter of old Giuseppa—was going to beauty school. The girls registered at the Supreme Beauty School of Beauty and Aesthetic Design, which sounded much fancier than it was. And their fathers paid in monthly installments. Santina and Teddie each walked out of their father's houses and met on the sidewalk in between each Monday, Wednesday, and Friday. And then they hurried the six blocks over to Supreme. Supreme was where they learned it all: shampooing, coloring, bleaching, tinting, frosting, teasing, teasing, and more teasing. They memorized the pressure points on the human skull and the many conflicting causes of dandruff. They sanitized combs in glass jars of blue Barbicide and swept hair into great piles, triple bagging it before putting it into the dumpsters to keep the rats out. As they learned, they experimented on each other's heads, and their hair grew higher and higher and more and more vibrant in color. Often with the help of pieces, but there was no shame in extra help.

By autumn, Santina's glossy black hair towered above her and swirled like an ice cream cone at the top. When she sat down in the red vinyl booths at The Busy Bee, people often gathered to look in and admire what was Santina's head and Teddie's art, for there's always an artist's hand at work in such a hairdo. Often a friend. Two flat tendrils swung in front of Santina's ears; these she'd sculpted herself. Her eyes rimmed with black liquid eyeliner, and her eyelashes were false and lush. She looked a lot like Cleopatra, everyone said.

In return, Santina did Teddie's hair, double processed it to some kind of blonde, shiny and brassy and gleaming. Santina excelled in her beauty classes. The course took her mind off the loss of college and the moon. A distraction but an insufficient one. The moon followed her whenever she went out at night, big or small, waxing or waning. It tailed her. And JFK's words grew more urgent in her dreams, as the words of the dead often do. Santina Prosperino knew others were taking her place—the race would be run without her. She pulled her chenille blanket hairless and had to hide it under her bed. By day, she studied the molecular workings of bleaches and permanent waves and kept moving—still halfheartedly trying to convince herself that this was good enough. At night she mourned until finally she resigned to convince herself to forget it.

She was getting closer to convincing herself when she and Teddie completed beauty school and landed jobs at the Curl and Twirl beauty shop, run by Ms. Marcella, who had a hair-do even taller than Santina's—and long blood-red fingernails. Ms. Marcella was the *height* of fashion in Mulberry Park and divorced to boot. Of course, Santina's father did not know about Ms. Marcella; had he known such a woman was instructing his daughter, Santina would have been trundled off to Secretarial School immediately. Teddie's father *did* know all about Ms. Marcella, but that's another story for another time.

Miss Marcella was demanding; sometimes she shrieked and sometimes she snapped, but never in front of customers. Despite the woman's temperament, she paid well and, well, she was the best hairdresser in town. She had a knack with mixing color that was part art, part chemistry, part magic. Miss M. gave a new lesson each morning, and taught them the finesse beauty school could not. She taught with the fastidiousness of a woman who had somehow earned her own shop, despite her great sin. But Ms. Marcella hogged the best clients. The girls spoiled to try out new styles on new heads and, once in a while, they did. But the clientele was predominantly ancient and Ms. Marcella herself would snatch up any younger clients. Santina and Teddie were left rolling sets on elderly women who came in once a week to be "done" exactly the same way there were "done" the week before. If the old women left looking exactly how they looked when they had entered three hours before, they were content. And it was important to keep them content.

This was the pattern of life for Santina and her friend for quite some time: meeting on the sidewalk, walking to work, sets, comb outs, spraying, collecting the tips, sweeping the floors, going to the shops or out for a Coke, going home. They had pocket money for whatever they wanted—within reason—and they met boys from high school at the Drive In—those who hadn't enlisted to fight in Vietnam, anyway. They went to movies in Oak Park and picnicked in twin sets at the forest preserve in River Forest. They each bought twelve-piece settings of what claimed to be fine china on layaway at Woolworths and stuffed their hope chests. After they'd collected the place servings, they bought the completer sets, and then the crystal. Santina liked to ping the rim of her champagne flutes and listen to the note ring out—when she was alone in her bedroom, which was often now that her sisters had both married and moved to the next street.

Santina gave half of her paycheck to her mother each Friday—she left the money under the infant of Prague on the entry table—but her tips were hers to keep. She and Teddie took up smoking cigarettes and penciling-in strong eyebrows high on their foreheads. They began to feel quite independent and decided between themselves and two other girls at the Curl and Twirl that they would pool their money and rent a flat. Everyone was in. It would be wonderful!

But, of course, when Santina came home lugging a big brown sack of sopping beefs topped with sweet peppers and hot oily *gardinera* all the way from Carm's in the city, her father said "No way in hell." King Massimo explained, "You leave this house when you get married, no sooner. What do you want people to think of you? What do you want people to think of this family? I know what goes on in those apartments! I know!"

This time he did not pull her face down to kiss her or wipe her tears with his kerchief. Instead, he slammed his fist on the table and then slammed it again to make certain he was understood. He was, as always, understood. Santina's mother was sorting the bill money into marked envelopes at the corner of the table, and Santina harbored no silly thoughts that her mother might stand up and intervene, that she was secretly enjoying her own fantasy of what it might have been like to live in a flat as a young woman, surrounded by friends and free to come and go as she pleased. Santina knew her mother thought none of these things. She simply counted and sorted her envelopes: gas bill, light bill, water bill, food.

Back at the Curl and Twirl, the other girls encouraged Santina to do it anyway. To move to the apartment with them. They gathered around her in a ring out by the dumpster behind the shop, patting their own flushed faces and French-inhaling in the cold, still air of their first winter there. They all talked tough.

"So, what if you are 'dead to him'? Just do it. He'll get over it," Teddie spat. "Dead to him" like this?" She laughed and bit her knuckle in a furious mimicry of her own father. "Like this?"

"Dead to me! Dead to me!" they all shrieked in unison, nearly falling to the snowy ground laughing. Even Shenandoah whose father was not Italian but whose new stepfather was.

"You know, they're all talk, these sons-a-bitch fathers," Teddie sighed. "I shit you not." Santina nodded, but they all knew it would never happen—the moving out. They all knew the father would *never* get over it. Never. And in the trade, Santina would have her friends and a lovely flat and her own key to a door of her own choosing for a while. But for how long? How long before life moved them on? Family was forever, and if she defied her father, she'd lose not just him but her mother, her brother, her sisters, her old nonno, her aunts, her uncles, her cousins, and all the neighbors over the age of twenty-five. And then who would she even *be*?

So, she didn't defy, but this time, Santina did keep asking for the permission she needed. She even jumped up and down and screamed at him. He was quite taken aback and dropped his glass of apricot nectar on the floor. She towered over him now with all that hair, and she glittered with earrings and flashed with lipstick, but still, she could not overpower him. "You will thank me," he assured her, "and you will realize one day that I saved you from the evils of this world. It wasn't easy, Santina, but I did it."

Santina wondered how satisfying it would be to knock him over, but only for a split second. She pushed the thought from her mind and went loudly out the door to Our Lady of the Flowers where she lit a candle, but not before she had fully envisioned her papa flying backwards into the metal kitchen cabinets like a bowling pin, at thirty-degree angle. At church, the candle sputtered as the yellow wick caught fire, and Father Picanto, who hadn't seen Santina Prosperino much since her confirmation nodded at her in approval. He reached up and patted her on the bouffant as he swished by in his robes in a way that communicated his main thought: she looked a bit overripe. Santina remained before her candle praying to Mary to make her father see the light just long enough to possibly do some good. But she was a pragmatic young woman, and so she gave up soon, and went to the restroom to check her bouffant for damage.

* * *

Santina could not know it yet, but in time all the girls will grow tired of Curl and Twirl, of Ms. Marcella, of standing for hours shampooing and snipping and teasing old, dry heads. They'll suspect they might be setting themselves up for unsightly varicose veins, standing on that hard tile floor day after day. They will gripe out back by the dumpster and when the patrons can't hear them over the hot-breathing hair dryers. But in truth, it's not just Santina who can't move out. None of them can. For all the provincial fathers of all the kitchens in all the land of Mulberry Park have said, "No!"

The girls will become dejected and their eyes will grow a little hard, but they will still be looking fine, plump on fries with red sauce and Coca-Cola from The Busy Bee and coiffed with care. They'll be toting patent leather clutches well-stocked with Juicy Fruit, rat's tail combs and jingling change, striding up and down the streets of town in a mist of Aqua-Net and semi-confidence that left a wake like boats had passed. Young men will notice, and one by one, the girls of Curl and Twirl will marry away. New girls will replace them, and Miss Marcella will continue initiating all those girls who really wanted to be astronauts and doctors and lawyers and marine biologists, painters, writers, inventors, along with those who really wanted to be hair-dressers. She will never have known the difference, and sometimes, neither will they.

When Santina marries in September of '66 her father will march through the church in his dark suit looking a lot like a deck of cards with its King of Clubs on top. He will have chosen the spread for the reception—waiting in the dark church basement—cold cut sandwiches, *taralli*, potato chips, pickles, and dishes of hot peppers and plates of cheese, olives, and bowls of fruit salad. And a cake, of course, not homemade, but from Palermo's bakery and topped with a tiny bride and a tiny groom. White cake with white frosting. Purity. A good wedding would ensure a good marriage.

Everyone will see him there in the very throes of marrying off his last daughter. And everyone will see Santina, the happy bride. She'll blush and adjust the long sleeves of her lace gown. Her enormous dark eyes solemn and quiet as they note the movements her father makes with his hands, like a man shucking the earth from them. *Finito.*

Yes, everyone will be there. Neighbors, friends, her little brother, Massimo Junior, who calls himself Ricky now. He will have come in on the train from college. Everyone will know he's close to flunking out, and not for lack of trying. Poor kid. She'll almost feel sorry for him over there in his wrinkled suit picking his teeth and leaning against the wall with the other groomsmen. Almost.

Her mother will wait in the pew, sitting quietly in a dark blue dress, a little net veil attached to her pillbox hat down over glasses. Santina will think absently about her own veil, about her family, about the cake in the basement, and about her handsome fiancé who waits at the altar. She'll feel grown up—like a woman. Beautiful. Good.

When Santina turns to admire her lengths of ivory silk with the train pooling behind her, and the matching slippers that peep out— no heel so she won't stand taller than her husband, she'll think he's handsome—rakish almost, but with sensitive eyes—and he's adopted, so no one will know if he's Italian or not. She'll hope he isn't.

Even later, on June 20th, 1969, the black and white television in Santina's living room will hum. Her husband, Billy, will move the rabbit's ears this way and that, searching for a signal until he gets it. The broadcast won't start for a few more hours, but he'll need to make sure all is ready. Santina will kneel on the shag carpeting in front of the massive ornate coffee table her Uncle Nemo will have sent from Naples. She will know it's hideous and beautiful at the same time, but she'll try to think of it as beautiful because it was too expensive to ever get rid of. Though as she spreads out the canapes and crudités, she'd made so carefully she'll gasp when it shows her its various uglinesses, scrollwork like slow-moving snails clustered upon one another, the whole thing dripping with gold edgings and done in a high gloss finish. She'll tuck her long feet under her and continue to arrange the food in concentric circles.

Her new home will not be in Mulberry Park but several towns away. Her family will drive over, just for the afternoon, all of them, just to watch the moon landing because she will have the biggest living room and the best TV. After she lays out the canapes and chills the white wine, after she vacuums the shag carpet and then rakes it, she will kiss her baby, all round dark eyes and thick little feet that bank about in the walker, getting stuck in corners.

Santina will have already baked a cake in the shape of the moon, for dessert, with cream cheese frosting and sprinkled with coconut. She will have indented areas to mimic the surface lakes of the moon. And she'll have laid out waxy paper plates, red and blue cartoonish rockets streaming across them. What the heck? Why not? She'll say. She'll think she's over all that now. The air-conditioner in the living room window will roar at a different frequency than the one in the bedroom, but she'll hear them both, and they'd sound like engines. Rocket engines, she'll think but then dismiss herself—never actually heard a rocket engine, has she? She'll wipe the baby's nose with a fresh tissue and take a breath. Ten minutes before the guests arrive; she will put out the shrimp platter.

Santina will be wearing pedal-pushers and a sleeveless blouse, pale yellow to match the baby's dress. On her feet, strappy leather sandals, her toes painted red. She'll think of Ms. Marcella but hardly be able to conjure her face anymore. It will have been so long by then. Three years. She will sniff and be reassured by the smell of her cologne. Heaven Scent. And when her Papa steps through the door, followed by her Mamma and her sisters and her brother and Billy's people and their friends and a handful of neighbors, Santina will be ready. She will kiss him and take his hat. He will make his way into the house, wearing pressed shirt and slacks despite the heat. Santina will hear him telling everyone how proud he was of America, showing those Ruskies what was what.

"Look at this house of my daughter and my son-in-law! What a great place, no?"

Massimo will pass through the house to the back patio, the train of guests following him. They will devour the canapes and shrimp; even the back-up plates which she'd stored in the old round fridge in the garage.

Out on the patio, Billy, brushing a forelock of hair out of his eyes, will fan the graying briquettes and, on go the dogs and burgers and hot Italian sausages, the marinated flank steak. Out go the potato salad, the slaw, the macaroni salad, the fruit ambrosia with shreds of coconut. Down go the wine and 7-Up, Kool-Aid for kids. The air will smell of firecrackers, Coppertone, and Cutter. Kids will run through the sprinkler near the statue of Mary, who's getting wet in her blue cement cape. The people will wait in the sun for the moon. Expectant.

And at the appointed hour, everyone will gather around the set, and the room will burgeon. Mothers will put the small children in front so that they see and never forget—even the toddlers, who will take it seriously. They will have hoped it was Mutual of Omaha's Wild Kingdom about to begin. Babies who cry will be taken from the room, but when her baby cries, Santina will not move. Teddie, who will be there of course, will put down her umpteenth cigarette of the day and pick up the baby for her friend, bouncing the fat little thing rapidly on her hip, her own preschooler safely cross-legged in front of the set. Massimo, still going on about the Russians, will have long ago forgotten that his daughter ever wanted to be an astronaut in the same way he's forgotten all the other foolish inclinations his children brought home, inclinations he'd had to stem. He will wait eagerly and impatiently for the thing to happen and hold his wife's hand. Squeeze it. "The moon," he'll whisper, "Can you imagine?"

All will go silent except for the hiss of static, and then from the set, very calm men's voices: Cronkite, Schirra, Mission Control, and Aldrin. A bubble of something swallowed will seem to be in their throats, all the throats, those speaking and of those listening alike.

In the living room, the television volume turned all the way up, the only person who will truly understand what's happening will be Santina.

The parents and children and neighbors and wine spilling onto her new carpeting will all recede behind her as she leans forward to see, moving two toddlers aside. She will watch the altitude, angle of descent, range to go superimposed across the broadcast. The rocket's tail will flash and flare in the dark of the screen. White hot. Pulsing. Alive. Long minute after long minute.

And then, slowly, Apollo II will land. The children on the floor, clapping. Cronkite in his tie, removing his glasses, rubbing his nose as if to stop himself from crying. Every hair on Santina's arms will be standing up, and on the nape of her neck, too. She will rub her own nose to keep from crying. "…and there's a foot coming down the steps," Cronkite will say. She will rub her nose harder. Lots of people will be crying, too, all for different reasons. Some for pride, others for relief, some from sheer elevation.

Even her father, Massimo, will sniff and dab with his pocket kerchief. But Santina, she will be the only one to howl. She'll howl for all the regular reasons, but also for the never-ending tension between the life she will have led and loved and the life she will never have gotten to try—for the shoebox under her childhood bed, her three acceptance letters, and the glassy eye of the white chicken, its small red comb wobbling as it found itself swinging in an orbit devised by another.

She will.

TWENTY

The Feast

Teddie Millefiore stepped closer to the mirrored medicine chest to make sure she was good. She didn't feel she had a particularly pretty face aside from her eyes, which were large, intelligent, and Milk Dud brown. Because she didn't like her own face much, she put extra effort into staying slim—difficult for a five-foot-one-inch young woman with a constant craving for French fries. She was a little plump, she thought, this summer, enough to have obscured her cheekbones and put her up a size in pedal-pushers. She felt her complexion was a strange mix: the olive undertone of her father's family and the paleness of her mother's. Sallow. She lit a Winston with the matches she'd set on the edge of the sink. Teddie took in a cleansing drag, threw the spent match in the toilet, flushed it down. Wondered vaguely where it would end up.

Beauty school, and now her work at the Curl and Twirl Salon, had taught her a few tricks.

Deftly, she jiggered the gray rat's tail comb up and down with one hand while lifting the hair at the crown of her head with the other, she teased her cotton-candy pink do—a recent experiment directly following platinum—to a height that made her appear taller, at least five foot four, maybe more. She clipped a couple of "pieces" in and turned her head to the side to make sure she was seamless. Hair satisfactory, she carefully adjusted the curve of her shaved and re-drawn eyebrows in mink-gray pencil before wetting a tiny brush between her lips and dipping it into cake eyeliner. With a twist of her wrist, Teddie created the Cleopatra effect. Had she been an older woman, the effect would have been garish, but youth saves us from so many things.

It was going to be one heck of a weekend, she thought. July second had, for as long as any living person in Mulberry Park could remember, been the feast day of Our Lady of the Flowers. It wasn't just the mass on Sunday that brought everyone out, though it was indeed beautiful with the thousands of gladiolas and the Latin mass. No, what got hearts beating was the feast week leading up to that mass.

And so, the avenue was blocked from cars with sawhorses and streamers. Lighted arches made a tunnel that gleamed well past midnight in gold and red and green. The oyster sellers, cannoli makers, beer and wine sellers came forth in dozens and dozens. The *lupini* man with his huge table sectioned into squares showed off salty *lupini,* roasted *cecis,* and nuts of all sorts, pumpkin seeds, squash seeds, and more. He stood chest puffed, shouting out, "*Lupini, Lupini!*" He was always the first to the scene, followed closely by the Italian ice man, his dry ice rising like a fog around him and his steel homemade tubs of lemon and cherry ices dazzling under the lights.

People who happened to live along the route put tables in front of their own houses to sell fresh bread, sausage and peppers, whorls of *braciole,* plates of *vermicelli, arancini,* lemon cookies—to make a few extra bucks. On the second night, the carnies came to set up rides and to open their games of chance with balls and darts and popguns There was real gambling as well, in dark rooms within the church basement and in tents with the flaps down. The iron horse man raced his iron horses and gave away prizes to children. Next month, he'd go to the Feast of St. Rocco in the city, and the one for whichever saint it was where they flew kids on wires over the crowds, dressed as death-defying angels. People knew about the feasts of other neighborhoods, but they never went to them. This feast was the only one that mattered for the people of Mulberry Park.

The nearly dead, the chronically infirm, the anti-social by nature along with the rest, always raised themselves to come into the streets—every night for five nights in a row. If you were alive, you were there. At least that's what Teddie believed. She'd never missed a feast, nor had her father. And she, this year, was more alive than ever before. She would be there.

She had a different outfit planned for each night of the five nights. It was her main focus because she'd graduated high school in May and there was nothing left to do but enjoy life. She was sure she was not one of those girls in a hurry to marry—though she dated often—and she didn't want to go to college—though her teachers had pressed her to give it a try. She had pocket money of her own, plenty of eyeliner, and newfound freedoms. So, it should have been the best feast year ever for her. But her sister Dolores was ruining it.

Yes, Dolores was getting married this week—and on Saturday, no less—the best night of the feast. And Teddie was really ticked off. She stood taller in the mirror and reminded herself it wasn't the only time Dolores had been unkind. There was the time Dolores had called Teddie over to that same mirror and said, "Let's compare necks." It had been a long time ago, but still Teddie remembered fourteen-year-old Dolores announcing that she obviously had the neck of a swan, and Teddie, the neck of an owl. How many inches long, she wondered now, was her neck actually. She pulled down the V neck of her knit top to elongate her line. Oh, everyone thought Dolores was scatterbrained and harmless, so much that Pa called her "Daisy Mae." But Teddie knew there was a kernel of meanness under all that harmless weirdo-ness. Not that she didn't have that same kernel herself. But how scattered could Dolores really be, having graduated college? Teddie loved her sister, of course, but the feast night wedding was making it difficult to like her.

Things had changed a lot since their mother had moved out, just after the feast the year before. Now Teddie had no curfew and she and her father lived like friendly roommates. Her brother, Big John, was married and gone off to be a teacher, and Dolores had been away at school, only coming home for some weekends—busy falling in love with a man who was not at all Italian and who was likely out at his stag party tonight in some strange town, Addison or Rosemont. Where he was from.

Well, if she had to miss the big night tomorrow, Teddie was going to get the most out of tonight—Friday night—the fourth night of the feast. She stepped away from the mirror and went to wait for her girlfriends on the front porch as she did each night. She stood on her front porch in the heat of the setting sun. She saw them coming up the sidewalk, like a string of beads as they picked up one girl here and one girl there, until they reached Teddie's house, laughing and patting their high hair. No girl would go to the feast alone, ever.

"The shit's going on?" Santina called out to Teddie, her black bouffant threatening to hit the porch ceiling as she bounced up the steps in platform shoes.

"Not much, not much at all."

"Dolores coming with us?"

"Her? Ha, she's down at the church cutting sandwiches into triangles."

"Should we go help, maybe?"

They looked at one another for an instant. They could go stand in the kitchen of the church slicing egg salad sandwiches and tuna sandwiches and ham sandwiches with mayo.

"Nope!" they yelled in unison. Five young women stepped off the porch with the sun sinking on their left and the allure of the feast on their right—they turned right into it. The feast took up about three city blocks in length, not much, but Teddie and her friends would walk miles and miles as they paraded up and down. A *passeggiata*. On Sunday, the old women would also walk miles, but on their bloodied knees and barefoot over the hot pavement with no water to drink. The old women would make their way through the whole town. And so, on Sunday they would be the center of attention—Teddie's grandmother among them—but tonight it was the young. It was profane. It was a *passeggiata* of lust, but highly choreographed lust with great hair. They walked as if they were horses with blinders, up and down, back and forth. Packs of young men and young women passed slowly by one other, trampling the *lupini* skins that piled up on the streets and craning their necks to get a good view of whoever caught the corner of their eye, without actually looking. Breasts sailed proudly forth under light cotton blouses, hips twisted in unconscious exaggeration, false eyelashes lowered. The young men in response rolled up their cigarette packs in their short sleeves, which gave a clear view of their biceps. Often, they whipped out a black comb to put their combed back hair right. Sometimes these guys pushed into each other to threaten fights that by design never happened—committed to just enough shoving and chicken-strutting for the girls to notice before a well-timed pulling away by a friend. Generally, the girl packs didn't fight one another. But it had happened in the past, and once that began, there was no pulling back. There were some real tough girls around, like Ignatzia Inamorato, but the police were there for that sort of thing.

As they walked, Teddie couldn't help but notice that the packs of older boys were fewer this year because of what was happening in Vietnam. All the kids knew exactly who was missing, and Teddie ticked those boys off in her mind as she squeezed *lupini* out of their skins and into her mouth, careful not to salt-up her frosted lipstick. Some, she also knew, were home on leave. In fact, she'd passed Rory Cannone and Sly Lamantia by the Ferris wheel. They looked more interesting now than they had in high school—all their baby fat gone and with a certain danger about them—mainly in the eyes. Josie agreed, but Santina said they looked malnourished and mean, and even stupider than ever.

The heat of the pavement didn't lessen, not even as darkness fell. Instead, it radiated, and this far from the lake, there was no breeze. Teddie's friend Shenandoah—whose parents had come up from Kentucky in what Shen called the great Hillbilly stampede, knew the food of the feast as well as any Sicilian, and she herded the little group to the Ice Man. The five leaned up against the back side of the stand, sucking lemon ice from white paper cups and listening to the sounds from the dunking booths, the thuds of the arms releasing and the splashes that followed. The three booths were large and made of painted wood with great tanks of water below. They were lined up, side by side, along 17th Avenue.

When Teddie turned to look, she saw it was the same as every year and it made her feel sick. Inside each booth was a Black man. In front of each booth was an Italian American man with a league baseball in his hand, and in front of the whole mess stood round-faced Woody Willardson. Woody always ran the booths, and Woody always collected the money. He didn't have to say much—unlike the *lupini* man and the games of chance men—he just let the Black men in his booths do the talking. They taunted the Italians as they were paid to do. As they were expected to do. And the Italians took their rage and their bigotry, and threw it in the form of baseballs, dunking their rivals. Teddie couldn't help notice how much those men in the booth looked like men in her own family and yet were different. Her school was in no way segregated, in fact, it was half Black and half White, but none of her Black friends ever came to the feast. And none of them lived in her neighborhood. They lived in neighbor-hoods made up of the same kinds of houses as Mulberry Park, large wood frame houses the Germans had built. They lived twenty blocks north or so, in Bellwood, Maywood. And likewise, Teddie seldom if ever went there.

Tonight, the Black men yelled "Wop! Wop! Wop!" and "You all just like us, 'specially you Sicilians WOPs, you *Afro Italians*!" And the Italian men outside the dunking booths were driven to such fury that they hurled baseballs at the dunking levers with no precision. The madder the Italian men got, the more money Woody made—and the drier the Black men stayed, high above the water. Though on a night like this, Teddie thought, they might be hoping to be dropped into the cool water of the tank. Sweltering. The jeering from both directions was like the buzz of hornets in the night air.

Teddie was a young woman who thought a lot about civil rights—she'd even written her term paper for graduation on voter suppression in the south. And she'd been lucky enough to have teachers who encouraged such things. Every day she read the news at the kitchen table. She wasn't the only one—most of her friends did too. At school, she had Black girlfriends—though never quite as close as her White ones. But it made her feel like she was doing the right thing.

Last year, the Black girls and the White greasers, Teddie's clique—had spearheaded a movement to unite to vote to overthrow the waspy White social climber domination of Prom Queen. It had worked.

So, Teddie felt she'd done some good there, too. And yet, Teddie Millefiore, despite her proximity to Black friends and her interest in equality, simply stood and watched the dunking booths, chatted about boys and Fanciful rinses and the ill-timing of her sister's wedding planning.

Teddie saw normality around her. She sensed that Woody was making a buck off of something very deep that existed here, in her people, but also in the country as a whole. And she wasn't shocked at all. Recently, she'd watched the schism in her own house over Martin Luther King Jr. and Robert F. Kennedy. Her uncles and father hated them and called them troublemakers. Her mother admired Dr. King quietly but complained about her Black coworkers at the Post Office even so. Her aunts wouldn't talk about Martin Luther King at all, which led Teddie to suspect they either disagreed with her uncles or simply had no idea what was going on outside their own kitchens. And didn't care. There was a lot of contention. Especially since JFK. But his brother, Robert, she was certain, this Kennedy would put it all to rights soon. He'd be another Lincoln. It might take time to make the world better, but it was coming. What she saw in front of her, the whizzing balls and jabs and choked rage spilling from water and box, was like watching an extended exorcism, she thought, one that would not end tonight. But one she believed would end soon.

She watched Woody collecting the money. Watched him egging on the crowd but also making sure the Italians didn't try to jump in the booths and drown the Black men, that too. Woody's money, you see, didn't all go to Woody. Some of it went to the church.

At midnight, Teddie and Santina and the rest, aching feet swelling in their tight shoes on the hot blacktop, limped back past the booths at the end of the night, the bitter end, the street sweepers were hard at work pushing their big mustache brooms, piling up the *lupini* shells like cicada skins. The crowds were nearly gone, but five or six neighborhood men remained at the booths, throwing out their backs, still, in incensed attempts to dunk their Black brothers—who still yelled, "Wop, wop, wop!" The Italian men struggled to differentiate themselves from what they'd clearly learned in their short time in the country, America did not value. And the Black men, well paid for the night, perhaps, released some rage of their own at this immigrant group who had been so willing to step on their heads in order to pull themselves up. Among the throwers, Teddie now saw both her own father and Santina's as well, middle aged men sweating in the close night air under the streetlights, each urging the other on in Sicilian. The railroad man and the factory accountant. Teddie did not point this out to Santina, though she was sure her friend had also noticed as well—so few people were left on the street. The effort it took not to look at her father was considerable, but the hatred that radiated from him was so intimate, had she looked she knew it would have been like staring at his naked body.

With the young men gone back into their homes, Teddie and her crew also headed home, dropping one at a time off along Singer Street and beyond, just as they'd first come together. Teddie was the first to disengage, and she waved goodbye and let herself in the screen door, letting it bang behind her. Her father was not home yet.

All day Saturday, Teddie did her best. After all, she *was* the maid of honor. Dolores wore an ivory wedding dress, in creamy satin, that pooled and draped from her slender body. The veil was like a crown. The Lutheran church was lovely, as was her sister, but these other people were maddeningly unaware of the street festival just blocks away, kicking off again.

Teddie wore a pale blue fitted long sheath with a matching pill-box hat, tiny mesh veil over her eyes. She adored her sister through the service and through the unending crustless sandwiches, white cake, and ambrosia salad with coconut shreds that followed. She drank punch, and she hugged her mother, Lena, who whispered in her ear that he'd better stay put for the night because this, this, her sister's wedding was *the* most important event for everyone in the family. Her mother and father had been successfully avoiding one another with kindness, but he nodded from across the room. All her aunts and uncles and cousins were there. Everyone she loved. And yet, she wanted nothing more than to be back out on the street where the action was.

By eight pm, the wedding reception had played itself out, though it showed no sign of ending—and the hall was booked until eleven. Dolores was unwrapping a Mixmaster with the speed of a sloth, while Teddie wrote down who had given what. Suddenly, she handed her pad and pen over to another bridesmaid, who suddenly felt important and took it happily—some simp from Dolores's college. Teddie excused herself to the bathroom for a good reason— to pee. But the momentary freedom exhilarated her, and while she washed her hands, she knew she had to escape. She fixed her lipstick, took the pins out of her hair, detaching the cap and setting it on the wide public sink. Without the cap, she looked almost normal. Teddie Millefiore snapped closed her evening bag, stepped out into the hall, and without a look back, clipped quickly past the reception room and out the front doors, nearly running towards the feast where all manners of things holy and profane—all mixed together—were playing out under the summer moon.

She promised she'd atone tomorrow, Sunday, and crawl with the wailing, old women on her knees following the statue of Our Lady up and down the streets, maybe crawl beside her grandma. Wear black stockings. She'd pay the price, willingly. And she was relatively sure all would be forgiven in time. She'd ask her father why he wasted his money to throw the ball at the Black men in the booths. Didn't he know it was wrong? And he'd tell her, "*Bedda*, everybody's got to have someone to look down on," without even missing a beat. She'd ask him again and again for the rest of his life, and his answer would never change. In time, she'd realize no Kennedy in the world was going to change it, either.

TWENTY ONE

Addio, Love Monster

L ate afternoons since Grandma had taken a turn for the worst, nineteen-year-old Teddie Millefiore had made it her practice to catch the bus right in front of Curl and Twirl Beauty Shop and ride it to the corner of Singer and Seventeenth Avenue. She always made sure to thank Gus, the driver, before stepping carefully down the twisting bus stairs. She hurried past the gas station, nodding to Mr. Sullivan who now manned the pumps there. And she ran up the porch stairs and into her house.

Once she got home, Teddie's new routine looked something like this: she went directly to the bedroom she'd shared with her older sister Dolores before Dolores left for college. Unzipping her pink work smock, she sniffed it under the arm holes to see if it needed washing, and then whether it needed washing or not, she tossed it in the general direction of her unmade bed. When her aim was good, the smock landed on the rumpled sheets; if she missed, on the cluttered floor. Before her mother had moved out last year, she'd have hung it immediately—in the required method: facing the same way as the rest of her things, each garment on its own paper-covered wire hanger. Martin's dry cleaners. Martinizing! the white paper skins proclaimed in red letters above the stylized image of a single red rose, so clean looking. Only seven hangers were even *in* the closet, the rest languished on the floor because *nowadays* Teddie Millefiore kept her room as she pleased. And when her smock hit the bed, it joined a selection of magazines, books, and Mounds Bar wrappers.

Next, Teddie strode into the house's one bathroom, where she sat on the pot to pee and smoke a Winston. And then, sometimes, another. In the mirror, she observed herself execute a French inhale for double the effect, and finally blew the smoke out the vent in the storm window as best she could. It was not easy; the vent was high and tiny. Teddie was short. But it was necessary because Teddie didn't smoke in front of her father, nor did she leave evidence of her smoking for him to discover. This is not to say Nicky Millefiore didn't know his youngest daughter smoked. He knew. And Teddie knew he knew. And he knew Teddie knew he knew. But that wasn't the point.

Since the divorce, Teddie and her dad lived as roommates—though he paid the utilities and the rent. But she wasn't to smoke in the house. Her mother had moved to a flat on the other side of town and her brother and sister were away. Big John was in the Peace Corps and Dolores had gone to the Normal School and then gotten married. The landlord was Grandma across the street, sick, in bed. There were certain agreements. Some were perpetual and some were new.

Today, like every day this past week, Teddie flushed the two butts and one spent match, twice to make sure they didn't re-surface. Then she took her bottle of Emeraude, roundish and yellowish, from the metal medicine chest and sprayed it high above her head, letting its mist fall, like she'd heard they do in France. It wasn't a big deal, not *really*. Everyone smoked. Her teachers smoked, her librarians smoked, Gus the bus driver smoked. Every doctor she'd ever known smoked in his office. More than that, Teddie's mother, uncles, cousins, friends: smoke, smoke, smoke. And Teddie's father smoked like a zealot. She misted a little more Emeraude just to be sure she'd covered it up.

As she left the bathroom, Teddie unsnapped her clutch-purse and rummaged for chewing gum. She pushed a stick of Wrigley's Spearmint into her mouth so that it bent like an accordion against her tongue. She yanked the last clean cardigan from her dresser drawer and shrugged it on, reapplied her lipstick, and pinched her cheeks. Then, chomping vigorously, Teddie Millefiore hurried across the street to Grandma.

When she opened the door to Grandma's bedroom, she found wet late-September was creeping in under the barely lifted window. Probably, her cousin Daniel had opened it—he was one of those weirdos that loves the cool weather, and he'd done the shift with Grandma just prior. The outside air was that strange mix of clean and filthy, spiced with exhaust from the diesel busses, black earth and spores from the last gasp of backyard gardens, sweet oil of frying donuts from the corner shop. And in an attempt to intercede for all that earthbound smell, the Autumn rain pulled down the smell of clouds themselves and folded it in. She shut the window to keep Grandma warm and calm.

Teddie got into the bed—sitting up—and smoothed a tartan blanket over herself and sleeping Grandma. Edged in satin but made of wool, it was an itchy sort of thing, probably picked up on clearance at Goldblatt's by someone out shopping for something else entirely. Must have come from one of the aunts. She could hear them all in Grandma's kitchen, running water, traipsing back and forth over the worn linoleum, combating drawers that wouldn't shut properly. Because the aunts lived upstairs or next door or across the street, now that Grandma was sick, they easily spent their days in her kitchen keeping an eye on things. Teddie had poked her head in to say hi when she'd come into the house and then hurried to Grandma, without stopping to visit. "*Aspette!*" they'd yelled, "come here and give us a kiss." But she'd just waved and hurried to Grandma's room, cracking her gum and rolling her eyes.

At just past four in the afternoon, and despite the closed bedroom door and the long hallway to the kitchen beyond, espresso and anisette wafted in under the door, replacing the outside smells that had come from the window. Espresso and anisette were smells so familiar that Teddie hardly noticed them at all. Peripheral. What *was* different than ever before though, and had become the hard stone of her attention, was the dwindling form of Grandma lying in the three-quarters bed. A changing grandma who, weak, always cold, and increasingly lonely had recently let it be known that she would be comforted *only* by her many grandchildren, and comforted best if they would lie down beside her to keep her warm and keep her company. A three-quarters bed doesn't leave much room, and Teddie's and Grandma's hips met just barely, like two violins side by side.

A family of cracks swept itself diagonally along the ceiling from above the door to the opposite corner, as if someone had slammed that door one time too many. Teddie had never noticed the cracks before but laying in her grandmother's bed these days opened new perspectives. And while she and her many cousins had spent their childhoods snatching Jordan almonds from the dark kitchen down the hall, or sitting on the east-facing front porch of the house at Grandma's feet to escape the direct afternoon sun, Teddie had seldom entered this bedroom before these last weeks. It wasn't that she'd been kept out; it was just that she was part of a family in which, under normal circumstances, children had no business in the bedrooms of adults. *La Famiglia* had perimeters.

Though everyone was going mod with foil wallpaper and shag carpets, Grandma's bedroom walls were still cloaked in turn-of-the century wallpaper. It was dense with violets, ferns, and curlicues, so the plain white crown molding above provided visual relief. Teddie drove her eyes round and round the molding's square track, listening to the air whistle on its way up Grandma's nose.

Softening her own spine down into the mattress, she winced. Her neck and shoulders pinched from all that bending over the shampoo bowls. Days when the Curl and Twirl didn't have a shampoo-girl in—which were many if not most—Teddie and the other beauticians shampooed their own ladies, bending low from the waist, massaging tired scalps, lathering and rinsing away Dippity-Doo and hairspray gum, chasing the suds down the drain with the new pink hand sprayers. Proud to be working women with money to fill their hope chests with stylish china patterns from Weiboldt's—on layaway.

Since she'd graduated high school and beauty school in June, Teddie had been working full time at the Curl and Twirl Beauty Shop. She enjoyed coloring most of all. Re-casting a client with dye or bleach felt like glorious alchemy but finding a client game enough to make the change was rare. So, often, she was let down. Most

Curl and Twirl clientele came in asking to be made to look exactly the same when they left as when they'd come in, though somehow also better. And that was another kind of alchemy, indeed. So, the beauticians experimented on one another after hours and walked the streets as hair-chameleons, changing before the neighborhood's eyes. In Mulberry Park, they were the last word in style.

Holding her head as straight as possible on her pillow, Teddie aimed not to flatten her hairdo which had required substantial ratting and teasing. Her backcombed pixie, made vibrant by Wella, level 3 RED, glowed. It was hot copper above her pale face, and that face was made paler with thick white lipstick. Teddie's lashes were curled, and her eyes were brown as the espresso her aunts swallowed from tiny cups in the kitchen.

The pear trees against Grandma's house were always the first of the season to pack it in. Slick yellow leaves uncoupled from their twigs and dropped with the rain. Many blew against the clapboard siding, slapping softly, sticking. The leaves reminded Teddie of *Colorforms*, and she envisioned peeling them away to rearrange them in patterns, maybe adding some maple and oak leaves when those began to fall.

Jutting from the pillow next to Teddie's, Grandma's nose was an angle iron. Asleep, her open mouth showed bottom teeth, stumpy and golden as corn kernels. A flannel nightgown rose high on Grandma's neck covering the old woman from head to toe. The bed felt like a cocoon—or was it a chrysalis? Teddie could never remember the difference.

When Grandma stirred, it was only to yawn or to whisper at Teddie, in English, "*You,* my favorite." Teddie gave her grandma a squeeze, knowing full well the old love monster had certainly said the same thing to Daniel not two hours ago, and to Big John before that. It wasn't that Grandma lied, no, whoever was hugging her at any given moment *was* her favorite. Teddie turned her head, still minding the hair, to look closely at the old lady beside her. She noticed tiny movements in the folds of Grandma's closed eyelids and wondered what sorts of dreams might come to very old women. She scooted closer, so close that the point of her chin rested against the side of

Grandma's neck. It smelled waxy, like mass candles, and Teddie and Grandma lay side by side just like that for a long time while the pear leaves layered into a skin on the dark side of the house.

As evening drew in, it got colder—wetter—windier. Uncles shoveled coal into the clanking furnace—blasting it high enough to braise Teddie's menopausal aunts, who panted and muttered over the kitchen sink. Splashing cold water onto their wrists, Aunt Pina reached over the sink to crank open the jalousie window, but it wasn't enough. So, they stuck their heads into the icebox, a trick they'd learned from Grandma's oldest daughter, Aunt Lucy-God-rest-her-soul.

The oldest woman in the kitchen, and Teddie could hear her now, was Grandma's seventy-nine-year-old niece and closest friend, Filomena Giaccina. Everyone, including Grandma, called her *Fi-la-mi-na-gi-a-chi* in a way that showed how much they loved the sound of the word she was. Filomena laughed a lot, usually while snorting and stomping her feet. She leaned in very close when she talked to people, and she locked eyes to see if they really meant what they said. Teddie was glad when Filomena Giaccina arrived from the other side of town with her big red suitcase and began sleeping in Grandma's spare room. The woman believed in house dresses and in crocheted house slippers. She believed in rainbow colored yarn, and when she wasn't taken up with keeping coffee and powdered sugar cookies on the table for everyone, she turned out slippers like a small factory. She also told each grandchild when their shift with grandma was. And she helped Grandma with the private things.

Often, when Teddie arrived for her daily time with Grandma, she'd open the bedroom door to find Filomena Giaccina standing quietly by Grandma's bed, their old hands clasped together like splayed tree roots. Aunt Fil, who was Filomena Giaccina's namesake, godchild, and opposite always hovered nearby. Aunt Fil, nearly forty years younger, silent but for the stacked bangle bracelets on her slender forearms, clacking with her every sigh. Teddie, who paid a lot of attention to appearances due to her line of work, wondered how, despite sharing a name, Aunt Fil looked like Vivian Leigh while old Filomena resembled Jimmy Durante with a permanent wave. This was not a value judgment; it was simply a fact. She couldn't imagine that age alone made the difference.

Staring at the ceiling gave Teddie lots of time to wonder if Grandma might get better. And while it was what she hoped for, she knew a little that it might not happen. The thing was: Grandma *never* got sick. No colds. No sick headaches. No burping *agita*. No *nothing*. Grandma never needed to shake things off because she'd always warded them off instead, with herbs or prayers or amulets. Always the healer, never the patient, but since she hadn't warded this thing off, who knew?

The next day, Teddie came again, precisely at four in the afternoon, smelling strongly of Emeraude, Wrigley's Spearmint gum, and cigarette smoke. Grandma was sleepy, so Teddie napped with her, the two of them snoring and dreaming until Teddie woke with some kind of foreboding, some kind of change in the timbre of voices from the kitchen. She rose and opened the bedroom door, lingering in the doorway and peering down the long hall. She walked toward the kitchen where five balding heads—her uncles' and her father's—nearly touched as the Millefiore men hunkered toward one another over Grandma's walnut plank kitchen table. Their pates had become purple and red and green under the light that shone through the stained-glass fruits of the heavy kitchen light fixture. Fortified by countless cups of coffee, and exhausted by worry, they murmured that it was time to call the doctor.

When they told old Filomena, who'd been busy filling the percolator with fresh grounds, she paused on the braided rug and leaned against the porcelain drainboard, setting down the coffee canister with a thump. Teddie saw her look down at the many colors of yarn that made up her little slippers and at the splatter of more colors in the rub beneath them. She remained very still while the men watched her, waiting. Then she looked up and simply nodded her head in approval, which was very unusual for Filomena Giaccina, who was a talker.

Even though *she* was further from the sound, down the hall, in her bed, somehow Grandma had heard it all, and she demanded in a weak groan from her pillow, "*Non, bambini vecchi, non medico*—no, old babies, no doctor." She called her children her "old babies" and her grandchildren "the new babies" just to keep things straight. The men at the table covered their ears to drown out their mother's entreaties. And when they removed their hands from their ears, they unbuttoned their work shirts and pulled the tails over their heads like awnings. Like that, torsos covered only with their white undershirts, they ran out into the rain. Next door, to use the phone at Aunt Agata's. It was just that there was no phone in Grandma's house, and even if there had been, they couldn't make such a call with her in the background.

Teddie had seen in the faces of her uncles and her father that they were terrified. Terrified to make the call and terrified not to make the call. Terrified of what it would mean. Teddie knew what everyone knew, that there *had* been one other time Grandma had taken to her bed. Just about half a century ago when she was newly widowed with eight children—seven still at home. And she'd methodically pulled down the Roman shades throughout the house, crept under her covers, and let her children fend for themselves. Like *animales*, they said when they told the story, sometimes trying to laugh. But they'd never forgotten what it had been like without her. It had been, the old babies sometimes whispered like a Greek chorus, *una lunga eclissi solare*—a long solar eclipse. The younger kids had stayed inside the darkened house, eating crusts of bread for days—and taking caponata from the stoneware crocks in the basement—dunking their crusts under the layer of oil into the fermented *melanzane*. The oldest three had been absent themselves—her uncles sawing trees in the WPA camp, and Aunt Lucy married and out of the house. They had no clue what was going on. Lucy would have known sooner except for the feud between her and her mother which simmered at a more rapid rate after the death of her father Giovanni.

When the children ran out of crusts, they had eaten bread crumbs that had been left scattered on the breadboard, pressing their fingers down against grit to pick it up. They'd never gone hungry before, and they were befuddled. But then they'd realized that they could go out the front door without being questioned or chased or beaten. And so, they had run wild, so wild that it was found out.

The corner shopkeeper told Filomena Giaccina they'd been seen on Croaker Street swiping bananas from the greengrocer's stand and two towns over sneaking into the films. Filomena Giaccina, Aunt Lucy, and the chief of police had to capture and drag them back home. Someone telegrammed the fearsome *Zia* Rocca to come all the way from New York to Chicago and get her cousin out of the bed. But, as the old babies said to one another, that was forever ago, and there was no *Zia* Rocca anymore. It was the doctor or nothing.

The next day, having been led down the hall by Filomena Giaccina, Dr. Cabrio knocked on the bedroom door too softly to be heard and then let himself in. When she saw the doctor standing over the bed, Teddie bolted upright and scrambled to the edge of the mattress. She wondered why she was so frightened, settling on the unsettling notion that it simply would have been terrifying to have been lying beside Grandma while the doctor pressed his cold stethoscope against her hard, old chest. It felt like the doctor might mix them up.

Her patent leather purse, which had slid across the varnished, wood floor from where she'd dropped it earlier, lay wide open, the cigarettes visible. She looked away in an entirely unsuccessful attempt to suffocate her craving and swung her foot to kick the purse the rest of the way under the bed.

The doctor spoke very simply.

"Donna Giuseppa," he'd said, "It's good to see you here with all your children and grandchildren."

Grandma eyed the doctor flatly from her bed, breathing heavier than before. She tried to wave him away, but her hand flopped onto the blanket like a speckled trout. She stared at it, blinking through cataracts. Dr. Cabrio also stared at Grandma's floppy hand. Flicking his pen against his little pad of paper to get the ink flowing, he wrote, "left hand weak and partly paralyzed. Rubbery appearance."

"Is she *left-handed*?" he asked Teddie in English with something smile-like playing under his moustache, *la sinestra*? The left, the sinister hand, yes, Teddie nodded. Grandma huffed a little in the bed, as if the left-handed-devil-curse-baloney had been the very thing which had drained her and sent her into infirmity.

Teddie drummed the fingers on her left and right hands simultaneously against the stretched chambray of her pedal-pushers. She couldn't conclude much from the accuracy of her tapping fingers—both sides seemed the same. Maybe she was ambidextrous? The doctor tried to get Grandma to talk to him. Grandma ignored him.

The entire Millefiore family, thus far, was a shade of olive particularly prone to sallowness, but today Grandma was colorful: daisy yellow with what looked like black eyes. Not dark circles—the entire family had those and wouldn't have even noted them—no, really like black eyes. When Dr. Cabrio lifted Grandma's slack hand, drawing her fingernails up close to his eyeballs, he sucked his teeth. Then he shined a penlight into Grandma's eyes with one hand, holding her lids open with the other, first the right, then the left, peering at the whites and stopping to make more notes. Watching as he etched word after word with his stick-pen, in those building block letters, Teddie came to understand that her grandma was truly dying. Each letter looked like a little tombstone.

But it's okay, she reminded herself. After all, wasn't it *Grandma* herself who'd taught Teddie that all things must die? Yes, indeed, it was. When Teddie was just seven, that's when she'd looked out the front window after breakfast only to see Grandma, *babushka-sciarpa* knotted under her throat and looking more than a little like a kitchen witch, marching at the coop behind Teddie's house. Grandma had already slaughtered all but the last two hens, the two that laid double-yolked eggs, enjoyed cuddles, and were happy to be wheeled about in doll buggies. Teddie and Dolores had let themselves believe double yolks meant Mamie and Maxine could remain in the coop forever.

"Please, Grandma! Not them!" Teddie had pleaded, hurrying out the front door in her short nightgown and bare feet, shivering.

"*All* of them," came the answer in Sicilian. "*Even these!*" Grandma had sung it out without even slowing her pace. And when she'd crossed back over the street, a hen under each arm, she'd turned to face Teddie who still stood frozen on the sidewalk.

"Delicious! You'll see!" Grandma yelled with cheer, "Everything dies!"

*   *   *

That tough grandma who'd marched over the street a decade before seemed so much smaller and quieter as the doctor wrapped-up his exam. Teddie pulled the wool blanket up even higher around Grandma's shoulders and settled back into the mattress herself, listening to the sounds a doctor makes leaving a room, the swishing of trouser legs, the clearing of the throat.

Though Dr. Cabrio had said nothing of great import in the bedroom, once in the kitchen, he spoke freely, and his voice—like the voices of all the Cabrios in Mulberry Park—was the kind of voice that carries, the kind that's come from people who for generations upon generations called from mountain top to mountain top. The walls of the old house were filled only with slats and Victorian-era newspapers, so his diagnosis bounded like a big dog.

"Well, it's simply organ failure," he began without preamble. "She's ninety-five, and every," he paused for effect, "Every. Single. Organ. Every single one is worn out." And then in a strangely hopeful tone he added, "The kidneys are going first."

The kitchen was silent.

"Renal failure," he supplemented as if the old babies hadn't understood. "We call this renal failure. She's dying."

"Does she know?" someone asked, but Teddie couldn't make out who it was.

"Well, yes, I mean, no," his tone buoyed into something paternal, "I'm sure she feels very weak, but I think it's best if you don't tell her. What good would that do?"

Teddie expected the kitchen to dissolve into wails or, at least, sobs. But instead, silence floated calmly until Dr. Cabrio was seen out. And even then, there were only surprised murmurs, too quiet to decipher.

Though her children had remained composed, the doctor's words had a distinct and opposite effect on Grandma herself who, with some kind of supernatural hearing, had understood the prognosis. And upon hearing it, her left hand did some extra-frantic flopping while both of her bare feet kicked at the enamel footboard and she groaned.

The kitchen still murmured and shuffled. Teddie could tell they were hugging one another in a clustering of sadness. Alone with Grandma, she stared at the little trout hand and wondered what to do. Grandma scowled at the ceiling and panted.

Clearly, now that the time was nigh, ninety-five years was not enough for Grandma. A hundred and ninety-five wouldn't have been enough for her. And then Teddie realized, and it felt similar to having a boulder dropped on her face, there'd be no day, ever, *she'd* be ready to die, either. And the longer *she* lived, the more she'd get used to being alive. The *less* she'd be willing to die. In due time, Teddie just knew the old woman resisting death would be herself. In another bed, in some other house but otherwise the same. She felt the marrow in her bones gurgle like a radiator and chewed what was left of the white lipstick from her lips.

Everyone knew, even the doctor knew, that Grandma couldn't go to the hospital to die. There were at least two reasons for this. First, Grandma, like most of the old-timers, believed hospitals to be fatal in their own right. You could die in your house too, sure, why not? But only if you were *meant to*. At the hospital, they'd kill you. For years Grandma had kept a mental list, sharing it often, a list of all the people in the neighborhood who'd gone to the hospital just a little sick and come out dead.

The second reason had nothing to do with the hospital itself but was something recently discovered about Grandma. Her daughters-in-law had dug for paperwork and visited the Social Security office downtown only to find that despite Grandma's recollections, she'd never actually become a citizen of the United States of America. And so, there was no Medicare for her.

"Look at her, *really*, how could we have thought she was a citizen?" Aunt Agata had whispered over her cup.

Aunt Betty, who almost never came over to the house till now, agreed, clinking the sugar spoon against the side of her plate, "She doesn't even speak English. She doesn't write American, neither. I mean, how would she even take the test? And *do you think*, I mean, *do you really think* she'd ever have bothered?"

"She hasn't left the neighborhood since 1934, that's thirty years," came a muffled voice.

"It's okay," Uncle Calogero said, "it's okay because it's only Americans that die in the hospital from being old. We wouldn't put her there anyway. What for? To die with strangers?" Because Uncle Calogero had come into the world during the journey from Sicily, he carried Sicily with him in ways his American-born siblings did not. He had more in common with his mother than he did with these other men at the table. "Hospitals are no place to die on purpose," he added.

"Well, Lucy-god-rest-her-soul almost died in the hospital," said the muffled voice. "I mean we tried to take her there but it was too late."

But Aunt Pina, the mail-order bride from Palermo, backed Uncle Calogero, "Not a-same," she said, "Not a-same at all."

Teddie had listened with some interest to that discussion as if she were listening to a radio program, each player's voice piping in from a distance with kitchen sound effects: chairs shoving across the lino-leum, the rinsing of cups, someone hunting for the flour-sack towels. She wondered why they were speaking in English for a moment but then realized it was to keep Grandma from listening-in. In reality, Grandma wasn't even trying to listen anymore. She just lay there like a sack, tired-out from her initial reaction to the doctor's news.

Noticing a washcloth half in and half out of the washbowl on the bedside table, Teddie reached for it. She meant to gently wipe Grandma's face, so she wrung it out well, twisting and twisting, but then she decided not to do anything with it, dropped it back in the bowl and let the water seep up to saturate the cotton threads. Teddie had nothing left herself.

Slipping her stockinged feet into her ballet flats, she stood up and bent to kiss the old woman on the forehead, and then—again—on the end of her nose.

"I love you, Grandma."

Teddie met her cousin Little John on her way out of the bed-room. He'd been coming in to take his turn, and she brought him up to speed. And then Teddie joined the kitchen table group. She poured herself a coffee—black—and munched a few Maurice Lenell pinwheel cookies with her father, her aunts, her uncles. But she stayed only a little while before trotting through the mist, back over the road, pink sugar stuck to her lipstick. Home to dinner of canned soup and sliced bread without butter. It was part of her diet regimen.

Unlike Teddie, Grandma did not sleep that night. She refused. The next afternoon Teddie heard about how Filomena Giaccina had dropped oil in water to see if this was the work of the evil eye, but the oil and water had indicated nothing could be blamed on *Malocchio,* both a relief and a disappointment. Grandma uttered not a syllable. Nor did she move so much as to twitch. Instead, she petrified herself in what Teddie was certain could only have been a strategy to expend no energy beyond keeping her eyes open and continuing to breathe. When the old babies turned the lights out in her bedroom, Grandma had stared out into the darkness, like an owl. But despite her will and her fear, within two days, she crumpled in the bed and finally slept.

On the day Grandma was overcome by sleep—and after a cup of coffee with Filomena Giaccina and Aunt Fil—Teddie slipped into bed with Grandma, smoothing the Goldblatt's blanket over them both. Grandma slept, but not a true sleep. Sometimes, a tear cut down one slack cheek, pausing in the deeper lines near her chin before sliding off her jaw into the sheets.

Dr. Cabrio stopped in to leave some pain medicine in case it was needed. "But really," he reminded the kitchen, "renal failure *is* a good way to go." His audience was seated at the table, all women at that moment, because the men were still at work at four on a Tuesday, hammering things, boxing things, lifting things at the Union Pacific or American Can or the Bobko Moving Company. He instructed the ladies there to stop pressing Grandma with the teas and tinctures they'd been brewing to bring her back to health—it only made more work for kidneys not up to doing any work at all. It was simply a matter of dying now, he said. "Not even water," he said.

Filomena Giaccina made the sign of the cross and then the protection from the evil eye behind Dr. Cabrio's back as he pulled his boxy trench coat over himself.

After the doctor left, Teddie felt antsy, too antsy to stay in bed. Grandma was not aware of her anyway, so she got up and began padding around Grandma's bedroom. She ran her hands over the enamel bed frame, plain ivory with a dark constellation of black spots where the paint was chipped away. She pressed her fingertips into the depressions—they looked deeper than they felt. Her father and his siblings had been born in this bed, all except Aunt Lucy, who had been born in Sicily and Uncle Calogero who had been born on the sea.

Teddie checked herself in the mirror; she needed to re-pin "pieces" that were coming loose from today's hairdo, one that required so much additional hair. She curled her lips over her teeth to hold bobby-pins in her mouth. Grandma's sleeping face—mouth wide open—floated behind her in the mirror's wide reflection. There was really no choice but to notice how her own nose jutted in an angularity like Grandma's. *More than similar*, she had to admit, as she peered closer. Just about identical. And it felt traitorous to be so young as Grandma lay dying. Pulling the bobby pins from between her lips, Teddie pinned and pinned the pieces back in until it was time to go home.

The next afternoon, when she rushed home from work it was to relieve her sister Dolores at Grandma's bedside. Dolores had taken the Greyhound home from The Normal School, where her new husband was now enrolled in graduate school and where she taught first grade DeKalb proper with her bachelor's degree. She dragged her sky-blue Samsonite suitcase from the station way over on Fifteenth to the house. It had no wheels. Teddie knew how her sister's face went pink from exertion, how her eyes watched the cracks in the pavement from behind thick glasses, so she wouldn't trip. She knew Dolores would be worn out already.

When Teddie arrived at Grandma's, Dolores had been there a few hours already, and so Teddie expected she would be ready to go—but maybe they could have a coffee in the kitchen with the aunts and catch up. But before Teddie could even greet her sister, Dolores erupted from the little bedroom in tears, ran down the hall, through the parlor and out the storm door, which banged closed behind her.

Her wails filled the street, loud and mournful. A dog, somewhere in the neighborhood, howled along, which set off a second dog as well. The aunts banged out the storm door, chasing Dolores down, capturing her. Hugging her. Teddie checked Grandma to make sure Dolores wasn't crying because Grandma had died on her shift. She hadn't. She was still breathing. Teddie stood up to make sure the window was shut. Dolores had always been that way.

Sitting on the edge of Grandma's bed, Teddie slipped off her shoes and prepared to lie down. She had the blanket lifted and one leg already under when Grandma turned over, stared blindly at her, and asked, "Mamma, Mamma, where are you, Mamma? *Aiutami!*"

In one spastic movement, Teddie hopped out of the bed. Grandma clawed weakly at the air above her own chest as if swimming or drowning, still wanting her Mamma.

The women in the kitchen came in to see for themselves, widened their eyes, and then went back to the kitchen to debate what to do next: should they give her the painkillers to make her stop? Technically, it wasn't what the painkillers were for, and really, the morphine could finish her off. But would that be so bad? Most didn't want to take that risk. Two thought that might be fine. The discussion became frantic and full of rattling saucers, pacing feet, Sicilian. Everyone knew the old babies wanted their Mamma to guide them, but she couldn't anymore. She wanted her own Mamma now.

When Teddie got to the kitchen, Grandma's African Violets in their little terra-cotta pots were shuddering on the enamel top of the Hoosier cabinet in the kitchen. Teddie carried them into the living room before they could be knocked over. Grandma had kept them for years in these same clay pots—they flowered now, living their planty lives in another dimension, she supposed. They were oblivious, and who would take care of them when Grandma was gone?

Aunt Pina and Aunt Fil said maybe the grandchildren shouldn't lie in with Grandma anymore. It was getting too bad now. They said these shouldn't be the last memories the kids should have of Grandma.

"Okay," Teddie said to them, "but I think I'll stay in her room for now anyway." She went back to Grandma's room and shoved the commode in the closet. Grandma was way past using that. She had made room for the prayer bench, and she dragged it away from the wall, parking it alongside the bed. She knelt to make some prayers, a mixture of what she'd seen and heard in both Catholic and Lutheran services. Teddie, the child of a Catholic father—who was technically excommunicated because he was divorced—and a Lutheran mother, had had her fair share of both. She knelt on the hard wood *prie dieu*, and it didn't take long for her to abandon the memorized prayers and compose her own. These she directed at the agonized face of Christ who bled brown enamel from nail holes in his wrists and feet high on his cross over Grandma's bed as well as at the almond eyes of the Black Madonna, who abided serene in the far windowsill.

Teddie wasn't sure what she should pray for, exactly. A full recovery? No, not only did that seem unlikely, it also seemed like a bad idea for some reason. A quick death? No, that felt callous. In the end, she prayed for Grandma to feel loved and to not be scared.

Then Grandma began really hollering, which was a shock. Because though she was tough and unrelenting, Grandma was not a woman who raised her voice. Not a woman who ever had to. She hollered for Grandpa. This was surprising as well. In fact, Teddie was so surprised she whipped her head around, numbing her tongue from a twanged tendon running to the top of her head. Why would Grandma call for *him*? A hundred times she had told Teddie, "They *make-a* me marry him. Pah! I no want him, I no choose him, I no *like* him!" Sometimes she'd even spit.

Teddie had never known her grandfather, and so in her imagination, he was always in the same pose she saw him take in the portrait that hung in the living room, serious, if a bit foolish looking, around the eyes. Somewhat unlikeable, somewhat unchooseable, and somewhat unwantable as well. But like him or not, Grandma now summoned him, and in earnest.

Teddie quietly left the bedroom and got her aunts, feeling now it must really be time to call the priest. Waiting for the priest in Grandma's kitchen, Teddie's was just one face of at least thirty, all resembling the next in some way, though some were truly ugly and some verifiably beautiful. They wedged in to wait. Filomena Giaccina plenished the kitchen, holding a burlap bag high, letting pistachios, red as red lipstick, cascade into Grandma's twin ceramic nut dishes. She passed around cups of coffee with saucers shuddering underneath. She kissed the people who were too quiet, pinched their faces. She shushed the people who were too loud.

Aunt Agata—with the detached focus only a daughter-in-law can muster—fluttered from person to person, hugging one after the other after the other, her white apron with the green brick-a-brack and ruffles standing like wings over her chubby shoulders. Aunt Fil, Grandma's only living daughter, her youngest child, stared up at the fruit on the light fixture, silent. Grandma's many sons, including Teddie's father, Nicky, sobbed, some quietly, some loudly. Sitting in kitchen chairs with their heads down, they wiped their big noses with big white handkerchiefs. Dolores was there, too, her hair in a schoolmarm bun, her poncho all green and black around her as she cried. And so was Teddie's mother, Lena, pulling out the tissues she stashed in the cuffs of her shirt, one by one. She'd come from her flat on the other side of town, saying no matter how much water had passed under the bridge, no matter how polluted that water was, her mother-in-law was the only mother she'd ever known. The family sat in chairs, leaned against walls, sat cross-legged on the floor if they were young enough to get down there. A great-grandchild toddled from the kitchen to the living room and back, pulling a quacking wooden duck on wheels, the red and white rope tight in his little fist.

Grandma was never alone in her bedroom waiting for the priest. People trailed in again and again in groups, alone, in groups again. Many cried harder as they emerged, but often chose to go a second or third time anyway. Teddie began to find it all dizzying. She was unsure at any moment who was in and who was out. She cried a little herself and held her mother's hand tentatively, as if she were ten years younger than she was.

At half past ten, Father Francis Fillo let himself into the house as only a priest can do, an air of sanctity clinging to him. He wiped his wet shoes on the carpet remnant by the front door and raised his hand to bless the kitchen, but he did not stop to greet any person. Instead, he tilted forward and launched himself for the hall, where Grandma's holy cabinet hung on brass hooks. Just as he'd done every Wednesday morning for the last seven years, ever since Grandma's arthritic hip got bad enough to keep her out of the pews at church. He gathered the host and his instruments.

It was too late for a confession, what with Grandma ignoring everyone in the room and speaking only with the long dead. Father tried, but it was impossible. "But," he soothed the family with his calm reason, "what could Giuseppa possibly confess this week that she hadn't confessed at her last confession? Or the one before that?" They chewed on what he had to say and thought, well, it might be so.

As many as could wedge into Grandma's bedroom with the priest wedged in, while being sure to leave him enough room to operate. He held the host to Grandma's lips. She was still moaning. She'd stopped calling for her husband and had gone back to calling for her Mamma.

Hands floating gracefully, the priest made the benediction. Incense smoked in the censer he'd carried over from the church. His voice was sonorous as he intoned the prayers, and he pushed his heavy black eyeglasses up the bridge of his nose when they slipped, without pausing at all. All the while he averted his eyes from the statue of the Black Madonna who stared blankly at him from her windowsill, her face unfathomable and pagan beyond redemption.

After the last rites, the priest remained in the home for a while to soothe the family, some of whom had become nervous again about not having a confession and argued with him on that account, respectfully of course. Filomena Giaccina reminded them that Grandma was much fonder of communion than confession—and she'd had her communion even though it could only be touched to her lips, not put in her mouth or she'd choke to death. Everyone knew that was true, including Father Fillo, and so they became calm, as calm as they could be in the hallway. In the bedroom, Grandma still suffered and called, weakly now, but still unceasingly.

Despite having received her last rites, Grandma did not die that day. She did not die later that night, either. And she still did not die by the following morning. Everyone told her it was okay, that they'd be okay if she went, that she could just go. But maybe she sensed they didn't really mean it. Or maybe she just wasn't ready and didn't care what anyone else thought about it. Or maybe she was in a place where she could neither see nor hear them, and in that place her heart simply continued to beat of its own stubborn volition.

People began to say she was refusing to die. And people worried about that. It wasn't right. At various hours of those long days, Father Fillo came in and out of the house. Teddie saw him every afternoon, holding his coffee cup on both hands to warm himself at the kitchen table. Filomena Giaccina was there with the window over the sink cracked open. Both of them, with wild hair and looking insane, smoking cigarettes. No one had ever seen Filomena Giaccina smoke before. The priest smoked all the time, though, and he handed Pall Malls over to Filomena and lit them with his fancy silver lighter.

He also went to Grandma's bedroom where he knelt in prayer, doing his best to ease Grandma out of the world, but also now *urging* her to go, sometimes even suggesting to God to help her go, and please, *Dio*, make it soon.

"This death," the aunts in the kitchen said, "is like a long childbirth—too much."

Teddie was at the Curl and Twirl, lathering and massaging the scalps of middle-aged strangers when Grandma finally did die. By the time she arrived home from work and heard the news, the men from Zimbardo's funeral home had already come and taken away the corpse. In fact, Grandma's dead body in the hearse and Teddie's live one on the bus must have passed one another somewhere on Seventeenth Avenue. Zimbardo's Funeral Home, after all, was just one part of a large, nondescript, brick building—long and rectangular as a shoe-box—that housed three other businesses: Belle-View Florist, Gagliardi's Bakery, and the Curl and Twirl Beauty Shop.

For the three days that led up to the wake, while at work at the Curl and Twirl, Teddie could not help but be intensely aware that Grandma's body rested on the other side of the wall, close to where she stood cutting and clipping and applying color. Close to where she hung her raincoat on the hook. *Very* close to where she ate her lunch. Her friends chatted with her over the heads of patrons, being extra-kind because they knew. The whole town knew. But Teddie couldn't follow their conversations. There's nothing so interesting it makes you forget your dead grandmother is on a slab next door. And yet, where else would she be? Teddie began making errors. She left patrons with noticeable scissor lines, over-teased and over-ratted until they looked either edgy far beyond the scope of Mulberry Park or like squirrels with the mange. Ms. Marcella gave her—and the rest of the girls—extra smoke breaks. She was Grandma's cousin's daughter's niece.

When the three nights of the wake finally began, things got stranger still. Ms. Marcella—who forbid tardiness—let Teddie come in late. But she also asked her to close up since she was going straight to Zimbardo's anyway. After the others left, Teddie locked the register, flipped the OPEN sign to CLOSED, and walked to the storeroom to change into black dress or black slacks and low heels. Each night, it was the same. She peeled away her work clothes in the narrow space with the concrete floor, feeling surrounded by chemicals and a crowd of beautician's mannequins, each with the same waspy face, differing only by extremes in hair and makeup. Each head without a body. She stood in her underwear and bra feeling like she should cry some more, but instead she just stood there not-crying.

On the third night, there was some relief just because it was the last night. Grandma would be off to the mausoleum tomorrow, which while certainly unpleasant, was an improvement from the unending wake.

Teddie's stomach growled, but she knew she'd have a big sandwich soon, in the maple-paneled backroom of the funeral home, warmed by the heat of so many bodies. Aunt Pina and Aunt Agata brought the sandwiches every night, mortadella and provolone on seeded bread with oil and vinegar. And bowls of olives and trays of cookies and lemonade. And *lupini*. Little Bradley would be toddling with his quacky duck on the perimeters of the room, and Filomena Giaccina would be talking to everyone she could, all those seated and shifting for comfort on extra folding chairs.

In the viewing room, there would be people to greet and grim details of death to repeat over and over and over again. People wanted to *know*. This was how they inured themselves to death and began to take away its power to shock. Neighbors and acquaintances would file in and out but the family would stay till the bitter end. And Grandma would lie so still, being nothing at all, not even a shell, just a sort of icon there in the front of the room.

Holding their elbows, Teddie would accompany the old-timers to the open casket, many of them looking almost ready for it themselves, and most of them limping or gasping or lurching. It was always a long trek during which the liver-spotted and the toothless whispered how Grandma had helped them, often many times, with something magical. "Of course," they said, "let's not talk about that when the priest comes close." When they kneeled before the body, Teddie wondered, did they see themselves there soon, or did it seem a relief it wasn't them there now? Most likely, she figured, it was both. And tonight, would be just like that. Again. For the last time.

Teddie tugged the edges of her new pixie, shaping it. She peered into the mirror at her station. She re-applied her lipstick and swished her collection of combs in their decanter of Barbicide, so blue and antiseptic. She glanced around her, at the empty stations—Nora's and Santina's, Judi's, the new girl Susan's, and Ms. Marcella's, first up front. They each left little clues as to who they were: a photo of a boyfriend here, a string of cheap beads there, a copy of *Scientific America* shoved behind Santina's tall pink aerosol of Aqua Net. On Teddie's station, beside the *Barbicide*, which everyone had, there was her color wheel, a glass jar of candy kisses, and the mass card she'd taken from last night's visitation. On it were all the usual mass card things: the ethereal rendering of Mary, mother of God, on the front. Her feet were in clouds, her head was veiled, and a blue gown swirled over her body like the hand of chastity. On the back of the mass card: Giuseppa Millefiore, born April 1871, Died September 24, 1965. And beneath that, the Hail Mary, simple and direct. Teddie picked up the mass card and slid it under the glass top of her station, Grandma's name facing up, the ninety-five years protected but visible under the glass.

Teddie picked up her purse and the duffel bag stuffed with her work clothes. She turned out the lights in the storeroom, leaving the mannequins in the dark, and then she shut off the lights in the rest of the shop. Ms. Marcella's extra set of keys jangled from her left hand as she wrestled the sticky lock for too long. But then it clicked, and she walked away from that door, pulling her red, polka dot raincoat around her, hurrying down the short sidewalk to the door of Zimbardo's. She was the first one there tonight, as she had been the nights before, and so she'd sit by Grandma for at least an hour as they waited for the wake to get rolling. It had taken her less than a minute to pass from Curl and Twirl into Zimbardo's and up the middle aisle to Grandma's casket. Interior walls, she now believed, meant very little. Everything, everything, everything is proximity.

Because her father was named executor of the will, Teddie accompanied him to the lawyer's directly after the funeral the next day so that he could be informed of his duties and so that she could help him. She stood behind his chair as he listened carefully, watching him nod, his brown tie too tight at his throat, his hands signing his name here and there—more writing than he'd done since he quit school in the eighth grade, she guessed.

It had taken some time at the lawyer's, and so when Teddie and her father Nicky finally arrived at Grandma's house, it was very dark out. They went inside, ready to re-join everyone, to begin executing the will. But the place was empty. And not just empty of people. It was really empty. What must have been a whirlwind of Millefiores, stepping over one another to get what they wanted, had carted away almost everything earlier in the day. Those many children and equally many in-laws, the herds of grandchildren and nieces and nephews, all wanting some part of Grandma to keep forever—and figuring all rules were done with. They'd cleaned the place out. Left behind were a half-burned broom in the kitchen, two heavy portraits on the living room wall—one of Grandma and one of Grandpa—the one where he looked unlikeable—and the chipped enamel bed in the bedroom—though its mattress and box spring were nowhere in sight.

Teddie watched her father take down the portraits, one then the other, leaning them carefully against the wall. And then he carried them, one at a time, across the street while Teddie began to dismantle the bed. With all of Grandma's lamps and her colorful kitchen fixture departed, the light was meager indeed. It came only from a bare bulb with a chain pull inside the closet. The walls seemed enormous, like in one of those dreams where a person finds extra rooms in the house they've always lived in. It made Teddie feel a little like she might be having a stroke, really. And she could still smell Grandma in every corner, not a perfume or a favorite soap, the actual smell of the person, layered deep. When she sighed, she heard Grandma's lifetime of sighs rise up and echo around her. Teddie kneeled on the bare and dusty bedroom floor, grit under her knees, and a rollie watching her from the mopboard. She figured she'd sweep it away with the burnt broom later. She began to work on the wing-nuts, which didn't loosen easily as they'd been in place since 1902. She gripped one between her thumb and forefinger, and though it pinched into her skin, she wouldn't give up. She twisted until she was sweating, even with the furnace low. There, alone, in the empty bedroom, Teddie re-knew what she'd always known, and what she would continue to discover over and over during her own long life, always as if it was a surprise, as if it was news: she was, indeed, her grandma's girl.

About the Author

Christina Marrocco works in memoir, short story, long fiction, and poetry. Her work has appeared in Silverbirch Press, The Laurel Review, House Mountain Review, VIA, Ovunque Siamo, and Red Fern Press. She lives outside of Chicago where she teaches Creative Writing and other courses at Elgin Community College.

Lessons in chem

Apple

HBO

Ntflix The Light I
Cannot see

After Life Pn

Made in the USA
Monee, IL
21 October 2023